美国文学经典教程

American Literary Canon: A Course Book

主　编　江宁康
编　者　（按姓氏拼音顺序）
　　　　程　爽　丁建宁　郝桂莲
　　　　江宁康　叶　英　朱丽田
参　编　高　巍　项歆妮　孔小纲　王　华

东南大学出版社
·南京·

图书在版编目(CIP)数据

美国文学经典教程/江宁康主编. —南京：东南大学出版社,2010.10(2019.12重印)
 ISBN 978-7-5641-2478-6

Ⅰ.①美… Ⅱ.①江… Ⅲ.①文学-作品综合集-美国 Ⅳ.①I 712.11

中国版本图书馆 CIP 数据核字(2010)第 200172 号

东南大学出版社出版发行
(南京四牌楼 2 号 邮编 210096)
出版人：江建中
江苏省新华书店经销　虎彩印艺股份有限公司印刷
开本：787mm×1092mm　1/16　印张：17　字数：424 千字
2010 年 11 月第 1 版　2019 年 12 月第 4 次印刷
ISBN 978-7-5641-2478-6
印数：6001~6500 册　定价：42.00 元
(凡因印装质量问题，可直接向读者服务部调换。电话：025-83792328)

Contents

Part One   From the Native to the National

Lesson 1   American Indian Legend .... (3)
Lesson 2   Christopher Columbus (1451—1506) .... (7)
Lesson 3   American Indian Oral Poetry .... (11)
Lesson 4   William Bradford (1590—1657) .... (14)
Lesson 5   Benjamin Franklin (1706—1790) .... (18)
Lesson 6   Washington Irving (1783—1859) .... (23)
Lesson 7   James Fennimore Cooper (1789—1851) .... (30)

Part Two   From Romanticism to Realism

Lesson 8   Edgar Allen Poe (1809—1849) .... (39)
Lesson 9   Ralph Waldo Emerson (1803—1882) .... (45)
Lesson 10   Henry David Thoreau (1817—1862) .... (52)
Lesson 11   Henry Wadsworth Longfellow (1807—1882) .... (59)
Lesson 12   Nathaniel Hawthorne (1804—1864) .... (63)
Lesson 13   Herman Melville (1819—1891) .... (70)
Lesson 14   Walt Whitman (1819—1892) .... (77)
Lesson 15   Emily Dickinson (1830—1886) .... (82)
Lesson 16   Samuel L. Clemens (Mark Twain, 1835—1910) .... (87)
Lesson 17   Henry James (1843—1916) .... (94)

Part Three   Fiction and Drama in the 20th Century (1)

Lesson 18   Willa Cather (1873—1947) .... (102)
Lesson 19   Jack London (1876—1916) .... (109)
Lesson 20   Sherwood Anderson (1876—1941) .... (114)
Lesson 21   F. Scott Fitzgerald (1896—1940) .... (120)

Lesson 22	Ernest Hemingway (1899—1961)	(127)
Lesson 23	Eugene Gladstone O'Neill (1888—1953)	(133)
Lesson 24	William Faulkner (1897—1962)	(141)

Part Four   American Poetry in the 20th Century

Lesson 25	Ezra Pound (1885—1972)	(149)
Lesson 26	Robert Frost (1874—1963)	(153)
Lesson 27	Langston Hughes (1902—1967)	(157)
Lesson 28	William Carlos Williams (1883—1963)	(161)
Lesson 29	Robert Lowell (1917—1977)	(165)
Lesson 30	Allen Ginsberg (1926—1997)	(169)
Lesson 31	Elizabeth Bishop (1911—1979)	(174)
Lesson 32	John Ashbery (1927—)	(179)

Part Five   Fiction and Drama in the 20th Century (2)

Lesson 33	Ralph Ellison (1914—1994)	(185)
Lesson 34	Arthur Miller (1915—2005)	(191)
Lesson 35	Edward Albee (1928—)	(199)
Lesson 36	Joseph Heller (1923—1999)	(208)
Lesson 37	John Updike (1932—2009)	(214)
Lesson 38	Saul Bellow (1915—2005)	(221)

Part Six   Postmodernism and Ethnic Literature

Lesson 39	John Barth (1930—)	(230)
Lesson 40	Kurt Vonnegut (1922—2007)	(236)
Lesson 41	Toni Morrison (1931—)	(241)
Lesson 42	Maxine Hong Kingston (1940—)	(246)
Lesson 43	Leslie Marmon Silko (1948—)	(251)
Lesson 44	E. L. Doctorow (1931—)	(258)
Lesson 45	Cormac McCarthy (1933—)	(263)

参考文献 (267)

后　记 (268)

Part One

From the Native to the National
第一部　从本土文学到民族文学

　　长期以来,美国文学被视为仅有二百多年历史的国家文学,其发展进程相当于中国古代明、清那样一个朝代文学的历史跨度;同时,美国文学也曾被视为继承了欧洲和英国文学的传统,是西方和英语文学的自然延续。但是,随着美国当代多元文化主义的兴起,20世纪后期的一些学者把美利坚民族的多族裔文化传承也纳入了文学史的视野,这就把美国文学发展史延伸了至少数百年。于是,近年来一些美国文学史和文学选集也把美利坚民族文学的起源延伸到本土印第安人的早期口头文学和民间传说,并把欧洲探险者如哥伦布等人的航海日记或书信见闻也作为美国文学的一部分加以整合。有鉴于此,近年来《诺顿美国文学选集》和《西斯美国文学选集》等厚重的美国文学作品选集都扩大了篇目遴选的范围,对于本土印第安人的口头文学作品和早期欧洲探险者的叙述等也给予了适当的收录,视其为美利坚民族文学的一个有机部分。事实上,在欧洲人到达北美大陆之前,本土印第安人就形成了500多种部落语言和文化,并在各自的文明进程中创造了不少歌谣、史诗、神话和传说等等,其文学母题和人物形象对于美国经典作家以及当代少数族裔作家的创作都产生了一定的影响。本土口头文学包含了创始神话,"恶作剧者"形象,萨满教咒语,易洛魁英雄传说,"狩猎歌"、"战争之歌"和"爱情之歌"等谣曲短歌,以及各种谚语和童话等等。这些本土文学传统虽然带有原始文化的痕迹,但对于美利坚民族语言和文化的形成具有十分重要的意义,当然也在一定程度上影响到这个新兴民族和国家的文学史建构。

　　哥伦布于1492年踏足美洲大陆之后,欧洲文化也逐渐传入北美。1607年,英国移民建立了第一个殖民地詹姆斯敦,这标志了英国文化和文学传统在北美大陆传播的开始。从此,以英语为媒介的早期美利坚民族文学逐渐形成,而1620年"五月花号"航船载来的清教徒们则带来了基督教的价值观念,对后来美国文学的形成产生了极其深远的影响。在17世纪的新英格兰地区,威廉·布拉德福(1590—1657)写的《普利茅斯种植园史》和当地出版的《海湾圣诗》(1640)等成了早期殖民地文学的代表之作,而约翰·温斯罗普(1588—1649)关于建立"山巅之城"的呼唤更给美国文学经典中的清教思想脉络打上了深刻的宗教印记。由于疾病、战争和杀戮等原因,北美大陆各殖民地上的印第安本土居民人口大幅减少,而大批欧洲移民的涌入使得殖民地的社会和文化产生了重要的演变,清教伦理和工商文化成为当地的主流价值观念,因此也给殖民地文学带来了深远的影响。在殖民地时期的北美文学发展中,还出现了一些女作家如安妮·布拉德里特(1612—1672)的诗歌创作,以及南方作家威廉·伯德(1674—1744)的日记体叙事文学等等。

　　在启蒙主义思潮的影响下,北美殖民地人民日益觉醒,而英国政府不断加重的经济剥削更是激起了殖民地人民的反抗意识。从18世纪的启蒙主义直到1775年美国独立战争爆发，北美殖民地文学出现了许多优秀的经典作家，其中以本杰明·富兰克林(1706—1790)为最重要的代表。富兰克林曾被大卫·休谟称为美国"第一位伟大的文学家"，他撰写的《穷理查历书》(1734)等作品对于倡导新教伦理和建立美利坚民族文化产生了十分深远的影响。在这一时期里，殖民地作家还面对着欧洲和英国文学的挑战，因为本土文学界仍然有不少人热衷模仿大西洋对岸的文学名家名作。值得一提的是，出生于英国的托马斯·潘恩(1737—1809)在美国独立战争前夕写出了文字激扬的《常识》(1776)一书，公开号召北美殖民地人民起来反抗，为摆脱大英帝国、争取民族独立而进行战斗。上述那些作品既是美国文化的思想来源，也是美国历史的生动记述，更是美国文学的不朽篇章。这些殖民地文学作品和本土印第安文学一样，对于美国独立以后的民族文学建构起到了筚路蓝缕、承前启后的重要作用。

　　随着美国革命的胜利，美国文学史进入了一个新的发展时期，或者说，严格意义上的"美国文学"开始了自己的文化独立旅程。出生在纽约的诗人菲利普·弗兰诺(1752—1832)在独立战争时期写下了许多热情充溢的诗篇，如《一首政治祷文》(1775)、《纪念勇敢的美国人》(1781)和《野生蜂蜜》(1786)等等。在小说创作上，查尔斯·布朗(1771—1810)的《维兰德》(1799)、华盛顿·欧文(1789—1859)的《见闻札记》(1820)和詹姆斯·库柏(1789—1851)的《间谍》(1821)等形成了美利坚民族文学的坚实基础。这些作品的出现标志了美利坚合众国的文学创建奠基，展示了用美国式英语描写的一幅幅本民族历史风情的鲜活画面，更是美国革命的一个重要胜利成果。在美国文学史上，欧文和库柏通常被视为美国文学之父，因为前者从各种当地民间传说中汲取艺术创作的灵感，并以美洲山川为背景，写出了充满本土特色的见闻札记和生动故事；而后者则在自称为"纯粹美国式作品"的《间谍》一书中对独立战争进行了深刻的叙述，其中的主人公哈维·伯奇充满了爱国主义精神，成为一位脍炙人口的革命英雄。这些美国文学的奠基之作不仅开始摆脱英国新古典主义文学的影响，为后来的美利坚民族文学繁荣提供了极其宝贵的艺术范本，而且为19世纪初美国浪漫主义文学的兴起开辟了艺术创新的道路。

Lesson 1　American Indian Legend

Ⅰ. A Brief Review.

The early Native American literary texts were orally created, linking the native people with plants and animals, rivers and rocks, and all things believed significant in local life. The texts of origin stories nurture and explore a spiritual kinship between nature and the native people in all forms. Coyote, raven, fox, hawk, turtle, rabbit and other animal characters in the stories are considered by many Native Americans to be their relatives. In the same way, oak, maple, pine, cedar, fir, corn, squash, berries and roots are viewed as relatives, too. According to local legends, the Animal People and Plant People participated in the building of a history before and after the arrival of humans. This history was kept through the spoken words and there was similarity related to the geographical features of the earth.

图1　Iroquious Indians' Place

Registering historic and geographical features of native societies, these texts include informal accounts of personal events and formally recited epics, which depict the creation of the world and other living things. Native American Indians' origin epics are the most distinctive, such as seven major types of origin epics, including *Earth Diver, Father Sky with Mother Earth, Emergence from an Underworld, Spider Weaving the World, Tricksters, Twins, and Dismemberment of a Giant*. None of these epics is unusual: they also appear in other cultures. A good storyteller in American Indian literature could make people feel that they were in another world with a new story, which often has a title, a beginning, and an ending.

The storyteller would often adopt the mode of story by repeating an incident for a specific number of times, connecting the sacred with the native culture. Through this way of repetition, the listeners could remember these tales. Besides, repetition added an aesthetic value and a dramatic effect to the tale for it could help the listener to foretell what could happen to the hero. Therefore, oral literature was usually difficult and boring to read. When transcribed in later years, oral literature loses its effect more or less because readers are not familiar with the worldview, ethics, socio-cultural settings, and personality traits of the Native American people. Furthermore, American Indian oral literature may serve as a chronology for the native people who tried to explain the history of human society and the formality of the cosmos from a primordial perspective. All in all, the role and importance of these tales, whatever type or form, within the domain of literature can be summed up in the Native reminder that "our stories were our libraries".

Ⅱ. Texts.

The Origin of Stories (Seneca)

There was once a boy who had no home. His parents were dead and his uncles would not care for him. In order to live this boy, whose name was Gaqka, or Crow, made a bower of branches for an abiding place and hunted birds and squirrels for food.

He had almost no clothing but was very ragged and dirty. When the people from the village saw him they called him Filth-Covered-One, and laughed as they passed by, holding their noses. No one thought he would ever amount to anything, which made him feel heavy-hearted. He resolved to go away from his tormentors① and become a great hunter.

One night Gaqka found a canoe②. He had never seen this canoe before, so he took it. Stepping in he grasped the paddle, when the canoe immediately shot into the air, and he paddled above the clouds and under the moon. For a long time he went always southward. Finally the canoe dropped into a river and then Gaqka paddled for shore.

On the other side of the river was a great cliff that had a face that looked like a man. It was at the forks of the river where this cliff stood. The boy resolved to make his home on the top of the cliff and so climbed it and built a bark cabin.

The first night he sat on the edge of the cliff he heard a voice saying, "Give me some tobacco." Looking around the boy, seeing no one, replied, "Why should I give tobacco?"

There was no answer and the boy began to fix his arrows for the next day's hunt. After a while the voice spoke again, "Give me some tobacco."

Gaqka now took out some tobacco and threw it over the cliff. The voice spoke again: "Now I will tell you a story."

Feeling greatly awed the boy listened to a story that seemed to come directly out of the rock upon which he was sitting. Finally the voice paused, for the story had ended. Then it spoke again saying, "It shall be the custom hereafter to present me with a small gift for my stories." So the boy gave the rock a few bone beads. Then the rock said, "Hereafter when I speak, announcing that I shall tell a story you must say, 'Nio,' and I speak you must say 'Hě'',' that I may know that you are listening. You must never fall asleep but continue to listen until I say 'Dā'neho nigagā' is.' (So thus finished is the length of my story). Then you shall give me presents and I shall be satisfied."

The next day the boy hunted and killed a great many birds. These he made into soup and roasts. He skinned the birds and saved the skins, keeping them in a bag.

That evening the boy sat on the rock again and looked westward at the sinking sun. He wondered if his friend would speak again. While waiting he chipped some new arrow-points, and made them very small so that he could use them in a blow gun. Suddenly, as he worked, he heard

---

① tormentors: 折磨人的人
② canoe: 独木舟,小划子

the voice again. "Give me some tobacco to smoke," it said. Gaqka threw a pinch of tobacco over the cliff and the voice said, "Hau'nio''," and commenced a story. Long into the night one wonderful tale after another flowed from the rock, until it called out, "So thus finished is the length of my story." Gaqka was sorry to have the stories ended but he gave the rock an awl made from a bird's leg and a pinch of tobacco.

The next day the boy hunted far to the east and there found a village. Nobody knew who he was but he soon found many friends. There were some hunters who offered to teach him how to kill big game, and these went with him to his own camp on the high rock. At night he allowed them to listen to the stories that came forth from the rock, but it would speak only when Gaqka was present. He therefore had many friends with whom to hunt.

Now after a time Gaqka made a new suit of clothing from deer skin and desired to obtain a decorated pouch①. He, therefore, went to the village and found one house where were two daughters living with an old mother. He asked that a pouch be made and the youngest daughter spoke up and said, "It is now finished. I have been waiting for you to come for it." So she gave him a handsome pouch.

Then the old mother spoke, saying, "I now perceive that my future son-in-law has passed through the door and is here." Soon thereafter, the younger woman brought Gaqka a basket of bread and said, "My mother greatly desires that you should marry me." Gaqka looked at the girl and was satisfied, and ate the bread. The older daughter was greatly displeased and frowned in an evil manner.

That night the bride said to her husband, "We must now go away. My older sister will kill you for she is jealous." So Gaqka arose and took his bride to his own lodge. So the rock spoke and began to relate wonder stories of things that happened in the old days. The bride was not surprised, but said, "This standing rock, indeed, is my grandfather. I will now present you with a pouch into which you must put a trophy for every tale related."

All winter long the young couple stayed in the lodge on the great rock and heard all the wonder tales of the old days. Gaqka's bag was full of stories and he knew all the lore of former times.
……

Everybody now thought Gaqka a great man and listened to his stories. He was the first man to find out all about the adventures of the old-time people. That is why there are so many legends now.

Ⅲ. Notes.

1. The word "Seneca" likely derives from the Mahican word, "a stone", or "rock", or the Iroquois name for "it is a standing or projecting stone." The "stone" probably refers to the site of an Oneida village, but the Dutch used the Mahican term generally to identify not only the Oneida, but also the Onondaga and the Cayuga, all of whom were closely linked with the Seneca. The Europeans

---

① pouch: 小袋子,荷包

eventually used the other tribes' true names as they learned them, but the name for the Seneca remained. Whatever the derivation of the term, their identity seems tied to their location, since the name for themselves can be translated into "the people of the great hill."

    2. In Iroquois story *The Origin of Stories*, Gaqka, the young hero, learns the art of storytelling from an anthropomorphic cliff. The characterizations would have resonated for a people whose identity was variously tied to a "great hill" and "projecting rock," and so it is conceivable that the story would have been originally told on the basic source of the legends themselves.

Ⅳ. Key Words(关键词).

oral myth and legend：口述神话与传说。印第安人是美洲土地上最早的主人，他们的原始文化和神话传说近年来被认为是美国文学的最早源头。印第安人没有文字，但有丰富的口头语和手势语。仅北美洲印第安人部族中就有500多种口头语，其中美国和加拿大有149种，大多数沿用至今。丰富多彩的印第安人口述神话、传说、故事、诗歌、民谣、格言等显示了印第安人丰富的想象力和聪明才智。

Origin stories：起源故事。印第安文化中关于"起源"的神话、故事、传说异常丰富，几乎囊括了印第安人生活的各个方面，是早期印第安文学的最主要内容之一。作为神话传说的"起源"可以使我们从一个方面了解印第安人的世界观以及他们对自然，生活等诸多方面的认识。各种"起源故事"传说构成了印第安人的文化之根，对于保护印第安人的文化记忆，确立其文化身份尤其重要。

Ⅴ. Questions.

    1. What is the basic function of Gaqka's story in American Indian culture?
    2. From this story can you figure out how the Indian individuals get their names?
    3. What is the role played by a story-teller in Indian tribal societies?

Lesson 2 Christopher Columbus (1451—1506)

I. A Brief Review.

Born in the Italian Republic of Genoa, Columbus explored the Mediterranean as a mariner and then went to the Italian merchant colony in Lisbon in the 1470s. After he married Felipa Perestrello e Moniz, member of an Italian-Portuguese noble family, he gained access to the Portuguese and Castilian royal courts. Convinced that Asia could be reached by sailing west from Europe, Columbus planned to make expedition to the American countries for the commercial purpose. When the Portuguese King John II refused his plan for a westward passage to Asia, Columbus turned to the Spanish monarchs, Isabella and Ferdinand. They disagreed with Columbus on his flawed geography, but they believed that the world was round and thus agreed to support Columbus's first voyage in early 1492.

图2　Christopher Columbus

Columbus's fleet sailed first to the Canary Islands and then headed westward with following winds. On 12 October, the fleet arrived at an island that Columbus renamed San Salvador. Believing they were in Asia, the crew called the natives "Indians". While visiting Cuba, Columbus could not find the vast chance for commerce and rich ports of Asia. He then sailed to the island he named Hispaniola and explored its northern coast. Columbus made three other voyages to the Caribbean islands and the mainland of Central and South America. During the second and third voyages, he was required to act as a colonial administrator as well. But his poor administrative skills instigated rebels and for this reason he was arrested by a royal investigator and sent back to Spain.

On his fourth and final voyage, Columbus mainly explored the coast of Central America, where he encountered fierce local resistance. In 1506, Columbus died. Like everyone else, Columbus was inevitably influenced by norms and beliefs about commerce, religion, and science of his time. He was deeply religious and hoped to supply funds to recapture Jerusalem from the Muslims to fulfill Christian crusading ideas and millenarian prophecies. Although he failed to find a new route to Asia, Columbus made the lands and peoples of the Western Hemisphere known to Europeans and started a chain of events that helped all societies in the world to be closely connected.

After the American Revolution, the use of Columbus as a founding figure of New World nations spread rapidly. In 1812, the newly founded capital of Ohio was named "Columbia".

Ⅱ. Texts.

Letter to Luis de Sant' Angel (1493)

......

  I understood sufficiently from other Indians... that this land... was an island; and so I followed its coast eastwardly for a hundred and seven leagues as far as where it terminated; from which headland I saw another island to the east [eighteen] leagues distant from this, to which I at once gave the name La Spanola. And I proceeded thither①, and followed the northern coast, as with La Juana, eastwardly for a hundred and [eight-eight] great leagues in a direct easterly course, as with La Juana.

  The which, and all the others, are more [fertile] to an excessive degree, and this extremely so. In it, there are many havens② on the seacoast, incomparable with any others that I know in Christendom, and plenty of rivers so good and great that it is a marvel. The lands thereof are high, and in it are many ranges of hills, and most lofty③ mountains incomparably beyond the Island of [Tenerife]; all most beautiful in a thousand shapes, and all accessible, and full of trees a thousand kinds, so lofty that they seem to reach the sky. And I am assured that they never lose their foliage; as may be imagined, since I saw them as green and as beautiful as they are in Spain during May...

  And the nightingale was singing, and other birds of a thousand sorts, in the month of November, round about the way I was going. There are palm trees of six or eight species, wondrous to see for their beautiful variety; but so are the other trees, and fruits, and plants therein. There are wonderful pine groves, and very large plains of verdure, and there is honey, and many kinds of birds, and many various fruits. In the earth there are many mines of metals; and there is a population of incalculable number. Spanola is a marvel; the mountains and hills, and plains, and fields, and land, so beautiful and rich for planting and sowing, for breeding cattle of all sorts, for building of towns and villages. There could be no believing, without seeing, such harbors as are here, as well as the many and great rivers, and excellent waters, most of which contain gold. In the trees and fruits and plants, there are great differences from those of Juana. In [La Spanola], there are many spiceries, and great mines of gold and other metals.

  The people of this island, and of all the others that I have found and seen, or not seen, all go naked, men and women, just as their mothers bring them forth; although some women cover a single place with the leaf of a plant, or a cotton something which they make for that purpose. They have no iron or steel, nor any weapons; nor are they fit thereunto; not be because they be not a well-formed people and of fair stature, but that they are most wondrously timorous. They have no other weapons than the stems of reeds in their seeding state, on the end of which they fix little sharpened stakes. Even these, they dare not use; for many times has it happened that I sent two or

---

① thither: 到那里;向那里
② havens: 安全场所;避难所
③ lofty: 巍峨的;高耸的

three men ashore to some village to parley, and countless numbers of them sallied forth, but as soon as they saw those approach, they fled away in such wise that even a father would not wait for his son. And this was not because any hurt had ever done to any of them: — but such they are, incurably timid. It is true that since they have become more assured, and are losing that terror, they are artless and generous with what they have, to such a degree as no one would believe but him who had seen it. Of anything they have, if it be asked for, they never say no, but do rather invite the person to accept it, and show as much lovingness as though they would give their hearts. And whether it be a thing of value, or one of little worth, they are straight ways content with whatsoever trifle of whatsoever kind may be given them in return for it. I forbade that anything so worthless as fragments of broken platters, and pieces of broken glass, and strap buckles, should be given them; although when they were able to get such things, they seemed to think they had the best jewel in the world…

And they knew no sect①, nor idolatry②; save that they all believe that power and goodness are in the sky, and they believed very firmly that I, with these ships and crew, came from the sky; and in such opinion, they received me at every place where I landed, after they had lost their terror. And this comes not because they are ignorant; on the contrary, they are men of very subtle wit, who navigate all those seas, and who give a marvelously good account of everything—but because they never saw men wearing clothes nor the like of our ships. And as soon as I arrived in the Indies, in the first island that I found, I took some of them by force to the intent that they should learn [our speech] and give me information of what there was in those parts. And so it was, that very soon they understood [us] and we them, what by speech or what by signs; and those [Indians] have been of much service… with loud cries of "Come! Come to see the people from heaven!" Then, as soon as their minds were reassured about us, every one came, men as well as women, so that there remained none behind, big or little; and they all brought something to eat and drink, which they gave with wondrous lovingness…

It seems to me that in all those islands, the men are all content with a single wife; and to their chief or king they give as many as twenty. The women, it appears to me, do more work than the men. Nor have I been able to learn whether they held personal property, for it seemed to me that whatever one had, they all took share of, especially of eatable things. Down to the present, I have not found in those islands any monstrous men, as many expected, but on the contrary all the people are very comely; nor are they black like those in Guinea, but have flowing hair; and they are not begotten where there is an excessive violence of the rays of the sun…. In those islands, where there are lofty mountains, the cold was very keen there, this winter; but they endued it by being accustomed thereto, and by the help of the meats which they eat with many and inordinately hot spices…

---

① sect: (宗教的) 派别; 宗派
② idolatry: (宗教的) 神像崇拜; 偶像崇拜

Ⅲ. Notes.

1. In this letter to one of his leading supporters in the Spanish court, Christopher Columbus described his reaction to the sights of the New World. In actuality, what he referred to as the island of Hispaniola is present-day Haiti and the Dominican Republic.

2. The last two voyages witnessed Columbus's failure to get along with the natives. He fled by his two remaining worn-out vessels to the Jamaican coast and spent a miserable year before being rescued. Finally, he arrived in Spain on 7 November 1504 with broken health and miserable memory.

Ⅳ. Key Words(关键词).

Explore: 探险。哥伦布的传奇一生与他伟大的航海冒险是不可分割的。没有了航海就没有哥伦布;离开了冒险就无以成就他发现美洲大陆的伟业。哥伦布在世界历史地理大发现中的地位远高于他在美国文学史上的地位,但美国文学的发展却绝不能回避哥伦布的贡献。自哥伦布的航海壮举开始,冒险渐渐地铸就了美利坚的民族特征之一。将目光投向未知的世界,勇于迎接所有的挑战的冒险精神不但成就了美利坚民族,也成就了美国文学。

Description: 描述。虽然哥伦布的主要历史贡献在于航海探险和新大陆的发现,哥伦布在他的日志和信件中对美洲作了极为生动的描述,而欧洲人正是从他的描述中第一次对壮丽的美洲有了印象。这在客观上激起了欧洲人对新大陆的向往,激励着越来越多的人不畏艰险来美洲寻梦,并最终完成了美洲国家的建立。从这个意义上来说,哥伦布对美洲的描述有其独特的文学价值。

Ⅴ. Questions.

1. What does Columbus' description of the indigenous people he encountered reveal his preconceptions of the New World?

2. Why was Columbus so amazed at the physical environment of the New World? Was it so different from the Old?

3. What were the European expectations of the New World?

Lesson 3　American Indian Oral Poetry

I. A Brief Review.

In Native American cultures, poems (more properly called "songs") were often presented orally for such tribal occasions as initiation rites, healings ceremonies, and planting or hunting rituals. The songs could be significant in the transmission of tribal history, standards of ethical conduct, and religious beliefs. Closely related to nearly every side of Indian life, there were many forms of local poetry, such as love songs, war songs, songs sung in stories, game songs, lullabies and other American songs in Native American cultures. While some

图 3　Native Indians in Hunting

songs were composed by individuals, others were borrowed from neighboring peoples. Tribal singers believed that words could magically connect them with the supernatural forces, so they often projected themselves into the future by "visualizing" the outcome they hoped to produce or by identifying with nature. Actually, these songs contributed largely to the cohesion of the community of Indian tribes.

Usually the songs were rhythmically chanted or sung in a tribal context to drums or musical accompaniment. Parallelisms and repetitions of similar or contrasting phrases were often used to create the effect of "rhyming thoughts" rather than the rhyming sounds. Repetition could become a powerful memorizing technique in the context of performed tribal ceremonies. Economy of language was also common in Native American oral poetry, as can be seen in this typical superb two-line poem "Spring Song" (Chippewa):

> *As my eyes search the prairie*
> *I feel the summer in the spring.*

Chanted over a long period of time in a performance context, these lines would have a strong impact on readers as the speaker invoked and anticipated the warmth and fullness of summer after a hard winter, although the precise and terse images of the lines may sometimes seem like imagist poetry to modern readers. Throughout hundreds years of the history of the United States, numerous Native People have created numerous orations including songs, many of them are considered the greatest in world literature.

Ⅱ. Texts.

Love Song①
(Aleut)
I cannot bear it, I cannot bear it at all.
I cannot bear to be where I usually am.
She is yonder, she moves near me, she is dancing.
I cannot bear it
If I may not smell her breath, the fragrance of her.

Formula to Secure Love②
(Cherokee)
Now! I am as beautiful as the very blossoms themselves
I am a man, you lovely ones, you women of the Seven Clans!③
Now! You women who reside among the Seven Peoples,
I have just come to intrude myself among you.

All of you have just come to gaze upon me alone, the most beautiful.
Now! You lovely women, already I just took your souls!

I am a man!
You women will live in the very middle of my soul.

Forever I will be as beautiful as the bright red blossoms!④

Song of War
(Blackfeet)
Old man on high [Sun],
help me,
that I may be saved from my dream!
Give me a good day!
I prey you, pity me!

---

① 选自居住在北美阿拉斯加的阿留申人的诗歌
② Formula to Secure Love: 切罗基族(北美易洛魁人的一支)有很多记载被称为 *i: gawe: sdi* 的巫术的手稿,这首切罗基族诗歌就记载于这样的手稿之上
③ 这首诗歌附有注释,称写给那些在成长中自助的青年,在念完四遍后向他所选的女子呼气。"七"在切罗基人中代表圆满
④ 红色在切罗基人中是胜利和力量的象征

Song of War

*Odjib'we*①

(*Anishinabe*)②

The Sioux women

pass to and fro wailing.

As they gather up their wounded men

the voice of their weeping comes back to me. ③

Ⅲ. Notes.

Some of native oral "poetry" are essentially analogized with modern poems. When old parts of the Navajo Blessing way Rite are translated and printed, for example, they read like poems on the page, and their appearance invites us to read them as if they were as self-contained and discrete as modern poems.

Ⅳ. Key Words(关键词).

Indian songs: 印第安诗歌。虽然在每一次提及时都被冠以"诗歌"之名,但它实际上并不符合中西文化及文学研究中对诗歌的通常定义和理解。毋宁说它是印第安人的"歌谣"。

Blackfeet: 黑脚族。历史上的印第安黑脚族以捕猎野牛为生,生活在现今美国蒙大拿及加拿大阿尔伯塔。黑脚族视太阳为生命之神,是他们祈祷的对象。诗歌中对"怜悯"的祈求表达了对太阳的敬畏和依靠。诗歌中的勇士因梦到即将到来的战斗而焦虑,因而祈求神灵的帮助。

Ⅴ. Questions.

1. From the selected Indian songs, can you find the object of Indian people's worship?
2. Would you try to make a comparison between Indian songs and typical English poems?
3. How do you understand the relationship between native songs and American multiculturism?

---

① Odjib'we 为自己的亲人复仇,立誓要追杀苏族人

② 即契帕瓦族印第安人,生活在明尼苏达、威斯康星及安大略西部,历史上曾因与苏族人争夺土地而成为死敌。弗朗丝·邓斯莫上世纪初在明尼苏达印第安人保留地得到这首诗歌

③ 这首诗歌是弗朗丝·邓斯莫收录的三首有关 Odjib'we 远征苏族人的诗歌中的一首,战斗发生在明尼苏达河上游苏族人的营地。据邓斯莫记载,"一支上百人的契帕瓦战斗队袭击了苏族人的营地,首先被杀的就是苏族人的首领。战斗中苏族妇女冲出来拽回受伤的男人,否则他们会被割下头皮。"

Lesson 4　William Bradford (1590—1657)

Ⅰ. **A Brief Review.**

　　Born near Doncaster, in Austerfield, Yorkshire, William Bradford lived with his relatives after his parents died at his early childhood. When he was about 12, he happened to witness a church service in the neighboring town of Scrooby. Determined to reform the church, Bradford joined a "Separatist" church by the age of 17, which was radical enough to separate from the official Church of England. Compared with the Puritans who wanted to purify the Church of England, the Separatists thought the Church was beyond redemption because of its unbiblical doctrines and teachings. Due to this dangerous decision, Separatist leaders were persecuted by the King of England. Bradford fled to the Netherlands in 1609 with many members of the congregation. However, urged by their English ally King James, the Netherlands harassed the refugees.

图4　William Bradford

　　As a result, members of the congregation decided to flee to the north of the Virginia Colony. There they could remain loyal to King James, while freeing from interference in their way of worship. William Bradford was responsible to make out the plan for this move. He carefully preserved many notes and documents for the beckoning future, from which he later crafted his journal known today as *Of Plymouth Plantation*. Bradford finally sailed for America with his wife and other passengers in 1620 from Leiden aboard the *Mayflower*. After 65 days at sea, the exhausted company finally dropped anchor off Cape Cod in November 1620. However, the Pilgrims were frightened by the Native People, so they sailed on to their final destination, Plymouth Harbor. The worst ordeal was that they did not have enough food. Nearly all became ill. Within five months half of the company died, including John Carver who had been elected their first governor. William Bradford succeeded Carver as Governor, which he would remain almost until his death in 1657, a total of 36 years of public service.

　　The Pilgrims found out that native corn was more suitable to the climate than their English seed. By autumn they had "fitted their houses against winter" and had "all things in good plenty." To celebrate their harvest, the governor started a Thanksgiving shared with their Wampanoag friends. They also remained on good terms with the Native People. Since Bradford was elected governor of the plantation, he underwent great hardships in governing such an unstable settlement. William Bradford died at Plymouth, and was interred at Plymouth Burial Hill. His life and influence have been chronicled by many. As the author of a manuscript journal and the long-term governor of Plymouth Colony, William Bradford's most well-known work by far is *Of Plymouth Plantation*, which recorded in detail the founding of the Massachusetts Bay Colony and the lives of the Puritan colonists from 1621 to 1646. It was a retrospective account of his recollections and observations, written in the form of two books.

Ⅱ. Texts.

Of Plymouth Plantation
Book Ⅱ
Chapter Ⅺ
The Remainder of Anno 1620

[The Mayflower Compact]

I shall a little return back, and begin with a combination made by them before they came ashore; being the first foundation of their government in this place.① Occasioned partly by the discontented and mutinous speeches that some of the strangers amongst them had let fall from them in the ship: That when they came ashore they would use their own liberty, for none had power to command them, the patent they had being for Virginia and not for New England, which belonged to another government, with which the Virginia Company had nothing to do. And partly that such an act by them done, this their condition considered, might be as firm as any patent, and in some respects more sure.

The form was as followeth

IN THE NAME OF GOD, AMEN.

We whose names are underwritten, the loyal subjects of our dread Sovereign Lord King James, by the Grace of God of Great Britain, France, and Ireland King, Defender of the Faith, etc.

Having undertaken, for the Glory of God and advancement of the Christian Faith and Honour of our King and Country, a Voyage to plant the First Colony in the Northern Parts of Virginia, do by these presents solemnly and mutually in the presence of God and one of another, Covenant and Combine ourselves together into a Civil Body Politic, for our better ordering and preservation and furtherance of the ends aforesaid; and by virtue hereof to enact, constitute and frame such just and equal Laws, Ordinances, Acts, Constitutions and Offices, from time to time, as shall be thought most meet and convenient for the general good of the Colony, unto which we promise all due submission and obedience. In witness whereof we have hereunder subscribed our names at Cape Cod, the 11th of November, in the year of the reign of our Sovereign Lord King James, of England, France and Ireland the eighteenth, and of Scotland the fifty-fourth. Anno Domini 1620.

After this they chose, or rather confirmed, Mr. John Carver (a man godly and well approved amongst them) their Governor for that year. And after they had provided a place for their goods,

---

① Place: 指 1620 年清教徒抵达时的普利茅斯

or common store (which were long in unlading for want of boats, foulness of the winter weather and sickness of divers) and begun some small cottages for their habitation; as time would admit, they met and consulted of laws and orders, both for their civil and military government as the necessity of their condition did require, still adding thereunto as urgent occasion in several times, and as cases did require.

……

But that which was most sad and lamentable was, that in two or three months' time half of their company died, especially in January and February, being the depth of winter, and wanting houses and other comforts; being infected with the scurvy and other diseases which this long voyage and their inaccommodate condition had brought upon them. So as there died some times two or three of a day in the foresaid time, that of 100 and odd persons, scarce fifty remained. And of these, in the time of most distress, there was but six or seven sound persons who to their great commendations, be it spoken, spared no pains night nor day, but with abundance of toil and hazard of their own health, fetched them wood, made them fires, dressed them meat, made their beds, washed their loathsome clothes, clothed and unclothed them. In a word, did all the homely and necessary offices for them which dainty and queasy stomachs cannot endure to hear named; and all this willingly and cheerfully, without any grudging in the least, showing herein their true love unto their friends and brethren; a rare example and worthy to be remembered. Two of these seven were Mr. William Brewster, their reverend Elder, and Myles Standish, their Captain and military commander, unto whom myself and many others were much beholden in our low and sick condition. And yet the Lord so upheld these persons as in this general calamity they were not at all infected either with sickness or lameness. And what I have said of these I may of many others who died in this general visitation, and others yet living; that whilst they had health, yea, or any strength continuing, they were not wanting to any that had need of them. And I doubt not but their recompense is with the Lord. ……

Ⅲ. Notes.

1. *Of Plymouth Plantation* refers to the most complete authority the Pilgrims founded in the early years of the Colony. The Bradford journal is the single most important source of information about the Pilgrims and Plymouth Colony. Bradford's history is a blend of fact and interpretation. The Bradford journal records not only the events of the first 30 years but also the reactions of the colonists.

2. The Bradford journal is regarded by historians as the preeminent work of 17th century America. It is Bradford's simple yet vivid story, as told in his journal, which has made the Pilgrims the much-loved "spiritual ancestors of all Americans".

Ⅳ. Key Words(关键词).

The Mayflower Compact: "五月花号公约"。在布莱福得牧师的带领下,为摆脱宗教迫害的35名清教徒及其他67人于1620年9月16日乘"五月花"号向美洲进发。11月21日抵达达科德角(今马萨诸塞州)。船上41名成年男子决定共同签署一份公约,名为"五月花号公约"。这份公约成为美国日后无数自治公约中的首例,它的形成表明了:人民可以由自己来决定自治管理的方式,不再由超越人民的强权来管理。这对王权与神权统治是重大反叛,可谓美国民主社会建设的里程碑。

Thanksgiving Day: 感恩节。清教徒在美洲的第一个冬天所遇到的饥荒与美国感恩节的传统有极为密切的联系。当"五月花"号帆船满载着102人到达美洲时,正值冬天。他们处在饥寒交迫之中,冬天过去时,活下来的移民只有50来人。这时,心地善良的印第安人给移民送来了生活必需品,还特地派人教他们怎样狩猎、养火鸡、捕鱼和种植玉米、南瓜等。在印第安人的帮助下,移民们终于获得了丰收。在欢庆丰收的日子,移民为了感谢上帝恩典和印第安人的真诚帮助,邀请他们参加庆祝仪式。在第一个感恩节的这一天,人们在清晨列队进入一间用作教堂的屋子,向上帝表达谢意,然后点起篝火举行盛大宴会。第二天和第三天又举行了摔跤、赛跑、唱歌、跳舞等活动。

V. Questions.

1. What is the significance of *Mayflower* in American history?
2. How did the newcomers cope with the starvation and hardship in their first winter?
3. Who was the first actual leader of all the pilgrims before Bradford?

Lesson 5　Benjamin Franklin (1706—1790)

Ⅰ. A Brief Review.

图 5　Benjamin Franklin

Benjamin Franklin, American printer and publisher, author, scientist, inventor, and diplomat, was born in Boston into a pious Puritan family, whose forebears had come to New England in 1683 to avoid the Restoration era. However, Franklin rejected the Calvinist theology of his father, and adopted the more secular world view of Sir Isaac Newton and John Locke, which added the tolerance of the new philosophy to his Puritan earnestness.

Due to the lack of formal education out of poverty, Franklin became an apprentice to his brother James, printer of a Boston newspaper. Refusing to suffer his brother's petty tyrannies, Franklin ran away to Philadelphia in 1723, where he set up his own press and published a newspaper (Pennsylvania Gazette), *Poor Richard's Almanac*, and a good share of the public printing. He received a comfortable income from his business for 20 more years and retired at the age of 42. Franklin became very popular in the publication of *Poor Richards Almanac* and later his famous *Autobiography*, in which he praised hard work, thriftiness, and honesty as the poor man's means for a successful career. He also applied his talent for hard work to science. After inventing the Pennsylvania fireplace (soon called the Franklin stove), he turned to electricity. In his famous kite experiment, he proved that lightning is a form of electricity. He was elected to the Royal Society in 1756 for his scientific ingenuity. Franklin the scientist seemed to confirm the 18th-century faith that men were able to understand themselves and the world in which they lived.

As an active politician, he signed the Declaration of Independence and negotiated with France and Britain on behalf of the newly formed government of the United States. As the only person to have signed the three most significant founding documents of the United States—"the Declaration of Independence" (1776), "the Treaty of Paris" (1783), and "the U. S. Constitution" (1787)—Benjamin Franklin is revered by later generations as an international celebrity in his day and a representative of the American character in history.

II. Texts.

The Way to Wealth

Courteous Reader,

  I have heard that nothing gives an author so great pleasure, as to find his works respectfully quoted by other learned authors. This pleasure I have seldom enjoyed; for though I have been, if I may say it without vanity, an eminent author of almanacs annually now a full quarter of a century, my brother authors in the same way, for what reason I know not, have ever been very sparing in their applauses; and no other author has taken the least notice of me, so that did not my writings produce me some solid pudding, the great deficiency of praise would have quite discouraged me.

  I concluded at length, that the people were the best judges of my merit; for they buy my works; and besides, in my rambles, where I am not personally known, I have frequently heard one or other of my adages repeated, with, as Poor Richard says, at the end on't; this gave me some satisfaction, as it showed not only that my instructions were regarded, but discovered likewise some respect for my authority; and I own, that to encourage the practice of remembering and repeating those wise sentences, I have sometimes quoted myself with great gravity.

  Judge then how much I must have been gratified by an incident I am going to relate to you. I stopped my horse lately where a great number of people were collected at a vendue① of merchant goods. The hour of sale not being come, they were conversing on the badness of the times, and one of the company called to a plain clean old man, with white locks, "Pray, Father Abraham, what think you of the times? Won't these heavy taxes quite ruin the country? How shall we be ever able to pay them? What would you advise us to?" Father Abraham stood up, and replied, "If you'd have my advice, I'll give it to you in short, for a word to the wise is enough, and many words won't fill a bushel, as Poor Richard says." They joined in desiring him to speak his mind, and gathering round him, he proceeded as follows:

  Friends, says he, and neighbors, the taxes are indeed very heavy, and if those laid on by the government were the only ones we had to pay, we might more easily discharge them; but we have many others, and much more grievous to some of us. We are taxed twice as much by our idleness, three times as much by our pride, and four times as much by our folly, and from these taxes the commissioners cannot ease or deliver us by allowing an abatement. However let us hearken to good advice, and something may be done for us; God helps them that help themselves②, as Poor Richard says, in his almanac of 1733.

  It would be thought a hard government that should tax its people one tenth part of their time, to be employed in its service. But idleness taxes many of us much more, if we reckon all that is spent in absolute sloth③, or doing of nothing, with that which is spent in idle employments or

---

① vendue: 这里指出售或拍卖
② God helps them that help themselves: 上帝帮助自助者
③ sloth: 指无所事事或懒散

amusements, that amount to nothing. Sloth, by bringing on diseases, absolutely shortens life. Sloth, like rust, consumes faster than labor wears, while the used key is always bright, as Poor Richard says. But dost thou love life, then do not squander time, for that's the stuff life is made of, as Poor Richard says. How much more than is necessary do we spend in sleep, forgetting that the sleeping fox catches no poultry, and that there will be sleeping enough in the grave, as Poor Richard says.

If time be of all things the most precious, wasting time must be, as Poor Richard says, the greatest prodigality, since, as he elsewhere tells us, lost time is never found again, and what we call time-enough, always proves little enough: let us then be up and be doing, and doing to the purpose; so by diligence shall we do more with less perplexity. Sloth makes all things difficult, but industry all easy, as Poor Richard says; and he that riseth late, must trot all day, and shall scarce overtake his business at night. While laziness travels so slowly, that poverty soon overtakes him, as we read in Poor Richard, who adds, drive thy business, let not that drive thee; and early to bed, and early to rise, makes a man healthy, wealthy and wise.

So what signifies wishing and hoping for better times. We may make these times better if we bestir ourselves. Industry need not wish, as Poor Richard says, and he that lives upon hope will die fasting. There are no gains, without pains, then help hands, for I have no lands, or if I have, they are smartly taxed. And, as Poor Richard likewise observes, he that hath a trade hath an estate, and he that hath a calling① hath an office of profit and honor; but then the trade must be worked at, and the calling well followed, or neither the estate, nor the office, will enable us to pay our taxes. If we are industrious we shall never starve; for, as Poor Richard says, at the working man's house hunger looks in, but dares not enter. Nor will the bailiff or the constable enter, for industry pays debts, while despair encreaseth them, says Poor Richard. What though you have found no treasure, nor has any rich relation left you a legacy, diligence is the mother of good luck, as Poor Richard says, and God gives all things to industry. Then plough deep, while sluggards sleep, and you shall have corn to sell and to keep, says Poor Dick. Work while it is called today, for you know not how much you may be hindered tomorrow, which makes Poor Richard say, one today is worth two tomorrows; and farther, have you somewhat to do tomorrow, do it today. If you were a servant, would you not be ashamed that a good master should catch you idle? Are you then your own master, be ashamed to catch yourself idle, as Poor Dick says. When there is so much to be done for yourself, your family, your country, and your gracious king, be up by peep of day; let not the sun look down and say, inglorious here he lies. Handle your tools without mittens; remember that the cat in gloves catches no mice, as Poor Richard says. 'Tis true there is much to be done, and perhaps you are weak handed, but stick to it steadily, and you will see great effects, for constant dropping wears away stones, and by diligence and patience the mouse ate in two the cable; and little strokes fell great oaks, as Poor Richard says in his almanac, the year I cannot just now remember.

---

① hath a calling: 宗教词语，指响应上帝的召唤

Methinks① I hear some of you say, must a man afford himself no leisure? I will tell thee, my friend, what Poor Richard says, employ thy time well if thou meanest to gain leisure; and, since thou art not sure of a minute, throw not away an hour. Leisure is time for doing something useful; this leisure the diligent man will obtain, but the lazy man never; so that, as Poor Richard says, a life of leisure and a life of laziness are two things. Do you imagine that sloth will afford you more comfort than labor? No, for as Poor Richard says, trouble springs from idleness, and grievous toil from needless ease. Many without labor would live by their wits only, but they break for want of stock. Whereas industry gives comfort, and plenty, and respect: fly pleasures, and they'll follow you. The diligent spinner has a large shift②, and now I have a sheep and a cow, everybody bids me good morrow, all which is well said by Poor Richard.

But with our industry, we must likewise be steady, settled and careful, and oversee our own affairs with our own eyes, and not trust too much to others; for, as Poor Richard says,

> I never saw an oft removed tree,
> Nor yet an oft removed family,
> That throve so well as those that settled be.

And again, three removes③ is as bad as a fire, and again, keep the shop, and thy shop will keep thee; and again, if you would have your business done, go; if not, send. And again,

> He that by the plough would thrive,
> Himself must either hold or drive.

"And again, the eye of a master will do more work than both his hands; and again, want of care does us more damage than want of knowledge; and again, not to oversee workmen is to leave them your purse open. Trusting too much to others' care is the ruin of many; for, as the almanac says, in the affairs of this world men are saved not by faith, but by the want of it; but a man's own care is profitable; for, saith Poor Dick, learning is to the studious, and riches to the careful, as well as power to the bold, and Heaven to the virtuous. And farther, if you would have a faithful servant, and one that you like, serve yourself. And again, he adviseth to circumspection and care, even in the smallest matters, because sometimes a little neglect may breed great mischief; adding, for want of a nail the shoe was lost; for want of a shoe the horse was lost, and for want of a horse the rider was lost, being overtaken and slain by the enemy, all for want of care about a horse-shoe nail. "So much for industry, my friends, and attention to one's own business; but to these we must add frugality, if we would make our industry more certainly successful. A man may, if he

---

① methinks: 旧用法,意为我认为
② shift: 这里指衣橱或衣柜
③ removes: 指迁移,搬迁

knows not how to save as he gets, keep his nose all his life to the grindstone, and die not worth a groat① at last. A fat kitchen makes a lean will, as Poor Richard says; and,

> Many estates are spent in the getting,
> Since women for tea forsook spinning and knitting,
> And men for punch forsook hewing and splitting.

If you would be wealthy, says he, in another almanac, think of saving as well as of getting: the Indies have not made Spain rich, because her outgoes are greater than her incomes.

Ⅲ. Notes.

1. His *Poor Richard's Almanac* includes such often-quoted adages as "A penny saved is two pence dear" (often misquoted as "A penny saved is a penny earned"), and "Fish and visitors stink in three days". Franklin was "the most accomplished American of his age and the most influential in inventing the type of society that America would become."

2. Franklin composed this essay for the twenty-fifth anniversary issue of his Almanac, the first issue of which, under the fictitious editorship of "Richard Saunders", appeared in 1733. For this essay Franklin brought together the best of his maxims in the guise of a speech by Father Abraham. It is frequently reprinted as the way to wealth, but is also known by earlier titles: *Poor Richard Improved* and *Father Abraham's Speech*.

Ⅳ. Key Words（关键词）.

American Spirit: 美国精神。美国精神不仅意味着自由、平等、博爱，而且还包含着美利坚民族性格中最为突出的特点，那就是开拓创新和勇于冒险的气质。富兰克林的个人成长历程突出体现了从第一批英国清教徒移民北美大陆时就开始形成并传承下来的顽强拼搏、艰苦创业、开拓进取的美国精神。

Wealth: 财富。美国文化向来重视俗世的成功与享受，而这一切在相当程度上取决于对物质财富的占有。本杰明。富兰克林认为："私有财富是社会的创造，又从属于社会的需要。"富兰克林的诸多论著生动表述了如何获得财富，如何利用财富，以及财富的人生意义等问题，对后世美国人的财富观产生了极为深远的影响。

Ⅴ. Questions.

1. What are the real taxes one has to pay in his life according to Father Abraham? And what are the smart ways to get rid of them?
2. To Poor Richard, what is the proper way to wealth?
3. What is the difference between leisure and laziness?

---

① groat: 指面值四便士的一种银币

Lesson 6　Washington Irving (1783—1859)

I. **A Brief Review.**

　　Washington Irving was born in New York City on April 3, 1783. His parents named their son after their hero general, George Washington. After the American Revolution, an increasing sense of national pride permeated the country and Americans began to call for an independent literature different from European models to express their Americanism. Irving was one of the pioneers whose writing will be remembered for generations in this regard.

　　His career as a writer started with his writing for journals and newspapers, such as *Morning Chronicle* (1802—03), which was edited by his brother Peter. From 1812 to 1814 he was an editor of *Analectic Magazine* in Philadelphia and New York. With the publication of *History of New York*, a satirical history of the Dutch regime in New York, under

图6　Washington Irving

pseudonym of "Dietrich Knickerbocker", Irving obtained national fame as an established writer. His *The Sketch Book* (1819—20), a collection of stories, made Irving even more successful that he became a full-time writer. Although heavily influenced by the German folktales, stories from this collection, such as "Rip Van Winkle" and "The Legend of Sleepy Hollow," presented a fine example of Irving's craft and served as models for the modern American short story. The publication of this book made Irving the first American author popular with audiences abroad.

　　Irving's translation of Navarette's *Columbus* and extensive research for *The Life and Voyages of Christopher Columbus* (1828) during his stay in Europe were considered the greatest of his historical and biographical works, which established Irving in these new genres. Irving remained abroad for seventeen years and then returned to America in 1832. Shortly after his return, Irving went to an expedition to the Western territories and visited the Osage and Pawnee Indian tribes. His works produced during this time had an American flavor and exploratory themes, such as *A Tour of the Prairies* (1835), *Astoria* (1836) and *Adventures of Captain Bonneville, USA* (1837). By 1842, Irving accepted a position as the minister to Spain, where he remained the minister until 1845 when his presence was requested in London as a representative for the United States to settle the issues concerning Oregon and the boundaries between the United States and Canada. By the end of 1846, Irving returned to America and continued working on his biographies and other works. Eight months after completing the final volume of *The Life of Washington* (1855—1859) at age seventy-six, Washington Irving died of heart attack on November 28, 1859.

As the founding father of American literature, Irving was popular and extolled by his contemporaries, and his position in American literature is prominent permanently for his establishment of the American national literature, his undisputable work as a storyteller, a biographer and a historian.

Ⅱ. Texts.

The Legend of Sleepy Hollow

(*Found among the Papers of the Late Dietrich Knickerbocker*)

I recollect that, when a stripling①, my first exploit in squirrel-shooting was in a grove of tall walnut-trees that shades one side of the valley. I had wandered into it at noon-time, when all nature is peculiarly quiet, and was startled by the roar of my own gun, as it broke the Sabbath stillness around, and was prolonged and reverberated by the angry echoes. If ever I should wish for a retreat, whither I might steal from the world and its distractions, and dream quietly away the remnant of a troubled life, I know of none more promising than this little valley.

From the listless repose of the place, and the peculiar character of its inhabitants, who are descendants from the original Dutch settlers, this sequestered② glen has long been known by the name of SLEEPY HOLLOW, and its rustic lads are called the Sleepy Hollow Boys throughout all the neighboring country. A drowsy, dreamy influence seems to hang over the land, and to pervade the very atmosphere. Some say that the place was bewitched by a high German③ doctor, during the early days of the settlement; others, that an old Indian chief, the prophet or wizard of his tribe, held his powwows there before the country was discovered by Master Hendrick Hudson④. Certain it is, the place still continues under the sway of some witching power, that holds a spell over the minds of the good people, causing them to walk in a continual reverie. They are given to all kinds of marvellous beliefs; are subject to trances and visions; and frequently see strange sights, and hear music and voices in the air. The whole neighborhood abounds with local tales, haunted spots, and twilight superstitions: stars shoot and meteors glare oftener across the valley than in any other part of the country, and the nightmare, with her whole nine fold, seems to make it the favorite scene of her gambols.

The dominant spirit, however, that haunts this enchanted region, and seems to be commander-in-chief of all the powers of the air, is the apparition of a figure on horseback without a head. It is said by some to be the ghost of a Hessian trooper⑤, whose head had been carried away

---

① stripling: 小伙子
② sequester: 与世隔绝的
③ High German: 德国南部
④ Hendrick Hudson: 为荷兰服务的英国航海家
⑤ the ghost of a Hessian trooper: 传说在美国独立战争时期的一次战役中头被炮弹打飞的一个德国赫塞骑兵的鬼魂

by a cannon-ball, in some nameless battle during the revolutionary war; and who is ever and anon① seen by the country folk, hurrying along in the gloom of night, as if on the wings of the wind. His haunts are not confined to the valley, but extend at times to the adjacent roads, and especially to the vicinity of a church at no great distance. Indeed, certain of the most authentic historians of those parts, who have been careful in collecting and collating the floating facts concerning this spectre, allege that the body of the trooper having been buried in the churchyard, the ghost rides forth to the scene of battle in nightly quest of his head; and that the rushing speed with which he sometimes passes along the Hollow, like a midnight blast, is owing to his being belated, and in a hurry to get back to the churchyard before daybreak.

Such is the general purport of this legendary superstition, which has furnished materials for many a wild story in that region of shadows; and the spectre is known, at all the country firesides, by the name of the Headless Horseman of Sleepy Hollow.

It is remarkable that the visionary propensity I have mentioned is not confined to the native inhabitants of the valley, but is unconsciously imbibed by every one who resides there for a time. However wide awake they may have been before they entered that sleepy region, they are sure, in a little while, to inhale the witching influence of the air, and begin to grow imaginative—to dream dreams, and see apparitions②.

I mention this peaceful spot with all possible laud; for it is in such little retired Dutch valleys, found here and there embosomed in the great State of New York, that population, manners, and customs, remain fixed; while the great torrent of migration and improvement, which is making such incessant changes in other parts of this restless country, sweeps by them unobserved. They are like those little nooks of still water which border a rapid stream; where we may see the straw and bubble riding quietly at anchor, or slowly revolving in their mimic harbor, undisturbed by the rush of the passing current. Though many years have elapsed since I trod the drowsy shades of Sleepy Hollow, yet I question whether I should not still find the same trees and the same families vegetating in its sheltered bosom③.

In this by-place of nature there abode, in a remote period of American history, that is to say, some thirty years since, a worthy wight of the name of Ichabod Crane, who sojourned, or, as he expressed it, "tarried," in Sleepy Hollow, for the purpose of instructing the children of the vicinity. He was a native of Connecticut; a State which supplies the Union with pioneers for the mind as well as for the forest, and sends forth yearly its legions of frontier woodsmen and country schoolmasters. The cognomen of Crane was not inapplicable to his person④. He was tall, but exceedingly lank, with narrow shoulders, long arms and legs, hands that dangled a mile out of his

---

① ever and anon: 时常
② see apparitions: 看到鬼魂显形
③ vegetating in its sheltered bosom: 在沉睡谷的荫庇下过着单调慵懒的生活
④ the cognomen of Crane was not inapplicable to his person: 这人姓克莱恩；克莱恩的意思是"鹤"，而他本人也确实有点像鹤

sleeves, feet that might have served for shovels, and his whole frame most loosely hung together. His head was small, and flat at top, with huge ears, large green glassy eyes, and a long snipe nose, so that it looked like a weather-cock, perched upon his spindle neck, to tell which way the wind blew. To see him striding along the profile of a hill on a windy day, with his clothes bagging and fluttering about him, one might have mistaken him for the genius① of famine descending upon the earth, or some scarecrow eloped from a corn-field.

His school-house was a low building of one large room, rudely constructed of logs; the windows partly glazed, and partly patched with leaves of old copy-books. It was most ingeniously secured at vacant hours, by a withe twisted in the handle of the door, and stakes set against the window-shutters; so that, though a thief might get in with perfect ease, he would find some embarrassment in getting out; an idea most probably borrowed by the architect, Yost Van Houten, from the mystery of an eelpot②. The school-house stood in a rather lonely but pleasant situation, just at the foot of a woody hill, with a brook running close by, and a formidable birch-tree growing at one end of it. From hence the low murmur of his pupils' voices, conning over their lessons, might be heard in a drowsy summer's day, like the hum of a bee-hive; interrupted now and then by the authoritative voice of the master, in the tone of menace or command; or, peradventure, by the appalling sound of the birch, as he urged some tardy loiterer along the flowery path of knowledge. Truth to say, he was a conscientious man, and ever bore in mind the golden maxim, "Spare the rod and spoil the child."③—Ichabod Crane's scholars certainly were not spoiled.

I would not have it imagined, however, that he was one of those cruel potentates of the school, who joy in the smart of④ their subjects; on the contrary, he administered justice with discrimination rather than severity; taking the burden off the backs of the weak, and laying it on those of the strong. Your mere puny stripling, that winced at the least flourish of the rod, was passed by with indulgence; but the claims of justice were satisfied by inflicting a double portion on some little, tough, wrong-headed, broad-skirted Dutch urchin, who sulked and swelled, and grew dogged and sullen beneath the birch. All this he called "doing his duty by their parents;" and he never inflicted a chastisement without following it by the assurance, so consolatory to the smarting urchin, that he would remember it, and thank him for it the longest day he had to live.

When school hours were over, he was even the companion and playmate of the larger boys; and on holiday afternoons would convoy some of the smaller ones home of a holy day, who happened to have pretty sisters, or good housewives for mothers, noted for the comforts of the cupboard. Indeed, it behooved him to keep on good terms with his pupils. The revenue arising from his school was small, and would have been scarcely sufficient to furnish him with daily bread, for he was a huge feeder, and, though lank, had the dilating powers of an anaconda; but to

---

① genius: 形象
② from the mystery of an eelpot: 袭用了捕鳝笼子的妙处
③ Spare the rod and spoil the child: 不动棍子,宠坏孩子
④ in the smart of: 以……的痛苦为代价

help out his maintenance, he was, according to country custom in those parts, boarded and lodged at the houses of the farmers, whose children he instructed. With these he lived successively a week at a time; thus going the rounds of the neighborhood, with all his worldly effects① tied up in a cotton handkerchief.

……

The schoolmaster is generally a man of some importance in the female circle of a rural neighborhood; being considered a kind of idle gentlemanlike personage, of vastly superior taste and accomplishments to the rough country swains, and, indeed, inferior in learning only to the parson. His appearance, therefore, is apt to occasion some little stir at the tea-table of a farm-house, and the addition of a supernumerary dish of cakes or sweetmeats, or, peradventure, the parade of a silver teapot. Our man of letters, therefore, was peculiarly happy in the smiles of all the country damsels. How he would figure among them in the churchyard, between services on Sundays; gathering grapes for them from the wild vines that overrun the surrounding trees; reciting for their amusement all the epitaphs on the tombstones; or sauntering, with a whole bevy of them, along the banks of the adjacent mill-pond; while the more bashful country bumpkins hung sheepishly back②, envying his superior elegance and address.

From his half itinerant life, also, he was a kind of travelling gazette③, carrying the whole budget of local gossip from house to house; so that his appearance was always greeted with satisfaction. He was, moreover, esteemed by the women as a man of great erudition, for he had read several books quite through, and was a perfect master of Cotton Mather's History of New England Witchcraft④, in which, by the way, he most firmly and potently believed.

He was, in fact, an odd mixture of small shrewdness and simple credulity. His appetite for the marvellous, and his powers of digesting it, were equally extraordinary; and both had been increased by his residence in this spellbound region. No tale was too gross or monstrous for his capacious swallow. It was often his delight, after his school was dismissed in the afternoon, to stretch himself on the rich bed of clover, bordering the little brook that whimpered by his school-house, and there con over old Mather's direful tales, until the gathering dusk of the evening made the printed page a mere mist before his eyes. Then, as he wended his way, by swamp and stream and awful woodland, to the farm-house where he happened to be quartered, every sound of nature, at that witching hour, fluttered his excited imagination: the moan of the whip-poor-will⑤ from the hill-side; the boding cry of the tree-toad, that harbinger of storm⑥; the dreary hooting of

---

① worldly effects: 现世的动产
② while the more bashful country bumpkins hung sheepishly back: 而那些比较怕羞的乡下佬羞怯地踌躇不前
③ travelling gazette: 逐户换阅的小报
④ History of New England Witchcraft:《新英格兰巫术史》
⑤ whip-poor-will: 北美夜鹰,一种夜间活动的鸟,以其所发声音而得名。
⑥ the boding cry of the tree-toad, that harbinger of storm: 预知暴风雨的树蟾蜍

the screech-owl①, or the sudden rustling in the thicket of birds frightened from their roost. The fire-flies, too, which sparkled most vividly in the darkest places, now and then startled him, as one of uncommon brightness would stream across his path; and if, by chance, a huge blockhead of a beetle came winging his blundering flight against him, the poor varlet was ready to give up the ghost, with the idea that he was struck with a witch's token②. His only resource on such occasions, either to drown thought, or drive away evil spirits, was to sing psalm tunes;—and the good people of Sleepy Hollow, as they sat by their doors of an evening, were often filled with awe, at hearing his nasal melody, "in linked sweetness long drawn out③," floating from the distant hill, or along the dusky road.

(*The following part of the story tells how Ichabod Crane's dreams of making his fortune on the frontier are just dreams and how his wish to win his love is demolished by a Yankee intruder, who is perceived as all brawn and no brains.*)

Ⅲ. Notes.

1. "The Legend of Sleepy Hollow" is one of Irving's most popular stories because of the engagingly drawn central character. The part we have chosen here opens with the narrator describing the story's setting, creating images of a quaint, cozy Dutch village, "one of the quietest places in the whole world," in a "remote period of American history" that seemed long-ago even to Irving's original readers.

2. Ichabod Crane is a schoolteacher and singing instructor, who comes from Connecticut. Ichabod Crane is a memorable comic figure in American literature: despite his supposedly superior education, he is a naive dreamer with a penchant for swallowing everything whole — superstitions as well as food.

Ⅳ. Key Words（关键词）.

Romanticism: 浪漫主义。它是十八世纪末十九世纪初在欧洲艺术、音乐和文学领域兴起的一项文艺运动。这种创作流派具有强烈的抒情性，强调主观世界的感受，主张对传统形式或古典主义进行革新，体现了资产阶级社会中个人主义高涨的时代潮流。

folklore: 民间故事。它是指一个民族流传下来的有关传统信仰、神话和习俗的故事。广义上讲就是民间社会创作并口头传播的文学作品。这些作品代代相传，通常会因记忆、特定需要以及个人特性加以变化。

legends: 传说。它是一个民族流传下来的各种民族起源、英雄故事、早期历史等传说故事。它具有记载民族集体记忆和民间艺术想象的重要历史意义和艺术价值。

---

① the dreary hooting of the screech-owl: 尖叫的猫头鹰凄厉的鸣声
② the poor varlet was ready to give up the ghost, with the idea that he was struck with a witch's token: 那可怜的教书匠简直要被吓死了,以为他被女巫的信物打中
③ in linked sweetness long drawn out: 用甜蜜、和谐、余音袅袅的音韵

V. Questions.

1. What kind of mood does the setting of this story create?

2. Who was the headless horseman? How did he lose his head? What was he doing out at night?

3. Why did the women in the countryside think he was an important person? How did they treat him?

Lesson 7　James Fennimore Cooper (1789—1851)

Ⅰ. A Brief Review.

Born on September 15, 1789 at Burlington, New Jersey, James Fennimore Cooper was the first successful novelist in the history of American literature. In 1790, his family moved to Cooperstown, New York, a frontier settlement founded by his father near Otsego Lake, where the landscape and history had great influence on many of his famous novels. An Indian massacre once happened in this area, but it was relatively peaceful during Cooper's boyhood when he saw frontiersmen and Indians on this land.

图7　James F. Cooper

Cooper's literary career covered a period of around 30 years with more than 50 publications. *Precaution* (1820) imitated the English novel of manners, while his next work, *The Spy* (1821), described the American Revolution with a patriotic theme and thus became immediately successful. With the publication of famous Leather-stocking Tales, the first of which was *The Pioneer* (1821), the second *The Last of the Mohicans* (1826), Cooper established his reputation as the first major American novelist.

Cooper also published *The Prairie* (1827), and *Notions of the Americans* (1828), in which he defended his country against European critics. His monumental work *History of the Navy of the United States of America* (1839) once again caused many disputes and lawsuits over his works, which cast long shadows on his later life. Cooper tried to reveal a deep tension between a lonely individual and society, nature and culture, spirituality and materialism in his portrait of the successive waves of the frontier settlements. He was the first to sound the recurring tragic note in American fiction by creating wild settings, new, distinctively American characters, and national themes. In his most important novels, the Leather-stocking Tales—which in the order of narrative are *The Deerslayer* (1841), *The Last of the Mohicans* (1826), *The Pathfinder* (1840), *The Pioneers* (1823), and *The Prairie* (1827)—Cooper skillfully dramatized the clash between the frontier wilderness and the encroaching civilization. The forthright frontiersman Natty Bumppo was their chief character, nicknamed Leather-stocking, who was the first famous frontiersman in American literature and the literary forerunner of countless cowboy and backwoods heroes.

The Leather-stocking Tales are notable for their descriptive power, their mastery of native background, and their romanticized portrayal of the Native American. Natty Bumppo, therefore, prefigures Herman Melville's Billy Budd and Mark Twain's Huck Finn. Although Cooper has been criticized for his extravagant plots, his conventional characters, and his stilted dialogue, he remains the vital and original writer of romances of the wilderness. He has thus enjoyed a high reputation for the founding of American national literature.

Ⅱ. Texts.

The Pioneers or The Source of the Susquehanna

"See, Winter comes, to rule the varied year,
Sullen and sad, with all his rising train;
Vapors, and clouds, and storms."

——Thomson①

Near the centre of the State of New York lies an extensive district of country whose surface is a succession of hills and dales, or, to speak with greater deference to geographical definitions, of mountains and valleys. It is among these hills that the Delaware takes its rise; and flowing from the limpid lakes and thousand springs of this region the numerous sources of the Susquehanna② meander through the valleys until, uniting their streams, they form one of the proudest rivers of the United States. The mountains are generally arable to the tops, although instances are not wanting where the sides are jutted with rocks that aid greatly in giving to the country that romantic and picturesque character which it so eminently possesses. The vales are narrow, rich, and cultivated, with a stream uniformly winding through each. Beautiful and thriving villages are found interspersed along the margins of the small lakes, or situated at those points of the streams which are favorable for manufacturing; and neat and comfortable farms, with every indication of wealth about them, are scattered profusely through the vales, and even to the mountain tops. Roads diverge in every direction from the even and graceful bottoms of the valleys to the most rugged and intricate passes of the hills. Academies and minor edifices of learning meet the eye of the stranger at every few miles as be winds his way through this uneven territory, and places for the worship of God abound with that frequency which characterize a moral and reflecting people, and with that variety of exterior and canonical government which flows from unfettered liberty of conscience. In short, the whole district is hourly exhibiting how much can be done, in even a rugged country and with a severe climate, under the dominion of mild laws, and where every man feels a direct interest in the prosperity of a commonwealth of which he knows himself to form a part. The expedients of the pioneers who first broke ground in the settlement of this country are succeeded by the permanent improvements of the yeoman who intends to leave his remains to molder under the sod which he tills, or perhaps of the son, who, born in the land, piously wishes to linger around the

---

① 引自英国诗人詹姆斯·汤姆森(James Thomson, 1700—1748)的长诗《四季》(*The Seasons*)

② the Susquehanna: 萨斯奎哈纳河，是美国东岸最长的河流，也是全美第十六长河流。身为贵格教派家庭后代的库柏，成长在父亲位于纽约州中部偏僻奥特希哥湖(Otsego Lake)的庄园，该地现即为库柏镇(Cooperstown)。在库柏的童年时期，此地虽然相当平静，过去却曾发生过印度安人大屠杀事件

grave of his father. Only forty years have passed since this territory was a wilderness.①

Our tale begins in 1793, about seven years after the commencement of one of the earliest of those settlements which have conduced to effect that magical change in the power and condition of the State to which we have alluded.

Very soon after the establishment of the independence of the States by the peace of 1783, the enterprise of their citizens was directed to a development of the natural advantages of their widely extended dominions. Before the war of the Revolution, the inhabited parts of the colony of New York were limited to less than a tenth of its possessions, a narrow belt of country, extending for a short distance on either side of the Hudson, with a similar occupation② of fifty miles on the banks of the Mohawk, together with the islands of Nassau and Staten, and a few insulated settlements on chosen land along the margins of streams, composed the country, which was then inhabited by less than two hundred thousand souls. Within the short period we have mentioned, the population has spread itself over five degrees of latitude and seven of longitude③, and has swelled to a million and a half of inhabitants, who are maintained in abundance, and can look forward to ages before the evil day must arrive when their possessions shall become unequal to their wants.

It was near the setting of the sun, on a clear, cold day in December, when a sleigh was moving slowly up one of the mountains in the district we have described. The day had been fine for the season, and but two or three large clouds, whose color seemed brightened by the light reflected from the mass of snow that covered the earth, floated in a sky of the purest blue. The road wound along the brow of a precipice, and on one side was upheld by a foundation of logs piled one upon the other, while a narrow excavation in the mountain in the opposite direction had made a passage of sufficient width for the ordinary travelling of that day. But logs, excavation, and every thing that did not reach several feet above the earth lay alike buried beneath the snow. A single track, barely wide enough to receive the sleigh, denoted the route of the highway, and this was sunk nearly two feet below the surrounding surface.

Sleigh is the word used in every part of the United States to denote a traineau. It is of local use in the west of England, whence it is most probably derived by the Americans. The latter draw a distinction between a sled, or sledge, and a sleigh, the sleigh being shod with metal. Sleighs are also subdivided into two-horse and one-horse sleighs. Of the latter, there are the cutter, with thills so arranged as to permit the horse to travel in the side track; the "pung," or "tow-pung" which is driven with a pole; and the "gumper," a rude construction used for temporary purposes in the new countries. Many of the American sleighs are elegant though the use of this mode of conveyance is much lessened with the melioration of the climate consequent to the clearing of the forests.

In the vale, which lay at a distance of several hundred feet lower, there was what, in the

---

① 本书于 1823 年写成,作者在《序》中指出殖民活动始于 1785 年

② occupation: 此处指上文中的"a narrow belt of country"

③ the population has spread itself over five degrees of latitude and seven of longitude: 人口已经扩散到宽为 5 纬度,长为 7 经度的区域内

language of the country, was called a clearing, and all the usual improvements of a new settlement; these even extended up the hill to the point where the road turned short and ran across the level land, which lay on the summit of the mountain; but the summit itself remained in the forest. There was glittering in the atmosphere, as if it was filled with innumerable shining particles; and the noble bay horses that drew the sleigh were covered, in many parts with a coat of hoar-frost. The vapor from their nostrils was seen to issue like smoke; and every object in the view, as well as every arrangement of the travellers, denoted the depth of a winter in the mountains. The harness, which was of a deep, dull black, differing from the glossy varnishing of the present day, was ornamented with enormous plates and buckles of brass, that shone like gold in those transient beams of the sun which found their way obliquely through the tops of the trees. Huge saddles, studded with nails and fitted with cloth that served as blankets to the shoulders of the cattle, supported four high, square-topped turrets, through which the stout reins led from the mouths of the horses to the hands of the driver, who was a negro, of apparently twenty years of age. His face, which nature had colored with a glistening black, was now mottled with the cold, and his large shining eyes filled with tears; a tribute to its power that the keen frosts of those regions always extracted from one of his African origin. Still, there was a smiling expression of good-humor in his happy countenance, that was created by the thoughts of home and a Christmas fireside, with its Christmas frolics. The sleigh was one of those large, comfortable, old-fashioned conveyances, which would admit a whole family within its bosom, but which now contained only two passengers besides the driver. The color of its outside was a modest green, and that of its inside a fiery red, The latter was intended to convey the idea of heat in that cold climate. Large buffalo-skins trimmed around the edges with red cloth cut into festoons, covered the back of the sleigh, and were spread over its bottom and drawn up around the feet of the travellers - one of whom was a man of middle age and the other a female just entering upon womanhood. The former was of a large stature; but the precautions he had taken to guard against the cold left but little of his person exposed to view①. A great-coat, that was abundantly ornamented by a profusion of furs, enveloped the whole of his figure excepting the head, which was covered with a cap of marten-skins lined with morocco②, the sides of which were made to fall, if necessary, and were now drawn close over the ears and fastened beneath his chin with a black rib bon. The top of the cap was surmounted with the tail of the animal whose skin had furnished the rest of the materials, which fell back, not ungracefully, a few inches behind the head. From beneath this mask were to be seen part of a fine, manly face, and particularly a pair of expressive large blue eyes, that promised extraordinary intellect, covert humor, and great benevolence. The form of his companion was literally hid beneath the garments she wore. There were furs and silks peeping from under a large camlet cloak with a thick flannel lining, that by its cut and size was evidently intended for a

---

① but the precautions he had taken to guard against the cold left but little of his person exposed to view: 为了防寒,他把自己包裹的那么严实,以至于身子露在外面的部分已经微乎其微了

② morocco: 摩洛哥羊皮革

masculine wearer. A huge hood of black silk, that was quilted with down, concealed the whole of her head, except at a small opening in front for breath, through which occasionally sparkled a pair of animated jet-black eyes.

Both the father and daughter (for such was the connection between the two travellers) were too much occupied with their reflections to break a stillness that derived little or no interruption from the easy gliding of the sleigh by the sound of their voices. The former was thinking of the wife that had held this their only child to her bosom, when, four years before, she had reluctantly consented to relinquish the society of her daughter in order that the latter might enjoy the advantages of an education which the city of New York could only offer at that period. A few months afterward death had deprived him of the remaining companion of his solitude①; but still he had enough real regard for his child not to bring her into the comparative wilderness in which he dwelt, until the full period had expired to which he had limited her juvenile labors. The reflections of the daughter were less melancholy, and mingled with a pleased astonishment at the novel scenery she met at every turn in the road.

The mountain on which they were journeying was covered with pines that rose without a branch some seventy or eighty feet, and which frequently doubled that height by the addition of the tops. Through the innumerable vistas that opened beneath the lofty trees, the eye could penetrate until it was met by a distant inequality in the ground②, or was stopped by a view of the summit of the mountain which lay on the opposite side of the valley to which they were hastening. The dark trunks of the trees rose from the pure white of the snow in regularly formed shafts, until, at a great height, their branches shot forth horizontal limbs, that were covered with the meagre foliage of an evergreen, affording a melancholy contrast to the torpor of nature below. To the travellers there seemed to be no wind; but these pines waved majestically at their topmost boughs, sending forth a dull, plaintive sound that was quite in consonance with the rest of the melancholy scene.

The sleigh had glided for some distance along the even surface, and the gaze of the female was bent in inquisitive and, perhaps, timid glances into the recesses of the forest, when a loud and continued howling was heard, pealing under the long arches of the woods like the cry of a numerous pack of hounds. The instant the sounds reached the ear of the gentleman he cried aloud to the black:

"Hol up, Aggy; there is old Hector; I should know his bay among ten thousand! The Leather-Stocking has put his hounds into the hills this clear day, and they have started their game. There is a deer-track a few rods ahead; and now, Bess, if thou canst③ muster courage enough to stand fire④, I will give thee a saddle for thy Christmas dinner."

---

① the remaining companion of his solitude: 此处指他的妻子
② inequality in the ground: 意为"hollow"
③ if thou canst: 此处为古语和诗歌语言用法,意为"if you can",本书语言虽为现代英语,但部分地方仍保留了一些最初殖民语言的形式
④ stand fire: 意为"承受枪声的惊扰"。父亲要停车射猎,先给娇惯的女儿打一剂"强心针"

The black drew up, with a cheerful grin upon his chilled features, and began thrashing his arms together in order to restore the circulation of his fingers, while the speaker stood erect and, throwing aside his outer covering, stepped from the sleigh upon a bank of snow which sustained his weight without yielding.

In a few moments the speaker succeeded in extricating a double-barrelled① fowling-piece from among a multitude of trunks and bandboxes. After throwing aside the thick mittens which had encased his hands, there now appeared a pair of leather gloves tipped with fur; he examined his priming, and was about to move forward, when the light bounding noise of an animal plunging through the woods was heard, and a fine buck darted into the path a short distance ahead of him. The appearance of the animal was sudden, and his flight inconceivably rapid; but the traveller appeared to be too keen a sportsman to be disconcerted by either. As it came first into view he raised the fowling-piece to his shoulder and, with a practised eye and steady hand, drew a trigger. The deer dashed forward undaunted, and apparently unhurt. Without lowering his piece, the traveller turned its muzzle toward his victim, and fired again. Neither discharge, however, seemed to have taken effect.

The whole scene had passed with a rapidity that confused the female, who was unconsciously rejoicing in the escape of the buck, as he rather darted like a meteor than ran across the road, when a sharp, quick sound struck her ear, quite different from the full, round reports of her father's gun, but still sufficiently distinct to be known as the concussion produced by firearms. At the same instant that she heard this unexpected report, the buck sprang from the snow to a great height in the air, and directly a second discharge, similar in sound to the first, followed, when the animal came to the earth, failing head long and rolling over on the crust with its own velocity. A loud shout was given by the unseen marksman, and a couple of men instantly appeared from behind the trunks of two of the pines, where they had evidently placed them selves in expectation of the passage of the deer.

……

Ⅲ. Notes.

1. In *The Pioneers*, James Fennimore Cooper thematically debates the complexity of landscape within a new American frontier. The battle between nature and civilization is a constant and competing force within the minds of the characters and in the general surroundings. In his preface to *The Pioneers*, Cooper explained that he wrote the novel, his third, for his own pleasure, "so it would be no wonder if it displeased everybody else; for what two thought alike, on a subject of the imagination!" The excerpted part we have taken here is from chapter 1, in which Cooper described the first meeting of Judge Temple and Natty Bumppo.

2. Cooper is cautiously optimistic about the future of exploring the wild land as he narrates that the local residents "can look forward to ages before the evil day must arrive when their

---

① double-barrelled: 双管的

possessions shall become unequal to their wants".

Ⅳ. Key Words(关键词).

American frontier: 美国边疆。它既是地理概念也是政治概念,指美国中西部直达太平洋沿岸的广袤边疆地区。"边疆"一词的使用对北美发展有特殊意义,因为美国历史上的开拓边疆不但给美国社会带来了极大的发展空间,而且形成了许多文学创作的灵感来源。

historical novel: 历史小说。小说中有虚构人物参与、影响或见证真实历史事件,和历史人物相互交织。如瓦尔特·司各特的《艾凡赫》,劳埃德·C·道格拉斯的《圣袍千秋》,以及詹姆斯·费尼莫·库柏的《最后的莫希干人》。

myth: 神话。它是关于超凡人物或超自然事件的传说故事。它通常想解释与常识或事实无关的奇怪现象,强调感性认知和非理性推理。神话不如传说的史实性强,但也是通过口口相传而延续的。库柏就被 D. H. 劳伦斯称作神话作家。

Ⅴ. Questions.

1. At the end of the first paragraph, Cooper wrote: "Only forty years have passed since this territory was a wilderness." What may this sentence imply?

2. Even in the first part of the novel, Natty is already in conflict with the forces of civilization. How?

3. Try to relate the events that Cooper described with real historical happenings.

Part Two

From Romanticism to Realism
第二部　从浪漫主义到现实主义

19世纪的美国浪漫主义文学始于欧文、库柏和布莱恩特(1794—1878)等人的早期文学创作,其代表性作家大多生活或创作于新英格兰地区,其思潮一直延续到美国内战前后,并在几位美国文学经典作家如爱默生(1803—1882)、梭罗(1817—1862)和朗费罗(1807—1882)等人的创作中达到了高峰,而沃尔特·惠特曼(1819—1892)则为美国浪漫主义文学烙上了伟大的民族精神印记。当然,美国启蒙思潮的高涨和浪漫主义文学的兴起都受到了欧洲现代思潮和文学运动的影响,特别是英国浪漫主义诗歌和法国浪漫主义小说对于新大陆文学的转折起到了重大的作用。但是,美国浪漫主义文学虽然发轫于欧洲浪漫主义文学之后,其表现的美国理想、民族风貌和时代精神却使美国文学的面貌焕然一新。正如被哈罗德·布鲁姆称为"美国文学经典核心"的惠特曼所言,"美国各州的风貌本身就是一首伟大的诗篇,它期待着与之丰沛广袤相媲美的艺术展示!"

美国文学的早期代表作除了欧文和库柏的小说以外,布莱恩特的诗歌创作可谓独树一帜。布莱恩特的抒情诗歌集《诗选》(1821)细腻地描写了新英格兰地区美丽的自然景观,在对飞鸟、丛林和鲜花等形象的描绘中表达了自己深沉的哲理思考和人生感慨。另一位浪漫主义诗人爱伦·坡(1809—1849)虽然以侦探小说鼻祖著称于世,但是他的诗歌如《乌鸦》(1845)等表现了浓厚的神秘和怪诞的哥特式风格,甚至对后来的欧洲象征派诗歌和唯美主义文学都产生了深远的影响。不过,美国浪漫主义文学思潮还是具有自身独特的思想特征,这就是美国的超验主义及其对一些作家的深刻影响,并使美国文学体现的民族精神上升到了一个新的高度。超验主义思想认为人的灵魂和上帝创造的世界是一个整体,而个人主义和亲近自然则体现了灵魂与上帝的统一。超验主义的代表人物之一、美国浪漫主义文学的中坚人物爱默生认为,大自然的万般物象就是上帝的神圣昭示,而人自身也体现了自然界的全部法则。爱默生在《论自然》和《美国学者》等文章中提出,建立新的美国信念和道德理想刻不容缓,因为美国这里"有新的土地、新的人群和新的观念,所以要呼唤我们自己的事业、法则和信仰"。另外一位浪漫主义作家梭罗不仅采纳了欧洲浪漫主义所主张的"回归自然"的号召,而且从古希腊文化和东方文化中汲取思想灵感,在他的散文代表作《瓦尔登》(1854)中充分表露了超验主义的情愫,把对自然荒野的热爱和对心灵隐秘的探索完美地结合在一起,为美国文学史留下了一篇影响深远的哲理散文。

在美国浪漫主义文学运动中,惠特曼的《草叶集》(1855)是对美利坚民族形象和时代精神的标举张扬。其中的《自我之歌》等篇章讴歌了人的主观意志和自我意识,赞美了从木匠到村妇的俗世众生。惠特曼的诗歌以极具语言冲击力的排比和象征等文体创新为美国诗歌和世界文学做出了可贵的贡献。另外,美国女诗人艾米莉·狄金森(1830—1886)的一千七百多首诗歌语言含蓄优美,形象活泼生动,对于人生、自然和上帝的内在关联和意义进行了深度思考和抒情表达。在美国浪漫主义文学的发展后期,与惠特曼几乎同时期的作家霍桑(1804—1864)和麦尔维尔(1819—1891)等人悉心小说创作,对工业革命初期的美国社会和时代氛围进行了生动的描绘,也为现实主义文学的崛起进行了艺术的铺垫。霍桑的《红字》(1850)以17世纪中期的新英格兰清教徒聚集地为背景,描写了一位坚强女性海斯特·白兰如何从"通奸犯"变成德行楷模的曲折经历,小说对教会和绅士的虚伪进行了深刻的揭露,歌颂了善良正直的人性美。小说在新英格兰乡镇生活描写和人物心理探寻这两方面都做到了精雕细琢,在叙述历史现实的同时还体现了浪漫主义文学的强大艺术感染力。与《红字》堪称双璧的《白鲸》(1851)则叙述了一个追捕白鲸的海上冒险故事,其中渲染了白鲸形象的神秘气氛和亚哈船长的冷酷性格,而通篇叙事所表现的强烈浪漫主义色彩大大地增强了这部作品在美国文学经典中的突出地位。

就在美国浪漫主义文学蔚成大观之际,美国文学中的现实主义创作思潮也在日渐崛起。希尔德列斯的长篇小说《白奴》(1836)和斯托夫人的小说《汤姆叔叔的小屋》(1852)等作品对于美国的蓄奴制进行了尖锐的批判,其中的现实主义场景描写深刻揭露了蓄奴制和种族压迫的罪恶,激起了广大读者的强烈共鸣。与英国现实主义文学思潮有所不同的是,美国现实主义文学的兴起与美国工业革命的步伐几乎是一致的,从浪漫主义文学对乡村田园生活的表现到现实主义文学对都市喧嚣的再现,19世纪的美国文学经历了一个从浪漫主义到现实主义的转型过程。由于美国内战结束以后的城市化进程不断加快,现实生活的艰难和人性阴暗面在物质欲望的刺激下不断膨胀成为时代的弊端。这种变化虽然使美国传统的新教伦理受到冲击,却也给美国的现实主义文学提供了丰富的创作素材和主题思想的灵感。于是,由乡土文学和都市文学两大题材所代表的现实主义文学潮流在19世纪后期兴起,以后一直延续到20世纪,并在小说创作中表现得尤为突出。

作为"现实主义文学奠基人"的豪威尔斯(1837—1920)对于美国文学的转型起了十分重要的作用。他在担任《大西洋月刊》等杂志主编时大力提倡现实主义的创作方法,而他的小说《塞拉斯·拉帕斯发迹史》(1885)也以现实主义的方法揭示了传统道德原则和唯利是图逻辑之间的剧烈冲突。与此同时,带有自然主义特征的小说如克莱恩(1871—1900)的小说《街头女梅杰》(1893)等也深入批判了物欲社会的罪恶。在美国现实主义文学的发展中,马克·吐温(1835—1910)和亨利·詹姆斯(1843—1916)是两位成就卓越的小说大师。马克·吐温与人合作的小说《镀金时代》(1874)无情地揭露了内战后美国社会金钱万能的腐败风气,而他在《哈克贝利·费恩历险记》(1884)中以通俗的语言和充沛的活力描写了密西西比河流域的人文景观,以带有地域色彩的生动描写叙述了费恩和吉姆两人共同奔向自由的冒险故事,歌颂了自由平等的崇高价值。另一位现实主义作家亨利·詹姆斯善于在国际性背景中描写美国民族性格的多重表现,他注重对人物心理活动进行分析和描写,这使他的小说获得了心理现实主义杰作的赞誉,如他的小说《黛西·米勒》(1879)和《一位女士的画像》(1881)等突出体现了作家对美国文化与欧洲传统之间差异的深切感受与认识。马克·吐温和亨利·詹姆斯的创作生涯一直延续到20世纪初期,他们的作品为美国现实主义文学创作做出了重要的贡献。

Lesson 8   Edgar Allen Poe (1809—1849)

I. A Brief Review.

Born on January 19, 1809 in Boston, Massachusetts, Poe had lost both parents at the age of two and was taken in by John Allan, a wealthy tobacco merchant of Richmond, Virginia. With the Allen family he went to England in 1815 and attended schools there, learning Latin and French as well as math and history. He returned to the U. S. and later entered the University of Virginia in February 1826. Due to his gambling debts and sour relation with Allen, Poe left family and had to quit school in March 1827. He enlisted in the U. S. Army in the same year and attained the rank of Sergeant-major. Poe gained an appointment to the U. S. Military Academy at the West Point, but his careless behavior got himself expelled by the West Point in 1831. After moving

图 8　Edgar Allen Poe

to New York City in May 1831, he published his *Poems* and began writing short stories for literary journals and periodicals. His first short story "Metzengerstein" was published in the Philadelphia *Saturday Courier* in January 1832. In the next year, his tale "A Ms. Found in a Bottle" won a writing competition sponsored by the weekly *Baltimore Saturday Visitor* and was then published in the issue of the *Visitor*, October 19, 1833.

As the editor of the *Southern Literary Messenger*, Poe published first printings of his now famous works such as "Morella," "Berenice," and parts of his only novel *The Narrative of Arthur Gordon Pym of Nantucket*. In 1838 he moved to Philadelphia, and lived there for about six years, writing and publishing many of his most noteworthy works, such as "The Fall of the House of Usher" (1839), "Murders in the Rue Morgue" (1841), "The Masque of the Red Death" (1842), and "The Black Cat" (1843). In September 1839, a Philadelphia firm published his *Tales of the Grotesque and Arabesque*, a two volume set, but it sold badly.

In April 1844 he removed his family to New York City, where he wrote for newspapers and magazines and held positions with the *New York Evening Mirror* (1844—1845), the *Broadway Journal* (1845—1846), and *Godey's Lady's Book* (1846). In January 1845 he published "The Purloined Letter" and his most famous poem "The Raven." "The Raven" was an instant success, the popularity of which led to the publication of a collection of his tales in July and *The Raven and Other Poems* in November.

His wife's death, together with Poe's own employment problems, had a substantial effect on Poe. He was seriously ill, drinking steadily and falling deeper into poverty. In his last years, Poe wrote some of his best verse—"Ulalume" (1847), "The Bells" (1849), and some critical essays, such as "Eureka: A Prose Poem" (1848) and "The Poetic Principle" (1850). On October 3, 1849, Poe was found unconscious on a street in Baltimore. He died four days later at age 40. The reason of his death remains a mystery. Now, Poe is widely recognized as the master of horror and mystery, the father of the detective story, and an originator of modern science fiction. He is also well-known for his poetry and criticism.

Ⅱ. Texts.

The Tell-Tale Heart

TRUE! —nervous—very, very dreadfully nervous I had been and am; but why will you say that I am mad? The disease had sharpened my senses—not destroyed—not dulled them. Above all was the sense of hearing acute. I heard all things in the heaven and in the earth. I heard many things in hell. How, then, am I mad? Hearken①! and observe how healthily - how calmly I can tell you the whole story.

It is impossible to say how first the idea entered my brain; but once conceived, it haunted me day and night. Object there was none. Passion there was none. I loved the old man. He had never wronged me. He had never given me insult. For his gold I had no desire. I think it was his eye! Yes, it was this! He had the eye of a vulture②—a pale blue eye, with a film over it. Whenever it fell upon me, my blood ran cold; and so by degrees—very gradually—I made up my mind to take the life of the old man, and thus rid myself of the eye forever.

Now this is the point. You fancy me mad. Madmen know nothing. But you should have seen me. You should have seen how wisely I proceeded—with what caution—with what foresight—with what dissimulation③ I went to work! I was never kinder to the old man than during the whole week before I killed him. And every night, about midnight, I turned the latch of his door and opened it—oh so gently! And then, when I had made an opening sufficient for my head, I put in a dark lantern, all closed, closed, that no light shone out, and then I thrust in my head. Oh, you would have laughed to see how cunningly I thrust it in! I moved it slowly—very, very slowly, so that I might not disturb the old man's sleep. It took me an hour to place my whole head within the opening so far that I could see him as he lay upon his bed. Ha! Would a madman have been so wise as this, and then, when my head was well in the room, I undid the lantern cautiously—oh, so cautiously—cautiously (for the hinges④ creaked) —I undid it just so much that a single thin ray fell upon the vulture eye. And this I did for seven long nights—every night just at midnight—but I found the eye always closed; and so it was impossible to do the work; for it was not the old man

---

① hearken: 倾听;谛听;留心
② vulture: 秃鹫;美洲鹫;贪得无厌者
③ dissimulation: 掩饰
④ hinge: 铰链;合叶

who vexed me, but his Evil Eye. And every morning, when the day broke, I went boldly into the chamber, and spoke courageously to him, calling him by name in a hearty tone, and inquiring how he has passed the night. So you see he would have been a very profound old man, indeed, to suspect that every night, just at twelve, I looked in upon him while he slept.

Upon the eighth night I was more than usually cautious in opening the door. A watch's minute hand moves more quickly than did mine. Never before that night had I felt the extent of my own powers—of my sagacity①. I could scarcely contain my feelings of triumph. To think that there I was, opening the door, little by little, and he not even to dream of my secret deeds or thoughts. I fairly chuckled at the idea; and perhaps he heard me; for he moved on the bed suddenly, as if startled. Now you may think that I drew back—but no. His room was as black as pitch with the thick darkness, (for the shutters were close fastened, through fear of robbers,) and so I knew that he could not see the opening of the door, and I kept pushing it on steadily, steadily.

I had my head in, and was about to open the lantern, when my thumb slipped upon the tin fastening, and the old man sprang up in bed, crying out—"Who's there?"

I kept quite still and said nothing. For a whole hour I did not move a muscle, and in the meantime I did not hear him lie down. He was still sitting up in the bed listening;—just as I have done, night after night, hearkening to the death watches in the wall.

Presently I heard a slight groan, and I knew it was the groan of mortal terror. It was not a groan of pain or of grief—oh, no!—it was the low stifled sound that arises from the bottom of the soul when overcharged with awe. I knew the sound well. Many a night, just at midnight, when all the world slept, it has welled up from my own bosom, deepening, with its dreadful echo, the terrors that distracted me. I say I knew it well. I knew what the old man felt, and pitied him, although I chuckled at heart. I knew that he had been lying awake ever since the first slight noise, when he had turned in the bed. His fears had been ever since growing upon him. He had been trying to fancy them causeless, but could not. He had been saying to himself—"It is nothing but the wind in the chimney—it is only a mouse crossing the floor," or "It is merely a cricket which has made a single chirp." Yes, he had been trying to comfort himself with these suppositions②: but he had found all in vain. All in vain; because Death, in approaching him had stalked with his black shadow before him, and enveloped the victim. And it was the mournful influence of the unperceived shadow that caused him to feel—although he neither saw nor heard—to feel the presence of my head within the room.

When I had waited a long time, very patiently, without hearing him lie down, I resolved to open a little—a very, very little crevice in the lantern. So I opened it—you cannot imagine how stealthily, stealthily—until, at length a simple dim ray, like the thread of the spider, shot from out the crevice and fell full upon the vulture eye.

It was open—wide, wide open—and I grew furious as I gazed upon it. I saw it with perfect

---

① sagacity: 聪慧;精明;洞察力
② supposition: 假定;推测

distinctness—all a dull blue, with a hideous veil over it that chilled the very marrow in my bones; but I could see nothing else of the old man's face or person: for I had directed the ray as if by instinct, precisely upon the damned spot.

And have I not told you that what you mistake for madness is but over-acuteness of the sense? —now, I say, there came to my ears a low, dull, quick sound, such as a watch makes when enveloped in cotton. I knew that sound well, too. It was the beating of the old man's heart. It increased my fury, as the beating of a drum stimulates the soldier into courage.

But even yet I refrained① and kept still. I scarcely breathed. I held the lantern motionless. I tried how steadily I could maintain the ray upon the eye. Meantime the hellish tattoo② of the heart increased. It grew quicker and quicker, and louder and louder every instant. The old man's terror must have been extreme! It grew louder, I say, louder every moment! —do you mark me well I have told you that I am nervous: so I am. And now at the dead hour of the night, amid the dreadful silence of that old house, so strange a noise as this excited me to uncontrollable terror. Yet, for some minutes longer I refrained and stood still. But the beating grew louder, louder! I thought the heart must burst. And now a new anxiety seized me—the sound would be heard by a neighbour! The old man's hour had come! With a loud yell, I threw open the lantern and leaped into the room. He shrieked once—once only. In an instant I dragged him to the floor, and pulled the heavy bed over him. I then smiled gaily, to find the deed so far done. But, for many minutes, the heart beat on with a muffled sound. This, however, did not vex me; it would not be heard through the wall. At length it ceased. The old man was dead. I removed the bed and examined the corpse. Yes, he was stone, stone dead. I placed my hand upon the heart and held it there many minutes. There was no pulsation. He was stone dead. His eye would trouble me no more.

If still you think me mad, you will think so no longer when I describe the wise precautions I took for the concealment of the body. The night waned, and I worked hastily, but in silence. First of all I dismembered the corpse. I cut off the head and the arms and the legs.

I then took up three planks from the flooring of the chamber, and deposited all between the scantlings. I then replaced the boards so cleverly, so cunningly, that no human eye—not even his—could have detected any thing wrong. There was nothing to wash out—no stain of any kind—no blood-spot whatever. I had been too wary for that. A tub had caught all—ha! ha!

When I had made an end of these labors, it was four o'clock—still dark as midnight. As the bell sounded the hour, there came a knocking at the street door. I went down to open it with a light heart, —for what had I now to fear? There entered three men, who introduced themselves, with perfect suavity③, as officers of the police. A shriek had been heard by a neighbour during the night; suspicion of foul④ play had been aroused; information had been lodged at the police office,

---

① refrain: 忍住;节制;克制
② tattoo: 连续有节奏的敲击
③ suavity: 温文;谦和
④ foul: 邪恶的;残酷的

and they (the officers) had been deputed to search the premises.

I smiled, —for what had I to fear? I bade the gentlemen welcome. The shriek, I said, was my own in a dream. The old man, I mentioned, was absent in the country. I took my visitors all over the house. I bade them search—search well. I led them, at length, to his chamber. I showed them his treasures, secure, undisturbed. In the enthusiasm of my confidence, I brought chairs into the room, and desired them here to rest from their fatigues, while I myself, in the wild audacity of my perfect triumph, placed my own seat upon the very spot beneath which reposed the corpse of the victim.

The officers were satisfied. My manner had convinced them. I was singularly at ease. They sat, and while I answered cheerily, they chatted of familiar things. But, ere long, I felt myself getting pale and wished them gone. My head ached, and I fancied a ringing in my ears: but still they sat and still chatted. The ringing became more distinct: —It continued and became more distinct: I talked more freely to get rid of the feeling: but it continued and gained definiteness—until, at length, I found that the noise was not within my ears.

No doubt I now grew very pale; —but I talked more fluently, and with a heightened voice. Yet the sound increased—and what could I do? It was a low, dull, quick sound—much such a sound as a watch makes when enveloped in cotton. I gasped for breath—and yet the officers heard it not. I talked more quickly—more vehemently; but the noise steadily increased. I arose and argued about trifles, in a high key and with violent gesticulations; but the noise steadily increased. Why would they not be gone? I paced the floor to and fro with heavy strides, as if excited to fury by the observations of the men—but the noise steadily increased. Oh God! what could I do? I foamed①—I raved②—I swore! I swung the chair upon which I had been sitting, and grated it upon the boards, but the noise arose over all and continually increased. It grew louder—louder—louder! And still the men chatted pleasantly, and smiled. Was it possible they heard not? Almighty God! —no, no! They heard! —they suspected! —they knew! —they were making a mockery of my horror! —this I thought, and this I think. But anything was better than this agony! Anything was more tolerable than this derision! I could bear those hypocritical smiles no longer! I felt that I must scream or die! and now—again! —hark! louder! louder! louder! louder!

"Villains!" I shrieked, "dissemble no more! I admit the deed! —tear up the planks! here, here! —It is the beating of his hideous heart!"

Ⅲ. Notes.

"The Tell-Tale Heart" (1843) is widely considered one of Poe's most famous macabre tales. It tells about the murder of an old man and its aftermath, exploring some recurrent themes, such as insanity, murder, death, terror, and guilt—with which Poe had an almost obsessive preoccupation. In the story Poe demonstrates his unrivalled talent to enter the dark recesses of the

---

① foam: 唾沫四溅
② rave: 口出呓语；说胡话

human soul, to probe the hidden depths of the mental world, and to expose the nightmares and hysteria lurking beneath the facade of normal behavior.

Ⅳ. **Key Words**(关键词).

Gothic Fiction: 哥特式小说。它是一种把恐怖与浪漫结合在一起的文学体裁,起源于英国作家霍勒斯·沃波尔于 1764 年发表的小说《奥特兰托城堡》。该体裁在 18 世纪后期和 19 世纪风行于欧美。哥特式小说的主要元素包括黑暗、死亡、腐烂、疯狂、秘密、家族诅咒、鬼魂、闹鬼的房屋、哥特式建筑、古老的城堡、神秘的氛围、心理上和生理上的恐怖、超自然或非自然的力量或现象等等。坡的恐怖故事也属于哥特式小说。坡的很多恐怖故事都带有诸多哥特式小说的特点,比如《厄舍府的倒塌》、《一桶蒙特亚白葡萄酒》、《黑猫》等。坡擅长于触及人内心深处的恐惧和欲望,特别会制造和渲染恐怖气氛,因而被誉为恐怖大师。

The Philosophy of Composition:《创作哲学》,是坡的一篇文论。在这篇文章中坡提出了自己关于文学创作的一些理论,譬如:作品中的每一个细节每一个情节都应该有助于创作意图的实现,与故事的结局相吻合;任何文学作品的长度都应该有个明确的限定,那就是能让人一口气读完;诗歌应该在启迪心灵的同时对读者施予强烈的刺激;诗歌中最美的情调是悲郁之情,而最悲郁的事莫过于美人的早逝,等等。虽然这篇文论主要谈及他对《乌鸦》一诗的创作,但是他的这些创作思想也充分体现在他其他体裁的文学创作之中。

Detective Story: 侦探小说,也叫"推理小说"。坡是侦探小说这一文学体裁的开山鼻祖,并且他的侦探故事创立了这一文学体裁的基本模式。后来者或许能以故事情节取胜,但很难超越坡当初创立下的这种模式,因为坡的侦探小说已经包括了所有后来同类故事的基本元素,比如:一个拥有超常的推理能力的侦探,一个忠诚但是稍显愚钝的朋友,一桩警察再怎么努力也破不了的案件,一位无辜的被怀疑对象,以及故事最后让整个谜团解开,等等。

Ⅴ. **Questions.**

1. What kind of role does the setting of the story play?

2. How do you think about Poe's use of the first person point of view in the story? What kind of effect does it create?

3. Why does the narrator insist on the fact that he is sane and healthy?

4. Can you tell if the narrator is a man or a woman? Why or why not? And what is Poe's purpose of writing in such a way?

Lesson 9 Ralph Waldo Emerson (1803—1882)

Ⅰ. **A Brief Review.**

Emerson is regarded as one of the most influential American writers, philosophers, and thinkers for leading the Transcendentalist Movement and advocating cultured independence and self-reliance. He had a great influence on other American writers, such as Melville, Henry David Thoreau, Nathaniel Hawthorne, Walt Whitman, and Emily Dickson.

Emerson was born into a family with a long line of ministry ancestors on May 25, 1803 in Boston, Massachusetts. He went to Boston Public Latin School at the age nine and to Harvard when he was fourteen. After his graduation in 1821, he tried teaching in school for several years. In 1825 he attended the Harvard Divinity School to study theology but was forced to interrupt his courses

图9 Ralph Waldo Emerson

because of vision problems. He was licensed to preach in 1826 and ordained minister of Boston's Second Church in 1829. However, his skepticism about Christianity and dislike of being merely the agent of received doctrines and rituals eventually caused his resignation from the ministry position in 1832. He sailed to Europe on Dec. 25, 1832 and traveled extensively across the Continent. In Europe, he met Samuel Taylor Coleridge, William Wordsworth, Walter Savage Lander, John Stuart Mill, and, particularly, Thomas Carlyle. This European tour exerted profound influence on the formation of his philosophy.

Around one year later, he returned to the United States. In 1837, he was invited to give an address to the Phi Beta Kappa Society at Harvard. His essay "The American Scholar" was recognized by most Americans as a clarion call for intellectual independence from Europe, from the past, and from all obstacles to originality. In the following years he delivered an address to the graduating class of the Harvard Divinity School on the state of Christianity; his unorthodox religious views aroused a brief, virulent series of attacks in the press. Emerson and members of the Transcendental Club were against the orthodoxy of Calvinism and the Rationalism of the Unitarian Church. They developed instead their own faith centering on the divinity of humanity and the natural world. Their ideas represented a battle between the younger and older generations, and signaled the emergence of a new national culture based on American history and society. Emerson thus became the central and most influential figure of the Transcendental Club.

In 1841, he published his second book, *Essays: First Series*, which included such famous essays as "Self-Reliance" and "The Over-Soul". He published *Essays: Second Series* in 1844 and *Poems* in 1846. These works laid the foundation for his national and international fame. In later years, he published *Nature, Addresses and Lectures* in 1849, *Representative Men* in 1850, *The Conduct of Life* in 1860, and *May-Day and Other Pieces* in 1867. These newer books were forceful and sold better because of his established fame. Unfortunately, Emerson's memory began to fail more than ten years before his death, so that he declined into a benign senility during which the English-speaking world, and even many who read him in translation, continued to honor the intellectual liberator that he had been in his middle life. He died on April 27, 1882 at home in Concord, Massachusetts.

Ⅱ. Texts.

Nature

To go into solitude, a man needs to retire as much from his chamber as from society. I am not solitary whilst I read and write, though nobody is with me. But if a man would be alone, let him look at the stars. The rays that come from those heavenly worlds, will separate between him and what he touches. One might think the atmosphere was made transparent with this design, to give man, in the heavenly bodies, the perpetual presence of the sublime. Seen in the streets of cities, how great they are! If the stars should appear one night in a thousand years, how would men believe and adore; and preserve for many generations the remembrance of the city of God which had been shown! But every night come out these envoys① of beauty, and light the universe with their admonishing smile.

The stars awaken a certain reverence, because though always present, they are inaccessible; but all natural objects make a kindred impression, when the mind is open to their influence. Nature never wears a mean appearance. Neither does the wisest man extort her secret, and lose his curiosity by finding out all her perfection. Nature never became a toy to a wise spirit. The flowers, the animals, the mountains, reflected the wisdom of his best hour, as much as they had delighted the simplicity of his childhood.

When we speak of nature in this manner, we have a distinct but most poetical sense in the mind. We mean the integrity of impression made by manifold natural objects. It is this which distinguishes the stick of timber of the wood-cutter, from the tree of the poet. The charming landscape which I saw this morning is indubitably made up of some twenty or thirty farms. Miller owns this field, Locke that, and Manning the woodland beyond. But none of them owns the landscape. There is a property in the horizon which no man has but he whose eye can integrate all the parts, that is, the poet. This is the best part of these men's farms, yet to this their warranty-

---

① envoy: 使者,代表

deeds① give no title②.

To speak truly, few adult persons can see nature. Most persons do not see the sun. At least they have a very superficial seeing. The sun illuminates only the eye of the man, but shines into the eye and the heart of the child. The lover of nature is he whose inward and outward senses are still truly adjusted to each other; who has retained the spirit of infancy even into the era of manhood. His intercourse with heaven and earth becomes part of his daily food. In the presence of nature, a wild delight runs through the man, in spite of real sorrows. Nature says, — he is my creature, and maugre③ all his impertinent griefs, he shall be glad with me. Not the sun or the summer alone, but every hour and season yields its tribute of delight; for every hour and change corresponds to and authorizes a different state of the mind, from breathless noon to grimmest midnight. Nature is a setting that fits equally well a comic or a mourning piece. In good health, the air is a cordial of incredible virtue. Crossing a bare common, in snow puddles, at twilight, under a clouded sky, without having in my thoughts any occurrence of special good fortune, I have enjoyed a perfect exhilaration. I am glad to the brink of fear. In the woods too, a man casts off his years, as the snake his slough, and at what period soever of life, is always a child. In the woods is perpetual youth. Within these plantations of God, a decorum and sanctity reign, a perennial festival is dressed, and the guest sees not how he should tire of them in a thousand years. In the woods, we return to reason and faith. There I feel that nothing can befall me in life—no disgrace, no calamity, (leaving me my eyes,) which nature cannot repair. Standing on the bare ground—my head bathed by the blithe air, and uplifted into infinite space—all mean egotism vanishes. I become a transparent eye-ball; I am nothing; I see all; the currents of the Universal Being circulate through me; I am part or particle of God. The name of the nearest friend sounds then foreign and accidental: to be brothers, to be acquaintances, master or servant, is then a trifle and a disturbance. I am the lover of uncontained and immortal beauty. In the wilderness, I find something more dear and connate than in streets or villages. In the tranquil landscape, and especially in the distant line of the horizon, man beholds somewhat as beautiful as his own nature.

The greatest delight which the fields and woods minister, is the suggestion of an occult④ relation between man and the vegetable. I am not alone and unacknowledged. They nod to me, and I to them. The waving of the boughs in the storm is new to me and old. It takes me by surprise, and yet is not unknown. Its effect is like that of a higher thought or a better emotion coming over me, when I deemed I was thinking justly or doing right.

Yet it is certain that the power to produce this delight, does not reside in nature, but in man, or in a harmony of both. It is necessary to use these pleasures with great temperance. For, nature is not always tricked in holiday attire, but the same scene which yesterday breathed perfume and

---

① warranty-deed: 担保契据
② title: 所有权
③ maugre: 尽管,不顾
④ occult: 难以理解的,奥秘的

glittered as for the frolic of the nymphs①, is overspread with melancholy today. Nature always wears the colors of the spirit. To a man laboring under calamity, the heat of his own fire hath sadness in it. Then, there is a kind of contempt of the landscape felt by him who has just lost by death a dear friend. The sky is less grand as it shuts down over less worth in the population.

The American Scholar

……

In this distribution of functions, the scholar is the delegated intellect. In the right state, he is, Man Thinking. In the degenerate state, when the victim of society, he tends to become a mere thinker, or, still worse, the parrot of other men's thinking.

In this view of him, as Man Thinking, the theory of his office is contained. Him nature solicits with all her placid, all her monitory pictures; him the past instructs; him the future invites. Is not, indeed, every man a student, and do not all things exist for the student's behoof? And, finally, is not the true scholar the only true master? But the old oracle said, "All things have two handles: beware of the wrong one." In life, too often, the scholar errs with mankind and forfeits his privilege. Let us see him in his school, and consider him in reference to the main influences he receives.

I. The first in time and the first in importance of the influences upon the mind is that of nature. Every day, the sun; and, after sunset, night and her stars. Ever the winds blow; ever the grass grows. Every day, men and women, conversing, beholding and beholden. The scholar is he of all men whom this spectacle most engages. He must settle its value in his mind. What is nature to him? There is never a beginning, there is never an end, to the inexplicable continuity of this web of God, but always circular power returning into itself. Therein it resembles his own spirit, whose beginning, whose ending, he never can find—so entire, so boundless…

……

II. The next great influence into the spirit of the scholar is the mind of the Past—in whatever form, whether of literature, of art, of institutions, that mind is inscribed. Books are the best type of the influence of the past, and perhaps we shall get at the truth—learn the amount of this influence more conveniently—by considering their value alone.

The theory of books is noble. The scholar of the first age received into him the world around; brooded thereon; gave it the new arrangement of his own mind, and uttered it again. It came into him, life; it went out from him, truth. It came to him, short-lived actions; it went out from him, immortal thoughts. It came to him, business; it went from him, poetry. It was dead fact; now, it is quick thought. It can stand, and it can go. It now endures, it now flies, it now inspires. Precisely in proportion to the depth of mind from which it issued, so high does it soar, so long does it sing.

Or, I might say, it depends on how far the process had gone, of transmuting life into truth. In

---

① nymph: 居于山林水泽的仙女

proportion to the completeness of the distillation, so will the purity and imperishableness of the product be. But none is quite perfect. As no air-pump can by any means make a perfect vacuum, so neither can any artist entirely exclude the conventional, the local, the perishable from his book, or write a book of pure thought, that shall be as efficient, in all respects, to a remote posterity, as to contemporaries, or rather to the second age. Each age, it is found, must write its own books; or rather, each generation for the next succeeding. The books of an older period will not fit this.

Yet hence arises a grave mischief. The sacredness which attaches to the act of creation, the act of thought, is transferred to the record. The poet chanting was felt to be a divine man: henceforth the chant is divine also. The writer was a just and wise spirit: henceforward it is settled, the book is perfect; as love of the hero corrupts into worship of his statue. Instantly, the book becomes noxious: the guide is a tyrant. The sluggish and perverted mind of the multitude, slow to open to the incursions of Reason, having once so opened, having once received this book, stands upon it, and makes an outcry, if it is disparaged. Colleges are built on it. Books are written on it by thinkers, not by Man Thinking; by men of talent, that is, who start wrong, who set out from accepted dogmas, not from their own sight of principles. Meek young men grow up in libraries, believing it their duty to accept the views, which Cicero①, which Locke②, which Bacon③, have given, forgetful that Cicero, Locke, and Bacon were only young men in libraries, when they wrote these books.

Hence, instead of Man Thinking, we have the bookworm. Hence, the book-learned class, who value books, as such; not as related to nature and the human constitution, but as making a sort of Third Estate with the world and the soul. Hence, the restorers of readings, the emendators, the bibliomaniacs of all degrees.

……

I read with joy some of the auspicious signs of the coming days, as they glimmer already through poetry and art, through philosophy and science, through church and state.

One of these signs is the fact, that the same movement which effected the elevation of what was called the lowest class in the state, assumed in literature a very marked and as benign an aspect. Instead of the sublime and beautiful; the near, the low, the common, was explored and poetized. That, which had been negligently trodden under foot by those who were harnessing and provisioning themselves for long journeys into far countries, is suddenly found to be richer than all foreign parts. The literature of the poor, the feelings of the child, the philosophy of the street, the meaning of household life, are the topics of the time. It is a great stride. It is a sign—is it not? — of new vigor, when the extremities are made active, when currents of warm life run into the hands and the feet.

I ask not for the great, the remote, the romantic; what is doing in Italy or Arabia; what is

---

① Cicero: 西塞罗(106—43BC,古罗马政治家、演说家和哲学家)
② Locke: 洛克(1632—1704,英国唯物主义哲学家)
③ Bacon: 培根(1214?—1292,英国哲学家和科学家)

Greek art, or Provencal① minstrelsy②; I embrace the common, I explore and sit at the feet of the familiar, the low. Give me insight into to-day, and you may have the antique and future worlds. What would we really know the meaning of? The meal in the firkin; the milk in the pan; the ballad in the street; the news of the boat; the glance of the eye; the form and the gait of the body; show me the ultimate reason of these matters; show me the sublime presence of the highest spiritual cause lurking, as always it does lurk, in these suburbs and extremities of nature; let me see every trifle bristling with the polarity that ranges it instantly on an eternal law; and the shop, the plough, and the ledger, referred to the like cause by which light undulates and poets sing; and the world lies no longer a dull miscellany and lumber-room, but has form and order; there is no trifle; there is no puzzle; but one design unites and animates the farthest pinnacle and the lowest trench.

This idea has inspired the genius of Goldsmith③, Burns④, Cowper⑤, and, in a newer time, of Goethe⑥, Wordsworth⑦, and Carlyle⑧. This idea they have differently followed and with various success. In contrast with their writing, the style of Pope⑨, of Johnson⑩, of Gibbon⑪, looks cold and pedantic. This writing is blood-warm. Man is surprised to find that things near are not less beautiful and wondrous than things remote. The near explains the far. The drop is a small ocean. A man is related to all nature. This perception of the worth of the vulgar is fruitful in discoveries. Goethe, in this very thing the most modern of the moderns, has shown us, as none ever did, the genius of the ancients.

……

Ⅲ. Notes.

1. The selected text is the First Chapter of *Nature*. In the Introduction, Emerson laments that people understand the world around us through impersonal history, stories and theories rather than observing it personally and experiencing it directly. He advocates casting off old ways of viewing the world and having a direct connection with nature, with God's divine creation. In Chapter One, he gives concrete examples of how to have such a direct contact with the universe, such as gazing at the stars at night, perceiving the landscape as an integrated whole, standing alone in the woods, etc.

---

① Provencal: 普罗旺斯的,普罗旺斯人的
② minstrelsy: 吟游诗人
③ Goldsmith: 哥尔德斯密(1730—1774,英国诗人、剧作家、小说家)
④ Burns: 彭斯(1759—1796,苏格兰诗人)
⑤ Cowper: 柯珀(1731—1800,英国诗人)
⑥ Goethe: 歌德(1749—1832,德国诗人、作家)
⑦ Wordsworth: 华兹华斯(1770—1850,英国诗人)
⑧ Carlyle: 卡莱尔(1795—1881,苏格兰散文作家和历史学家)
⑨ Pope: 蒲柏(1688—1744,英国诗人)
⑩ Johnson: 约翰逊(1709—1784,英国作家、评论家)
⑪ Gibbon: 吉本(1737—1794,英国历史学家)

2. The text is a selection from "The American Scholar," which is considered to be America's "Intellectual Declaration of Independence." In this essay, Emerson defines the duties of the scholar, puts forth the idea that the scholar is the "Man Thinking," discusses the influence of nature, history, books, and action on the education of the thinking man and, above all else, declares the end of American dependence upon European Literature.

Ⅳ. Key Words(关键词).

Transcendentalist Movement: "超验主义运动"。它也叫"新英格兰超验主义"或"美国文艺复兴",是19世纪30年代兴起于美国新英格兰地区的一场重要的思想运动。它强调精神获救,强调个人的重要性,相信万物本质上的统一,相信人性中包含着神性,认为自然界是"超灵"或上帝的象征,提倡人与上帝、与大自然直接交流,主张超越经验和理性,通过直觉去认识真理。在文学领域,超验主义的主要代表人物有爱默生和梭罗。

Unitarianism: "神体一位论派"。这是16世纪宗教改革运动中产生的一个派别,18世纪传入美国。该派别认为:一、崇信唯一的上帝,否认圣父、圣子、圣灵三位一体说,否认基督神性。二、人具有善恶两种本性,人有能力通过遵循正确的宗教教义,良好的教育和真诚的努力达到圆满的道德及灵性高度。三、重视人类的理性的作用,对凡是理性不能说明的教义均予以否定。四、反对加尔文的"原罪"说和预定论,主张基督救赎是为了全人类,因而也被称为"普世派"(Universalist)。该教派对超验主义运动的产生起了很大的作用。

Calvinism: "加尔文主义"。这是16世纪宗教改革家、神学家约翰·加尔文所提出,一般被归结为五个要点:一、人类由于亚当的堕落而在本性中拒绝神,无力向善;二、神拣选人是无条件的,而不是基于人在伦理道德上的优点;三、有限的救赎,这是说耶稣只为上帝拣选的人赎罪,而不是为所有的人赎罪;四、不可抗拒的恩典,这是指圣灵向"选民"发出特别的呼唤,使他们获得救赎,这种恩典是不能抗拒的;五、人的本性要偏离神,但神却能保守信徒已经得到的救赎。加尔文主义是清教徒思想的核心,对美国文化的形成和发展产生了巨大且深远的影响。

Ⅴ. Questions.

1. How does Emerson define Nature, Me and Not Me?
2. How do you understand this sentence "Every man's condition is a solution in hieroglyphic to those inquiries he would put"?
3. What is Emerson's definition of "a poet"?
4. What differs the "Man Thinking" from the "mere thinker"?

Lesson 10 Henry David Thoreau (1817—1862)

Ⅰ. **A Brief Review.**

Born into a relatively poor family on July 12, 1817 in Concord, Massachusetts, Thoreau was an American essayist, poet and philosopher, famous mainly for his book *Walden*. Despite the family's lack of means, Thoreau was able to accept a fine education. He studied at Concord Academy from 1828 to 1833 and entered Harvard in 1833. During his college years, he devoted himself principally to the study of literature and read Ralph Waldo Emerson's *Nature*, which was probably the earliest intellectual influence upon him.

After his graduation in 1837, Thoreau returned to Concord, taught briefly in the public school and resigned two weeks later. Thoreau established a friendship with his neighbor Ralph Waldo Emerson and became a member of the Transcendental Club that met regularly at Emerson's home. In 1841, Thoreau accepted an invitation to live at Emerson's

图 10　Henry D. Thoreau

home, nominally to earn his living as a gardener, tutor of the children, and literary assistant to Emerson, but actually to devote much of his time to reading and writing, talking with other Transcendentalists, assisting from time to time in editing the transcendental periodical *Dial*. He returned to Concord in 1844. Instead of going back to the Emerson household, he rejoined the family business. In March 1845, with Emerson's permission, he began to build a cabin in the woods on Emerson's property at the Northwest end of Walden Pond. He lived there alone for more than two years in speculating and writing his book.

In 1849, he published at his own expense his first book *A Week on the Concord and Merrimack Rivers*, which is a memorial to a river trip he took with his brother in 1839. His second book *Walden* was published on August 9, 1854. Unlike the first book, *Walden* enjoyed moderate success, and occasioned comments in some widely read newspapers and magazines. In the 1850s, Thoreau became very active in anti-slavery matters. He lectured on "Slavery in Massachusetts" at an anti-slavery meeting at Framingham, Massachusetts on July 4, 1854, attacking the Fugitive Slave Law of 1850. During this period, however, he increasingly suffered from tuberculosis, a disease he contracted in 1835. He died on May 6, 1862.

During his life time, Thoreau published only *Week* and *Walden* in book forms. In the years following his death, editions of his previously unpublished works came out, among which were

Excursions (1863), *The Maine Woods* (1864), *Cape God* (1864), and *A Yankee in Canada, with Anti-Slavery and Reform Papers* (1866).

Ⅱ. Texts.

Walden

Chapter Ⅱ. Where I Lived, and What I Lived for

……

When first I took up my abode① in the woods, that is, began to spend my nights as well as days there, which, by accident, was on Independence Day, or the Fourth of July, 1845, my house was not finished for winter, but was merely a defence against the rain, without plastering or chimney, the walls being of rough, weather-stained boards, with wide chinks, which made it cool at night. The upright white hewn studs and freshly planed door and window casings gave it a clean and airy look, especially in the morning, when its timbers were saturated with dew, so that I fancied that by noon some sweet gum would exude from them. To my imagination it retained throughout the day more or less of this auroral② character, reminding me of a certain house on a mountain which I had visited a year before. This was an airy and unplastered cabin, fit to entertain a travelling god, and where a goddess might trail her garments. The winds which passed over my dwelling were such as sweep over the ridges of mountains, bearing the broken strains, or celestial③ parts only, of terrestrial music. The morning wind forever blows, the poem of creation is uninterrupted; but few are the ears that hear it. Olympus④ is but the outside of the earth everywhere.

The only house I had been the owner of before, if I except a boat, was a tent, which I used occasionally when making excursions in the summer, and this is still rolled up in my garret; but the boat, after passing from hand to hand, has gone down the stream of time. With this more substantial shelter about me, I had made some progress toward settling in the world. This frame, so slightly clad, was a sort of crystallization around me, and reacted on the builder. It was suggestive somewhat as a picture in outlines. I did not need to go outdoors to take the air, for the atmosphere within had lost none of its freshness. It was not so much within doors as behind a door where I sat, even in the rainiest weather. The Harivansa⑤ says, "An abode without birds is like a meat without seasoning." Such was not my abode, for I found myself suddenly neighbor to the birds; not by having imprisoned one, but having caged myself near them. I was not only nearer to some of those which commonly frequent the garden and the orchard, but to those smaller and more

---

① abode: 住所
② auroral: (像)黎明的,(像)曙光的
③ celestial: 天的;天上的;天空的
④ Olympus: 奥林匹斯山(诸神的住所);天堂;天国
⑤ Harivansa:《哈利梵萨》,是印度史诗《摩诃婆罗多》(Mahabharata)的附诗

thrilling songsters of the forest which never, or rarely, serenade a villager—the wood thrush, the veery, the scarlet tanager, the field sparrow, the whip-poor-will, and many others.

I was seated by the shore of a small pond, about a mile and a half south of the village of Concord and somewhat higher than it, in the midst of an extensive wood between that town and Lincoln, and about two miles south of that our only field known to fame, Concord Battle Ground; but I was so low in the woods that the opposite shore, half a mile off, like the rest, covered with wood, was my most distant horizon. For the first week, whenever I looked out on the pond it impressed me like a tarn high up on the side of a mountain, its bottom far above the surface of other lakes, and, as the sun arose, I saw it throwing off its nightly clothing of mist, and here and there, by degrees, its soft ripples or its smooth reflecting surface was revealed, while the mists, like ghosts, were stealthily withdrawing in every direction into the woods, as at the breaking up of some nocturnal① conventicle②. The very dew seemed to hang upon the trees later into the day than usual, as on the sides of mountains.

This small lake was of most value as a neighbor in the intervals of a gentle rain-storm in August, when, both air and water being perfectly still, but the sky overcast, mid-afternoon had all the serenity of evening, and the wood thrush sang around, and was heard from shore to shore. A lake like this is never smoother than at such a time; and the clear portion of the air above it being, shallow and darkened by clouds, the water, full of light and reflections, becomes a lower heaven itself so much the more important. From a hill-top near by, where the wood had been recently cut off, there was a pleasing vista southward across the pond, through a wide indentation in the hills which form the shore there, where their opposite sides sloping toward each other suggested a stream flowing out in that direction through a wooded valley, but stream there was none. That way I looked between and over the near green hills to some distant and higher ones in the horizon, tinged with blue. Indeed, by standing on tiptoe I could catch a glimpse of some of the peaks of the still bluer and more distant mountain ranges in the northwest, those true-blue coins from heaven's own mint, and also of some portion of the village. But in other directions, even from this point, I could not see over or beyond the woods which surrounded me. It is well to have some water in your neighborhood, to give buoyancy to and float the earth. One value even of the smallest well is that when you look into it you see that earth is not continent but insular. This is as important as that it keeps butter cool. When I looked across the pond from this peak toward the Sudbury meadows, which in time of flood I distinguished elevated perhaps by a mirage in their seething valley, like a coin in a basin, all the earth beyond the pond appeared like a thin crust insulated and floated even by this small sheet of intervening water, and I was reminded that this on which I dwelt was but dry land.

Though the view from my door was still more contracted, I did not feel crowded or confined in the least. There was pasture enough for my imagination. The low shrub oak plateau to which the

---

① nocturnal: 夜的，夜间发生的
② conventicle: 集会

opposite shore arose stretched away toward the prairies of the West and the steppes of Tartary, affording ample room for all the roving families of men. "There are none happy in the world but beings who enjoy freely a vast horizon"—said Damodara①, when his herds required new and larger pastures.

  Both place and time were changed, and I dwelt nearer to those parts of the universe and to those eras in history which had most attracted me. Where I lived was as far off as many a region viewed nightly by astronomers. We are wont to imagine rare and delectable places in some remote and more celestial corner of the system, behind the constellation of Cassiopeia's Chair②, far from noise and disturbance. I discovered that my house actually had its site in such a withdrawn, but forever new and unprofaned, part of the universe. If it were worth the while to settle in those parts near to the Pleiades③ or the Hyades④, to Aldebaran⑤ or Altair⑥, then I was really there, or at an equal remoteness from the life which I had left behind, dwindled and twinkling with as fine a ray to my nearest neighbor, and to be seen only in moonless nights by him. Such was that part of creation where I had squatted;

> "There was a shepherd that did live,
> And held his thoughts as high
> As were the mounts whereon his flocks
> Did hourly feed him by."

  What should we think of the shepherd's life if his flocks always wandered to higher pastures than his thoughts?

  Every morning was a cheerful invitation to make my life of equal simplicity, and I may say innocence, with Nature herself. I have been as sincere a worshipper of Aurora⑦ as the Greeks. I got up early and bathed in the pond; that was a religious exercise, and one of the best things which I did. They say that characters were engraven on the bathing tub of King Tchingthang⑧ to this effect: "Renew thyself completely each day; do it again, and again, and forever again." I can understand that. Morning brings back the heroic ages. I was as much affected by the faint hum of a mosquito making its invisible and unimaginable tour through my apartment at earliest dawn, when I was sitting with door and windows open, as I could be by any trumpet that ever sang of

---

① Damodara: 达摩达拉,是印度神话史诗中一位名叫毗瑟拏(Vishnu)的守护神之第 367 个名字
② Cassiopeia's Chair: 仙后座
③ Pleiades: 昴星团
④ Hyades: (位于金牛星座中的)毕(宿)
⑤ Aldebaran: 毕宿五,金牛座 α 星
⑥ Altair: 牵牛星,天鹰座 α 星
⑦ Aurora: 古罗马神话中的曙光女神
⑧ King Tchingthang: 中国商朝的开国君主成汤王

fame. It was Homer's① requiem②; itself an Iliad③ and Odyssey④ in the air, singing its own wrath and wanderings. There was something cosmical about it; a standing advertisement, till forbidden, of the everlasting vigor and fertility of the world. The morning, which is the most memorable season of the day, is the awakening hour. Then there is least somnolence in us; and for an hour, at least, some part of us awakes which slumbers all the rest of the day and night. Little is to be expected of that day, if it can be called a day, to which we are not awakened by our Genius⑤, but by the mechanical nudgings of some servitor, are not awakened by our own newly acquired force and aspirations from within, accompanied by the undulations of celestial music, instead of factory bells, and a fragrance filling the air—to a higher life than we fell asleep from; and thus the darkness bear its fruit, and prove itself to be good, no less than the light. That man who does not believe that each day contains an earlier, more sacred, and auroral hour than he has yet profaned, has despaired of life, and is pursuing a descending and darkening way. After a partial cessation of his sensuous life, the soul of man, or its organs rather, are reinvigorated each day, and his Genius tries again what noble life it can make. All memorable events, I should say, transpire in morning time and in a morning atmosphere. The Vedas⑥ say, "All intelligences awake with the morning." Poetry and art, and the fairest and most memorable of the actions of men, date from such an hour. All poets and heroes, like Memnon⑦, are the children of Aurora, and emit their music at sunrise. To him whose elastic and vigorous thought keeps pace with the sun, the day is a perpetual morning. It matters not what the clocks say or the attitudes and labors of men. Morning is when I am awake and there is a dawn in me. Moral reform is the effort to throw off sleep. Why is it that men give so poor an account of their day if they have not been slumbering? They are not such poor calculators. If they had not been overcome with drowsiness, they would have performed something. The millions are awake enough for physical labor; but only one in a million is awake enough for effective intellectual exertion, only one in a hundred millions to a poetic or divine life. To be awake is to be alive. I have never yet met a man who was quite awake. How could I have looked him in the face?

We must learn to reawaken and keep ourselves awake, not by mechanical aids, but by an infinite expectation of the dawn, which does not forsake us in our soundest sleep. I know of no more encouraging fact than the unquestionable ability of man to elevate his life by a conscious endeavor. It is something to be able to paint a particular picture, or to carve a statue, and so to make a few objects beautiful; but it is far more glorious to carve and paint the very atmosphere and

---

① Homer: 荷马(古希腊吟游盲诗人)
② requiem: 挽歌;挽诗
③ Iliad: 《伊利亚特》,古希腊史诗
④ Odyssey: 《奥德赛》,古希腊史诗
⑤ Genius: 古罗马神话中的守护神
⑥ Vedas: (印度最古老的经典)《吠陀经》
⑦ Memnon: 门农(古希腊神话中埃塞俄比亚人之王)

medium through which we look, which morally we can do. To affect the quality of the day, that is the highest of arts. Every man is tasked to make his life, even in its details, worthy of the contemplation of his most elevated and critical hour. If we refused, or rather used up, such paltry information as we get, the oracles would distinctly inform us how this might be done.

I went to the woods because I wished to live deliberately, to front only the essential facts of life, and see if I could not learn what it had to teach, and not, when I came to die, discover that I had not lived. I did not wish to live what was not life, living is so dear; nor did I wish to practise resignation, unless it was quite necessary. I wanted to live deep and suck out all the marrow of life, to live so sturdily and Spartan①-like as to put to rout all that was not life, to cut a broad swath and shave close, to drive life into a corner, and reduce it to its lowest terms, and, if it proved to be mean, why then to get the whole and genuine meanness of it, and publish its meanness to the world; or if it were sublime, to know it by experience, and be able to give a true account of it in my next excursion. For most men, it appears to me, are in a strange uncertainty about it, whether it is of the devil or of God, and have somewhat hastily concluded that it is the chief end of man here to "glorify God and enjoy him forever."

……

Ⅲ. Notes.

The selected text is from the second chapter of *Walden*. In this chapter, Thoreau explains why he chose to live alone in a small, simple cabin at Walden Pond, and why he writes this book. He finds that many of his contemporaries do not understand the real meaning of life, that they are too much involved in material concerns to achieve spiritual wholeness. Thoreau states his understanding of life, offers means of self-culture, describes the beauty of nature, celebrates the unity of nature, humanity and divinity—a central idea of transcendentalism, and promotes his philosophy of life—"simplicity, simplicity, simplicity."

Ⅳ. Key Words(关键词).

Nature: 自然。超验主义者认为自然不仅仅是物质而已,它有生命,是精神或"超灵"的外衣,是神的一种呈现方式;它充溢着神的精神和力量,具有丰富的象征意义。超验主义者相信自然对人在思想和情感上的健康有滋补和康复作用,因此,主张人类走近自然,与自然相融合,在自然中去探求真与美,从而达到人在道德上的完善和精神上的升华。梭罗在瓦尔登湖边的独居试验正是把超验主义者的这种思想付诸于实践。他在《瓦尔登》中描写的自然风光都带有某种象征意义,可以对人产生净化和启迪的作用。

Simplicity: 简朴。这是梭罗生活哲学中的一个重要组成部分。梭罗认为在他所处的时代,人们越来越沉湎于对物质的追求而忽略了精神上的需求。他认为生活之富足和生命之意义体现在丰富的思想和深刻的见解之上而不是体现在对物质的积累之上。因此,他倡导一种简单的生活观念,崇尚一种简朴的生活方式,主张人们应该尽可能地简化物质生活,降

---

① Spartan:(古希腊奴隶制城邦)斯巴达的;斯巴达人的;(以简朴、刻苦、黩武为特征的)斯巴达式的

低物质需求，摆脱物质对人的控制，把更多的时间和精力用于丰富人的内心世界，追求精神上的独立和道德上的完善。

Awaken: 清醒。梭罗认为芸芸众生大多是一些半睡半醒的人，他们的灵魂并没有完全清醒。对梭罗来说，清醒即生活，只有完全清醒的人才是真正活着的人，只有了解生活真谛的人才是完全清醒的人，而生活的真谛便是：真正富有的生活不是物质上的而是精神上的。梭罗写道："数百万人清醒得足以从事体力劳动，但只有百万分之一的人清醒得足以运用智力，亿分之一的人清醒得足以过上诗意且神圣的生活。"

V. Questions.

1. How does Thoreau feel about the "civilized" life of his time?
2. How do you understand the phrase "…when I came to die, discover that I had not lived"?
3. Thoreau calls upon people to simplify their life. How would you simplify your own life?
4. What symbolic meaning does Thoreau's morning bath in the pond have?

Lesson 11　Henry Wadsworth Longfellow (1807—1882)

Ⅰ. **A Brief Review.**

A popular poet in his day, Longfellow was born into a well-to-do family in Portland, Maine, on February 27, 1807. He was a student at Bowdoin College, where he met Nathaniel Hawthorne and Franklin Pierce, the 14th president of the United States (1853—1857), as his fellow students. After he graduated in 1825, he went to Europe and cultivated his preference for European culture and literature. Four years later, he returned to the United States and then found a position as a professor at Harvard in 1837. Longfellow published his first volume of poetry, *Voices of the Night* and the prose romance *Hyperion* in 1839. He continued to publish a small collection, *Poems on Slavery*, to demonstrate his public support of abolitionism. In 1854, Longfellow retired from Harvard in order to engage himself completely in literary writing. In his later years, he turned to translation of Dante's *Divine Comedy* and his last collection of poems was published in 1882.

图 11　Henry W. Longfellow

Longfellow enjoyed his popularity as a poet during his life time. His early poems were mostly collected in *Voices of the Night* (1839), which was well accepted and assured him as a famous poet. "A Psalm of Life" was one of the best-known poems from this volume. His later poetry collections include *Ballads and Other Poems* (1841), *Poems on Slavery* (1842), *Birds of Passage* (1845), *Tales of a Wayside Inn* (1863), and *In the Harbor* (1882). Longfellow experimented with many poetic forms, including hexameter and free verse. Many of his works helped shape the American character and its legacy, particularly with the poem "Paul Revere's Ride". He was such an admired figure in the United States during his life time that his 70th birthday in 1877 took on the air of a national holiday with parades, speeches, and the reading of his poetry.

In terms of American poetic tradition, his poetry shows great versatility, using anapestic and trochaic forms, blank verse, heroic couplets, ballads and sonnets. Usually he conceived the subject of his poetic creation for a long time before deciding on the right metrical form for it. Though much of his work is categorized as lyric poetry, many of his poems are recognized for melody-like musicality today.

II. Texts.

A Psalm of Life①

What the Heart of the Young Man Said to the Psalmist

I

Tell me not, in mournful numbers,
 "Life is but an empty dream!"
For the soul is dead that slumbers②,
And things are not what they seem.

II

Life is real! Life is earnest!
And the grave is not its goal;
"Dust thou art, to dust returnest③,"
Was not spoken of the soul.

III

Not enjoyment, and not sorrow,
Is our destined end or way;
But to act to each to-morrow
Finds us farther than to-day.

IV

Art is long, and Time is fleeting,
And our hearts, though stout and brave,
Still, like muffled drums, are beating
Funeral marches to the grave.

V

In the world's broad field of battle,
In the bivouac④ of Life,
Be not like dumb, driven cattle!
Be a hero in the strife!

VI

Trust no Future, howe'er pleasant!
Let the dead Past bury its dead!

---

① Psalm: 赞美诗,圣诗,圣歌
② slumber: 睡眠,沉睡
③ Dust thou art, to dust returnest: 你本是尘土,还将回到尘土,出自《圣经》
④ bivouac: 露营地,野营

Act,—act in the living Present!
Heart within, and God o'erhead!
             VII
Lives of great men all remind us
We can make our lives sublime,
And, departing, leave behind us
Footprints on the sands of time;
             VIII
Footprints, that perhaps another,
Sailing o'er life's solemn main,
A forlorn① and shipwrecked brother,
Seeing, shall take heart again.
             IX
Let us, then, be up and doing,
With a heart for any fate;
Still achieving, still pursuing
Learn to labor and to wait.

Excelsior②

The shades of night were falling fast,
As through an Alpine village passed
A youth, who bore, 'mid snow and ice.
A banner with the strange device
Excelsior!

His brow was sad; his eye beneath,
Flashed like a falchion③ from its sheath,
And like a silver clarion④ rung
The accents of that unknown tongue,
Excelsior!

In happy homes he saw the light
Of household fires gleam warm and bright;

---

① forlorn: 被遗弃的,孤苦伶仃的,可怜的
② Excelsior: 精益求精
③ falchion: 外刃大弯刀
④ clarion: 号角

Above, the spectral glaciers shone,
And from his lips escaped a groan,
Excelsior!
……

Ⅲ. Notes.

1. The poem "A Psalm of Life" comes from the volume *Voices of the Night*, the major collection of Longfellow's early poems. To a great extent, this poem is simple and straight, but its mind-set is outdated, which characterizes the ethos of a naïve and aspiring nation. Most critics pay less attention to this poem now. The "psalm", as the epigraph says, issues from "the heart of a young man". It could be Longfellow himself to do the psalm because he lost his first wife in 1835.

2. The poem "Excelsior" depicts a young man, wearing the banner "Excelsior" which is translated in Latin as "ever higher", passing through a town. This young man climbs higher and higher, ignoring all the warnings, until he is nearly close to be lifeless. The faithful hound finally finds him half-buried in the snow when he clasps the banner "Excelsior" in his hands.

Ⅳ. Key Words（关键词）.

American Romanticism: 美国浪漫主义文学。它开始于19世纪上半叶,深受西欧浪漫主义文学的影响。当时,随着美国资本主义的迅速发展,人们的民族意识和爱国热情十分高涨,摆脱英国文学束缚、重视人的精神创造和追求自由的超验主义风行一时,并使美国浪漫主义文学得到了蓬勃发展。朗费罗翻译了许多欧洲国家的诗歌,为在美国倡导浪漫主义文学起了很大的作用。

Lyric poems: 抒情诗。它是诗歌的一种,以集中抒发诗人在生活中激发起来的思想感情来反映生活为特征,诗中没有完整的故事情节,不具体描写人物和景物。朗费罗一生创作了大量的抒情诗、叙事诗、歌谣和诗剧,诗中充满了乐观主义的情绪,曾在美国和欧洲广为流传,并受到赞赏。

Optimism: 乐观主义。朗费罗是19世纪美国最伟大的浪漫主义诗人之一,他的诗歌中反映的主题一般都包含积极向上的,诗中充满奋发向上的精神。就算是面对死亡时,他也在诗歌中抒发了一种入世的豪迈情怀,坦然面对必将来临的死亡。因此,他的诗歌具有十分强烈的感染力。

Ⅴ. Questions.

1. In "A Psalm of Life", who, in your opinion, is the psalmist of this poem?

2. In "A Psalm of Life", how to paraphrase the sentence "And, departing, leave behind us Footsteps on the sands of time"?

3. What is the symbolic meaning of the banner "Excelsior"?

Lesson 12　Nathaniel Hawthorne (1804—1864)

Ⅰ. **A Brief Review.**

A novelist and short story writer, Hawthorne was born on July 4, 1804 in Salem, Massachusetts. Among his ancestors were some influential Puritan magnates and judges, including William Hathorne, a colonial magistrate, who was a notorious persecutor of Quakers. While in college, Hawthorne added the "w" to his last name so as to distance himself from his ancestors because of their shameful deeds. His father, a sea captain, died when Hawthorne was four years old, leaving the family dependent on relatives. Hawthorne was raised secluded from the world by his mother, and thus had formed in an early age the habits of solitude and self-sufficiency that he retained throughout his life. He was fond of reading books and roaming alone in the woods. His early encounter with English canonic writers,

图 12　Nathaniel Hawthorne

such as Shakespeare, Milton, Pope and Henry Fielding, helped him tremendously in his later years of creative writing.

In 1821, with the aid of his prosperous maternal uncles, Hawthorne entered Bowdoin College in Maine, where he had as classmates some prominent literary figures, such as Henry Wadsworth Longfellow. After graduating from Bowdoin College in 1825, Hawthorne returned to Salem and wrote numerous sketches and stories. He published his first novel *Fanshawe* in 1828. In the meantime, he wrote a series of books for children, such as *Grandfather's Chair* (1841), *Famous Old People* (1841), *Liberty Tree* (1841), and *Biographical Stories for Children* (1842).

His most famous work *The Scarlet Letter* came out in the spring of 1850 and attained an immediate success, earning him considerable fame in both the United States and Great Britain. At the end of March 1850, Hawthorne moved with his family to Lenox, Massachusetts, where he became a close friend of Herman Melville. In the next few years he produced in rapid succession *The House of the Seven Gables* (1851), *The Blithedale Romance* (1852), *The Snow-Image and Other-Twice-Told Tales* (1852). Hawthorne died on May 19, 1864 in Plymouth, New Hampshire. After his death, his wife Sophia Hawthorne edited and published his notebooks: *Passage from the American Notebooks* (1868), *Passages from the English Notebooks* (1870), and *Passages from the French and Italian Notebooks* (1871).

Hawthorne's Puritan family background exerted great influence on his imagination, giving him a dark vision of human nature. He believed that evil was as old as human beings. He was one of the first American writers to tell the dark truth of society, to explore the psychological conflicts and hidden motivations of his characters. It is well recognized that his many narratives are set in colonial New England; many of his stories feature moral allegories with a Puritan inspiration. Inherent evil and sin of humanity seem to be recurrent themes of his writing while allegory and symbol remain his favorite means of expression.

Ⅱ. Texts.

The Scarlet Letter

Chapter II. The Market-Place

The grass-plot before the jail, in Prison Lane, on a certain summer morning, not less than two centuries ago, was occupied by a pretty large number of the inhabitants of Boston, all with their eyes intently fastened on the iron-clamped① oaken door. Amongst any other population, or at a later period in the history of New England, the grim rigidity that petrified the bearded physiognomies② of these good people would have augured some awful business in hand. It could have betokened nothing short of the anticipated execution of some rioted culprit, on whom the sentence of a legal tribunal③ had but confirmed the verdict of public sentiment. But, in that early severity of the Puritan character, an inference of this kind could not so indubitably be drawn. It might be that a sluggish bond-servant, or an undutiful child, whom his parents had given over to the civil authority, was to be corrected at the whipping-post. It might be that an Antinomian④, a Quaker⑤, or other heterodox religionist, was to be scourged out of the town, or an idle or vagrant Indian, whom the white man's firewater had made riotous about the streets, was to be driven with stripes into the shadow of the forest. It might be, too, that a witch, like old Mistress Hibbins⑥, the bitter-tempered widow of the magistrate, was to die upon the gallows. In either case, there was very much the same solemnity of demeanour on the part of the spectators, as befitted a people among whom religion and law were almost identical, and in whose character both were so thoroughly interfused, that the mildest and severest acts of public discipline were alike made venerable and awful. Meagre⑦, indeed, and cold, was the sympathy that a transgressor might look for, from such bystanders, at the scaffold. On the other hand, a penalty which, in our days, would infer a degree of mocking infamy and ridicule, might then be invested with almost as stern a

---

① iron-clamped: 用铁加固的
② physiognomy: 面容；面相
③ tribunal: 法庭
④ Antinomian: （基督教）反律法主义的(人)，持唯信仰伦の(人)
⑤ Quaker: （基督教）贵格会教徒，教友会派教徒
⑥ Mistress Hibbins: 即安·希宾斯(Ann Hibbins, ?—1656)，马萨诸塞湾殖民地理查德·贝林厄姆(Richard Bellingham, 1592—1672)总督之妹,其丈夫威廉·希宾斯也是殖民地时期的一个重要人物。1655年安·希宾斯因被指控为女巫而受到审判并于次年在波士顿被处以绞刑
⑦ meagre: （尤指食物)质量差的,粗劣的,不足的；(思想等)不丰富的,贫瘠的

dignity as the punishment of death itself.

It was a circumstance to be noted on the summer morning when our story begins its course, that the women, of whom there were several in the crowd, appeared to take a peculiar interest in whatever penal infliction might be expected to ensue. The age had not so much refinement, that any sense of impropriety restrained the wearers of petticoat and farthingale from stepping forth into the public ways, and wedging their not unsubstantial persons, if occasion were, into the throng nearest to the scaffold at an execution. Morally, as well as materially, there was a coarser fibre in those wives and maidens of old English birth and breeding than in their fair descendants, separated from them by a series of six or seven generations; for, throughout that chain of ancestry, every successive mother had transmitted to her child a fainter bloom, a more delicate and briefer beauty, and a slighter physical frame, if not character of less force and solidity than her own. The women who were now standing about the prison-door stood within less than half a century of the period when the man-like Elizabeth① had been the not altogether unsuitable representative of the sex. They were her countrywomen: and the beef and ale of their native land, with a moral diet not a whit more refined, entered largely into their composition. The bright morning sun, therefore, shone on broad shoulders and well-developed busts, and on round and ruddy cheeks, that had ripened in the far-off island, and had hardly yet grown paler or thinner in the atmosphere of New England. There was, moreover, a boldness and rotundity of speech among these matrons, as most of them seemed to be, that would startle us at the present day, whether in respect to its purport or its volume of tone.

"Good wives," said a hard-featured dame of fifty, "I'll tell ye a piece of my mind. It would be greatly for the public behoof if we women, being of mature age and church-members in good repute, should have the handling of such male factresses② as this Hester Prynne. What think ye, gossips? If the hussy stood up for judgment before us five, that are now here in a knot together, would she come off with such a sentence as the worshipful magistrates have awarded? Marry, I trow not."

"People say," said another, "that the Reverend Master Dimmesdale, her godly pastor, takes it very grievously to heart that such a scandal should have come upon his congregation."

"The magistrates are God-fearing gentlemen, but merciful overmuch—that is a truth," added a third autumnal matron. "At the very least, they should have put the brand of a hot iron on Hester Prynne's forehead. Madame Hester would have winced at that, I warrant me. But she——the naughty baggage——little will she care what they put upon the bodice of her gown Why, look you, she may cover it with a brooch, or such like. heathenish③ adornment, and so walk the streets as brave as ever"

"Ah, but," interposed, more softly, a young wife, holding a child by the hand, "let her

---

① Elizabeth: 即英国女王伊丽莎白一世
② malefactress: 女罪犯;作恶的女人,坏女人
③ heathenish: (似)异教徒的

cover the mark as she will, the pang of it will be always in her heart."

"What do we talk of marks and brands, whether on the bodice of her gown or the flesh of her forehead?" cried another female, the ugliest as well as the most pitiless of these self-constituted judges. "This woman has brought shame upon us all, and ought to die; Is there not law for it? Truly there is, both in the Scripture and the statute-book. Then let the magistrates, who have made it of no effect, thank themselves if their own wives and daughters go astray".

"Mercy on us, goodwife" exclaimed a man in the crowd, "is there no virtue in woman, save what springs from a wholesome fear of the gallows? That is the hardest word yet Hush now, gossips for the lock is turning in the prison-door, and here comes Mistress Prynne herself."

The door of the jail being flung open from within there appeared, in the first place, like a black shadow emerging into sunshine, the grim and gristly presence of the town-beadle, with a sword by his side, and his staff of office in his hand. This personage prefigured and represented in his aspect the whole dismal severity of the Puritanic① code of law, which it was his business to administer in its final and closest application to the offender. Stretching forth the official staff in his left hand, he laid his right upon the shoulder of a young woman, whom he thus drew forward, until, on the threshold of the prison-door, she repelled him, by an action marked with natural dignity and force of character, and stepped into the open air as if by her own free will. She bore in her arms a child, a baby of some three months old, who winked and turned aside its little face from the too vivid light of day; because its existence, heretofore, had brought it acquaintance only with the grey twilight of a dungeon, or other darksome apartment of the prison.

When the young woman—the mother of this child—stood fully revealed before the crowd, it seemed to be her first impulse to clasp the infant closely to her bosom; not so much by an impulse of motherly affection, as that she might thereby conceal a certain token, which was wrought or fastened into her dress. In a moment, however, wisely judging that one token of her shame would but poorly serve to hide another, she took the baby on her arm, and with a burning blush, and yet a haughty smile, and a glance that would not be abashed, looked around at her townspeople and neighbours. On the breast of her gown, in fine red cloth, surrounded with an elaborate embroidery and fantastic flourishes of gold thread, appeared the letter A. It was so artistically done, and with so much fertility and gorgeous luxuriance of fancy, that it had all the effect of a last and fitting decoration to the apparel which she wore, and which was of a splendour in accordance with the taste of the age, but greatly beyond what was allowed by the sumptuary② regulations of the colony.

The young woman was tall, with a figure of perfect elegance on a large scale. She had dark and abundant hair, so glossy that it threw off the sunshine with a gleam; and a face which, besides being beautiful from regularity of feature and richness of complexion, had the impressiveness belonging to a marked brow and deep black eyes. She was ladylike, too, after the manner of the

---

① Puritanic: 道德或宗教上极拘谨的;清教徒似的;禁欲的,苦行的
② sumptuary: (按道德或宗教观念等)节制个人(衣食等)消费的,规定个人费用的

feminine gentility of those days; characterised by a certain state and dignity, rather than by the delicate, evanescent, and indescribable grace which is now recognised as its indication. And never had Hester Prynne appeared more ladylike, in the antique interpretation of the term, than as she issued from the prison. Those who had before known her, and had expected to behold her dimmed and obscured by a disastrous cloud, were astonished, and even startled, to perceive how her beauty shone out, and made a halo① of the misfortune and ignominy in which she was enveloped. It may be true that, to a sensitive observer, there was some thing exquisitely painful in it. Her attire, which indeed, she had wrought for the occasion in prison, and had modelled much after her own fancy, seemed to express the attitude of her spirit, the desperate recklessness of her mood, by its wild and picturesque peculiarity. But the point which drew all eyes, and, as it were, transfigured the wearer—so that both men and women who had been familiarly acquainted with Hester Prynne were now impressed as if they beheld her for the first time—was that SCARLET LETTER, so fantastically embroidered and illuminated upon her bosom. It had the effect of a spell, taking her out of the ordinary relations with humanity, and enclosing her in a sphere by herself.

"She hath good skill at her needle, that's certain," remarked one of her female spectators; "but did ever a woman, before this brazen hussy, contrive such a way of showing it? Why, gossips②, what is it but to laugh in the faces of our godly magistrates, and make a pride out of what they, worthy gentlemen, meant for a punishment?"

"It were well," muttered the most iron-visaged of the old dames, "if we stripped Madame Hester's rich gown off her dainty shoulders; and as for the red letter which she hath stitched so curiously, I'll bestow a rag of mine own rheumatic flannel to make a fitter one!"

"Oh, peace, neighbours—peace!" whispered their youngest companion; "do not let her hear you! Not a stitch in that embroidered letter but she has felt it in her heart."

The grim beadle now made a gesture with his staff. "Make way, good people—make way, in the King's name!" cried he. "Open a passage; and I promise ye, Mistress Prynne shall be set where man, woman, and child may have a fair sight of her brave apparel from this time till an hour past meridian. A blessing on the righteous colony of the Massachusetts, where iniquity is dragged out into the sunshine! Come along, Madame Hester, and show your scarlet letter in the market-place!"

A lane was forthwith opened through the crowd of spectators. Preceded by the beadle, and attended by an irregular procession of stern-browed men and unkindly visaged women, Hester Prynne set forth towards the place appointed for her punishment. A crowd of eager and curious schoolboys, understanding little of the matter in hand, except that it gave them a half-holiday, ran before her progress, turning their heads continually to stare into her face and at the winking baby in her arms, and at the ignominious letter on her breast. It was no great distance, in those days, from

---

① halo:(圣人、天使等头上的)光轮
② gossip:(古)伙伴、密友、女友

the prison door to the market-place. Measured by the prisoner's experience, however, it might be reckoned a journey of some length; for haughty as her demeanour was, she perchance① underwent an agony from every footstep of those that thronged to see her, as if her heart had been flung into the street for them all to spurn and trample upon. In our nature, however, there is a provision, alike marvellous and merciful, that the sufferer should never know the intensity of what he endures by its present torture, but chiefly by the pang that rankles after it. With almost a serene deportment, therefore, Hester Prynne passed through this portion of her ordeal, and came to a sort of scaffold, at the western extremity of the market-place. It stood nearly beneath the eaves of Boston's earliest church, and appeared to be a fixture there.

In fact, this scaffold constituted a portion of a penal machine, which now, for two or three generations past, has been merely historical and traditionary among us, but was held, in the old time, to be as effectual an agent, in the promotion of good citizenship, as ever was the guillotine among the terrorists of France. It was, in short, the platform of the pillory; and above it rose the framework of that instrument of discipline, so fashioned as to confine the human head in its tight grasp, and thus hold it up to the public gaze. The very ideal of ignominy was embodied and made manifest in this contrivance of wood and iron. There can be no outrage, methinks, against our common nature—whatever be the delinquencies of the individual—no outrage more flagrant than to forbid the culprit to hide his face for shame; as it was the essence of this punishment to do. In Hester Prynne's instance, however, as not unfrequently in other cases, her sentence bore that she should stand a certain time upon the platform, but without undergoing that gripe about the neck and confinement of the head, the proneness to which was the most devilish characteristic of this ugly engine. Knowing well her part, she ascended a flight of wooden steps, and was thus displayed to the surrounding multitude, at about the height of a man's shoulders above the street.

Had there been a Papist among the crowd of Puritans, he might have seen in this beautiful woman, so picturesque in her attire and mien, and with the infant at her bosom, an object to remind him of the image of Divine Maternity②, which so many illustrious painters have vied with one another to represent; something which should remind him, indeed, but only by contrast, of that sacred image of sinless motherhood, whose infant was to redeem the world. Here, there was the taint of deepest sin in the most sacred quality of human life, working such effect, that the world was only the darker for this woman's beauty, and the more lost for the infant that she had borne.

……

III. Notes.

The Scarlet Letter is a novel about sin, guilt, punishment, and atonement. The excerpt is part of the second chapter of the novel. The first chapter sets the story in the seventeenth century puritanical Boston, and gives a dark and gloomy picture of the prison, from which the protagonist

---

① perchance: (古)容或;间或
② Divine Maternity: 指圣母玛丽亚

Hester Prynne is to come out. In depicting the prison, Hawthorne conveys his understanding of humanity, that is, sin is an inherent human nature. In the second chapter, through unsympathetic description of the crowd who condemns Hester the adulteress, Hawthorne reaffirms his belief in humanism. Also in the second chapter, Hawthorne begins his characterization of Hester as a positive figure of the good and honesty.

Ⅳ. Key Words（关键词）.

Puritanism: "清教主义"或"清教思想"。它起源于16世纪末英国的宗教改革，因其要求清除英国国教中的天主教残余影响而得名。清教主义以加尔文的学说为基础，相信"原罪说"、"获救预定论"、"全然堕落"和"有限的赎罪"等宗教思想，承认《圣经》为唯一权威，反对国王和主教的专制，认为一个人事业上的成功表明他是上帝的选民，并因此提倡一种勤勉工作、俭朴生活的道德观念。在17世纪和18世纪，由于在英国国内遭到迫害，大批清教徒逃亡到北美大陆，在新英格兰地区建立起殖民地。他们相信自己是上帝的选民，希望在美洲这个新世界里建立起自己的"山巅之城"。

Dark Romanticism: "黑色浪漫主义"。它是19世纪美国超验主义运动中产生的一种亚文学类型。它深受超验主义的影响，但在一些观点上又与之有所不同。坡、霍桑和麦尔维尔都是这种浪漫主义的代表作家。超验主义者认为人的本质是向善的，人性中包含着神性；而黑色浪漫主义者笔下的人物更倾向于犯罪和自甘堕落；虽然像超验主义者一样相信自然富有灵性，但黑色浪漫主义者将其视为一种阴暗，腐败和神秘的力量，认为它展现给人的往往是邪恶和可怕的事实，即使个人在道路上不断努力也不会改变社会，其结果只能是以失败而告终。

Ⅴ. Questions.

1. Could you point out the symbols Hawthorne uses in the selected text? How do they relate to the themes, plot and characters?
2. Why does Hawthorne depict Hester the adulteress in such sympathetic language?
3. What is your impression of the Puritan women in the story?

Lesson 13 Herman Melville (1819—1891)

Ⅰ. **A Brief Review.**

Born on August 1, 1819 in New York City, Melville was the third of the eight children in a distinguished family. He went to Albany Academy in October 1830 but dropped out of school two years later when his father died bankrupt. At nineteen, Melville decided to make his living at sea and signed a contract as a cabin boy on the *St. Lawrence*, a New York-Liverpool merchant marine. Coming back from Liverpool, he set sail again in January 1841 on the *Acushnet*, a whaler bound for the South Seas. On this voyage, he learned to hunt, kill and harvest whales, and to process whale oil aboard ship.

图 13 Herman Melville

In October 1844, Melville returned to New York and determined to write about his sea adventures. Within two or three months, he began writing his first novel *Typee*, an autobiographical novel based largely on his experiences among the Typee people of the Marquesas Islands in 1842. With the help of his brother Gansevoort, who was then the secretary for U. S. legation in London, the novel finally came out in London and then in the United States in 1846. It made an immediate success and remained his most popular novel during his lifetime. In 1850, on a trip to his uncle Thomas's old place in Pittsfield, Massachusetts, Melville met and made friends with Nathaniel Hawthorne, who lived in nearby Lenox. Under the influence of Hawthorne, he completed and published *Moby-Dick* in 1851, dedicating it to Hawthorne as noted in the novel. The book, however, was a critical and commercial failure upon its release, though it has come to be recognized as "a great American novel and a treasure of world literature" nowadays.

His next book *Pierre*, a psychological as well as autobiographical novel, came out in 1852 and met with negative responses from the public. Henceforth, his fame suffered a decline. His last full-length novel, *The Confidence Man*, a dense allegory of American materialism, came out in 1857. Ever since then, he wrote very little prose and his novels were almost forgotten. His last novel *Billy Budd*, which he began to write around 1886, was published posthumously in 1924, when a Melville revival launched his widespread fame as a great American writer.

II. Texts.

Moby Dick

Chapter 41

I, Ishmael, was one of that crew; my shouts had gone up with the rest; my oath had been welded with theirs; and stronger I shouted, and more did I hammer and clinch my oath, because of the dread in my soul. A wild, mystical, sympathetical feeling was in me; Ahab's quenchless feud seemed mine. With greedy ears I learned the history of that murderous monster against whom I and all the others had taken our oaths of violence and revenge.

For some time past, though at intervals only, the unaccompanied, secluded White Whale had haunted those uncivilized seas mostly frequented by the Sperm Whale fishermen. But not all of them knew of his existence; a few of them, comparatively, had knowingly seen him; while the number who as yet had actually and knowingly given battle to him, was small indeed. For, owing to the large number of whale-cruisers①; the disorderly way they were sprinkled over the entire watery circumference②, many of them adventurously pushing their quest along solitary latitudes, so as seldom or never for a whole twelvemonth or more on a stretch, to encounter a single news-telling sail③ of any sort; the inordinate length of each separate voyage; the irregularity of the times of sailing from home; all these, with other circumstances, direct and indirect, long obstructed the spread through the whole world-wide whaling-fleet of the special individualizing tidings concerning Moby Dick. It was hardly to be doubted, that several vessels reported to have encountered, at such or such a time, or on such or such a meridian, a Sperm Whale of uncommon magnitude and malignity④, which whale, after doing great mischief to his assailants, has completely escaped them; to some minds it was not an unfair presumption, I say, that the whale in question must have been no other than Moby Dick. Yet as of late the Sperm Whale fishery had been marked by various and not unfrequent instances of great ferocity, cunning, and malice in the monster attacked; therefore it was, that those who by accident ignorantly gave battle to Moby Dick; such hunters, perhaps, for the most part, were content to ascribe the peculiar terror he bred, more, as it were, to the perils of the Sperm Whale fishery at large, than to the individual cause. In that way, mostly, the disastrous encounter between Ahab and the whale had hitherto been popularly regarded.

And as for those who, previously hearing of the White Whale, by chance caught sight of him; in the beginning of the thing they had every one of them, almost, as boldly and fearlessly lowered for him, as for any other whale of that species. But at length, such calamities did ensue in these assaults—not restricted to sprained wrists and ankles, broken limbs, or devouring

---

① whale-cruiser: 捕鲸船
② circumference: 圆周;周长;物体或图形的周界或表面
③ news-telling sail: 报告信息的船只
④ malignity: 极度的恶意;恶毒;危险性

amputations—but fatal to the last degree of fatality; those repeated disastrous repulses, all accumulating and piling their terrors upon Moby Dick; those things had gone far to shake the fortitude of many brave hunters, to whom the story of the White Whale had eventually come.

  Nor did wild rumors of all sorts fail to exaggerate, and still the more horrify the true histories of these deadly encounters. For not only do fabulous rumors naturally grow out of the very body of all surprising terrible events—as the smitten tree gives birth to its fungi; but, in maritime life, far more than in that of terra firma①, wild rumors abound, wherever there is any adequate reality for them to cling to. And as the sea surpasses the land in this matter, so the whale fishery surpasses every other sort of maritime life, in the wonderfulness and fearfulness of the rumors which sometimes circulate there. For not only are whalemen as a body unexempt from that ignorance and superstitiousness② hereditary to all sailors; but of all sailors, they are by all odds the most directly brought into contact with whatever is appallingly astonishing in the sea; face to face they not only eye its greatest marvels, but, hand to jaw, give battle to them. Alone, in such remotest waters, that though you sailed a thousand miles, and passed a thousand shores, you would not come to any chiselled hearth-stone③, or aught hospitable beneath that part of the sun; in such latitudes and longitudes, pursuing too such a calling as he does, the whaleman is wrapped by influences all tending to make his fancy pregnant with many a mighty birth. No wonder, then, that ever gathering volume from the mere transit over the wildest watery spaces, the outblown rumors of the White Whale did in the end incorporate with themselves all manner of morbid hints, and half-formed foetal suggestions of supernatural agencies, which eventually invested Moby Dick with new terrors unborrowed from anything that visibly appears. So that in many cases such a panic did he finally strike, that few who by those rumors, at least, had heard of the White Whale, few of those hunters were willing to encounter the perils of his jaw.

  But there were still other and more vital practical influences at work. Nor even at the present day has the original prestige of the Sperm Whale, as fearfully distinguished from all other species of the leviathan④, died out of the minds of the whalemen as a body. There are those this day among them, who, though intelligent and courageous enough in offering battle to the Greenland⑤ or Right⑥ whale, would perhaps—either from professional inexperience, or incompetency, or timidity, decline a contest with the Sperm Whale; at any rate, there are plenty of whalemen, especially among those whaling nations not sailing under the American flag, who have never hostilely encountered the Sperm Whale, but whose sole knowledge of the leviathan is restricted to the ignoble monster primitively pursued in the North; seated on their hatches, these men will

---

① terra firma: （拉丁语）陆地，坚实的土地
② superstitiousness: 迷信；迷信思想
③ chiselled hearth-stone: 铺砌整齐的壁炉基石，转义为温暖的家
④ leviathan: （《圣经·以赛亚书》中象征邪恶的）海中怪兽；海中巨兽
⑤ Greenland: 格陵兰岛（世界第一大岛，位于北冰洋同大西洋之间）
⑥ Right: 真正的；货真价实的；十足的

hearken with a childish fireside interest and awe, to the wild, strange tales of Southern whaling. Nor is the preeminent tremendousness of the great Sperm Whale anywhere more feelingly comprehended, than on board of those prows which stem him.

And as if the now tested reality of his might had in former legendary times thrown its shadow before it; we find some book naturalists—Olassen and Povelson①—declaring the Sperm Whale not only to be a consternation to every other creature in the sea, but also to be so incredibly ferocious as continually to be athirst② for human blood. Nor even down to so late a time as Cuvier's③, were these or almost similar impressions effaced. For in his Natural History, the Baron himself affirms that at sight of the Sperm Whale, all fish (sharks included) are "struck with the most lively terrors," and "often in the precipitancy of their flight dash themselves against the rocks with such violence as to cause instantaneous death." And however the general experiences in the fishery may amend such reports as these; yet in their full terribleness, even to the bloodthirsty item of Povelson, the superstitious belief in them is, in some vicissitudes of their vocation, revived in the minds of the hunters.

So that overawed by the rumors and portents concerning him, not a few of the fishermen recalled, in reference to Moby Dick, the earlier days of the Sperm Whale fishery, when it was oftentimes hard to induce long practised Right whalemen to embark in the perils of this new and daring warfare; such men protesting that although other leviathans might be hopefully pursued, yet to chase and point lances at such an apparition as the Sperm Whale was not for mortal man. That to attempt it, would be inevitably to be torn into a quick eternity. On this head, there are some remarkable documents that may be consulted.

Nevertheless, some there were, who even in the face of these things were ready to give chase to Moby Dick; and a still greater number who, chancing only to hear of him distantly and vaguely, without the specific details of any certain calamity, and without superstitious accompaniments were sufficiently hardy not to flee from the battle if offered.

One of the wild suggestions referred to, as at last coming to be linked with the White Whale in the minds of the superstitiously inclined, was the unearthly conceit that Moby Dick was ubiquitous; that he had actually been encountered in opposite latitudes at one and the same instant of time.

Nor, credulous as such minds must have been, was this conceit altogether without some faint show of superstitious probability. For as the secrets of the currents in the seas have never yet been divulged, even to the most erudite research; so the hidden ways of the Sperm Whale when beneath the surface remain, in great part, unaccountable to his pursuers; and from time to time have originated the most curious and contradictory speculations regarding them, especially

---

① Olassen and Povelson: 18 世纪丹麦生物学家和游记作家,生卒年不详,著有《冰岛游记》一书
② athirst:（古）渴的;渴望的
③ Cuvier: 乔治·居维叶男爵(Baron George Cuvier 1769—1832),法国博物学家和动物学家,即下文中提到的"the Baron"

concerning the mystic modes whereby, after sounding to a great depth, he transports himself with such vast swiftness to the most widely distant points. It is a thing well known to both American and English whale-ships, and as well a thing placed upon authoritative record years ago by Scoresby①, that some whales have been captured far north in the Pacific, in whose bodies have been found the barbs of harpoons darted in the Greenland seas. Nor is it to be gainsaid, that in some of these instances it has been declared that the interval of time between the two assaults could not have exceeded very many days. Hence, by inference, it has been believed by some whalemen, that the Nor' West Passage②, so long a problem to man, was never a problem to the whale. So that here, in the real living experience of living men, the prodigies related in old times of the inland Strello mountain③ in Portugal (near whose top there was said to be a lake in which the wrecks of ships floated up to the surface); and that still more wonderful story of the Arethusa fountain④ near Syracuse⑤(whose waters were believed to have come from the Holy Land⑥ by an underground passage; these fabulous narrations are almost fully equalled by the realities of the whalemen.

Forced into familiarity, then, with such prodigies as these; and knowing that after repeated, intrepid assaults, the White Whale had escaped alive; it cannot be much matter of surprise that some whalemen should go still further in their superstitions; declaring Moby Dick not only ubiquitous, but immortal (for immortality is but ubiquity in time); that though groves of spears should be planted in his flanks, he would still swim away unharmed; or if indeed he should ever be made to spout thick blood, such a sight would be but a ghastly deception; for again in unensanguined billows hundreds of leagues away, his unsullied jet would once more be seen.

But even stripped of these supernatural surmisings, there was enough in the earthly make and incontestable character of the monster to strike the imagination with unwonted power. For, it was not so much his uncommon bulk that so much distinguished him from other sperm whales, but, as was elsewhere thrown out——a peculiar snow-white wrinkled forehead, and a high, pyramidical white hump. These were his prominent features; the tokens whereby, even in the limitless, uncharted seas, he revealed his identity, at a long distance, to those who knew him.

The rest of his body was so streaked, and spotted, and marbled with the same shrouded hue, that, in the end, he had gained his distinctive appellation of the White Whale; a name, indeed, literally justified by his vivid aspect, when seen gliding at high noon through a dark blue sea,

---

① Scoresby: 即威廉·斯科斯比(William Scoresby. Jr., 1789—1857),英国北极探险者,博物学家,科学家
② Nor' West Passage: 即西北航道(Northwest Passage),是由格陵兰岛经加拿大北极群岛到阿拉斯加北岸的航道,是沟通大西洋和太平洋的最短航道
③ Strello Mountain: 即埃什特雷拉山(Serra da Estrela),是葡萄牙境内最高的山脉
④ Arethusa Fountain: 希腊神话中,阿瑞托莎(山林中的仙女)在河神 Alpheus 追她时,化为了一股泉水,遁入地下一直流到了西西里的锡拉库扎与大海相汇
⑤ Syracuse: 锡拉丘斯(意大利西西里岛东南岸城市)
⑥ Holy Land: (基督教)圣地(指巴勒斯坦);宗教圣地

leaving a milky-way wake of creamy foam, all spangled with golden gleamings.

   Nor was it his unwonted magnitude, nor his remarkable hue, nor yet his deformed lower jaw, that so much invested the whale with natural terror, as that unexampled, intelligent malignity which, according to specific accounts, he had over and over again evinced in his assaults. More than all, his treacherous retreats struck more of dismay than perhaps aught else. For, when swimming before his exulting pursuers, with every apparent symptom of alarm, he had several times been known to turn round suddenly, and, bearing down upon them, either stave their boats to splinters, or drive them back in consternation to their ship.

   Already several fatalities had attended his chase. But though similar disasters, however little bruited ashore, were by no means unusual in the fishery; yet, in most instances, such seemed the White Whale's infernal aforethought of ferocity, that every dismembering or death that he caused, was not wholly regarded as having been inflicted by an unintelligent agent.

   Judge, then, to what pitches of inflamed, distracted fury the minds of his more desperate hunters were impelled, when amid the chips of chewed boats, and the sinking limbs of torn comrades, they swam out of the white curds of the whale's direful wrath into the serene, exasperating sunlight, that smiled on, as if at a birth or a bridal.

   His three boats stove around him, and oars and men both whirling in the eddies; one captain, seizing the line-knife from his broken prow, had dashed at the whale, as an Arkansas duellist① at his foe, blindly seeking with a six inch blade to reach the fathom-deep life of the whale. That captain was Ahab. And then it was, that suddenly sweeping his sickle-shaped lower jaw beneath him, Moby Dick had reaped away Ahab's leg, as a mower a blade of grass in the field. No turbaned Turk, no hired Venetian② or Malay③, could have smote him with more seeming malice. Small reason was there to doubt, then, that ever since that almost fatal encounter, Ahab had cherished a wild vindictiveness against the whale, all the more fell for that in his frantic morbidness he at last came to identify with him, not only all his bodily woes, but all his intellectual and spiritual exasperations. The White Whale swam before him as the monomaniac incarnation of all those malicious agencies which some deep men feel eating in them, till they are left living on with half a heart and half a lung. That intangible malignity which has been from the beginning; to whose dominion even the modern Christians ascribe one-half of the worlds; which the ancient Ophites④ of the east reverenced in their statue devil; Ahab did not fall down and worship it like them; but deliriously transferring its idea to the abhorred white whale, he pitted himself, all mutilated, against it. All that most maddens and torments; all that stirs up the lees of things; all truth with malice in it; all that cracks the sinews and cakes the brain; all the subtle demonisms of life and thought; all evil, to crazy Ahab, were visibly personified, and made practically assailable

---

① Arkansas duellist: 边疆未开发地区的斗殴者
② Venetian: (意大利)威尼斯人
③ Malay: (主要居住在马来半岛及马来群岛一带的)马来人
④ Ophites: 源自希腊语中的ophis(蛇)一词,意即以蛇为崇拜对象的人

in Moby Dick. He piled upon the whale's white hump the sum of all the general rage and hate felt by his whole race from Adam down; and then, as if his chest had been a mortar, he burst his hot heart's shell upon it.

......

Ⅲ. Notes.

Moby Dick is a highly symbolic and metaphorical novel. Ostensibly it is a story about Captain Ahab's monomaniacal chase of Moby Dick, the white sperm whale that destroyed his former ship and bit off his leg. Fundamentally the book explores multiple relationships between man and Nature, God and Nature, individual and individual, and different social, racial and religious groups of the nineteenth century in America. In the selected chapter, Ishmael, a sailor on the Pequod, the whaling ship run by Ahab, narrates various fancies, rumors, legends, and portents concerning Moby Dick. He also tells about why Ahab had such an obsession in hunting down the white whale.

Ⅳ. Key Words（关键词）.

Whaling: 捕鲸业。这不仅指以投掷系有绳索的鱼叉、标枪等方式猎捕鲸鱼，而且还指在捕鲸船上对猎捕到的鲸鱼进行粗加工，提取鲸油、鲸骨等材料。在人类发现石油的用途以前，鲸油是非常贵重的工业原料和理想的照明燃料。此外，鲸骨也有多种用途。因此自古以来就有捕鲸业。在麦尔维尔所处的19世纪，工业革命更是促进了捕鲸业的发展。捕鲸业在美国欣欣向荣，成了美国经济的一个重要支柱产业。每一年都有数百艘船从新英格兰地区尤其是新贝德福德和兰塔基特的港口出发，去世界各地捕猎鲸鱼。

Sperm Whale: 抹香鲸。是世界上最大的齿鲸。它的头部巨大，占了身体的1/3。脑子有大约9公斤重，是所有动物中最大的脑。雄性抹香鲸的最大体长可达20米左右，雌性可达13米左右。抹香鲸以枪乌贼和鱼为食，能潜入3千米的深海处，分布于世界各大洋，以出产龙涎香而得名。抹香鲸的肤色一般是深灰色或黑色，偶尔也有浅灰色。麦尔维尔笔下的抹香鲸莫比·迪克有着白色的皮肤，这种与众不同的肤色给其增添了一种神秘而不祥的意味。

Ⅴ. Questions.

1. What are the rumors about Moby Dick? What image of Moby Dick do these rumors create?

2. What is Ishmael's interpretation of the terror that Moby-Dick inspires?

3. What symbolic meaning does Moby-Dick have? Point out some other symbols used in this chapter.

Lesson 14   Walt Whitman (1819—1892)

Ⅰ. **A Brief Review.**

Walt Whitman was born on 31 May, 1819 in West Hills, a village near Hempstead in Long Island, New York. His father was a farmer and carpenter. When the family moved to Brooklyn later, young Walt attended public school and loved taking the ferry, which became a theme in many of his later works. His visits to his grandparents' farm on Long Island and its shores left him deep impression of the American rural life. Largely self-taught, Whitman attended lectures and visited museums and libraries where he studied theatre, history, geography as well as western literary canon.

图 14   Walt Whitman

Designated as the founding father of free verse, Walt Whitman is an American canonical poet among the most influential poets in the history of American literature. He has been claimed as America's first "poet of democracy" with strong American characteristics. His work breaks the boundaries of poetic form and is generally prose-like. His use of free verse has influenced generations of American poets, presenting a great inspiring example for the beat-generation writing (such as Ginsberg and Kerouac). In his poems, unusual images and symbols including rotting leaves, tufts of straw, and debris are depicted and the themes refer openly to slavery, freedom, death, and sexuality.

Whitman wrote in the preface to the 1855 edition of *Leaves of Grass*, "The proof of a poet is that his country absorbs him as affectionately as he has absorbed it." He believed there was a vital, symbiotic relationship between the poet and society, which was emphasized especially in "Song of Myself". Whitman's major work, his self-published collection of twelve poems, *Leaves of Grass*, came out first in 1855 with his own money. *Leaves of Grass* was an attempt at reaching out to the common people of all walks. Though at first his poems stirred little interest in the literary world, Ralph Waldo Emerson wrote of *Leaves of Grass* as "the most extraordinary piece of wit and wisdom that America has yet produced." In the months following the first edition of *Leaves of Grass*, critical responses began focusing more on the potentially offensive sexual themes. In the end, the edition went to retail, with 20 additional poems, in August 1856. *Leaves of Grass* was revised again in 1867 and released several more times throughout the remaining years of Whitman's life. Walt Whitman died on 26 March, 1892 in Camden, New Jersey.

Expressing his philosophy on such issues as democracy, war, politics, race, and slavery, some of his poems were patriotic and some celebrated nature and love with vivid descriptions of the human body. During his life he was confident that what he was doing was important though he caused much controversy; some of his works were banned for a time and he had many critics including D. H. Lawrence and Oliver Wendell Holmes. He also gained many admirers in North America and Europe including Lord Alfred Tennyson, Henry David Thoreau, Oscar Wilde, Pablo Neruda, William Carlos William, Allan Ginsberg and Langston Hughes. Today *Leaves of Grass* has been translated into dozens of foreign languages and is read widely around the world.

Ⅱ. Texts.

Leaves of Grass

Song of Myself

I celebrate myself,
And what I assume you shall assume,
For every atom belonging to me as good belongs to you.

I loafe① and invite my soul,
I lean and loafe at my ease…. observing a spear of summer grass.

Houses and rooms are full of perfumes…. the shelves are crowded with perfumes,
I breathe the fragrance myself, and know it and like it,
The distillation would intoxicate me also, but I shall not let it.

The atmosphere is not a perfume…. it has no taste of the distillation…. it is odorless,
It is for my mouth forever…. I am in love with it,
I will go to the bank by the wood and become undisguised and naked,
I am mad for it to be in contact with me.

The smoke of my own breath,
Echos, ripples, and buzzed whispers…. loveroot, silkthread, crotch and vine,
My respiration and inspiration…. the beating of my heart…. the passing of blood and air through my lungs,
The sniff of green leaves and dry leaves, and of the shore and dark colored searocks, and of hay in the barn,
The sound of the belched words of my voice…. words loosed to the eddies of the wind,
A few light kisses…. a few embraces…. a reaching around of arms,

---

① loafe: 惠特曼杜撰的词语,实为 loaf,意为无所事事,闲逛

The play of shine and shade on the trees as the supple boughs wag,

The delight alone or in the rush of the streets, or along the fields and hill-sides,

The feeling of health.... the full-noon trill.... the song of me rising from bed and meeting the sun.

Have you reckoned a thousand acres much? Have you reckoned the earth much?

Have you practiced so long to learn to read?

Have you felt so proud to get at the meaning of poems?

Stop this day and night with me and you shall possess the origin of all poems,

You shall possess the good of the earth and sun... there are millions of suns left,

You shall no longer take things at second or third hand... nor look through the eyes of the dead.... nor feed on the spectres in books,

You shall not look through my eyes either, nor take things from me,

You shall listen to all sides and filter them from yourself.

……

Swiftly arose and spread around me the peace and joy and knowledge that pass all the art and argument of the earth;

And I know that the hand of God is the elderhand of my own,

And I know that the spirit of God is the eldest brother of my own,

And that all the men ever born are also my brothers.... And the women my sisters and lovers,

And that a kelson① of the creation is love;

And limitless are leaves still or drooping in the fields,

And brown ants in the little wells beneath them,

And mossy scabs of the wormfence, and heaped stones, and elder and mul-len and pokeweed.

A child said, What is the grass? fetching it to me with full hands;

How could I answer the child?... I do not know what it is any more than he.

I guess it must be the flag of my disposition, out of hopeful green stuff woven.

Or I guess it is the handkerchief of the Lord,

A scented gift and remembrancer designedly dropped,

Bearing the owner's name someway in the corners, that we may see and remark, and say Whose?

---

① kelson: 原指船龙骨上部的紧固件,这里转喻精髓

Or I guess the grass is itself a child.... The produced babe of the vegetation.

Or I guess it is a uniform hieroglyphic,
And it means, Sprouting alike in broad zones and narrow zones,
Growing among black folks as among white,
Kanuck①, Tuckahoe②, Congressman, Cuff ③, I give them the same, I receive them the same.
……

Ⅲ. Notes.

1. This most famous work was one of the original twelve pieces in the 1855 edition of *Leaves of Grass*. Like most of the other poems, it too was revised extensively, reaching its final permutation in 1881. "Song of Myself" is a sprawling combination of biography, sermon, and poetic meditation. Whitman uses symbols and sly commentary to get at important issues. "Song of Myself" is composed more of vignettes than lists: Whitman uses small, precisely drawn scenes to do his work here. Whitman's grand poem is, in its way, an American epic. It loosely follows a quest pattern. "Missing me one place search another," he tells his reader, "I stop somewhere waiting for you." In its catalogues of American life and its constant search for the boundaries of the self, "Song of Myself" has much in common with classical epic.

2. Whitman creates two great characters in this poem: "I" and "you." The "I" becomes a model voice of American democracy. The "you" becomes an identity space the reader is invited to occupy. It is possible to hear the "you" in "Song" as addressed to the entire nation or the entire world, and it is also possible to hear it as intimately addressed only to the individual reader at a particular moment. "Song" opens with "I" and ends with "you," and the poem enacts a transfer of the absorptive energy from poet to reader, who by the final lines is sent off alone to continue the journey the poem began.

Ⅳ. Key Words(关键词).

I：在《自我之歌》中，"我"是一个中心意象。诗中从开篇到结束，惠特曼竭力赞美着自我。"我"具有多种含义，既指诗人自己，又指所有美国人，甚至全人类。通过对我的张扬，诗人表达了强烈自信以及对生活的无比热爱。惠特曼把对"自我"的赞美放置在美国和人类世界的广阔背景中，塑造了一个既平凡，又伟大，灵魂与肉体高度同一的自我形象，歌颂了美国人民的勃勃生机，渲染了美利坚民族的新兴力量与民主理想。

Leaves of Grass: 在《自我之歌》中，"草叶"始终象征着充满活力、自由、平等与爱的力量。作为世界上最平凡、最微贱的东西，草是散漫的，无所拘束的。小草虽受风雨摧残、被

---

① Kanuck: 加拿大人的别称，尤指法裔加拿大人
② Tuckahoe: 美国弗吉尼亚人的别称
③ Cuff: 原指手铐，此处转喻受奴役的穷苦人

人们践踏,但却到处生长,永远生机勃勃。在惠特曼看来,"一片草叶不亚于星球的运转。"草叶本身的生生死死,循环不息的特征,象征着生命—死亡—新生的不断循环,诗人对草叶的顽强生命力的颂扬,实际上是对普通民众优秀品质和高贵精神的赞美和讴歌。

Ⅴ. Questions.

1. What is your interpretation of the symbol of the leaves of grass?
2. By reading the poem, can you find how Whitman celebrates common people and life?
3. What is the characteristics of Whitman's free verse?

Lesson 15 Emily Dickinson (1830—1886)

I. A Brief Review.

Born into a family with strong social background, Dickinson lived an introverted and reclusive life in Amherst, Massachusetts. After she studied at the Amherst Academy for seven years in her youth, she attended Mount Holyoke Female Seminary in South Hadley. After one year, however, severe homesickness led her to return home. By the 1860s, Dickinson lived in almost total physical isolation from the outside world, but actively maintained correspondence with her friends and read western literature widely.

图 15 Emily Dickinson

The first half of the 1860s proved to be Dickinson's most productive writing period. Amounting to more than 1700 poems, Dickinson's poetry reflects her profound thinking about nature and God. The speakers of her poems generally live in a state of want, but her poems are also marked by the intimate recollection of inspirational moments which suggest the possibility of happiness and freedom. Her work was heavily influenced by the Metaphysical poets of seventeenth-century England, as well as her reading of / The Book of Revelation /. She grew up in a Puritan New England town, which encouraged a Calvinist and conservative approach to Christianity and caused somewhat suspicious ideas on the human salvation.

She admired the poetry of Robert and Elizabeth Barrett Browning, as well as John Keats. Though she was dissuaded from reading the verse of her contemporary Walt Whitman by rumor of its disgracefulness, the two poets are now connected by the distinguished place they hold as the founders of a uniquely American poetic voice. While Dickinson was extremely prolific as a poet, who regularly enclosed poems in letters to friends, she was not publicly recognized during her lifetime. The first volume of her work was published posthumously in 1890 and the last in 1955. She died at the age of 55 in Amherst in 1886.

Although most of her acquaintances were probably aware of Dickinson's writing, it was not until after Emily's younger sister discovered her cache of poems that the breadth of Dickinson's work became apparent. These booklets were made by folding and sewing five or six sheets of stationery paper and copying, which seem to be final versions of her poems in an order that many critics believe to be more than chronological. The handwritten poems show a variety of dash-like marks of various sizes and directions (some are even vertical). A complete and mostly unaltered collection of her poetry became available for the first time in 1955.

Emily Dickinson did not write in traditional iambic pentameter (a convention of English-speaking poetry for centuries), and did not even use a five-foot line. Her line lengths vary from four syllables or two feet to often eight syllables or four feet. Since many of her poems were written in common meter or ballad-meter with a regular rhyme scheme, some of these poems could be sung to the melodies of old, popular songs that use the same meter, employing alternating lines of iambic tetrameter and iambic trimeter. Familiar examples of such songs are "O Little Town of Bethlehem" and "Amazing Grace".

Ⅱ. Texts.

Poems of Emily Dickinson

67
Success is counted sweetest
By those who ne'er succeed.
To comprehend a nectar
Requires sorest need.

Not one of all the purple Host
Who took the Flag today
Can tell the definition
So clear of Victory

As he defeated—dying—
On whose forbidden ear
The distant strains of triumph
Burst agonized and clear!
     c. 1859

130
These are the days when Birds come back—
A very few—a Bird or two—
To take a backward look.

These are the days when skies resume
The old—old sophistries① of June—
A blue and gold mistake.

---

① Sophistries: 诡辩

Oh fraud that cannot cheat the Bee—
Almost thy plausibility
Induces my belief.

Till ranks of seeds their witness bear—
And softly thro' the altered air
Hurries a timid leaf.

Oh Sacrament of summer days,
Oh Last Communion① in the Haze—
Permit a child to join.

Thy sacred emblems to partake—
They consecrated bread to take
And thine immortal wine!

      c. 1859

199
I'm "wife"—I've finished that—
That other state—
I'm Czar—I'm "Woman" now—
It's safer so—

How odd the Girl's life looks
Behind this soft Eclipse—
I think that Earth feels so
To folks in Heaven—now—

This being comfort—then—
That other kind—was pain—
But why compare?
I'm "Wife"! Stop there!

      c. 1860

668
"Nature" is what we see—
The Hill—the Afternoon—

---

① Last Communion: 基督最后的晚餐, 此处借喻秋天万物凋零

Squirrel—Eclipse—the Bumble bee—
Nay—Nature is Heaven—
Nature is what we hear—
The Bobolink—the Sea—
Thunder—the Cricket—
Nay—Nature is Harmony—
Nature is what we know—
Yet have no art to say—
So impotent Our Wisdom is
To her Simplicity

      c. 1863

686
They say that "Time assuages"—
Time never did assuage—
An actual suffering strengthens
As Sinews do, with age—

Time is a Test of Trouble—
But not a Remedy—
If such is prove, it prove too
There was no Malady—

      c. 1863

Ⅲ. Notes.

1. While Dickinson wrote love poetry that indicates a strong attachment, it proved impossible to know the object of her feelings, or even how much was fed by her poetic imagination. The chief tension in her work comes from a different source: her inability to accept the orthodox religious faith of her day and her longing for its spiritual comfort. She called immortality "the flood subject," and she alternated confident statements of belief with lyrics of despairing uncertainty, which seemed to be both reverent and rebellious.

2. Noted for its aphoristic style, its wit, its delicate metrical variation and irregular rhymes, its directness of statement, and its bold and startling imagery, her poetry has won enormous acclaimation and had a great influence on 20th-century American poetic writing.

Ⅳ. Key Words(关键词).

Thematic variety: 主题多样性。狄金森一生所写诗作数量庞大,所涉及的主题众多,包括神与人的关系、信仰的真相、日常生活中死亡与受难的阴影、永恒、自然、爱与诗的哲学等诗人在生活中的所见,所思,所悟。

Self-searching: 自我探寻。狄金森的诗用词质朴,节奏顿挫突兀,常用独特的标点符号既让人感觉深奥莫测,又平淡如水,充满恬淡之情,总体上表现出诗人对自我心灵的一种探寻。整个诗集可称得上是一部诗人的精神自传史。

V. Questions.

1. Can you select some major themes of Dickinson's poems and give an interpretation to them?

2. Can you find the main stylistic features of Dickinson's poems?

3. Describe some of the reasons why Dickinson did not gain fame as a poet during her life time.

Lesson 16 Samuel L. Clemens
(Mark Twain, 1835—1910)

Ⅰ. A Brief Review.

Clemens was born on November 30, 1835 in Florida, Missouri, into a Virginian family. His father was a lawyer and store owner, but the family was never well-off. Four years after his birth, Samuel Clemens's family moved to Hannibal, Missouri, a fast-growing town on the Mississippi River. At thirteen he became a printer's apprentice, and four years later he left Hannibal to work in printing shops and on newspapers from Iowa to New York. In February 1863, he first signed a story with the pen name that he would make famous: *Mark Twain*. It was the riverboat man's term for water two fathoms, or twelve feet deep—meaning just barely deep enough to navigate safely.

图 16 Mark Twain

In 1865 a national magazine published his retelling of a tale he had heard from miners, "The Celebrated Jumping Frog of Calaveras County", which was an instant success. As a reporter for several newspapers, he traveled to Hawaii, Europe, and the Middle East. The book he wrote about his travels, *The Innocents Abroad,* made him famous. More books followed, including *Roughing It*, *The Adventures of Tom Sawyer*, *The Adventures of Huckleberry Finn*, and *The Prince and the Pauper.* In 1882, after a short break for pursuing inspiration, Twain restarted the work on the manuscript of *The Adventures of Huckleberry Finn*, developing the story of the young, white boy named Huck and the enslaved, black man named Jim. He worked sporadically over the next two years and finished the manuscript in July of 1883.

In this prominent novel, Huck's journey down the Mississippi River has been called an odyssey by some and a pilgrimage by others. Indeed, characteristics of each are much like Homer's *Odyssey* with an episodic structure—it is composed of a series of episodes. Some consider the novel the picaresque genre, which originated in Spain and depicted in realistic detail the adventures of a hero, often with satiric or humorous effects. Twain did not consider the novel his best work, and he was completely unprepared for the negative reception that would follow. In a caustic review immediately following *Huck Finn's* publication, *Life* magazine condemned the book that contained graphic instances of nudity and death. The Concord Public Library followed by declaring that the book held little humor and regarded it as the "veriest trash." However, majority of readers celebrated the novel as representing a fresh, vibrant, and democratic spirit of the United States. This novel has remained an inseparable part of American literary canon till now.

Ⅱ. Texts.

Adventures of Huckleberry Finn

Chapter XLII.

THE old man was uptown again before breakfast, but couldn't get no track① of Tom; and both of them set at the table thinking, and not saying nothing, and looking mournful, and their coffee getting cold, and not eating anything. And by and by the old man says:

"Did I give you the letter?"

"What letter?"

"The one I got yesterday out of the post-office."

"No, you didn't give me no letter."

"Well, I must a forgot it."

So he rummaged② his pockets, and then went off somewhere where he had laid it down, and fetched it, and give it to her. She says:

"Why, it's from St. Petersburg—it's from Sis."

I allowed another walk would do me good; but I couldn't stir. But before she could break it open she dropped it and run—for she see something. And so did I. It was Tom Sawyer on a mattress; and that old doctor; and Jim, in HER calico③ dress, with his hands tied behind him; and a lot of people. I hid the letter behind the first thing that come handy, and rushed. She flung herself at Tom, crying, and says:

"Oh, he's dead, he's dead, I know he's dead!"

And Tom he turned his head a little, and muttered something or other, which showed he warn't in his right mind; then she flung up her hands, and says:

"He's alive, thank God! And that's enough!" and she snatched a kiss of him, and flew for the house to get the bed ready, and scattering orders right and left at the niggers and everybody else, as fast as her tongue could go, every jump of the way.

I followed the men to see what they were going to do with Jim; and the old doctor and Uncle Silas followed after Tom into the house. The men was very huffy④, and some of them wanted to hang Jim for an example to all the other niggers around there, so they wouldn't be trying to run away like Jim done, and making such a raft of⑤ trouble, and keeping a whole family scared most to death for days and nights. But the others said, don't do it, it wouldn't answer at all; he ain't our nigger, and his owner would turn up and make us pay for him, sure. So that cooled them down a

---

① no track: 这里 no 无实意,文中多出类似口语表达法;另外,作者特意使文中有一些语法不规范的句子,如"I must a forgot it". 显示说话者教育水平较低。

② rummage: 翻找,搜查

③ calico: (单面)印花棉布

④ huffy: 怒气冲冲的,不悦的

⑤ a raft of: (美口)大量,许多

little, because the people that's always the most anxious for to hang a nigger that hain't done just right is always the very ones that ain't the most anxious to pay for him when they've got their satisfaction out of him.

They cussed Jim considerble①, though, and give him a cuff or two side the head once in a while, but Jim never said nothing, and he never let on to know me, and they took him to the same cabin, and put his own clothes on him, and chained him again, and not to no bed-leg this time, but to a big staple drove into the bottom log, and chained his hands, too, and both legs, and said he warn't to have nothing but bread and water to eat after this till his owner come, or he was sold at auction② because he didn't come in a certain length of time, and filled up our hole, and said a couple of farmers with guns must stand watch around about the cabin every night, and a bulldog tied to the door in the daytime; and about this time they was through with the job and was tapering off with a kind of generl good-bye cussing, and then the old doctor comes and takes a look, and says:

"Don't be no rougher on him than you're obleeged to, because he ain't a bad nigger. When I got to where I found the boy I see I couldn't cut the bullet out without some help, and he warn't in no condition for me to leave to go and get help; and he got a little worse and a little worse, and after a long time he went out of his head, and wouldn't let me come a-nigh him any more, and said if I chalked his raft he'd kill me, and no end of wild foolishness like that, and I see I couldn't do anything at all with him; so I says, I got to have HELP somehow; and the minute I says it out crawls this nigger from somewheres and says he'll help, and he done it, too, and done it very well. Of course I judged he must be a runaway nigger, and there I WAS! and there I had to stick right straight along all the rest of the day and all night. It was a fix, I tell you! I had a couple of patients with the chills, and of course I'd of liked to run up to town and see them, but I dasn't, because the nigger might get away, and then I'd be to blame; and yet never a skiff come close enough for me to hail. So there I had to stick plumb until daylight this morning; and I never see a nigger that was a better nuss or faithfuller, and yet he was risking his freedom to do it, and was all tired out, too, and I see plain enough he'd been worked main hard lately. I liked the nigger for that; I tell you, gentlemen, a nigger like that is worth a thousand dollars—and kind treatment, too. I had everything I needed, and the boy was doing as well there as he would a done at home—better, maybe, because it was so quiet; but there I WAS, with both of 'm on my hands, and there I had to stick till about dawn this morning; then some men in a skiff come by, and as good luck would have it the nigger was setting by the pallet with his head propped on his knees sound asleep; so I motioned them in quiet, and they slipped up on him and grabbed him and tied him before he knowed what he was about, and we never had no trouble. And the boy being in a kind of a flighty sleep, too, we muffled the oars and hitched the raft on, and towed her over very nice and quiet,

---

① They cussed Jim considerble: 他们狠狠地骂他，这里 considerable 应该是副词形式，文中多处类似直接写成形容词形式

② auction: 拍卖

and the nigger never made the least row nor said a word from the start. He ain't no bad nigger, gentlemen; that's what I think about him."

Somebody says:

"Well, it sounds very good, doctor, I'm obleeged to say."

Then the others softened up a little, too, and I was mighty thankful to that old doctor for doing Jim that good turn; and I was glad it was according to my judgment of him, too; because I thought he had a good heart in him and was a good man the first time I see him. Then they all agreed that Jim had acted very well, and was deserving to have some notice took of it, and reward. So every one of them promised, right out and hearty, that they wouldn't cuss him no more.

Then they come out and locked him up. I hoped they was going to say he could have one or two of the chains took off, because they was rotten heavy, or could have meat and greens with his bread and water; but they didn't think of it, and I reckoned it warn't best for me to mix in, but I judged I'd get the doctor's yarn① to Aunt Sally somehow or other as soon as I'd got through the breakers that was laying just ahead of me—explanations, I mean, of how I forgot to mention about Sid being shot when I was telling how him and me put in that dratted② night paddling around hunting the runaway nigger.

But I had plenty time. Aunt Sally she stuck to the sick-room all day and all night, and every time I see Uncle Silas mooning around I dodged him.

Next morning I heard Tom was a good deal better, and they said Aunt Sally was gone to get a nap. So I slips to the sick-room, and if I found him awake I reckoned we could put up a yarn for the family that would wash. But he was sleeping, and sleeping very peaceful, too; and pale, not fire-faced the way he was when he come. So I set down and laid for him to wake. In about half an hour Aunt Sally comes gliding in③, and there I was, up a stump again! She motioned me to be still, and set down by me, and begun to whisper, and said we could all be joyful now, because all the symptoms was first-rate, and he'd been sleeping like that for ever so long, and looking better and peacefuller all the time, and ten to one he'd wake up in his right mind.

So we set there watching, and by and by he stirs a bit, and opened his eyes very natural, and takes a look, and says:

"Hello!—why, I'm at HOME! How's that? Where's the raft?"

"It's all right," I says.

"And JIM?"

"The same," I says, but couldn't say it pretty brash④. But he never noticed, but says:

"Good! Splendid! NOW we're all right and safe! Did you tell Aunty?"

I was going to say yes; but she chipped in and says: "About what, Sid?"

---

① yarn: (非正式)冒险故事,奇闻轶事
② drat: (旧)讨厌,该死
③ comes gliding in: (神态)悠闲地(走进来)
④ brash: 无礼的,粗鲁的

"Why, about the way the whole thing was done."

"What whole thing?"

"Why, THE whole thing. There ain't but one; how we set the runaway nigger free—me and Tom."

"Good land! Set the run—What IS the child talking about! Dear, dear, out of his head again!"

"NO, I ain't out of my HEAD; I know all what I'm talking about. We DID set him free—me and Tom. We laid out to do it, and we DONE it. And we done it elegant, too." He'd got a start, and she never checked him up, just set and stared and stared, and let him clip along, and I see it warn't no use for ME to put in. "Why, Aunty, it cost us a power of work—weeks of it—hours and hours, every night, whilst you was all asleep. And we had to steal candles, and the sheet, and the shirt, and your dress, and spoons, and tin plates, and case-knives, and the warming-pan, and the grindstone, and flour, and just no end of things, and you can't think what work it was to make the saws, and pens, and inscriptions, and one thing or another, and you can't think HALF the fun it was. And we had to make up the pictures of coffins and things, and nonnamous letters from the robbers, and get up and down the lightning-rod, and dig the hole into the cabin, and made the rope ladder and send it in cooked up in a pie, and send in spoons and things to work with in your apron pocket—"

"Mercy sakes!"

"—and load up the cabin with rats and snakes and so on, for company for Jim; and then you kept Tom here so long with the butter in his hat that you come near spiling the whole business, because the men come before we was out of the cabin, and we had to rush, and they heard us and let drive at us, and I got my share, and we dodged out of the path and let them go by, and when the dogs come they warn't interested in us, but went for the most noise, and we got our canoe, and made for the raft, and was all safe, and Jim was a free man, and we done it all by ourselves, and WASN'T it bully, Aunty!"

"Well, I never heard the likes of it in all my born days! So it was YOU, you little rapscallions①, that's been making all this trouble, and turned everybody's wits clean inside out and scared us all most to death. I've as good a notion as ever I had in my life to take it out o' you this very minute. To think, here I've been, night after night, a—YOU just get well once, you young scamp②, and I lay I'll tan the Old Harry out o' both o' ye!"

But Tom, he WAS so proud and joyful, he just COULDN'T hold in, and his tongue just WENT it—she a-chipping in, and spitting fire all along, and both of them going it at once, like a cat convention; and she says:

"WELL, you get all the enjoyment you can out of it NOW, for mind I tell you if I catch you

---

① rapscallions: 原义指"流氓,混蛋",这里指"毛孩子"

② scamp: 无赖,流氓

meddling with him again—①"

"Meddling with WHO?" Tom says, dropping his smile and looking surprised.

"With WHO? Why, the runaway nigger, of course. Who'd you reckon?"

Tom looks at me very grave, and says:

"Tom, didn't you just tell me he was all right? Hasn't he got away?"

"HIM?" says Aunt Sally; "the runaway nigger? 'Deed he hasn't. They've got him back, safe and sound, and he's in that cabin again, on bread and water, and loaded down with chains, till he's claimed or sold!"

Tom rose square up in bed, with his eye hot, and his nostrils opening and shutting like gills, and sings out to me:

"They hain't no RIGHT to shut him up! SHOVE!—and don't you lose a minute. Turn him loose! he ain't no slave; he's as free as any cretur② that walks this earth!"

"What DOES the child mean?"

"I mean every word I SAY, Aunt Sally, and if somebody don't go, I'LL go. I've knowed him all his life, and so has Tom, there. Old Miss Watson died two months ago, and she was ashamed she ever was going to sell him down the river, and SAID so; and she set him free in her will."

"Then what on earth did YOU want to set him free for, seeing he was already free?"

"Well, that IS a question, I must say; and just like women! Why, I wanted the ADVENTURE of it; and I'd a waded neck-deep in blood to—goodness alive, AUNT POLLY!"

If she warn't standing right there, just inside the door, looking as sweet and contented as an angel half full of pie, I wish I may never!

Aunt Sally jumped for her, and most hugged the head off of her, and cried over her, and I found a good enough place for me under the bed, for it was getting pretty sultry③ for us, seemed to me. And I peeped out, and in a little while Tom's Aunt Polly shook herself loose and stood there looking across at Tom over her spectacles—kind of grinding him into the earth, you know. And then she says:

"Yes, you BETTER turn y'r head away—I would if I was you, Tom."

"Oh, deary me!" says Aunt Sally; "IS he changed so? Why, that ain't TOM, it's Sid; Tom's—Tom's—why, where is Tom? He was here a minute ago."

"You mean where's Huck FINN—that's what you mean! I reckon I hain't raised such a scamp as my Tom all these years not to know him when I SEE him. That WOULD be a pretty howdy-do④. Come out from under that bed, Huck Finn."

---

① for mind I tell you if I catch you meddling with him again—: 但是记住了, 别让我抓到你又和他鬼混在一起

② cretur: 应该是 creature, "人"

③ sultry: 闷热的, 酷热的

④ howdy-do: 口语, 指问候, 打招呼

So I done it. But not feeling brash.

……

Ⅲ. Notes.

In this chapter, the doctor returns to town with wounded Tom and Jim. Some of the local men treat Jim roughly and chain him hand and foot inside the shed. The doctor intervenes, telling the crowd how Jim helps him nurse Tom. The next morning, Tom wakes up and demands that Jim is a free man because the Widow freed him just before she passed away. At that moment, Aunt Polly arrives, and Tom and Huck are forced to reveal their true identities.

Ⅳ. Key Words（关键词）.

Irony: 反讽。它是运用机智,特别是讽刺、挖苦和嘲笑,来批评缺点。马克·吐温作品的显著特征是俏皮、幽默而又尖锐的社会讽刺。他的小说语言风趣幽默,意味隽永,但又不止于幽默本身,他以幽默为武器,对美国资本主义社会的金钱崇拜、道德的虚伪、政治的腐败、宗教的伪善、永不满足的贪欲等等进行了嘲笑、讽刺和抨击。

Colloquial Style: 会话体。《哈克贝利·费恩历险记》为美国的小说语言带来了极为深远的影响,奠定了美国文学会话体的写作风格。马克·吐温的写作文笔自然,不加雕饰,语汇和句法简单质朴,句子多为短句,有时甚至不符合语法规则,贴近普通人的日常生活表达,在语言选择上力求淋漓尽致地体现美国特色。该小说开创了美国小说语言的口语化先河,对后世美国作家的影响极大。

Local Color: 地方色彩。作为19世纪美国现实主义文学主要奠基人之一的马克·吐温,在现实主义小说创作理论方面,为美国文学的发展做出了卓越的贡献。他主张创作具有美国地域及乡土气息的文学作品,提倡作家从自己熟悉的地方着手,运用最普通大众的语言,描摹他们的生活,刻画他们的性格及灵魂,以此来展现美国人民和美国生活的全貌。

Ⅴ. Questions.

1. Discuss Twain's use of dialects in the chapter. What effect does this usage have on the reader?

2. The revelation at the novel's end that Tom has known all along that Jim is a free man is startling. Is Tom inexcusably cruel?

3. What techniques does Twain use to create sympathy for his characters, in particular, Jim? Are these techniques effective?

Lesson 17　Henry James (1843—1916)

Ⅰ. A Brief Review.

As an American-born writer, gifted with talents in literature, psychology, and philosophy, Henry James is mostly famous for his novels characterized by psychological realism. He is also well recognized as an influential critic, but his principal interest is to relate the confrontation between American culture and European culture.

图 17　Henry James

James was born in New York, into a wealthy, somewhat aristocratic family. At the age of nineteen he briefly attended Harvard Law School, but he seemed to be more interested in literature than studying law. He lived with his family for a time in Boston, where he became acquainted with New England authors and friends of his father, such as Hawthorn, and began his friendship with William Dean Howells. After 1866, James lived in Europe, where he met Turgenev, Flaubert, and Zola in Paris. The outbreak of the First World War was a shock for James and in 1915 he became a British citizen.

His writing first achieved recognition as having the so-called international theme. In the "international novels", persons of various nationalities who represented characteristics of their own country were brought together. He wrote novels that mainly portrayed Americans living abroad. The two groups, the Americans and the Europeans, were more often depicted in contrast with one idealistic and the other sophisticated. In *The American* (1877), he successfully depicted the encounter of the value of the New World represented by the naive young American, Christopher Newman, with the traditional value of the Old World. *Daisy Miller* (1878) won for him the widespread popularity. In general, Henry James uses his narratives to discuss what he thinks misunderstanding or prejudice between American and European cultures, which is the major theme of *The Portrait of a Lady* (1881).

After the failure of his "dramatic experiment", James returned to his fiction writing with international or cosmopolitan subjects. The three great novels of the last period, *The Wings of the Dove* (1902), *The Ambassadors* (1903), and *The Golden Bowl* (1904), all return to his international theme, yet are more concerned with the psychology of his characters, and with a more subtle style. These novels have received intense critical study even today.

II. Texts.

Daisy Miller

A Study

I

At the little town of Vevey, in Switzerland, there is a particularly comfortable hotel. There are, indeed, many hotels, for the entertainment of tourists is the business of the place, which, as many travelers will remember, is seated upon the edge of a remarkably blue lake①——a lake that it behooves every tourist to visit. The shore of the lake presents an unbroken array of establishments of this order, of every category, from the "grand hotel" of the newest fashion, with a chalk-white front, a hundred balconies, and a dozen flags flying from its roof, to the little Swiss pension of an elder day, with its name inscribed in German-looking lettering upon a pink or yellow wall and an awkward summerhouse in the angle of the garden. One of the hotels at Vevey, however, is famous, even classical, being distinguished from many of its upstart neighbors by an air both of luxury and of maturity. In this region, in the month of June, American travelers are extremely numerous; it may be said, indeed, that Vevey assumes at this period some of the characteristics of an American watering place. There are sights and sounds which evoke a vision, an echo, of Newport and Saratoga. There is a flitting hither and thither of "stylish" young girls, a rustling of muslin flounces, a rattle of dance music in the morning hours, a sound of high-pitched voices at all times. You receive an impression of these things at the excellent inn of the "Trois Couronnes"② and are transported in fancy to the Ocean House or to Congress Hall. But at the "Trois Couronnes," it must be added, there are other features that are much at variance with these suggestions: neat German waiters, who look like secretaries of legation; Russian princesses sitting in the garden; little Polish boys walking about held by the hand, with their governors; a view of the sunny crest of the Dent du Midi and the picturesque towers of the Castle of Chillon.

I hardly know whether it was the analogies or the differences that were uppermost in the mind of a young American, who, two or three years ago, sat in the garden of the "Trois Couronnes", looking about him, rather idly, at some of the graceful objects I have mentioned. It was a beautiful summer morning, and in whatever fashion the young American looked at things, they must have seemed to him charming. He had come from Geneva the day before by the little steamer, to see his aunt, who was staying at the hotel—Geneva having been for a long time his place of residence. But his aunt had a headache—his aunt had almost always a headache—and now she was shut up in her room, smelling camphor, so that he was at liberty to wander about. He was some seven-and-twenty years of age; when his friends spoke of him, they usually said that he was at Geneva "studying". When his enemies spoke of him, they said—but, after all, he had no enemies; he was an extremely amiable fellow, and universally liked. What I should say is, simply, that when

---

① blue lake: 这里指日内瓦湖
② Trois Couronnes: 法语词,即:Three Crowns

certain persons spoke of him they affirmed that the reason of his spending so much time at Geneva was that he was extremely devoted to a lady who lived there——a foreign lady——a person older than himself. Very few Americans——indeed, I think none——had ever seen this lady, about whom there were some singular stories. But Winterbourne had an old attachment for the little metropolis of Calvinism①; he had been put to school there as a boy, and he had afterward gone to college there——circumstances which had led to his forming a great many youthful friendships. Many of these he had kept, and they were a source of great satisfaction to him.

After knocking at his aunt's door and learning that she was indisposed, he had taken a walk about the town, and then he had come in to his breakfast. He had now finished his breakfast; but he was drinking a small cup of coffee, which had been served to him on a little table in the garden by one of the waiters who looked like an attache. At last he finished his coffee and lit a cigarette. Presently a small boy came walking along the path—an urchin② of nine or ten. The child, who was diminutive③ for his years, had an aged expression of countenance, a pale complexion, and sharp little features. He was dressed in knickerbockers, with red stockings, which displayed his poor little spindle-shanks; he also wore a brilliant red cravat. He carried in his hand a long alpenstock, the sharp point of which he thrust into everything that he approached—the flowerbeds, the garden benches, the trains of the ladies' dresses. In front of Winterbourne he paused, looking at him with a pair of bright, penetrating little eyes.

"Will you give me a lump of sugar?" he asked in a sharp, hard little voice——a voice immature and yet, somehow, not young.

Winterbourne glanced at the small table near him, on which his coffee service rested, and saw that several morsels of sugar remained. "Yes, you may take one," he answered; "but I don't think sugar is good for little boys."

This little boy stepped forward and carefully selected three of the coveted fragments, two of which he buried in the pocket of his knickerbockers, depositing the other as promptly in another place. He poked his alpenstock, lance-fashion, into Winterbourne's bench and tried to crack the lump of sugar with his teeth.

"Oh, blazes; it's har-r-d!" he exclaimed, pronouncing the adjective in a peculiar manner.

Winterbourne had immediately perceived that he might have the honor of claiming him as a fellow countryman. "Take care you don't hurt your teeth," he said, paternally.

"I haven't got any teeth to hurt. They have all come out. I have only got seven teeth. My mother counted them last night, and one came out right afterward. She said she'd slap me if any more came out. I can't help it. It's this old Europe. It's the climate that makes them come out. In America they didn't come out. It's these hotels."

---

① Metropolis of Calvinism: 日内瓦:是约翰·加尔文(1509—1564)实行一系列宗教改革的地方。被称为"新教的罗马,加尔文的圣城"

② urchin: 肮脏的街头小乞丐

③ diminutive: (正式)小的,矮的

Winterbourne was much amused. "If you eat three lumps of sugar, your mother will certainly slap you," he said.

"She's got to give me some candy, then," rejoined his young interlocutor①. "I can't get any candy here—any American candy. American candy's the best candy."

"And are American little boys the best little boys?" asked Winterbourne.

"I don't know. I'm an American boy," said the child.

"I see you are one of the best!" laughed Winterbourne.

"Are you an American man?" pursued this vivacious infant. And then, on Winterbourne's affirmative reply—"American men are the best," he declared.

His companion thanked him for the compliment, and the child, who had now got astride of his alpenstock, stood looking about him, while he attacked a second lump of sugar. Winterbourne wondered if he himself had been like this in his infancy, for he had been brought to Europe at about this age.

"Here comes my sister!" cried the child in a moment. "She's an American girl."

Winterbourne looked along the path and saw a beautiful young lady advancing. "American girls are the best girls," he said cheerfully to his young companion.

"My sister ain't the best!" the child declared. "She's always blowing at me."

"I imagine that is your fault, not hers," said Winterbourne. The young lady meanwhile had drawn near. She was dressed in white muslin, with a hundred frills and flounces, and knots of pale-colored ribbon. She was bareheaded, but she balanced in her hand a large parasol②, with a deep border of embroidery; and she was strikingly, admirably pretty. "How pretty they are!" thought Winterbourne, straightening himself in his seat, as if he were prepared to rise.

The young lady paused in front of his bench, near the parapet③ of the garden, which overlooked the lake. The little boy had now converted his alpenstock into a vaulting④ pole, by the aid of which he was springing about in the gravel and kicking it up not a little.

"Randolph," said the young lady, "what *are* you doing?"

"I'm going up the Alps," replied Randolph. "This is the way!" And he gave another little jump, scattering the pebbles about Winterbourne's ears.

"That's the way they come down," said Winterbourne.

"He's an American man!" cried Randolph, in his little hard voice.

The young lady gave no heed to this announcement, but looked straight at her brother. "Well, I guess you had better be quiet," she simply observed.

It seemed to Winterbourne that he had been in a manner presented. He got up and stepped slowly toward the young girl, throwing away his cigarette. "This little boy and I have made

---

① interlocutor: 参加谈话者,对话者
② parasol: 遮阳伞
③ parapet: 矮墙,护墙
④ vault: 撑杆跳

acquaintance," he said, with great civility①. In Geneva, as he had been perfectly aware, a young man was not at liberty to speak to a young unmarried lady except under certain rarely occurring conditions; but here at Vevey, what conditions could be better than these?——a pretty American girl coming and standing in front of you in a garden. This pretty American girl, however, on hearing Winterbourne's observation, simply glanced at him; she then turned her head and looked over the parapet, at the lake and the opposite mountains. He wondered whether he had gone too far, but he decided that he must advance farther, rather than retreat. While he was thinking of something else to say, the young lady turned to the little boy again.

"I should like to know where you got that pole," she said.

"I bought it," responded Randolph.

"You don't mean to say you're going to take it to Italy?"

"Yes, I am going to take it to Italy," the child declared.

The young girl glanced over the front of her dress and smoothed out a knot or two of ribbon. Then she rested her eyes upon the prospect again. "Well, I guess you had better leave it somewhere," she said after a moment.

"Are you going to Italy?" Winterbourne inquired in a tone of great respect.

The young lady glanced at him again. "Yes, sir," she replied. And she said nothing more.

"Are you-a-going over the Simplon②?" Winterbourne pursued, a little embarrassed.

"I don't know," she said. "I suppose it's some mountain. Randolph, what mountain are we going over?"

"Going where?" the child demanded.

"To Italy," Winterbourne explained.

"I don't know," said Randolph. "I don't want to go to Italy. I want to go to America."

"Oh, Italy is a beautiful place!" rejoined the young man.

"Can you get candy there?" Randolph loudly inquired.

"I hope not," said his sister. "I guess you have had enough candy, and mother thinks so too."

"I haven't had any for ever so long——for a hundred weeks!" cried the boy, still jumping about.

……

Ⅲ. Notes.

His writing from the point of view of a character within the novel allows him to explore the phenomena of consciousness and perception. His style has been compared to impressionist painting. Therefore, an extraordinary richness of syntax, characterization, point of view, symbolic resonance, metaphor, and organizing rhythms treat this complex subject well. The

---

① civility: 彬彬有礼,礼貌,客气
② the Simplon: 瑞士和意大利之间横穿阿尔卑斯山的一个山口

adaptions of his fiction for stage, film, and television make him more popular to people of all around the world.

IV. Key Words（关键词）.

psychological realism: 心理现实主义。主要是通过对人物心理描写来反映社会精神演变的现实主义小说流派。亨利·詹姆斯是这一流派的开创者。心理现实主义是以现实主义为基础，通过心理描写与心理分析来揭示人物的内心世界。它包括"心理"和"现实"两个方面，相互补充、相互依存，构成一个不可分割的有机整体。一方面，心理现实主义通过人物的心理来反映现实和客观世界；另一方面，心理内容的描写又与客观现实相结合，在创作中使客观的现实世界和主观的精神世界统一起来。

International theme: 国际主题。它是詹姆斯小说创作主要的主题之一。他在"国际主题"小说里大致刻画两种人物：世故势利、老练圆滑的欧洲人（包括欧化的美国人），和留在欧洲大陆、天真无邪如天使一般的美国少女。美国少女通常被塑造成道德高尚、超凡脱俗的形象，具有美国人完美的道德及强烈的责任感，与詹姆斯笔下缺乏道德观念的欧洲人形成了强烈的对比。

V. Questions.

1. What do you think are proper behaviors of a lady when she first encounters a gentleman in the Victorian period?

2. Discuss the importance of setting in *Daisy Miller*. What tension exists in this tourist resort?

3. How do you think James chose to call his heroine "Daisy Miller"? Is the name of "Winterbourne" significant?

4. Discuss the narrative voice James chose to recount the story between Daisy and Winterbourne.

Part Three

Fiction and Drama in the 20th Century（1）
第三部　20 世纪美国小说与戏剧（Ⅰ）

美国文学在 20 世纪上半叶经历了从现实主义到现代主义的发展过程,并日益融入西方文学的主流之中。但是,具有美国本土作家特征的一些文学流派也产生了不少重要的作品,例如"意象派"诗人庞德和"迷惘的一代"作家海明威等人的诗歌和小说创作等等。20 世纪初期,美国的工业化和城市化运动迅猛发展,大批人口从农村流向都市,更有大批的移民从世界各地涌入美国。到了 1900 年,美国人口达到 7600 万以上,许多现代化大企业如化工、纺织、炼油、钢铁和汽车制造等等大型工业企业不断出现,为美国社会带来了巨大的变化。同时,第一次世界大战破坏了欧洲的社会和文化,却给美国人带来了巨大的政治机遇和商业利益,使得美国在一战后迅速跃升为世界性的资本主义强国。这些社会变化给美国文学带来了许多新的素材和创作灵感,而美国的传统价值观念和工业化社会享乐风气之间的矛盾为许多美国作家提供了不少值得深思的小说和戏剧的主题。在这一时期,美国文学开始进入了一个崭新的发展阶段:年轻一代作家不断进入经典作家行列,文学流派和文学运动五彩纷呈,思想深刻、艺术精湛的小说和戏剧也日益增多。例如,除了现实主义文学继续繁荣以外,现代主义诗歌、"迷惘的一代"小说以及表现主义戏剧等等都出现了不少传世之作,而黑人文学也开始崛起于文坛。这些新的发展都为美国文学走向世界文学舞台奠定了坚实的基础。

在 20 世纪上半叶,美国现实主义作家仍然占据着文学创作领域中的重要位置,特别是对美国小说的繁荣做出了很大的贡献。美国心理现实主义大师亨利·詹姆斯的小说《信使》(1903)等探索了人物内心的种种复杂感受,对美国新兴文化与欧洲传统文化进行了深入的比较和艺术表现。与亨利·詹姆斯风格类似的女作家伊迪斯·沃顿在小说《天真时代》(1920)中进一步探索了纽约上层社会在现代都市社会的人生沉浮。在具有强烈社会批判色彩的现实主义小说中,德莱赛的《嘉莉妹妹》(1900)和杰克·伦敦的《马丁·伊顿》(1909)等作品揭示了美国人在心灵获救和物欲横流之间的深刻矛盾心理,描写了社会底层人民通过个人奋斗而取得了物质上的成功,但又马上面临着精神的痛苦或幻灭的故事。另一位美国作家菲茨杰拉德(1896—1940)虽然创作生涯不长,但是他的小说《伟大的盖茨比》(1925)以流畅的叙述再现了一个"美国梦"破灭的悲剧,从而为美国现实主义文学留下了一部经典之作。在这期间,美国出现了第一位获得诺贝尔文学奖(1930 年奖)的作家辛克莱尔·刘易斯(1885—1951),他的小说《巴比特》(1922)揭露了商业社会中的伪善和庸碌,增强了美国现实主义文学的世界性声誉。

20 世纪上半叶,"迷惘的一代"小说创作为美国文学带来了更大的国际声誉,特别是海明威(1899—1961)的小说如《永别了武器》(1929)等作品描写了战争的残酷和人性的复杂,其中的"硬汉"人物为美国文学史留下了令人难忘的艺术形象。在此期间,美国南方文学也迎来了自己的文学复兴,其代表性的成就以威廉·福克纳(1897—1962)的小说创作为标志。福克纳的小说如《喧嚣与骚动》(1929)等作品集中描写了南方乡镇的奇人奇事,其中的多重叙述视角和人物心理分析使作者成为西方现代主义文学运动的不朽代表。与南方文学复兴相呼应的是美国西部文学的不断发展,例如薇拉·凯瑟(1873—1947)的边疆题材小说《我的安东尼娅》(1918)等作品描写了移民开拓边疆的艰辛和人格的尊严,在美国文学中可谓独树一帜。20世纪20年代里,美国黑人文学经历了"哈莱姆文艺复兴"时期,其中的著名诗人如兰斯顿·休斯(1902—1967)善于把黑人音乐和民间歌谣结合起来进行创作,如诗歌《黑人的河》(1921—1925)等,为美国文学增添了一道亮丽的风景。同时,美国黑人作家杜波伊斯(1868—1963)写有散文集如《黑人的灵魂》(1903)等等,其清澈的语言和深沉的感情打动着饱受压迫的黑人读者,而他对于种族歧视和阶级压迫所表达的强烈抗议和批判则对后来的美国族裔文学发展产生了巨大的影响。值得一提的是,美国作家舍伍德·安德森(1876—1941)不但以自己风格独特的小说如《俄亥俄州的温斯堡:小城故事集》(1919)等在艺术创新方面作出了贡献,而且他还参加了当时的"芝加哥文艺复兴"运动,并在以后年月里大力提携了不少年轻的美国小说家。

美国现代戏剧在20世纪上半期经历了从崛起到繁荣的快速发展阶段。由于美国没有欧洲那样悠久的戏剧历史,其现代戏剧的出现可说是姗姗来迟,正如哈罗德·布鲁姆所谓的,美国这个极具戏剧性的国家却缺少戏剧的传统。从19世纪中期到20世纪初期,美国的两次工业革命带来了城市人口膨胀和消费文化的发展,商业性的戏剧演出和专业剧团日益增多,人们休闲娱乐的时间增多,这些都使戏剧繁荣有了较好的社会物质基础。这一时期的戏剧家成果颇丰,其中以尤金·奥尼尔(1888—1953)的戏剧成就为最。奥尼尔适逢其会,既秉承了父亲的舞台天赋,又在西方戏剧经典作品的熏陶下培育了自己的戏剧理念和艺术风格。1916年,他的独幕剧《东航卡迪夫》以独特的心理表现技巧引起人们广泛的注意,而他的《毛猿》(1922)则以强烈的表现主义手法揭示了存在的荒谬和人生的悲欢。美国在一战以后还出现了埃尔默·赖斯(1892—1967)、约翰·劳森(1895—1977)、克利福德·奥德兹(1906—1963)和桑顿·怀尔德(1897—1975)等著名剧作家。他们的戏剧创作既有表现主义的艺术特征,也有现实主义的批判力度,还有"表演主义"戏剧的实验创新。这些剧作家不但专心于戏剧艺术形式的革故鼎新,而且严肃地关注社会人生的种种矛盾,他们的艺术成果为美国戏剧的崛起和发展作出了很大的贡献。

Lesson 18   Willa Cather (1873—1947)

I. A Brief Review.

Born on a small farm in Virginia in 1873, Willa Sibert Cather was a Pulitzer-winning American author. Her writing career started at college when she regularly contributed to *Nebraska State Journal*. After her graduation, she joined the editorial staff of *McClure's* and co-authored with Georgina M. Wells, a critical biography of Mary Baker Eddy, the founder of *Christian Science*. In Pittsburgh, she met Isabelle McClung and lived in her home from 1901 to 1906. Throughout her life, Cather remained devoted to McClung, who died in 1938.

图 18   Willa Cather

Her most famous works were *O Pioneer!* (1913), *The Song of the Lark* (1915), and *My Antonia* (1918), which depicted some western heroines: Alexandra Bergson in *O Pioneer!* (1913), Thea Kronberg in *The Song of the Lark* (1915), and Antonia Shimerda in *My Antonia* (1918). These three novels described in details the lives of Nebraska settlers— Bohemian Czech, German, Danish, Swedish, Norwegian, French, Russian, and "Americans" from the East. Cather recognized that even by the 1920s, these pioneering settlers had disappeared, therefore she extolled her frontier characters for their endurance and accomplishment. In 1923, she was awarded the Pulitzer Prize for her work *One of Ours*. Around 1922, Cather was faced with a great crisis, which was caused by her poor health, dissatisfaction with the progress of her career, and alarm at the increasing mechanization and mass-produced quality of American life. She joined the Episcopal Church, and her novels took a new direction. Important books from her "middle period" dealt with spiritual and cultural crises in the lives of the main characters including *A Lost Lady* (1923) and *The Professor's House* (1925).

Her third writing stage began with the publication of *Death Comes for the Archbishop* (1923), which was based on the career of Jean Baptiste Lamy (1814—1888), archbishop of New Mexico, and the priest Joseph Marchebeuf, his close friend and collaborator. Another historical novel, *Shadows on the Rock* (1931) was set even further back, in seventeenth-century Quebec. In both books, an image of high French culture, ceremonial spirituality, and the American landscape contrasted to the material trivia and empty banality of contemporary life. Cather was celebrated by critics like H. L. Mencken for her writing in plainspoken language about ordinary people. However, later critics tended to attack Cather for her lack of interest in economics and her conservative politics. Discouraged by negative criticism of her work, Cather became reclusive, burned letters, and even forbade anyone publishing her letters.

Throughout Cather's life, her most significant friendships were with women and showed no romantic interest in men. Since the 1980s, however, feminist and other academic writers have appreciated highly Cather's literary accomplishment as well as the influence of her female friendships on her work. Most recently, her work has been viewed as the vanguard of Ecocriticism, a contemporary theoretical approach to the analysis of art that seeks out ecological awareness.

Ⅱ. Texts.

My Antonia(1918).

The Shimerdas

I

I first heard of Antonia on what seemed to me aninterminable journey across the great midland plain of North America. I was ten years old then; I had lost both my father and mother within a year, and my Virginia relatives were sending me out to my grandparents, who lived in Nebraska. I travelled in the care of a mountain boy, Jake Marpole, one of the "hands" on my father's old farm under the Blue Ridge, who was now going West to work for my grandfather. Jake's experience of the world was not much wider than mine. He had never been in a railway train until the morning when we set out together to try our fortunes in a new world.

We went all the way in day-coaches, becoming more sticky and grimy① with each stage of the journey. Jake bought everything the newsboys offered him: candy, oranges, brass collar buttons, a watch-charm, and for me a "Life of Jesse James", which I remember as one of the most satisfactory books I have ever read. Beyond Chicago we were under the protection of a friendly passenger conductor, who knew all about the country to which we were going and gave us a great deal of advice in exchange for our confidence. He seemed to us an experienced and worldly man who had been almost everywhere; in his conversation he threw out lightly the names of distant states and cities. He wore the rings and pins and badges of different fraternal② orders to which he belonged. Even his cuff-buttons were engraved with hieroglyphics③, and he was more inscribed④ than an Egyptian obelisk⑤.

Once when he sat down to chat, he told us that in the immigrant car ahead there was a family from "across the water" whose destination was the same as ours.

"They can't any of them speak English, except one little girl, and all she can say is 'We go

---

① grimy: 沾满污垢的;满是灰尘的;肮脏的
② fraternal: 兄弟的,兄弟般的
③ hieroglyphics: 象形文字
④ inscribed: 写;刻;题
⑤ obelisk: 方尖石塔,短剑号,疑问记号

Black Hawk, Nebraska.' She's not much older than you, twelve or thirteen, maybe, and she's as bright as a new dollar. Don't you want to go ahead and see her, Jimmy? She's got the pretty brown eyes, too!"

This last remark made me bashful, and I shook my head and settled down to "Jesse James". Jake nodded at me approvingly and said you were likely to get diseases from foreigners.

I do not remember crossing the Missouri River, or anything about the long day's journey through Nebraska. Probably by that time I had crossed so many rivers that I was dull to them. The only thing very noticeable about Nebraska was that it was still, all day long, Nebraska.

I had been sleeping, curled up in a red plush① seat, for a long while when we reached Black Hawk. Jake roused me and took me by the hand. We stumbled down from the train to a wooden siding, where men were running about with lanterns. I couldn't see any town, or even distant lights; we were surrounded by utter darkness. The engine was panting② heavily after its long run. In the red glow from the fire-box, a group of people stood huddled together on the platform, encumbered③ by bundles④ and boxes. I knew this must be the immigrant family the conductor had told us about. The woman wore a fringed⑤ shawl⑥ tied over her head, and she carried a little tin trunk in her arms, hugging it as if it were a baby. There was an old man, tall and stooped. Two half-grown boys and a girl stood holding oilcloth bundles, and a little girl clung to her mother's skirts. Presently a man with a lantern approached them and began to talk, shouting and exclaiming. I pricked up⑦ my ears, for it was positively the first time I had ever heard a foreign tongue.

Another lantern came along. A bantering⑧ voice called out: "Hello, are you Mr. Burden's folks? If you are, it's me you're looking for. I'm Otto Fuchs. I'm Mr. Burden's hired man, and I'm to drive you out. Hello, Jimmy, ain't you scared to come so far west?'

I looked up with interest at the new face in the lantern-light. He might have stepped out of the pages of "Jesse James". He wore a sombrero⑨ hat, with a wide leather band and a bright buckle, and the ends of his moustache were twisted up stiffly, like little horns. He looked lively and ferocious, I thought, and as if he had a history. A long scar ran across one cheek and drew the corner of his mouth up in a sinister⑩ curl. The top of his left ear was gone, and his skin was brown

---

① plush: 豪华的;舒适的;高级的
② pant: 波动,晃动,振动
③ encumbered: 妨碍,阻碍,阻塞,拖累
④ bundles: 捆,包,
⑤ fringed: 具流苏的
⑥ shawl: 围巾,披肩
⑦ prick up: 竖起
⑧ banter: (善意地)取笑,逗弄
⑨ sombrero: (墨西哥的)宽边帽
⑩ sinister: 危险的,不吉祥的,凶兆的,险恶的

as an Indian's. Surely this was the face of a desperado①. As he walked about the platform in his high-heeled boots, looking for our trunks, I saw that he was a rather slight man, quick and wiry, and light on his feet. He told us we had a long night drive ahead of us, and had better be on the hike. He led us to a hitching-bar where two farm-wagons were tied, and I saw the foreign family crowding into one of them. The other was for us. Jake got on the front seat with Otto Fuchs, and I rode on the straw in the bottom of the wagon-box, covered up with a buffalo hide. The immigrants rumbled off into the empty darkness, and we followed them.

I tried to go to sleep, but the jolting② made me bite my tongue, and I soon began to ache all over. When the straw settled down, I had a hard bed. Cautiously I slipped from under the buffalo hide, got up on my knees and peered over the side of the wagon. There seemed to be nothing to see; no fences, no creeks or trees, no hills or fields. If there was a road, I could not make it out in the faint starlight. There was nothing but land: not a country at all, but the material out of which countries are made. No, there was nothing but land—slightly undulating③, I knew, because often our wheels ground against the brake as we went down into a hollow and lurched④ up again on the other side. I had the feeling that the world was left behind, that we had got over the edge of it, and were outside man's jurisdiction⑤. I had never before looked up at the sky when there was not a familiar mountain ridge against it. But this was the complete dome of heaven, all there was of it. I did not believe that my dead father and mother were watching me from up there; they would still be looking for me at the sheep-fold down by the creek, or along the white road that led to the mountain pastures. I had left even their spirits behind me. The wagon jolted on, carrying me I knew not whither. I don't think I was homesick. If we never arrived anywhere, it did not matter. Between that earth and that sky I felt erased, blotted out⑥. I did not say my prayers that night: here, I felt, what would be would be.

II

I do not remember our arrival at my grandfather's farm sometime before daybreak, after a drive of nearly twenty miles with heavy work-horses. When I awoke, it was afternoon. I was lying in a little room, scarcely larger than the bed that held me, and the window-shade at my head was flapping softly in a warm wind. A tall woman, with wrinkled brown skin and black hair, stood looking down at me; I knew that she must be my grandmother. She had been crying, I could see, but when I opened my eyes she smiled, peered at me anxiously, and sat down on the foot of my bed.

"Had a good sleep, Jimmy?" she asked briskly. Then in a very different tone she said, as if to

---

① desperado: 亡命徒,暴徒
② jolting: 摇动
③ undulate: 波动;起伏;呈波浪形
④ lurch: 蹒跚而行,颠簸着行进
⑤ jurisdiction: 管辖区域;管辖范围
⑥ blot out: 毁灭,覆盖

herself, "My, how you do look like your father!" I remembered that my father had been her little boy; she must often have come to wake him like this when he overslept. "Here are your clean clothes," she went on, stroking my coverlid with her brown hand as she talked. "But first you come down to the kitchen with me, and have a nice warm bath behind the stove. Bring your things; there's nobody about."

"Down to the kitchen" struck me as curious; it was always "out in the kitchen" at home. I picked up my shoes and stockings and followed her through the living-room and down a flight of stairs into a basement. This basement was divided into a dining-room at the right of the stairs and a kitchen at the left. Both rooms were plastered① and whitewashed—the plaster laid directly upon the earth walls, as it used to be in dugouts. The floor was of hard cement. Up under the wooden ceiling there were little half-windows with white curtains, and pots of geraniums② and wandering Jew in the deep sills③. As I entered the kitchen, I sniffed a pleasant smell of gingerbread baking. The stove was very large, with bright nickel trimmings, and behind it there was a long wooden bench against the wall, and a tin washtub, into which grandmother poured hot and cold water. When she brought the soap and towels, I told her that I was used to taking my bath without help.

"Can you do your ears, Jimmy? Are you sure? Well, now, I call you a right smart little boy."

It was pleasant there in the kitchen. The sun shone into my bath-water through the west half-window, and a big Maltese cat came up and rubbed himself against the tub, watching me curiously. While I scrubbed, my grandmother busied herself in the dining-room until I called anxiously, "Grandmother, I'm afraid the cakes are burning!" Then she came laughing, waving her apron before her as if she were shooing chickens.

She was a spare④, tall woman, a little stooped, and she was apt to carry her head thrust forward in an attitude of attention, as if she were looking at something, or listening to something, far away. As I grew older, I came to believe that it was only because she was so often thinking of things that were far away. She was quick-footed and energetic in all her movements. Her voice was high and rather shrill, and she often spoke with an anxious inflection, for she was exceedingly desirous that everything should go with due order and decorum⑤. Her laugh, too, was high, and perhaps a little strident⑥, but there was a lively intelligence in it. She was then fifty-five years old, a strong woman, of unusual endurance.

After I was dressed, I explored the long cellar next the kitchen. It was dug out under the wing of the house, was plastered and cemented, with a stairway and an outside door by which the men

---

① plastered: 灰泥，用灰泥抹(墙等)
② geranium: 天竺葵
③ sill: 窗台(板);门槛
④ spare: 薄弱的,瘦的
⑤ decorum: 端庄得体
⑥ strident: (指声音)尖锐的;刺耳的

came and went. Under one of the windows there was a place for them to wash when they came in from work.

　　While my grandmother was busy about supper, I settled myself on the wooden bench behind the stove and got acquainted with the cat—he caught not only rats and mice, but gophers①, I was told. The patch of yellow sunlight on the floor travelled back toward the stairway, and grandmother and I talked about my journey, and about the arrival of the new Bohemian family; she said they were to be our nearest neighbors. We did not talk about the farm in Virginia, which had been her home for so many years. But after the men came in from the fields, and we were all seated at the supper table, then she asked Jake about the old place and about our friends and neighbors there.

　　……

Ⅲ. Notes.

　　My Ántonia tells the stories of several immigrant families who move to rural Nebraska to start new lives in America. The story has a particular focus on a Bohemian family, the Shimerdas, whose eldest daughter is named Ántonia. Antonia is a bold and free-hearted young woman, who becomes the center of narrator Jim Burden's attention. The narrator Jim Burden, who arrives in Nebraska on the same train as the Shimerdas, develops strong feelings for Ántonia, but the romantic interests ultimately disappear due to the uncontrolled changes that occur in people's lives. In the novel, there are many elements that clearly document the struggles of the hard-working immigrants in that difficult environment.

Ⅳ. Key Words（关键词）.

　　Modernism: 现代主义。美国现代主义文学运动开始于19世纪末期,在20世纪20年代的时候达到了高峰,延续到第二次世界大战以后。美国现代主义作家通过形式、技巧和风格的大胆实验和创新,如故意打破叙事时空顺序,大量运用梦境,心理时间,黑色幽默及魔幻、意象、象征和意识流等手法去表现生活和人的性格,注重对人物内心世界的挖掘,把人的个性和复杂的心理体验充分地表现出来。薇拉·凯瑟是20世纪初美国小说的杰出代表,她的《我的安东尼娅》运用了丰富而复杂的象征,具有明显的现代主义特征。

　　Pioneering Spirit: 拓荒精神。薇拉·凯瑟(Willa Cather,1873—1947)是美国公认的20世纪美国最杰出的小说家之一,她的作品主要是以西部边疆拓荒生活为题材,歌颂了欧洲移民在西部拓荒过程中所体现的人性之美以及不怕困难、勇往直前的拓荒精神,被认为是美国拓荒经历的象征。

Ⅴ. Questions.

　　1. In the novel, setting is extremely important. What function does the setting play in the first part?

---

① gopher: 囊地鼠

2. How do you explain the sentence "I had the feeling that the world was left behind, that we had got over the edge of it, and were outside man's jurisdiction."?

3. Why does Jim feel "erased" and "blotted out" as he travels on the wagon to his grandfather's house?

Lesson 19 Jack London (1876—1916)

Ⅰ. **A Brief Review.**

Born on January 12, 1876 in San Francisco, Jack London was an American author, journalist, and social activist. From his earliest youth, London supported himself by doing menial and dangerous jobs, experiencing profoundly the struggle for survival that most other writers and intellectuals knew only from observation or books. By 1883, London was determined to educate himself to improve his own condition. He quickly completed high school and spent a semester as a special student at the University of California. Embracing the hopeful socialism of Marx on the one hand and the rather darker view of Nietzche and Darwinism on the other, London believed at the same time in the inevitable triumph of the working class and in the evolutionary necessity of the survival of the strongest individuals.

图 19 Jack London

London recorded his sincere intellectual and personal involvement in that socialist movement in such novels as *The People of the Abyss* (1903), *The Iron Heel* (1908), *War of the Classes* (1905), and *Revolution* (1910); and dramatized his competing, deeply felt commitment to the fundamental reality of the law of survival and the will to power in his most popular novels, *The Call of the Wild* (1903) and *The Sea-Wolf* (1904). The contradiction between these competing beliefs is most vividly projected in the patently autobiographical novel *Martin Eden* (1909), a central document for the London scholar. The most enduringly popular of his stories involved the primitive (and melodramatic) struggle between strong and weak individuals in the context of irresistible natural forces such as the wild sea or the Arctic wastes.

London continued to write until his death in 1916. He had written too much yet too fast, with too little concern for the stylistic and formal refinement and subtlety of characterization that ranked high with critics. Like his contemporaries Stephen Crane and Franx Norris, London was interested in the violence that tested human character. Today, London's stories of humanity in and against nature continue to be popular all over the world. London's novels have been reevaluated also by many critics from an eco-critical perspective.

II. Texts.

The Law of Life

......

  He did not complain. It was the way of life, and it was just. He had been born close to the earth, close to the earth had he lived, and the law thereof was not new to him. It was the law of all flesh. Nature was not kindly to the flesh. She had no concern for that concrete thing called the individual. Her interest lay in the species, the race. This was the deepest abstraction old Koskoosh's barbaric① mind was capable of, but he grasped it firmly. He saw it exemplified in all life. The rise of the sap, the bursting greenness of the willow bud, the fall of the yellow leaf — in this alone was told the whole history. But one task did Nature set the individual. Did he not perform it, he died. Did he perform it, it was all the same, he died. Nature did not care; there were plenty who were obedient, and it was only the obedience in this matter, not the obedient, which lived and lived always. The tribe of Koskoosh was very old. The old men he had known when a boy, had known old men before them. Therefore it was true that the tribe lived, that it stood for the obedience of all its members, way down into the forgotten past, whose very resting places were unremembered. They did not count; they were episodes. They had passed away like clouds from a summer sky. He also was an episode, and would pass away. Nature did not care. To life she set one task, gave one law. To perpetuate was the task of life, its law was death. A maiden was a good creature to look upon, full-breasted and strong, with spring to her step and light in her eyes. But her task was yet before her. The light in her eyes brightened, her step quickened, she was now bold with the young men, now timid, and she gave them of her own unrest. And ever she grew fairer and yet fairer to look upon, till some hunter, able no longer to withhold himself, took her to his lodge to cook and toil for him and to become the mother of his children. And with the coming of her offspring her looks left her. Her limbs dragged and shuffled②, her eyes dimmed and bleared, and only the little children found joy against the withered cheek of the old squaw③ by the fire. Her task was done. But a little while, on the first pinch of famine or the first long trail, and she would be left, even as he had been left, in the snow, with a little pile of wood. Such was the law.

  He placed a stick carefully upon the fire and resumed his meditations. It was the same everywhere, with all things. The mosquitoes vanished with the first frost. The little tree-squirrel crawled away to die. When age settled upon the rabbit it became slow and heavy, and could no longer outfoot④ its enemies. Even the big bald-face grew clumsy and blind and quarrelsome, in the

---

① barbaric: 半开化的;野蛮的
② shuffle: 拖着脚步走
③ squaw: 北美印第安女子或妻子
④ outfoot: 超过

end to be dragged down by a handful of yelping① huskies. He remembered how he had abandoned his own father on an upper reach of the Klondike one winter, the winter before the missionary came with his talk-books and his box of medicines. Many a time had Koskoosh smacked his lips over the recollection of that box, though now his mouth refused to moisten. The "painkiller" had been especially good. But the missionary was a bother after all, for he brought no meat into the camp, and he ate heartily, and the hunters grumbled. But he chilled his lungs on the divide by the Mayo, and the dogs afterwards nosed the stones away and fought over his bones.

Koskoosh placed another stick on the fire and harked② back deeper into the past. There was the time of the Great Famine, when the old men crouched empty-bellied to the fire, and from their lips fell dim traditions of the ancient day when the Yukon ran wide open for three winters, and then lay frozen for three summers. He had lost his mother in that famine. In the summer the salmon run③ had failed, and the tribe looked forward to the winter and the coming of the caribou④. Then the winter came, but with it there were no caribou. Never had the like been known, not even in the lives of the old men. But the caribou did not come, and it was the seventh year, and the rabbits had not replenished, and the dogs were naught⑤ but bundles of bones. And through the long darkness the children wailed and died, and the women, and the old men; and not one in ten of the tribe lived to meet the sun when it came back in the spring. That was a famine!

But he had seen times of plenty, too, when the meat spoiled on their hands, and the dogs were fat and worthless with over-eating—times when they let the game go unkilled, and the women were fertile, and the lodges were cluttered⑥ with sprawling ⑦ men-children and women-children. Then it was the men became high-stomached, and revived ancient quarrels, and crossed the divides to the south to kill the Pellys, and to the west that they might sit by the dead fires of the Tananas. He remembered, when a boy, during a time of plenty, when he saw a moose pulled down by the wolves. Zing-ha lay with him in the snow and watched—Zing-ha, who later became the craftiest of hunters, and who, in the end, fell through an air-hole on the Yukon. They found him, a month afterward, just as he had crawled half-way out and frozen stiff to the ice.

But the moose. Zing-ha and he had gone out that day to play at hunting after the manner of their fathers. On the bed of the creek they struck the fresh track of a moose, and with it the tracks of many wolves. "An old one," Zing-ha, who was quicker at reading the sign, said—"an old one who cannot keep up with the herd. The wolves have cut him out from his brothers, and they will never leave him." And it was so. It was their way. By day and by night, never resting, snarling

---

① yelp: 发出短而尖的叫声
② hark: 回忆起(过去的事)
③ salmon run: 一年一度的鱼讯
④ caribou: (北美洲产的) 驯鹿
⑤ naught: 零, 无价值
⑥ clutter: 胡乱塞满
⑦ sprawling: 无计划的扩展

on his heels, snapping at his nose, they would stay by him to the end. How Zing-ha and he felt the blood-lust quicken! The finish would be a sight to see!

Eager-footed, they took the trail, and even he, Koskoosh, slow of sight and an unversed① tracker, could have followed it blind, it was so wide. Hot were they on the heels of the chase, reading the grim tragedy, fresh-written, at every step. Now they came to where the moose had made a stand. Thrice the length of a grown man's body, in every direction, had the snow been stamped about and uptossed. In the midst were the deep impressions of the splay-hoofed② game, and all about, everywhere, were the lighter footmarks of the wolves. Some, while their brothers harried③ the kill, had lain to one side and rested. The full-stretched impress of their bodies in the snow was as perfect as though made the moment before. One wolf had been caught in a wild lunge④ of the maddened victim and trampled to death. A few bones, well picked, bore witness.

Again, they ceased the uplift of their snowshoes at a second stand. Here the great animal had fought desperately. Twice had he been dragged down, as the snow attested⑤, and twice had he shaken his assailants clear and gained footing once more. He had done his task long since, but none the less was life dear to him. Zing-ha said it was a strange thing, a moose once down to get free again; but this one certainly had. The Shaman would see signs and wonders in this when they told him.

And yet again, they come to where the moose had made to mount the bank and gain the timber. But his foes had laid on from behind, till he reared and fell back upon them, crushing two deep into the snow. It was plain the kill was at hand, for their brothers had left them untouched. Two more stands were hurried past, brief in time-length and very close together. The trail was red now, and the clean stride of the great beast had grown short and slovenly⑥. Then they heard the first sounds of the battle — not the full-throated chorus of the chase, but the short, snappy⑦ bark which spoke of close quarters and teeth to flesh. Crawling up the wind, Zing-ha bellied it through the snow, and with him crept he, Koskoosh, who was to be chief of the tribesmen in the years to come. Together they shoved⑧ aside the under branches of a young spruce⑨ and peered forth. It was the end they saw.

The picture, like all of youth's impressions, was still strong with him, and his dim eyes watched the end played out as vividly as in that far-off time. Koskoosh marvelled at this, for in the days which followed, when he was a leader of men and a head of councillors, he had done great

---

① unversed: 无经验的, 不熟练的
② splay-hoofed: 长着外翻的蹄子的
③ harry: 一再袭击, 侵扰
④ lunge: 猛冲, 刺入
⑤ attest: 作证, 证明
⑥ slovenly: 邋遢的; 不整洁的
⑦ snappy: 短小而粗暴的
⑧ shoved: 推, 挤
⑨ spruce: 云杉

deeds and made his name a curse in the mouths of the Pellys, to say naught of the strange white man he had killed, knife to knife, in open fight.

For long he pondered on the days of his youth, till the fire died down and the frost bit deeper.

……

Ⅲ. Notes.

The Law of Life relates a moving story that an ancient Indian tribe was about to start its annual migration while the former headman was too old to follow. Being left with a pile of fagots, he was aware that death was befalling him. In the last moments of his life, huddling up close to the fire, he meditated on the law of life.

Ⅳ. Key Words (关键词).

Naturalism: 自然主义。它起源于法国,在很大程度上继承了现实主义的一些理念,但在具体创作中却与现实主义不同。自然主义利用环境和遗传来解释人的行为,认为环境的力量超过或压倒了人的力量,个人受到生存本能的控制,对具有决定性作用的事情几乎无能为力。《生存法则》这部短篇小说就具有浓重的自然主义色彩,它以极地为背景,以原始的印第安部落为描写对象,将人的社会属性降低到动物本性,强调人的自然属性和动物本能。

Determination: 命定论。它指人生中的一切事情都是注定的,是由人所无法控制的力量决定的,人的任何企图改变命运的努力都是徒劳的。如在《生命法则》中,部落将老人抛弃,而老人坦然地接受了这一安排就带有明显的宿命论意味。

Ⅴ. Questions.

1. What function does the setting perform in the story?
2. Why does the writer use the words "daughter's daughter" instead of "granddaughter", and "men-children and women-children" instead of "boys and girls"?
3. What does the reminiscence of the hunting scene symbolize?

Lesson 20　Sherwood Anderson (1876—1941)

Ⅰ. **A Brief Review.**

Born in Cameden, Ohio in 1876, Sherwood Anderson was a novelist and short story writer. Anderson never finished high school and held various jobs. When he was approaching middle age, he decided to become a successful writer. Living in Chicago, New Orleans, and Paris, he worked passionately to make up for his late start, producing novels, short stories, essays, and an autobiography.

In 1912, he returned to Chicago and met the writers and artists whose activities were creating the Chicago Renaissance: the novelists Floyd Dell and Theodore Dreiser; the poets Edgar Lee Masters, Vachel Lindsay, and Carl Sandburg; the editors Harriet Monroe of *Poetry* and Margaret C. Anderson of the *Little Review*. His first major publication

图 20　Sherwood Anderson

was *Windy McPherson's Son* (1916), the story of a man who runs away from a small Iowa town in futile search for life's meaning; his second was *Marching Men* (1917), telling about a charismatic lawyer who tries unsuccessfully to recognize the factory system in a small town. These books reveal three recurrent themes: the individual quest for self and social betterment, the small-town environment, and the distrust of modern industrial society. However, his works lack the interest in exploration into human psychology and the sense of conflict between inner and outer worlds.

In 1916, Anderson began writing and publishing the tales that were brought together in *Winesburg, Ohio*, a book which contains details about the lives of a number of people and Anderson calls these characters "grotesques." Measuring society by a utopian standard of free emotional and sensual expression, Anderson's attitude toward the characters mixes compassion for the individual with dismay at a social order that can do so much damage. In his literary career, he encouraged simplicity and directness of style, made attractive the use of the point of view of outsiders as a way of criticizing conventional society, and gave the craft of the short story a decided push toward stories presenting a slice of life or a significant moment as opposed to panorama and summary.

His best work was represented by short stories published in three volumes: *The Triumph of the Egg* (1921), *Horses and Men* (1923), and *Death in the Woods and Other Stories* (1933). He also wrote a number of novels, including *Poor White* (1920), *Many Marriages* (1923), *Beyond Desire* (1932) as well as free verse, prose poems, plays, essays and a series of autobiographical volumes. During the 1930s Anderson, along with many other writers, was active in liberal causes. He died at sea on the way to South America while on a goodwill mission for the State Department.

Ⅱ. Texts.

Winesburg, Ohio (1919)

Mother

Elizabeth Willard, the mother of George Willard, was tall and gaunt① and her face was marked with smallpox scars. Although she was but forty-five, some obscure disease had taken the fire out of her figure. Listlessly she went about the disorderly old hotel looking at the faded wallpaper and the ragged carpets and, when she was able to be about, doing the work of a chambermaid among beds soiled② by the slumbers③ of fat traveling men. Her husband, Tom Willard, a slender, graceful man with square shoulders, a quick military step, and a black mustache trained to turn sharply up at the ends, tried to put the wife out of his mind. The presence of the tall ghostly figure, moving slowly through the halls, he took as a reproach④ to himself. When he thought of her he grew angry and swore. The hotel was unprofitable and forever on the edge of failure and he wished himself out of it. He thought of the old house and the woman who lived there with him as things defeated and done for. The hotel in which he had begun life so hopefully was now a mere ghost of what a hotel should be. As he went spruce⑤ and business-like through the streets of Winesburg, he sometimes stopped and turned quickly about as though fearing that the spirit of the hotel and of the woman would follow him even into the streets. "Damn such a life, damn it!" he sputtered⑥ aimlessly.

Tom Willard had a passion for village politics and for years had been the leading Democrat in a strongly Republican community. Some day, he told himself, the tide of things political will turn in my favor and the years of ineffectual service count big in the bestowal⑦ of rewards. He dreamed of going to Congress and even of becoming governor. Once when a younger member of the party arose at a political conference and began to boast of his faithful service, Tom Willard grew white with fury. "Shut up, you," he roared, glaring about. "What do you know of service? What are you but a boy? Look at what I've done here! I was a Democrat here in Winesburg when it was a

---

① gaunt:（因疾病、饥饿或焦虑等）瘦削的;憔悴的
② soil: 弄脏;污辱
③ slumber: 睡眠
④ reproach: 带来羞辱的人或事;羞耻,丢脸
⑤ spruce: 衣着整洁的;漂亮的
⑥ sputter: 气急败坏地说
⑦ bestowal: 赠与,给与

crime to be a Democrat. In the old days they fairly hunted us with guns."

Between Elizabeth and her one son George there was a deep unexpressed bond of sympathy, based on a girlhood dream that had long ago died. In the son's presence she was timid and reserved, but sometimes while he hurried about town intent upon his duties as a reporter, she went into his room and closing the door knelt by a little desk, made of a kitchen table, that sat near a window. In the room by the desk she went through a ceremony that was half a prayer, half a demand, addressed to the skies. In the boyish figure she yearned to see something half forgotten that had once been a part of herself recreated. The prayer concerned that. "Even though I die, I will in some way keep defeat from you," she cried, and so deep was her determination that her whole body shook. Her eyes glowed and she clenched her fists. "If I am dead and see him becoming a meaningless drab① figure like myself, I will come back," she declared. "I ask God now to give me that privilege. I demand it. I will pay for it. God may beat me with his fists. I will take any blow that may befall if but this my boy be allowed to express something for us both." Pausing uncertainly, the woman stared about the boy's room. "And do not let him become smart and successful either," she added vaguely.

The communion between George Willard and his mother was outwardly a formal thing without meaning. When she was ill and sat by the window in her room he sometimes went in the evening to make her a visit. They sat by a window that looked over the roof of a small frame building into Main Street. By turning their heads they could see, through another window, along an alleyway that ran behind the Main Street stores and into the back door of Abner Groff's bakery. Sometimes as they sat thus a picture of village life presented itself to them. At the back door of his shop appeared Abner Groff with a stick or an empty milk bottle in his hand. For a long time there was a feud② between the baker and a grey cat that belonged to Sylvester West, the druggist. The boy and his mother saw the cat creep into the door of the bakery and presently emerge followed by the baker, who swore and waved his arms about. The baker's eyes were small and red and his black hair and beard were filled with flour dust. Sometimes he was so angry that, although the cat had disappeared, he hurled③ sticks, bits of broken glass, and even some of the tools of his trade about. Once he broke a window at the back of Sinning's Hardware Store. In the alley the grey cat crouched behind barrels filled with torn paper and broken bottles above which flew a black swarm of flies. Once when she was alone, and after watching a prolonged and ineffectual outburst on the part of the baker, Elizabeth Willard put her head down on her long white hands and wept. After that she did not look along the alleyway any more, but tried to forget the contest between the bearded man and the cat. It seemed like a rehearsal of her own life, terrible in its vividness.

In the evening when the son sat in the room with his mother, the silence made them both feel awkward. Darkness came on and the evening train came in at the station. In the street below feet

---

① drab: 无生气的,乏味的,单调的
② feud: 长期不和;世仇
③ hurl: 猛投,用力掷

tramped up and down upon a board sidewalk. In the station yard, after the evening train had gone, there was a heavy silence. Perhaps Skinner Leason, the express agent, moved a truck the length of the station platform. Over on Main Street sounded a man's voice, laughing. The door of the express office banged. George Willard arose and crossing the room fumbled① for the doorknob. Sometimes he knocked against a chair, making it scrape along the floor. By the window sat the sick woman, perfectly still, listless. Her long hands, white and bloodless, could be seen drooping over the ends of the arms of the chair. "I think you had better be out among the boys. You are too much indoors," she said, striving to relieve the embarrassment of the departure. "I thought I would take a walk," replied George Willard, who felt awkward and confused.

One evening in July, when the transient guests who made the New Willard House their temporary home had become scarce, and the hallways, lighted only by kerosene② lamps turned low, were plunged in gloom, Elizabeth Willard had an adventure. She had been ill in bed for several days and her son had not come to visit her. She was alarmed. The feeble blaze of life that remained in her body was blown into a flame by her anxiety and she crept out of bed, dressed and hurried along the hallway toward her son's room, shaking with exaggerated fears. As she went along she steadied herself with her hand, slipped along the papered walls of the hall and breathed with difficulty. The air whistled through her teeth. As she hurried forward she thought how foolish she was. "He is concerned with boyish affairs," she told herself. "Perhaps he has now begun to walk about in the evening with girls."

Elizabeth Willard had a dread of being seen by guests in the hotel that had once belonged to her father and the ownership of which still stood recorded in her name in the county courthouse. The hotel was continually losing patronage③ because of its shabbiness and she thought of herself as also shabby. Her own room was in an obscure corner and when she felt able to work she voluntarily worked among the beds, preferring the labor that could be done when the guests were abroad seeking trade among the merchants of Winesburg.

By the door of her son's room the mother knelt upon the floor and listened for some sound from within. When she heard the boy moving about and talking in low tones a smile came to her lips. George Willard had a habit of talking aloud to himself and to hear him doing so had always given his mother a peculiar pleasure. The habit in him, she felt, strengthened the secret bond that existed between them. A thousand times she had whispered to herself of the matter. "He is groping④about, trying to find himself," she thought. "He is not a dull clod⑤, all words and smartness. Within him there is a secret something that is striving to grow. It is the thing I let be killed in myself."

---

① fumble: 乱摸, 笨拙地弄
② kerosene: 煤油;火油
③ patronage: (顾客的)光顾,惠顾
④ grope: 探索,搜寻
⑤ clod: 傻瓜,笨蛋

In the darkness in the hallway by the door the sick woman arose and started again toward her own room. She was afraid that the door would open and the boy come upon her. When she had reached a safe distance and was about to turn a corner into a second hallway she stopped and bracing herself with her hands waited, thinking to shake off a trembling fit of weakness that had come upon her. The presence of the boy in the room had made her happy. In her bed, during the long hours alone, the little fears that had visited her had become giants. Now they were all gone. "When I get back to my room I shall sleep, " she murmured gratefully.

......

With a little broken sob in her throat Elizabeth Willard blew out the light that stood upon the table and stood weak and trembling in the darkness. The strength that had been as a miracle in her body left and she half reeled across the floor, clutching at the back of the chair in which she had spent so many long days staring out over the tin roofs into the main street of Winesburg. In the hallway there was the sound of footsteps and George Willard came in at the door. Sitting in a chair beside his mother he began to talk. "I'm going to get out of here, " he said. "I don't know where I shall go or what I shall do but I am going away."

The woman in the chair waited and trembled. An impulse came to her. "I suppose you had better wake up, " she said. "You think that? You will go to the city and make money, eh? It will be better for you, you think, to be a business man, to be brisk and smart and alive?" She waited and trembled.

The son shook his head. "I suppose I can't make you understand, but oh, I wish I could, " he said earnestly. "I can't even talk to father about it. I don't try. There isn't any use. I don't know what I shall do. I just want to go away and look at people and think."

Silence fell upon the room where the boy and woman sat together. Again, as on the other evenings, they were embarrassed. After a time the boy tried again to talk. "I suppose it won't be for a year or two but I've been thinking about it, " he said, rising and going toward the door. "Something father said makes it sure that I shall have to go away." He fumbled with the doorknob. In the room the silence became unbearable to the woman. She wanted to cry out with joy because of the words that had come from the lips of her son, but the expression of joy had become impossible to her. "I think you had better go out among the boys. You are too much indoors, " she said. "I thought I would go for a little walk, " replied the son stepping awkwardly out of the room and closing the door.

Ⅲ. Notes.

1. *Mother* tells a story of an unhappy mother, Elizabeth Willard, who feels a ferocious bond with her son George, a bond that she cannot express in words. She had dreams and hope when she was young. But her husband, Tom Willard, who always considers himself smart and successful (he is really neither), disparages and ridicules her until she is physically ill. Her self-esteem has sunk so low that she cannot even talk to her son. When she finds her son's dreams beaten down as hers, her hatred towards her husband almost leads to violence, but she is too weak to commit it.

2. Stylistically Anderson strives for a simple and concise prose, using brief or at least uncomplex sentences and an unsophisticated vocabulary appropriate to the muffled awareness and limited resources of his typical characters. Structurally, his stories move toward a moment when the character breaks out in some frenzied gesture of release which discloses a hidden inner self. In both style and structure Anderson's works have important influences on other writers including Ernest Hemingway, William Faulkner, John Steinbek, J. D. Salinger, among others.

Ⅳ. Key Words (关键词).

Realism: 是指19世纪30年代后在欧洲文学艺术中占主导地位的一种文艺思潮和文艺运动。这一文艺思潮后来影响到美国,时至19世纪末,它已经成为美国文学的主潮,涌现出一批以豪威尔斯为首的现实主义作家。他们注重揭露社会的阴暗面,给予黑暗的社会以猛烈的抨击,努力真实地刻画人们的生活,如实地反映生活的本来面貌,并力求深入细致地揭示人物内心的矛盾变化,塑造典型的人物性格。舍伍德·安德森就是20世纪早期美国现实主义文学的先驱者之一,在美国文学史上具有很重要的地位,海明威、菲茨杰拉德、福克纳、斯坦贝克、考德威尔等都受过他的很人影响。

Grotesque: 畸形。安德森在《俄亥俄州温斯堡》中刻画了一群畸形人,他们渴望爱与理解,但在和别人交流的时候却存在着严重的交际障碍,不能清楚地表达自己的情感和思想等。究其原因是他们或受社会传统的束缚,或受正统道德观念的压制,因而丧失了通过语言和行动将自己的情感表达出来的能力,于是形成一个隔离的群体,成为精神方面的畸形人。

Ⅴ. Questions.

1. At the beginning of the story, the writer says that "some obscure disease had taken the fire out of her figure." Do you think Mrs. Willard really had some disease?
2. Why did Mrs. Willard go to her son George's room when he was not in?
3. Why did Mrs. Willard "not let him (George) become smart and successful either"?

Lesson 21　F. Scott Fitzgerald (1896—1940)

Ⅰ. **A Brief Review.**

　　Born in St. Paul, Minnesota, on September 24, 1896, Francis Scott Fitzgerald was a short-story writer and novelist. Fitzgerald attended the St. Paul Academy where his first writing of a detective story appeared in print in the school newspaper when he was thirteen. Fitzgerald attended the Princeton Class in 1917 when he contributed regularly to the *Princeton Tiger* humor magazine and the *Nassau Literary Magazine*. On academic probation and unlikely to be able to graduate, Fitzgerald joined the army in 1917 and was commissioned a second lieutenant in the infantry. After his discharge in 1919, he went to New York City to seek his fortune.

　　Fitzgerald quit his job and started to rewrite his novel *This Side of Paradise* (1920), which was an immediate success and made the twenty-four-year-old author famous almost overnight. A week later, he married Zelda Sayre in New York. Living an extravagant life as young celebrities, the couple spent more than the money that Fitzgerald made from two collections of short stories——*Flappers and Philosophers* (1921) and *Tales of the Jazz Age* (1922)——and a second novel, *The Beautiful and Damned* (1922). The luxury life kept the Fitzgeralds in debts and the work pace as well as anxiety soon made them worn out.

　　Published in 1924, *The Great Gatsby* marked a striking advance in Fitzgerald's technique, utilizing a complex structure and a controlled narrative point of view. His fourth novel, *Tender Is the Night* (1934) examined the deterioration of Dick Diver, a brilliant American psychiatrist, during the course of his marriage to a wealthy mental patient. Its theme was concerned with American materialism, which was typical of Fitzgerald's fiction but seemed somewhat irrelevant to a country falling deep in depression. The new book was taken as a sign that Fitzgerald had lost touch of his age. His Hollywood novel, *The Love of the Last Tycoon* was about his experience as a Hollywood screen writer. Fitzgerald died on December 21, 1940.

　　To an extent, Fitzgerald's reputation still suffers from his image as a Jazz Age playboy. However, by the 1960s he had achieved a secure place among America's enduring writers. The invariable conclusion of all who have studied Fitzgerald's manuscripts is that he used to be very serious in his approach to writing and formed himself into an accomplished craftsman and meticulous reviser, whose best work, touched with genius, belonged to the best of his contemporaries.

图21　F. Scott Fitzgerald

Ⅱ. Texts.

The Great Gatsby

Chapter 9

AFTER TWO YEARS I remember the rest of that day, and that night and the next day, only as an endless drill of police and photographers and newspaper men in and out of Gatsby's front door. A rope stretched across the main gate and a policeman by it kept out the curious, but little boys soon discovered that they could enter through my yard, and there were always a few of them clustered open-mouthed about the pool. Some one with a positive manner, perhaps a detective, used the expression "madman" as he bent over Wilson's body① that afternoon, and the adventitious authority of his voice set the key for the newspaper reports next morning.

Most of these reports were a nightmare — grotesque, circumstantial, eager, and untrue. When Michaelis's testimony at the inquest brought to light Wilson's suspicions of his wife I thought the whole tale would shortly be served up in racy pasquinade — but Catherine, who might have said anything, didn't say a word. She showed a surprising amount of character about it too — looked at the coroner with determined eyes ender that corrected brow of hers, and swore that her sister had never seen Gatsby, that her sister was completely happy with her husband, that her sister had been into no mischief whatever. She convinced herself of it, and cried into her handkerchief, as if the very suggestion was more than she could endure. So Wilson was reduced to a man "deranged② by grief" in order that the case might remain in its simplest form. And it rested there.

But all this part of it seemed remote and unessential. I found myself on Gatsby's side, and alone. From the moment I telephoned news of the catastrophe to West Egg Village, every surmise about him, and every practical question, was referred to me. At first I was surprised and confused; then, as he lay in his house and didn't move or breathe or speak, hour upon hour, it grew upon me that I was responsible, because no one else was interested — interested, I mean, with that intense personal interest to which every one has some vague right at the end.

I called up Daisy③ half an hour after we found him, called her instinctively and without hesitation. But she and Tom had gone away early that afternoon, and taken baggage with them.

"Left no address?"

"No."

"Say when they'd be back?"

"No."

"Any idea where they are? How I could reach them?"

"I don't know. Can't say."

---

① Wilson's body: Wilson 的尸体。Wilson 经营一个汽车行,妻子在一次车祸中丧生。他误以为 Gatsby 是肇事者,因此将他杀死,后自杀而死

② derange: 使精神错乱

③ Daisy: 原为 Gatsby 的情人,后来嫁给 Tom

I wanted to get somebody for him. I wanted to go into the room where he lay and reassure him: "I'll get somebody for you, Gatsby. Don't worry. Just trust me and I'll get somebody for you—"

Meyer Wolfsheim's name wasn't in the phone book. The butler gave me his office address on Broadway, and I called Information, but by the time I had the number it was long after five, and no one answered the phone.

"Will you ring again?"

"I've rung them three times."

"It's very important."

"Sorry. I'm afraid no one's there."

I went back to the drawing-room and thought for an instant that they were chance visitors, all these official people who suddenly filled it. But, as they drew back the sheet and looked at Gatsby with unmoved eyes, his protest continued in my brain:

"Look here, old sport①, you've got to get somebody for me. You've got to try hard. I can't go through this alone."

Some one started to ask me questions, but I broke away and going upstairs looked hastily through the unlocked parts of his desk — he'd never told me definitely that his parents were dead. But there was nothing—only the picture of Dan Cody②, a token of forgotten violence, starting down from the wall.

Next morning I sent the butler to New York with a letter to Wolfsheim, which asked for information and urged him to come out on the next train. The request seemed superfluous③ when I wrote it. I was sure he'd start when he saw the newspapers, just as I was sure there'd be a wire from Daisy before noon — but neither a wire nor Mr. Wolfsheim arrived; no one arrived except more police and photographers and newspaper men. When the butler brought back Wolfsheim's answer I began to have a feeling of defiance④, of scornful solidarity between Gatsby and me against them all.

……

After that I felt a certain shame for Gatsby—one gentleman to whom I telephoned implied that he had got what he deserved. However, that was my fault, for he was one of those who used to sneer most bitterly at Gatsby on the courage of Gatsby's liquor, and I should have known better than to call him.

The morning of the funeral I went up to the New York to see Meyer Wolfsheim; I couldn't seem to reach him any other way. The door that I pushed open, on the advice of an elevator boy,

---

① old sport: 老朋友

② Dan Cody: 小说中几次提到这个名字,靠开发金银矿发家的人,Gatsby 年轻时曾在此人手下工作,但在小说中从未露面

③ superfluous: 过多的,过剩的,多余的

④ defiance: 违抗,挑衅的态度,蔑视

was marked "The Swastika Holding Company", and at first there didn't seem to be any one inside. But when I'd shouted "hello" several times in vain, an argument broke out behind a partition, and presently a lovely Jewess appeared at an interior door and scrutinized me with black hostile eyes.

"Nobody's in," she said. "Mr. Wolfsheim's gone to Chicago."

The first part of this was obviously untrue, for some one had begun to whistle "The Rosary," tunelessly, inside.

"Please say that Mr. Carraway wants to see him."

"I can't get him back from Chicago, can I?"

At this moment a voice, unmistakably Wolfsheim's, called "Stella!" from the other side of the door.

"Leave your name on the desk," she said quickly. "I'll give it to him when he gets back."

"But I know he's there."

She took a step toward me and began to slide her hands indignantly up and down her hips.

"You young men think you can force your way in here any time," she scolded. "We're getting sickantired① of it. When I say he's in Chicago, he's in Chicago."

I mentioned Gatsby.

"Oh-h!" She looked at me over again. "Will you just — What was your name?"

She vanished. In a moment Meyer Wolfsheim stood solemnly in the doorway, holding out both hands. He drew me into his office, remarking in a reverent voice that it was a sad time for all of us, and offered me a cigar.

"My memory goes back to when first I met him," he said. "A young major just out of the army and covered over with medals he got in the war. He was so hard up he had to keep on wearing his uniform because he couldn't buy some regular clothes. First time I saw him was when he come into Winebrenner's poolroom at Forty-third Street and asked for a job. He hadn't eat anything for a couple of days. 'Come on have some lunch with me,' I said. He ate more than four dollars' worth of food in half an hour."

"Did you start him in business?" I inquired.

"Start him! I made him."

"Oh."

"I raised him up out of nothing, right out of the gutter. I saw right away he was a fine-appearing, gentlemanly young man, and when he told me he was an Oggsford② I knew I could use him good. I got him to join up in the American Legion③ and he used to stand high there. Right off he did some work for a client of mine up to Albany. We were so thick like that in everything" — he held up two bulbous fingers — "always together."

---

① sickantired: sick and tired
② Oggsford: Oxford
③ American Legion: 美国军团(美国退伍军人组织)

I wondered if this partnership had included the World's Series transaction① in 1919.

"Now he's dead," I said after a moment. "You were his closest friend, so I know you'll want to come to his funeral this afternoon."

"I'd like to come."

"Well, come then."

The hair in his nostrils quivered slightly, and as he shook his head his eyes filled with tears.

"I can't do it — I can't get mixed up in it," he said.

"There's nothing to get mixed up in. It's all over now."

"When a man gets killed I never like to get mixed up in it in any way. I keep out. When I was a young man it was different — if a friend of mine died, no matter how, I stuck with them to the end. You may think that's sentimental, but I mean it — to the bitter end."

I saw that for some reason of his own he was determined not to come, so I stood up.

"Are you a college man?" he inquired suddenly.

For a moment I thought he was going to suggest a "gonnegtion②," but he only nodded and shook my hand.

"Let us learn to show our friendship for a man when he is alive and not after he is dead," he suggested. "After that my own rule is to let everyone alone."

When I left his office the sky had turned dark and I got back to West Egg in a drizzle. After changing my clothes I went next door and found Mr. Gatz walking up and down excitedly in the hall. His pride in his son and in his son's possessions was continually increasing and now he had something to show me.

"Jimmy sent me this picture." He took out his wallet with trembling fingers. "Look there."

It was a photograph of the house, cracked in the corners and dirty with many hands. He pointed out every detail to me eagerly. "Look there!" and then sought admiration from my eyes. He had shown it so often that I think it was more real to him now than the house itself.

"Jimmy sent it to me. I think it's a very pretty picture. It shows up well."

"Very well. Had you seen him lately?"

"He come out to see me two years ago and brought me the house I live in now. Of course we was broke up when he run off from home, but I see now there was a reason for it. He knew he had a big future in front of him. And ever since he made a success he was very generous with me."

……

Gatsby's house was still empty when I left — the grass on his lawn had grown as long as mine. One of the taxi drivers in the village never took a fare past the entrance gate without stopping for a minute and pointing inside; perhaps it was he who drove Daisy and Gatsby over to East Egg the night of the accident, and perhaps he had made a story about it all his own. I didn't want to hear it and I avoided him when I got off the train.

---

① World's Series transaction: 世界棒球赛的那场交易
② Gonnegtion: connection 联结处

I spent my Saturday nights in New York because those gleaming, dazzling parties of his were with me so vividly that I could still hear the music and the laughter, faint and incessant, from his garden, and the cars going up and down his drive. One night I did hear a material car① there, and saw its lights stop at his front steps. But I didn't investigate. Probably it was some final guest who had been away at the ends of the earth and didn't know that the party was over.

On the last night, with my truck packed and my car sold to the grocer, I went over and looked at that huge incoherent failure of a house once more. On the white steps an obscene word, scrawled by some boy with a piece of brick, stood out clearly in the moonlight, and I erased it, drawing my shoe raspingly along the stone. Then I wandered down to the beach and sprawled out on the sand.

Most of the big shore paces were closed now and there were hardly any lights except the shadowy, moving glow of a ferryboat across the Sound②. And as the moon rose higher the inessential houses began to melt away until gradually I became aware of the old island③ here that flowered once for Dutch sailors' eyes — a fresh, green breast of the new world. Its vanished trees, the trees that had made way for Gatsby's house, had once pandered in whispers to the last and greatest of all human dreams; for a transitory enchanted moment man must have held his breath in the presence of this continent, compelled into an aesthetic contemplation he neither understood nor desired, face to face for the last time in history with something commensurate to his capacity for wonder.

And as I sat there brooding on the old, unknown world, I thought of Gatsby's wonder when he first picked out the green light④ at the end of Daisy's dock. He had come a long way to this blue lawn, and his dream must have seemed so close that he could hardly fail to grasp it. He did not know that it was already behind him, somewhere back in that vast obscurity beyond the city, where the dark fields of the republic rolled on under the night.

Gatsby believed in the green light, the orgiastic future that year by year recedes before us. It eluded us then, but that's no matter — tomorrow we will run faster, stretch out our arms farther… And one fine morning —

So we beat on, boats against the current, borne back ceaselessly into the past.

Ⅲ. Notes.

1. *The Great Gatsby* tells the story of Jay Gatsby, a man who orders his life around one desire: to be reunited with Daisy Buchannan, the love he lost five years earlier. Gatsby's quest leads him from poverty to wealth, into the arms of his beloved, and eventually to death. This novel is a concentrated meditation on "the American dream," understood as the faith that anyone,

---

① a material car: a real car 小汽车
② Sound: Long Island Sound 长岛海峡
③ the old island: Long Island 长岛
④ the green light: 小说中最主要的意象之一，暗指 Gatsby 对光明和美好未来的向往

even of the most humble origins, can attain wealth and social standing in the United States through talent and individual initiative.

2. The part we have chosen is the last chapter of the book, in which the narrator, Nick, is left to organize Gatsby's funeral, but finds that few people cared for Gatsby. In the end, Nick comes to realize that greed and dishonesty have irrevocably corrupted both the "American Dream" and the dreams of individual Americans.

Ⅳ. Key Words (关键词).

The "American Dream": 美国梦。它是一种相信只要通过自己的不懈奋斗就能获得美好生活的理想。它表现了美国人自强不息和自给自足的乐观主义精神,是许多美国文学作品、电影和其他艺术形式所钟爱的主题。美国梦教育人们成功是来自于自己的勤奋工作、勇气和决心,而非依赖于特定的社会阶级和其他人的援助,并且任何人都有可能通过自己的努力去获得物质财富。因此,美国梦吸引了世界各地的人们来到美国去实现自己的财富梦想,这成为人们移居美国的主要原因。

The Jazz Age: "爵士乐时代"。它是由菲茨杰拉德杜撰出来的,指的是第一次世界大战结束到经济大萧条以前约十年的时间。在那个特殊时期,传统的新教理论已经土崩瓦解,享乐主义开始大行其道。用菲茨杰拉德自己的话来说,"这是一个奇迹的时代,一个艺术的时代,一个挥金如土的时代,也是一个充满嘲讽的时代。"

Satire: 讽刺。它是一种文学手法,通常以机智风趣的批评态度,对人类不良的或愚蠢的行为进行揭露或批判。严格地说,讽刺是一种俗称类型,常采用夸张或反讽等方式,以产生幽默效果为目的。

Ⅴ. Questions.

1. How is the setting, East Egg and West Egg related with the major theme of the novel?
2. What is the narrator's attitude towards Gatsby's story?
3. What caused Gatsby's tragedy? Would his dream become possible if he were not dead?

Lesson 22 Ernest Hemingway (1899—1961)

Ⅰ. **A Brief Review.**

Born on July 21, 1899 in Oak Park, Illinois, Hemingway attended the public school in Oak Park where he published his earliest stories and poems in the school newspaper. Upon his graduation in 1917, Hemingway became a reporter for *The Kansas City Star*. In WWI, Hemingway joined a volunteer ambulance unit and was wounded in the battlefield. Later he worked as a reporter for Canadian and American newspapers to visit Europe for reporting such events as the Greek Revolution.

In 1920, Hemingway went with his wife Hadley Richerdson to Paris to join the group of expatriate Americans there, and came to know Gertrude Stein, Sherwood Anderson, Ezra Pound, F. Scott Fitzgerald, and others who

图 22 Ernest Hemingway

were mostly better known than he was. With their help he published in 1925 one of his major short story collections, *In Our Time*. His experience with those English and American expatriates in Paris became the basis of his first important work, *The Sun Also Rises* (1926), in which a group of young foreigners were wounded both physically and emotionally by war, and were too knowledgeable, too self-aware to return to the simple life.

His second collection of short stories, *Men without Women* (1927), represents Hemingway at his most experimental, journalistic reporting techniques used in a fiction that was almost telegraphic in style and presentation, depending on direct description and dialogue with a minimum of narrator commentary and interpretation. His second novel, *A Farewell to Arms* (1929), set during the First World War, is about an American army officer, Frederick Henry, who deserts with a British nurse, Katherine Barkely, makes a "separate peace" which is shattered by Katherine's death in childbirth. The novel gained enormous critical and commercial success. His next important novel, *For Whom the Bell Tolls* (1940), is based on his experiences as a reporter during the civil war in Spain as the background. This is another novel in which he portrays a hero who lives with dignity and grace while playing an unwinnable game with a submissive heroine.

Hemingway's success in the 1920s made him a celebrity and gave him tremendous pressure in his later life, which made a new theme——that of the writer trying to preserve his talent against such threats as success, money, sex, and fame——entered his work in the mid-1930s, such as *The Snows of Kilimanjaro* (1936), and once again in a more allegorical manner in his novella, *The Old Man and the Sea* (1952), a story of an old fisherman's journey, his long and lonely struggle with a fish and the sea, and his victory in defeat.

Hemingway's legacy to American literature is his style: straightforward prose, spare dialogue, and the predilection for understatement are particularly effective in his short stories. His mastery of the art of narrative, most recently demonstrated in *The Old Man and the Sea*, and his influence on contemporary style won him the Nobel Prize for Literature in 1953. The number of followers of Hemingway style is enormous, and his work has remained more popular with a large audience than any other American writers of his era.

Ⅱ. Texts.

A Clean, Well-lighted Place

It was late and every one had left the café except an old man who sat in the shadow the leaves of the tree made against the electric light. In the daytime the street was dusty, but at night the dew settled the dust and the old man liked to sit late because he was deaf and now at night it was quiet and he felt the difference. The two waiters inside the café knew that the old man was a little drunk, and while he was a good client they knew that if he became too drunk he would leave without paying, so they kept watch on him.

"Last week he tried to commit suicide," one waiter said.

"Why?"

"He was in despair."

"What about?"

"Nothing."

"How do you know it was nothing?"

"He has plenty of money."

They sat together at a table that was close against the wall near the door of the café and looked at the terrace where the tables were all empty except where the old man sat in the shadow of the leaves of the tree that moved slightly in the wind. A girl and a soldier went by in the street. The street light shone on the brass number on his collar. The girl wore no head covering and hurried beside him.

"The guard will pick him up①," one waiter said.

"What does it matter if he gets what he's after?"

"He had better get off the street now. The guard will get him. They went by five minutes ago."

The old man sitting in the shadow rapped on his saucer with his glass. The younger waiter went over to him.

"What do you want?"

The old man looked at him. "Another brandy," he said.

---

① The guard will pick him up: (宵禁期间) 卫兵会将他抓起来的

"You will be drunk, " the waiter said. The old man looked at him. The waiter went away.

"He'll stay all night, " he said to his colleague. "I'm sleepy now. I never get into bed before three o'clock. He should have killed himself last week. "

The waiter took the brandy bottle and another saucer from the counter inside the café and marched out to the old man's table. He put down the saucer and poured the glass full of brandy.

"You should have killed yourself last week, " he said to the deaf man. The old man motioned with his finger. "A little more, " he said. The waiter poured on into the glass so that the brandy slopped over and ran down the stem into the top saucer of the pile. "Thank you, " the old man said. The waiter took the bottle back inside the café. He sat down at the table with his colleague again.

"He's drunk now, " he said.

"He's drunk every night. "

"What did he want to kill himself for?"

"How should I know. "

"How did he do it?"

"He hung himself with a rope. "

"Who cut him down?①"

"His niece. "

"Why did they do it?"

"Fear for his soul. ②"

"How much money has he got?"

"He's got plenty. "

"He must be eighty years old. "

"Anyway I should say he was eighty. "

"I wish he would go home. I never get to bed before three o'clock. What kind of hour is that to go to bed?"

"He stays up because he likes it. "

"He's lonely. I'm not lonely. I have a wife waiting in bed for me. "

"He had a wife once too. "

"A wife would be no good to him now. "

"You can't tell. He might be better with a wife. "

"His niece looks after him. You said she cut him down. "

"I know. "

"I wouldn't want to be that old. An old man is a nasty thing. "

"Not always. This old man is clean. He drinks without spilling. Even now, drunk. Look at him. "

---

① Who cut him down? 是谁把绳子剪断救下他的?
② 基督教认为自杀是一种罪,因此灵魂不能得救

"I don't want to look at him. I wish he would go home. He has no regard for those who must work."

The old man looked from his glass across the square, then over at the waiters.

"Another brandy," he said, pointing to his glass. The waiter who was in a hurry came over.

"Finished," he said, speaking with that omission of syntax stupid people employ when talking to drunken people or foreigners. "No more tonight. Close now."

"Another," said the old man.

"No. Finished." The waiter wiped the edge of the table with a towel and shook his head.

The old man stood up, slowly counted the saucers, took a leather coin purse from his pocket and paid for the drinks, leaving half a peseta① tip.

The waiter watched him go down the street, a very old man walking unsteadily but with dignity.

"Why didn't you let him stay and drink?" the unhurried waiter asked. They were putting up the shutters. "It is not half past two."

"I want to go home to bed.'

"What is an hour?"

"More to me than to him."

"An hour is the same."

"You talk like an old man yourself. He can buy a bottle and drink at home."

"It's not the same."

"No, it is not," agreed the waiter with a wife. He did not wish to be unjust. He was only in a hurry.

"And you? You have no fear of going home before your usual hour?"

"Are you trying to insult me?"

"No, hombre②, only to make a joke."

"No," the waiter who was in a hurry said, rising from pulling down the metal shutters. "I have confidence. I am all confidence."

"You have youth, confidence, and a job," the older waiter said. "You have everything."

"And what do you lack?"

"Everything but work."

"You have everything I have."

"No. I have never had confidence and I am not young."

"Come on. Stop talking nonsense and lock up."

"I am of those who like to stay late at the café," the old waiter said. "With all those who do not want to go to bed. With all those who need a light for the night."

"I want to go home and into bed."

---

① peseta: 比塞塔, 西班牙货币单位
② hombre: （西班牙文）男人, 老兄

"We are of two different kinds," the old waiter said. He was now dressed to go home. "It is not only a question of youth and confidence although those things are very beautiful. Each night I am reluctant to close up because there may be some one who needs the café."

"Hombre, there are bodegas open all night long."

"You do not understand. This is a clean and pleasant café. It is well lighted. The light is very good and also, now, there are shadows of the leaves."

"Good night," said the younger waiter.

"Good night," the other said. Turning off the electric light he continued the conversation with himself. It is the light of course but it is necessary that the place be clean and pleasant. You do not want music. Certainly you do not want music. Nor can you stand before a bar with dignity although that is all that is provided for these hours. What did he fear? It was not fear or dread. It was a nothing that he knew too well. It was all a nothing and a man was nothing too. It was only that and light was all it needed and a certain cleanness and order. Some lived in it and never felt it but he knew it all was nada① y② pues③ nada y nada y pues nada. Our nada who art in nada, nada be thy name thy kingdom nada thy will be nada in nada as it is in nada. Give us this nada our daily nada and nada us our nada as we nada our nadas and nada us not into nada but deliver us from nada; pues nada. Hail nothing full of nothing, nothing is with thee. ④ He smiled and stood before a bar with a shining steam pressure coffee machine.

"What's yours?" asked the barman.

"Nada."

"Otro loco mas,⑤" said the barman and turned away.

"A little cup," said the waiter.

The barman poured it for him.

"The light is very bright and pleasant but the bar is unpolished," the waiter said.

The barman looked at him but did not answer. It was too late at night for conversation.

"You want another copita⑥?" the barman asked.

"No, thank you," said the waiter and went out. He disliked bars and bodegas. A clean, well-lighted café was a very different thing. Now, without thinking further, he would go home to his room. He would lie in the bed and finally, with daylight, he would go to sleep. After all, he said to himself, it is probably only insomnia. Many must have it.

---

① nada:（西班牙文）虚无
② y:（西班牙文）所以,那么
③ pues:（西班牙文）既然,那么
④ Our nada who art...nothing is with thee: 这是一段模仿祷告词,其中动词和名词等实词都由"nada"一词取代,表示一切事物和行为都是虚无的
⑤ Otro loco mas:（西班牙文）又一个疯子
⑥ copita: 西班牙等地产的浅黄或深褐色葡萄酒

Ⅲ. Notes.

1. This exceptional minimalist short story centers around the conversation of two waiters in a comfortable, homey Spanish cafe. They are discussing one of the customers, a quiet, dignified old man who comes into the cafe every evening and runs up a tab which he is careful to pay before leaving for the night.

2. Hemingway manages to evoke the universal and timeless dichotomy between the young waiter, who, with his whole life ahead of him, is "all confidence" and the elderly patron of the cafe who realizes there is literally nothing to live for. The story's admirers argue that "A Clean, Well-Lighted Place" is a masterpiece by Hemingway because he captures in both form and content an irreducible and tragic essence of life.

Ⅳ. Key Words (关键词).

Iceberg theory: 冰山理论。它用来描述美国作家海明威的写作风格。海明威以"冰山"为喻,认为作者只应描写"冰山"露出水面的小部分,而沉浸水下的大部分应该通过文本的提示和比喻让读者去想象补充。

Hemingway Code Hero: 海明威式的"硬汉"形象。海明威作品中的主人公通常都是"硬汉"形象,以百折不挠的大丈夫气概来与世界斗争。海明威把"硬汉"定义为勇敢无畏、顽强不屈的形象。"硬汉"往往有某种身体或心理创伤,象征悲剧缺陷或性格中的软弱性,这一切要到人物表现出男子气概时才得以战胜。

The Lost Generation: 迷惘的一代。它指那些经历过第一次世界大战,二十世纪初期侨居在欧洲的作家。他们经历过一战后对传统的道德和价值观产生了怀疑,变得悲观失望。海明威就是"迷惘的一代"的代表人物。

Ⅴ. Questions.

1. How did Hemingway use the contrast between light and dark in the story to illustrate his theme?

2. What does the old man's deafness imply?

3. "Nothing," or the Spanish equivalent "nada," is the most important word in this short story, how is it related to "the Lost Generation"?

4. This is a story that clearly demonstrates the techniques of Hemingway's signature writing style. Try to show how economic Hemingway's writing is.

Lesson 23　Eugene Gladstone O'Neill (1888—1953)

Ⅰ. A Brief Review.

Born in a Broadway hotel room in Times Square on Oct. 16, 1888, Eugene Gladstone O'Neill was generally acclaimed as America's greatest dramatist. The difficult life his family led in hotel rooms, on trains and backstage made Eugene feel insecure in his early years and resulted in his mother's drug addiction. However, the theatre had a great impact on his literay career and the peasant Irish Catholicism of his parents aroused a high sense of religion that distinguished O'Ncill's plays. In 1906, O'Neill attended Princeton University for one year, after which he left school to begin what he later regarded as his real education in "life experience".

图 23　Eugene G. O'Neill

His first play *Bound East for Cardiff* appeared in the summer of 1916, set in a quiet fishing village of Provincetown, Mass., where a group of young writers and painters launched an experimental theatre. His first full-length play, *Beyond the Horizon,* produced in Broadway on Feb. 2, 1920, impressed the critics with its tragic realism and won for O'Neill the first of four Pulitzer prizes in drama. Important works of this period include *The Emperor Jones* (1920), in which, under stress, civilized veneer gives way to primitive fear; *The Hairy Ape* (1922), where a lower-class sailor, becoming aware of how he is viewed by the upper class, degenerates into what he is perceived to be; *Desire under the Elms* (1924), about family conflicts and desires; *The Great God Brown* (1926), exposing the inner life of a business magnate, and *Strange Interlude* (1928), similarly uncovering the hidden life of a beautiful woman.

Influenced by the popularization of certain ideas of Sigmund Freud, he began to experiment in making the hidden aspects of experience visible, which was applied to a cycle of nine autobiographical dramas about the O'Neills, whom he was to name the Tyrones. During the 30's and the 40's of the 20th century, O'Neill produced some major works including *Mourning Becomes Electra* (1931), a three-part drama based on the Greek dramatist Sophocles and *The Iceman Cometh* (1939), a study of man's need to cling to his hope for a better life. His autobiographical works of this period included: *A Touch of the Poet*, written between 1935 and 1942, centered on his father; *A Moon for the Misbegotten*, written in 1943, was about Jamie, his brother; *Long Day's Journey into Night*, written between 1939 and 1940, related the story of a four-member family with dramatic focus on his mother. However, none of these autobiographical plays came out in his lifetime. O'Neill's final years were spent in grim frustration and he died in a Boston hotel, as broken and tragic a figure as any he had created for the stage.

O'Neill was the first American dramatist to see the stage as a literary medium and the only American playwright ever to receive the Nobel Prize for Literature (1936). Through his efforts, the American theatre grew up during the 1920s, developing into a cultural medium that could take its place with the best in American fiction, painting, and music. Imbued with the tragic sense of life, O'Neill strove for a contemporary drama that had its roots in the most powerful of ancient Greek tragedies—a drama that could rise to the heights of Shakespeare.

II. Texts.

Long Day's Journey into Night

Act III

SCENE—*The same. It is around half past six in the evening. Dusk is gathering in the living room, an early dusk due to the fog which has rolled in from the Sound*① *and is like a white curtain drawn down outside the windows. From a lighthouse beyond the harbor's mouth, a foghorn is heard at regular intervals, moaning like a mournful whale in labor, and from the harbor itself, intermittently, comes the warning ringing of bells on yachts at anchor.*

The tray with the bottle of whiskey, glasses, and pitcher of ice water is on the table, as it was in the pre-luncheon scene of the previous act.

Mary and the second girl, Cathleen, are discovered. The latter is standing at left of table. She holds an empty whiskey glass in her hand as if she'd forgotten she had it. She shows the effects of drink. Her stupid, good-humored face wears a pleased and flattered simper.

Mary is paler than before and her eyes shine with unnatural brilliance. The strange detachment in her manner has intensified. She has hidden deeper within herself and found refuge and release in a dream where present reality is but an appearance to be accepted and dismissed unfeelingly—even with a hard cynicism—or entirely ignored. There is at times an uncanny gay, free youthfulness in her manner, as if in spirit she were released to become again, simply and without self-consciousness, the naïve, happy, chattering schoolgirl of her convent days. She wears the dress into which she had changed for her drive to town, a simple, fairly expensive affair, which would be extremely becoming if it were not for the careless, almost slovenly way she wears it. Her hair is no longer fastidiously in place. It has a slightly disheveled, lopsided look. She talks to Cathleen with a confiding familiarity, as if the second girl were an old, intimate friend. As the curtain rises, she is standing by the screen door looking out. A moan of the foghorn is heard.

MARY [*amused—girlishly*]   That foghorn! Isn't it awful, Cathleen?

CATHLEEN [*talks more familiarly than usual but never with intentional impertinence*

---

① Sound: 指下文中的 foghorn

because she sincerely likes her mistress] It is indeed, Ma'am. It's like a banshee①.

MARY [*Goes on as if she hadn't heard. In nearly all the following dialogue there is the feeling that she has Cathleen with her merely as an excuse to keep talking.*] I don't mind it tonight. Last night it drove me crazy. I lay awake worrying until I couldn't stand it any more.

CATHLEEN Bad cess to it.② I was scared out of my wits riding back from town. I thought that ugly monkey, Smythe, would drive us in a ditch or against a tree. You couldn't see your hand in front of you. I'm glad you had me sit in back with you, Ma'am. If I'd been in front with that monkey—He can't keep his dirty hands to himself. Give him half a chance and he's pinching me on the leg or you-know-where—asking your pardon, Ma'am, but it's true.

MARY [*dreamily*] It wasn't the fog I minded, Cathleen, I really love fog.

CATHLEEN They say it's good for the complexion.

MARY It hides you from the world and the world from you. You feel that everything has changed, and nothing is what it seemed to be. No one can find or touch you any more.

CATHLEEN I wouldn't care so much if Smythe was a fine, handsome man like some chauffeurs I've seen—I mean, if it was all in fun, for I'm a decent girl. But for a shriveled runt like Smythe—! I've told him, you must think I'm hard up that I'd notice a monkey like you. I've warned him, one day I'll give a clout that'll knock him into next week. And so I will!

MARY It's the foghorn I hate. It won't let you alone. It keeps reminding you, and warning you, and calling you back. [*She smiles strangely.*] But it can't tonight. It's just an ugly sound. It doesn't remind me of anything. [*She gives a teasing, girlish laugh.*] Except, perhaps, Mr. Tyrone's snores. I've always had such fun teasing him about it. He has snored ever since I can remember, especially when he's had too much to drink, and yet he's like a child, he hates to admit it. [*She laughs, coming to the table.*] Well, I suppose I snore at times, too, and I don't like to admit it. So I have no right to make fun of him, have I? [*She sits in the rocker at right of table.*]

CATHLEEN Ah, sure, everybody healthy snores. It's a sign of sanity, they say. [*then, worriedly*] What time is it, Ma'am? I ought to go back in the kitchen. The damp is in Bridget's rheumatism③ and she's like a raging devil. She'll bite my head off.

[*She puts her glass on the table and makes a movement toward the back parlor.*]

MARY [*with a flash of apprehension*] No, don't go, Cathleen. I don't want to be alone, yet.

CATHLEEN You won't be for long. The Master and the boys will be home soon.

MARY I doubt if they'll come back for dinner. They have too good an excuse to remain in the barrooms where they feel at home.

[*Cathleen stares at her, stupidly puzzled. Mary goes on smilingly.*]

---

① banshee: （英国古代民间传说中的）报丧女妖
② Bad cess to it: （爱尔兰语）真倒霉
③ rheumatism: 风湿病

Don't worry about Bridget. I'll tell her I kept you with me, and you can take a big drink of whiskey to her when you go. She won't mind then.

CATHLEEN [*grins—at her ease again*] No, Ma'am. That's the one thing can make her cheerful. She loves her drop.

MARY Have another drink yourself, if you wish, Cathleen.

CATHLEEN I don't know if I'd better, Ma'am. I can feel what I've had already. [*reaching for bottle*] Well, maybe one more won't harm. [*She pours a drink.*] Here's your good health, Ma'am. [*She drinks without bothering about a chaser.*]

MARY [*dreamily*] I really did have good health once, Cathleen. But that was long ago.

CATHLEEN [*worried again*] The Master's sure to notice what's gone from the bottle. He has the eye of a hawk for that.

MARY [*amusedly*] Oh, we'll play Jamie's trick on him. Just measure a few drinks of water and pour them in.

CATHLEEN [*does this—with a silly giggle*] God save me, it'll be half water. He'll know by the taste.

MARY [*indifferently*] No, by the time he comes home he'll be too drunk to tell the difference. He has such a good excuse, he believes, to drown his sorrows.

CATHLEEN [*philosophically*] Well, it's a good man's failing. I wouldn't give a trauneen① for a teetotaler. They've no high spirits. [*then, stupidly puzzled*] Good excuse? You mean Master Edmund. Ma'am? I can tell the Master is worried about him.

MARY [*stiffens defensively—but in a strange way the reaction has a mechanical quality, as if it did not penetrate to real emotion*] Don't be silly, Cathleen. Why should he be? A touch of grippe is nothing. And Mr. Tyrone never is worried about anything, except money and property and the fear he'll end his days in poverty. I mean, deeply worried. Because he cannot really understand anything else. [*She gives a little laugh of detached, affectionate amusement.*] My husband is a very peculiar man, Cathleen.

CATHLEEN [*vaguely resentful*] Well, he's a fine, handsome, kind gentleman just the same, Ma'am. Never mind his weakness.

MARY Oh, I don't mind. I've loved him dearly for thirty-six years. That proves I know he's lovable at heart and can't help being what he is, doesn't it?

CATHLEEN [*hazily reassured*] That's right. Ma'am. Love him dearly, for any fool can see he worships the ground you walk on. [*fighting the effect of her last drink and trying to be soberly conversational*] Speaking of acting, Ma'am, how is it you never went on the stage?

MARY [*resentfully*] I? What put that absurd notion in your head? I was brought up in a respectable home and educated in the best convent in the Middle West. Before I met Mr. Tyrone I hardly knew there was such a thing as a theater. I was a very pious girl. I even dreamed of becoming a null. I've never had the slightest desire to be an actress.

---

① trauneen: (爱尔兰语)很低面值的硬币

CATHLEEN [*bluntly*]　　Well, I can't imagine you a holy nun, Ma'am. Sure, you never darken the door of a church①. God forgive you.

MARY [*ignores this*]　　I've never felt at home in the theater. Even though Mr. Tyrone has made me go with him on all his tours, I've had little to do with the people in his company, or with anyone on the stage. Not that I have anything against them. They have always been kind to me, and I to them. But I've never felt at home with them. Their life is not my life. It has always stood between me and—[*she gets up—abruptly*] But let's not talk of old things that couldn't be helped. [*She goes to the porch door and stares out.*] How thick the fog is. I can't see the road. All the people in the world could pass by and I would never know. I wish it was always that way. It's getting dark already. It will soon be night, thank goodness. [*she turns back—vaguely*] It was kind of you to keep me company this afternoon, Cathleen. I would have been lonely driving uptown alone.

CATHLEEN　　Sure, wouldn't I rather ride in a fine automobile than stay here and listen to Bridget's lies about her relations? It was like a vacation. Ma'am. [*she pauses—then stupidly*] There was only one thing I didn't like.

MARY [*vaguely*]　　What was that, Cathleen?

CATHLEEN　　The way the man in the drugstore acted when I took in the prescription for you. [*indignantly*] The impidence② of him!

MARY [*with stubborn blankness*]　　What are you talking about? What drugstore? What prescription? [*then hastily, as Cathleen stares in stupid amazement*] Oh, of course, I'd forgotten. The medicine for the rheumatism in my hands.③ What did the man say? [*then with indifference*] Not that it matters, as long as he filled the prescription.

CATHLEEN　　It mattered to me, then! I'm not used to being treated like a thief. He gave me a long look and says insultingly, "Where did you get hold of this?" and I says, "It's none of your damned business, but if you must know, it's for the lady I work for, Mrs. Tyrone, who's sitting out in the automobile." That shut him up quick. He gave a look out at you and said, "Oh," and went to get the medicine.

MARY [*vaguely*]　　Yes, he knows me. [*She sits in the armchair at right rear of table. She adds in a calm, detached voice*] I have to take it because there is no other that can stop the pain—all the pain—I mean, in my hands. [*She raises her hands and regards them with melancholy sympathy. There is no tremor in them now.*] Poor hands! You'd never believe it, but they were once one of my good points, along with my hair and eyes, and I had a fine figure too. [*Her tone has become more and more far-off and dreamy.*] They were a musician's hands. I used to love the piano. I worked so hard at my music in the Convent—if you can call it work when you do something you love. Mother Elizabeth and my music teacher both said I had more talent than any

---

①　darken the door of a church: 光顾教堂
②　impidence: impudence
③　这里实际上是止痛用的吗啡

student they remembered. My father paid for special lessons. He spoiled me. He would do anything I asked. He would have sent me to Europe to study after I graduated from the Convent. I might have gone—if I hadn't fallen in love with Mr. Tyrone. Or I might have become a nun. I had two dreams. To be a nun, that was the more beautiful one. To become a concert pianist, that was the other. [*She pauses, regarding her hands fixedly. Cathleen blinks her eyes to fight off drowsiness and a tipsy feeling.*] I haven't touched a piano in so many years. I couldn't play with such crippled fingers, even if I wanted to. For a time after my marriage I tried to keep up my music. But it was hopeless. One-night stands, cheap hotels, dirty trains, leaving children, never having a home—[*she stares at her hands with fascinated disgust.*] See, Cathleen, how ugly they are! So maimed and crippled! You would think they'd been through some horrible accident! [*She gives a strange little laugh.*] So they have, come to think of it. [*She suddenly thrusts her hands behind her back.*] I won't look at them. They're worse than the foghorn for reminding me—[*then with defiant self-assurance*] But even they can't touch me now. [*She brings her hands from behind her back and deliberately stares at them—calmly*] They're far away. I see them, but the pain has gone.

CATHLEEN [*stupidly puzzled*] You've taken some of the medicine? It made you act funny, Ma'am. If I didn't know better, I'd think you'd a drop taken.

MARY [*dreamily*] It kills the pain. You go back until at last you are beyond its reach. Only the past when you were happy is real. ①[*She pauses—as if her words had been an evocation which called back happiness she changes in her whole manner and facial expression. She looks younger. There is a quality of an innocent convent girl about her, and she smiles shyly.*] If you think Mr. Tyrone is handsome now, Cathleen, you should have seen him when I first met him. He had the reputation of being one of the best looking men in the country. The girls in the Convent who had seen him act, or seen his photographs, used to rave about him. He was a great matinee idol then, you know. Women used to wait at the stage door just to see him come out. You can imagine how excited I was when my father wrote me he and James Tyrone had become friends, and that I was to meet him when I came home for Easter vacation. I showed the letter to all the girls, and how envious they were! My father took me to see him act first. It was a play about the French Revolution and the leading part was a nobleman. I couldn't take my eyes off him. I wept when he was thrown in prison—and then was so mad at myself because I was afraid my eyes and nose would be red. My father had said we'd go backstage to his dressing room right after the play, and so we did. [*She gives a little excited, shy laugh.*] I was so bashful all I could do was stammer and blush like a little fool. But he didn't seem to think I was a fool. I know he liked me the first moment we were introduced. [*coquettishly*] I guess my eyes and nose couldn't have been red, after all. I was really very pretty then, Cathleen. And he was handsomer than my wildest dream, in his make-up and his nobleman's costume that was so becoming to him. He was different from all ordinary men, like someone from another world. At the same time he was simple, and kind,

---

① 这里指服用吗啡以后忘记眼前的痛苦,沉浸在过去的欢乐幻觉中

and unassuming, not a bit stuck-up or vain. I fell in love right then. So did he, he told me afterwards. I forgot all about becoming a nun or a concert pianist. All I wanted was to be his wife. [*She pauses, staring before her with unnaturally bright, dreamy eyes, and a rapt, tender, girlish smile.*] Thirty-six years ago, but I can see it as clearly as if it were tonight! We've loved each other ever since. And in all those thirty-six years, there has never been a breath of scandal about him. I mean, with any other woman. Never since he met me. That has made me very happy. Cathleen. It has made me forgive so many other things.

……

Ⅲ. Notes.

1. Completed in 1940, *Long Day's Journey into the Night* is an autobiographical play Eugene O'Neill wrote. Because of the highly personal writing about his family, it was not to be released until 25 years after his death. It tells of the "Tyrones"—a fictional name for what is clearly the O'Neills: The youngest son (Edmond) is sent to a sanitarium to recover from tuberculosis; he despises his father for sending him; his mother is wrecked by narcotics; and his older brother by drink. In real-life these factors conspired to turn O'Neill into who he was—a tormented individual and a brilliant playwright.

2. In Act Ⅲ, the family is biding time waiting for dinner to be served. However, the process of having meals together breaks down over the course of the day. From the part we have chosen, we can see a more fully developed idea of Mary's desire for a home, and the wish to delve back into past memories.

Ⅳ. Key Words（关键词）.

tragedy: 悲剧。它是从古希腊悲剧传统中发展起来的,剧中人物往往受到命运的摆布,历经种种坎坷,最终以悲剧性的灾难为结局。在现代戏剧中,悲剧往往将社会的丑恶看作导致剧中人物毁灭的原因,例如莎剧《哈姆雷特》。

Expressionism: 印象主义。它出现在19世纪后期到20世纪初的文学艺术作品中,用来表达即时的瞬间印象,甚至是扭曲和夸张的情感。借助这种艺术风格,艺术家想描绘的并非客观现实,而是其对周围事物产生的主观情感和反应。他们通过歪曲、夸张、荒诞的手法增强艺术效果。奥尼尔的很多作品就带有印象派色彩。

Broadway Theatre: 百老汇剧院。它通常简称百老汇,在纽约市剧院区,以贯通曼哈顿区中心广场的一条大街命名,聚集了多家较大的剧院。在说英语国家中,百老汇剧院被认为是最高水准的商业剧院。

Ⅴ. Questions.

1. What dreams did Mary use to have before her marriage? How does she think of those dreams now?

2. Why did Mary start to use "the medicine" again?

3. How does O'Neill make use of stage directions in the play? How do they enlighten our

reading of the play?
4. How do drugs and alcohol function within the play?

Lesson 24 William Faulkner (1897—1962)

Ⅰ. A Brief Review.

Born in New Albany, Mississippi, William Faulkner was a Nobel-winning novelist and short story writer. Faulkner lived most of his life in Oxford in north-central Mississippi. About the age of 13, he began to write poetry. During the First World War, he joined the Royal Canadian Air Force and had basic training in Toronto. But the war was over before he could make his first solo flight. After the war he studied literature at the University of Mississippi but left there after a short time without taking a degree in 1920.

His first book, *The Marble Faun* (1924), a collection of poems, did not gain much recognition. His first novel, *Soldier's Pay* (1926), was centered on the return of a soldier,

图 24 William Faulkner

who was physically and psychologically disabled in WW I. The next novel was *Mosquitoes*, a satirical portrait of the Bohemian life, of artists and intellectuals, in New Orleans. During these years, Faulkner met and mingled with other literary figures and learned about the ideas of Sigmund Freud and the experimental writing of James Joyce. Faulkner's first masterwork was *The Sound and the Fury* (1929), which gained him recognition as a writer. The following work, *As I Lay Dying* (1930), a similar patchwork narrative, was also focused on a loss, the death of a mother. Though artistically creative, these works did not draw a very wide audience. Faulkner had to write and sell short stories to national magazines for extra money. He also wrote for the movies in Hollywood over the next 20 years to meet his financial needs. Besides scriptwriting, he continued to produce brilliant and inventive novels, such as *Light in August*, and *Absalom, Absalom!*.

In 1940, Faulkner published the first volume of the Snopes trilogy, *The Hamlet*, which was to be followed by two volumes, *The Town* (1957) and *The Mansion* (1959), all of them tracing the rise of the insidious Snopes family to positions of power and wealth in the community. Faulkner's national reputation received a boost in 1946 with the publication of *The Portable Faulkner*, edited by the critic Malcolm Cowley, which rescued him from near-oblivion. His anti-racist novel *Intruder in the Dust* (1948) won him the Nobel Prize in 1950. He died of a heart attack in 1962, which was partly brought by his heavy drinking.

Faulkner's legacy to American Literature lies in his invention of a host of characters typical of the historical growth and subsequent decadence of the South, his construction of the imaginary Yoknapatawpha County and its inhabitants, his creation of a saga of the Sartoris and Compson families, and the emergence of ruthless and brash newcomers, the Snopeses.

Ⅱ. Texts.

As I Lay Dying

Cora①

So I saved out the eggs and baked yesterday. The cakes turned out right well. We depend a lot on our chickens. They are good layers, what few we have left after the possums and such. Snakes too, in the summer. A snake will break up a hen-house quicker than anything. So after they were going to cost so much more than Mr Tull thought, and after I promised that the difference in the number of eggs would make it up, I had to be more careful than ever because it was on my final say-so we took them. We could have stocked cheaper chickens, but I gave my promise as Miss Lawington② said when she advised me to get a good breed, because Mr Tull himself admits that a good breed of cows or hogs pays in the long run. So when we lost so many of them we couldn't afford to use the eggs ourselves, because I could not have had Mr Tull chide me when it was on my say-so we took them. So when Miss Lawington told me about the cakes I thought that I could bake them and earn enough at one time to increase the net value of the flock the equivalent of two head. And that by saving the eggs out one at a time, even the eggs wouldn't be costing anything. And that week they laid so well that I not only saved out enough eggs above what we had engaged to sell, to bake the cakes with, I had saved enough so that the flour and the sugar and the stove wood would not be costing anything. So I baked yesterday, more careful than ever I baked in my life, and the cakes turned out right well. But when we got to town this morning Miss Lawington told me the lady had changed her mind and was not going to have the party after all.

"She ought to take those cakes anyway," Kate says.

"Well," I say, "I reckon she never had no use for them now."

"She ought to taken them," Kate says. "But those rich town ladies can change their minds. Poor folks cant."

Riches is nothing in the face of the Lord, for He can see into the heart. "Maybe I can sell them at the bazaar Saturday," I say. They turned out real well.

"You cant get two dollars a piece for them," Kate says.

"Well, it isn't like they cost me anything," I say. I saved them out and swapped a dozen of them for the sugar and flour. It isn"t like the cakes cost me anything, as Mr Tull himself realises that the eggs I saved were over and beyond what we had engaged to sell, so it was like we had found the eggs or they had been given to us.

"She ought to taken those cakes when she same as gave you her word," Kate says. The Lord can see into the heart. If it is His will that some folks has different ideas of honesty from other folks, it is not my place to question His decree.

---

① 这一部分是从 Cora 的角度叙述的。整个故事是从不同的十五个人物角度分别叙述的
② 福克纳在他另一部作品《村子》的初稿里也提到这位劳温顿小姐，说她是个到农村向大众示范宣讲农业技术的"县级示讲员"

"I reckon she never had any use for them," I say. They turned out real well, too.

The quilt is drawn up to her chin, hot as it is, with only her two hands and her face outside. She is propped on the pillow, with her head raised so she can see out the window, and we can hear him every time he takes up the adze or the saw. If we were deaf we could almost watch her face and hear him, see him. Her face is wasted away so that the bones draw just under the skin in white lines. Her eyes are like two candles when you watch them gutter down into the sockets of iron candle-sticks. But the eternal and the everlasting salvation and grace is not upon her.

"They turned out real nice," I say. "But not like the cakes Addie used to bake." You can see that girl's washing and ironing in the pillow-slip, if ironed it ever was. Maybe it will reveal her blindness to her, laying there at the mercy and the ministration of four men and a tom-boy girl.① "There's not a woman in this section could ever bake with Addie Bundren," I say. "First thing we know she'll be up and baking again, and then we wont have any sale for ours at all." Under the quilt she makes no more of a hump than a rail would, and the only way you can tell she is breathing is by the sound of the mattress shucks. Even the hair at her cheek does not move, even with that girl standing right over her, fanning her with the fan. While we watch she swaps the fan to the other hand without stopping it.

"Is she sleeping?" Kate whispers.

"She's just watching Cash yonder②," the girl says. We can hear the saw in the board. It sounds like snoring. Eula turns on the trunk and looks out the window. Her necklace looks real nice with her red hat. You wouldn't think it only cost twenty-five cents.

"She ought to taken those cakes," Kate says.

I could have used the money real well. But it's not like they cost me anything except the baking. I can tell him that anybody is likely to make a miscue, but it's not all of them that can get out of it without loss, I can tell him. It's not everybody can eat their mistakes, I can tell him.

Someone comes through the hall. It is Darl. He does not look in as he passes the door. Eula watches him as he goes on and passes from sight again toward the back. Her hand rises and touches her beads lightly, and then her hair. When she finds me watching her, her eyes go blank.

Darl

Pa and Vernon are sitting on the back porch. Pa is tilting snuff from the lid of his snuff-box into his lower lip, holding the lip outdrawn between thumb and finger. They look around as I cross the porch and dip the gourd into the water bucket and drink.

"Where's Jewel?" pa says. When I was a boy I first learned how much better water tastes when it has set a while in a cedar bucket. Warmish-cool, with a faint taste like the hot July wind in cedar trees smells. It has to set at least six hours, and be drunk from a gourd. Water should never be drunk from metal.

---

① tom-boy girl: 顽皮的、爱打闹闹的女孩
② yonder: 在那边,在远处

And at night it is better still. I used to lie on the pallet in the hall, waiting until I could hear them all asleep, so I could get up and go back to the bucket. It would be black, the shelf black, the still surface of the water a round orifice in nothingness, where before I stirred it awake with the dipper I could see maybe a star or two in the bucket, and maybe in the dipper a star or two before I drank. After that I was bigger, older. Then I would wait until they all went to sleep so I could lie with my shirt-tail up, hearing them asleep, feeling myself without touching myself, feeling the cool silence blowing upon my parts and wondering if Cash was yonder in the darkness doing it too, had been doing it perhaps for the last two years before I could have wanted to or could have.

Pa's feet are badly splayed①, his toes cramped and bent and warped, with no toenail at all on his little toes, from working so hard in the wet in homemade shoes when he was a boy. Beside his chair his brogans sit. They look as though they had been hacked with a blunt axe out of pig-iron. Vernon has been to town. I have never seen him go to town in overalls. His wife, they say. She taught school too, once.

I fling the dipper dregs to the ground and wipe my mouth on my sleeve. It is going to rain before morning. Maybe before dark. "Down to the barn," I say. "Harnessing the team."

Down there fooling with that horse. He will go on through the barn, into the pasture. The horse will not be in sight: he is up there among the pine seedlings, in the cool. Jewel whistles, once and shrill. The horse snorts, then Jewel sees him, glinting for a gaudy instant among the blue shadows. Jewel whistles again; the horse comes dropping down the slope, stiff-legged, his ears cocking and flicking, his mismatched eyes rolling, and fetches up twenty feet away, broadside on, watching Jewel over his shoulder in an attitude kittenish② and alert.

"Come here, sir," Jewel says. He moves. Moving that quick his coat, bunching, tongues swirling like so many flames. With tossing mane and tail and rolling eye the horse makes another short curvetting rush and stops again, feet bunched, watching Jewel. Jewel walks steadily toward him, his hands at his sides. Save for Jewel's legs they are like two figures carved for a tableau savage in the sun.

When Jewel can almost touch him, the horse stands on his hind legs and slashes down at Jewel. Then Jewel is enclosed by a glittering maze of hooves as by an illusion of wings; among them, beneath the upreared chest, he moves with the flashing limberness of a snake. For an instant before the jerk comes onto his arms he sees his whole body earth-free, horizontal, whipping snake-limber, until he finds the horse's nostrils and touches earth again. Then they are rigid, motionless, terrific, the horse back-thrust on stiffened, quivering legs, with lowered head; Jewel with dug heels, shutting off the horse's wind with one hand, with the other patting the horse's neck in short strokes myriad and caressing, cursing the horse with obscene ferocity.

They stand in rigid terrific hiatus, the horse trembling and groaning. Then Jewel is on the horse's back. He flows upward in a stooping swirl like the lash of a whip, his body in midair

---

① slay-footed: 八字脚的,外翻足的
② kittenish: 小猫般淘气的;顽皮的

shaped to the horse. For another moment the horse stands spraddled, with lowered head, before it bursts into motion. They descend the hill in a series of spine-jolting jumps, Jewel high, leech-like on the withers, to the fence where the horse bunches to a scuttering halt again.

"Well," Jewel says, "you can quit now, if you got a-plenty."

Inside the barn Jewel slides running to the ground before the horse stops. The horse enters the stall, Jewel following. Without looking back the horse kicks at him, slamming a single hoof into the wall with a pistol-like report. Jewel kicks him in the stomach; the horse arches his neck back, crop-toothed; Jewel strikes him across the face with his fist and slides on to the trough and mounts upon it. Clinging to the hay-rack he lowers his head and peers out across the stall tops and through the doorway. The path is empty; from here he cannot even hear Cash sawing. He reaches up and drags down hay in hurried armsful and crams it into the rack.

"Eat," he says. "Get the goddamn stuff out of sight while you got a chance, you pussel-gutted① bastard. You sweet son of a bitch," he says.

*Jewel*②

It's because he stays out there, right under the window, hammering and sawing on that goddamn box. Where she's got to see him. Where every breath she draws is full of his knocking and sawing where she can see him saying See. See what a good one I am making for you. I told him to go somewhere else. I said Good God do you want to see her in it. It's like when he was a little boy and she says if she had some fertilizer she would try to raise some flowers and he taken the bread pan and brought it back from the barn full of dung.

And now them others sitting there, like buzzards. Waiting, fanning themselves. Because I said If you wouldn't keep on sawing and nailing at it until a man cant sleep even and her hands laying on the quilt like two of them roots dug up and tried to wash and you couldn't get them clean. I can see the fan and Dewey Dell's arm. I said if you'd just let her alone. Sawing and knocking, and keeping the air always moving so fast on her face that when you're tired you cant breathe it, and that goddamn adze going One lick less. One lick less. One lick less until everybody that passes in the road will have to stop and see it and say what a fine carpenter he is. If it had just been me when Cash fell off of that church and if it had just been me when pa laid sick with that load of wood fell on him, it would not be happening with every bastard in the country coming in to stare at her because if there is a God what the hell is He for. It would just be me and her on a high hill and me rolling the rocks down the hill at their faces, picking them up and throwing them down the hill faces and teeth and all by God until she was quiet and not that goddamn adze going One lick less. One lick less and we could be quiet.

---

① pussel-gutted: 肥胖的
② Jewel 是将要死去的 Addie Bundren 的非婚生儿子,他的父亲是当地一位名为 Whitfield 的牧师

Ⅲ. **Notes.**

1. *As I Lay Dying* focuses on the death of Addie Bundren, the wife of Anse Bundren, a poor Mississippi farmer and her family's commitment to honoring the matriarch's wish to be laid to rest among her relatives and friends in Jefferson, Mississippi, the town from which she originates.

2. The story is seen through eyes of fifteen different characters. The excerpt here is the first four sections out of the total fifty-nine, from which we can see a dying woman lying on the bed told from three different narrative perspectives.

Ⅳ. **Key Words（关键词）.**

interior monologue: 内心独白。它指小说和诗歌中表达的人物内心想法、记忆和印象等等，使读者直接听到人物内心思想活动的表达，而不是通过作者的客观叙述。它广泛用于现代诗歌和小说，尤其是詹姆斯·乔伊斯、威廉·福克纳和其他作家的意识流风格的作品中。

Stream-of-consciousness: 意识流。它是一种叙事技巧，产生无数连续不断的印象，有视觉的、听觉的、触觉的、联想的和潜意识的。这些印象影响个人的意识。作家可以把似乎不连贯的思想片段、不合语法的句子结构组合在一起，通过自由联想来达到揭示人物心理真实活动的目的。在现代主义运动中，意识流小说也是一个重要的文学流派。

Southern Renaissance: 南方文艺复兴。它指20世纪20年代到30年代美国南方文学的复兴，其代表人物有威廉·福克纳、凯瑟琳·波特和田纳西·威廉斯等人。它主要涉及南方保守的地域文化，注重描写乡村生活，关注种族矛盾和乡村衰败等重大社会问题。南方文艺复兴的代表作家常常运用现代叙事技巧，如意识流和其它叙事技巧。

Ⅴ. **Questions.**

1. The novel begins as Addie Bundren's sons work for her dying wishes. Her eldest son, Cash, is perpetually working on her coffin, sawing outside for everyone to see. What does this show?

2. What kind of situation is the family in? Try to illustrate.

3. What kind of person is Cora according to the part you have read?

4. Is Faulkner's writing style different from those we have read before?

Part Four

American Poetry in the 20th Century
第四部 20世纪美国诗歌

美国诗歌具有悠久的历史,但20世纪的美国诗歌却经历了曲折的发展过程,即从世纪初现代诗歌的勃兴、二战后诗歌的标新立异、再到世纪末诗歌创作的雅俗并举等不同的发展阶段,其中还出现了几位具有世界影响力的重要诗人。美国早期诗歌包含了两个源远流长的传统,即本土印第安民间歌谣和殖民地宗教诗歌等诗歌传统,以后经过惠特曼和狄金森等作家的努力,美国诗歌形成了自身的民族文学风格。美国诗歌风格既有浪漫主义的激扬蹈厉,也有现实主义的直面人生,还有超验主义的清新隽永。20世纪初,《诗刊》(1912)的出版标志了美国现代诗歌蓬勃发展的开端,从那时起直到二战结束,美国诗人中出现了几位现代主义的诗歌大师,如意象派代表诗人庞德和象征主义诗人T. S.艾略特等人,而弗罗斯特(1874—1963)、斯蒂文斯(1879—1955)、玛丽安·摩尔(1887—1972)和卡洛斯·威廉斯(1883—1963)等诗人的创作也为美国诗坛的繁荣做出了极大的贡献。二战以后,一些著名诗人仍然吟咏不已,更多的年轻诗人却以文化反叛的心态在诗歌舞台上争奇斗艳,少数族裔诗人进一步崭露头角。20世纪50年代,"垮掉派"诗人如艾伦·金斯伯格(1926—1997)等推出了极为叛逆的《嚎叫》等诗作,为美国文学和当代诗坛带来了狂飙新声。20世纪中期出现的一些诗歌流派如"黑山派"、"纽约派"和"中西部文艺复兴派"等在二战后也转化为不同的创作倾向,而战后出现的"自由派"和"新惠特曼派"等也和"垮掉派"等当代诗歌流派一样,其中的不少作品艺术标新有余,激情表达充沛,但思想深度有限。尽管如此,20世纪的美国诗歌创作仍然做到了有声有色、佳作不断。

庞德(1885—1972)是美国现代诗歌的奠基者,也是西方现代主义文学的重要代表。他曾经长居欧洲,在那里受到了现代主义思潮和东方文学如中国古典诗歌的影响,认为"意象"是诗人情感和思绪结合的瞬间传达。1914年,他出版了《意象派诗选》,推重自己的意象派诗歌原则。从1917年开始,他在《诗刊》等杂志上陆续发表了题为《诗篇》的意象派诗歌,直到1969年共发表了一百多首,内容涵盖天上地下,东方西方。庞德提倡的"意象派"诗歌创作不仅对美国诗坛,而且对世界文坛都产生了十分深远的影响。20世纪上半叶的另一位重要诗人是罗伯特·弗罗斯特(1874—1963),他少年时生活在美国东部乡村,因此对田园景观感触颇深。他的短诗《雪夜驻足林边》韵律整齐、感情真挚、意境深远,是美国诗歌的名篇。T. S.艾略特(1888—1965)虽然后来移居英国,但是他的诗作饱含人生哲理,表现技巧奇特,是美国现代主义诗歌的一座里程碑。例如,他的长诗《荒原》(1922)承接了西方人文思想的主题,却充满了人世幻灭的意象,成为西方现代主义诗歌的标志性作品。

20世纪美国诗歌还包括了黑人作家如兰斯顿·休斯的开创性作品以及对黑人大众影响很大的当代女诗人玛雅·安吉洛的诗歌创作。前者运用了爵士乐的节奏和黑人民歌的因素,后者则抒发了黑人的战斗精神和传扬非洲古老文化,正如前者在自己诗歌中所吟唱的:"我的灵魂像河流一样深沉。"他们的诗歌在广大读者中传唱不已,历久弥新。美国诗歌虽然在20世纪经历了高峰和低谷的起伏,但是,一些执着的诗人还是一如既往地对诗歌创作倾注了心血。卡洛斯·威廉斯就是长期进行诗歌创作的代表性人物。他的诗集《气质》(1913)带有意象派的特征,而他后来创作的诗作《佩特生》(1946—1958)却杂糅了各种写作文体,在五卷之巨的诗篇中全面表现了他对美国风土人情的热爱和留恋。在美国诗人中,像卡洛斯·威廉斯这样注意艺术创新的作家还有爱德华·卡明斯(1894—1962)等人。卡明斯的诗歌特别注重形式创新,甚至在诗行排列结构和标点符号运用上也表现了独特的风格。另一位诗人哈特·克莱恩(1899—1932)则对美国都市景观进行了描述,以奇特的想象来回穿梭在城市和田园之间,其诗歌带有相当的写实和抒情结合的特征。

20世纪50年代以后,美国社会的政治运动和文化思潮风起云涌,激进思想影响了许多年轻的诗人和作家,一批带有强烈反叛精神的诗歌也出现在美国文坛上。同时,美国社会的大众传媒和电子音像制品等对于文学创作形成了极大的冲击,许多诗人竭力在诗歌形式上找到突破口。在这方面,诗人艾伦·金斯伯格是一位典型的代表。他在长诗《嚎叫》(1956)对于美国社会进行了激烈的批判,例如诗中写道:"我见到这一代最出色的头脑也毁于疯狂,饿着肚裸着身大发歇斯底里。"这真实地传达了当时的社会风气和文化氛围,其文体形式也显示了令人瞠目的语言创新。"垮掉派"诗人中还有加里·斯奈德(1930—)等人,其诗歌创作受到东方文化的影响,表现了较深的哲理思考。从诗风传承上来看,金斯伯格的诗歌充满了与传统决裂的粗犷激情,而罗伯特·洛威尔(1917—1977)的诗歌则发挥了承上启下的作用,把传统诗风和实验技巧结合在一起,例如他的自白体诗《人生探寻》(1959)等等。二战后的其他诗人还包括极具个性的女诗人西尔维娅·普拉斯(1932—1963)和伊丽莎白·毕晓普(1911—1979)。前者的诗集《爱丽尔》(1965)借鉴了通俗文学的技巧,表达了女性的自我意识和尊严;后者的诗歌继承了狄金森的诗风,在对自然万物的体察中表现了个人的自由想象空间。在当代美国诗歌的众多流派中,"纽约派"诗人的诗歌创作值得人们注意,因为他们的诗歌不但表现了艺术技巧上的先锋性,而且在思想主题上也带有自我反思的意味。总之,二战以后的美国诗歌成就是卓越的,其中新人辈出,流派纷呈,对美国文学发展作出了很大的贡献。

Lesson 25　Ezra Pound (1885—1972)

Ⅰ. **A Brief Review.**

Born in Idaho and raised in Pennsylvania, Ezra Pound was an American expatriate, poet, musician and critic. Pound attended Hamilton College and the University of Pennsylvania, where he studied various languages. In 1908 he sailed for Europe, where he became a dominant figure in Anglo-American verse, helping promote writers such as William Butler Yeats, James Joyce, Ernest Hemingway, Robert Frost, D. H. Lawrence, and T. S. Eliot. Pound was also largely responsible for the appearance of Imagism and Vorticism, which were deeply rooted in the ideogrammatic method he had developed through his study of Chinese and Japanese literature and arts. Works connected with these two movements were published in his Vorticist magazine BLAST and his editorial work with literary magazines Egoist and

图 25　Ezra Pound

Poetry. After World War I, Pound published two of his most important poems, "Homage to Sextus Propertius" (1919) and "Hugh Selwyn Mauberley" (1920). He also began publishing *The Cantos*, most of which would be written between 1915 and 1962. *The Cantos* consists of a long, incomplete poem in 120 sections, each of which is referred to as a canto (Italian for song). The poem is dense and abstract with no single narrative or narrator, resembling more a collage of disparate but thematically related fragments.

With the onset of the Great Depression, Pound increasingly pursued his interest in history and economics, became obsessed with monetary reform, and declared his admiration for Benito Mussolini. In World War II he made pro-fascist radio broadcasts and was detained by U. S. forces for treason in 1945. He was initially held at Pisa, where he wrote *The Pisan Cantos* (1948, Bollingen Prize), and subsequently held in an American mental hospital until 1958, when he returned to Italy. Pound died on November 1, 1972 in Venice's Civil Hospital from an intestinal blockage.

Despite the vicissitudes of public opinion, Pound secures an important position in English literature as the first poet to successfully employ free verse in extended compositions. Almost every 'experimental' poet in English since the early twentieth century has been considered to be in his debt. The vital role he played in the modernist movement is impossible to be ignored. Pound received various appraisals over the years, ranging from the genius of his age to an egocentric madman. In all, Pound's genius is undeniable, and although at times the ferocity of his inquisitiveness led him into "wrecks and errors", he remains one of the most important figures in

American literature.

II. Texts.

Portrait d'une Femme①

Your mind and you are our Sargasso Sea②,
London has swept about you this score years
And bright ships left you this or that in fee:
Ideas, old gossip, oddments of all things,
Strange spars of knowledge and dimmed wares of price.
Great minds have sought you—lacking someone else.
You have been second always. Tragical?
No. You preferred it to the usual thing:
One dull man, dulling and uxorious,
One average mind—with one thought less, each year.
Oh, you are patient, I have seen you sit
Hours, where something might have floated up.
And now you pay one. Yes, you richly pay.
You are a person of some interest, one comes to you
And takes strange gain away:
Trophies fished up; some curious suggestion;
Fact that leads nowhere; and a tale or two,
Pregnant with mandrakes③, or with something else
That might prove useful and yet never proves,
That never fits a corner or shows use,
Or finds its hour upon the loom of days:
The tarnished, gaudy, wonderful old work;
Idols and ambergris and rare inlays,
These are your riches, your great store; and yet
For all this sea-hoard of deciduous things,
Strange woods half sodden, and new brighter stuff:
In the slow float of differing light and deep,
No! there is nothing! In the whole and all,
Nothing that's quite your own.

---

① Portrait d'une Femme:（法语）指贵妇画像
② Sargasso Sea: 指北大西洋的一片海域,航船到此会行动缓慢
③ Mandrakes: 曼德拉草,传说中具有魔力的植物,碰触后会蜷缩,据信可以助孕

Yet this is you.

A Pact

I make a pact with you, Walt Whitman—
I have detested you long enough.
I come to you as a grown child
Who has had a pig-headed father;
I am old enough now to make friends.
It was you that broke the new wood,
Now is a time for carving.
We have one sap and one root—
Let there be commerce between us.

In a Station of the Metro①

The apparition of these faces in the crowd;
Petals on a wet, black bough.

Ⅲ. Notes.

1. Opinion varies on the style of Pound's poetry. Critics generally agree that he was a strong lyricist, as particularly evident in his early poetry. He drew on literature varying from medieval and ancient Chinese poetry to contemporary literature. Pound wanted his poetry to represent an "objective presentation of material which he believed could stand on its own" without use of symbolism or romanticism. It was in the Chinese writing system that he found what he most closely wanted. In his view, imagism was a form of minimalism, represented by his two-line poem "In a Station of the Metro".

2. As a translator, Pound was a pioneer with a great gift of language and an incisive intelligence. Pound did much to introduce Provencal and Chinese poetry, the Noh, Anglo-Saxon poetry and the Confucian classics to Western readers. He also translated and championed Greek and Latin classics and helped keep these alive for poets at a time when classical education was in decline.

Ⅳ. Key Words (关键词).

Pound and Imagism: 庞德和意象派。庞德是 20 世纪初意象派诗歌的奠基人,他是英美诗歌界在现代主义运动中一位重要的诗人。庞德提倡诗歌应遵循意象的准确性,使用清晰精准的语言,强调回归到比较古典的风格,主张尝试非传统的诗歌格式。庞德以及他的

---

① a Station of the Metro: 这里指巴黎的一处地铁站

跟随者认为应由意象产生情感,而不是作者告诉读者应该有何种感情。

意象主义三点宣言:1913 年休姆、庞德和弗林特等在伦敦发表意象主义三点宣言,要求直接表现主客观事物,删除一切无助于"表现"的词语,以口语节奏代替传统格律。庞德曾把"意象"称为"一刹那间思想和感情的复合体"。

Ⅴ. **Questions.**

1. Can you give a brief interpretation to the image of the lady in "Portrait d'une Femme"?
2. Why did Pound compare himself to a grown child before Walt Whitman in "A Pact"?
3. What do "petals" and "bough" stand for in "In a Station of the Metro"?

Lesson 26 Robert Frost (1874—1963)

Ⅰ. **A Brief Review.**

Born in 1874 in San Francisco, California, Robert Frost was regarded as one of American most notable 20th-century poets. After his study at Dartmouth College and Harvard University, Robert Frost worked on his farm and then moved to England, where he started his literary career at the age of 38. He published his first collections, *A Boy's Will* (1913) and *North of Boston* (1914), which immediately earned his reputation as a successful poet. At the outbreak of war, he returned to the United States of America and lived in New Hampshire where he continued to devote himself to writing poetry. He used colloquial language, familiar rhythms, and common symbols to express both its pastoral ideals and its dark complexities. His collections during this period include *New Hampshire* (1923, Pulitzer Prize), *Collected Poems* (1930, Pulitzer Prize), *A Further Range* (1936, Pulitzer

图 26 Robert Frost

Prize), and *A Witness Tree* (1942, Pulitzer Prize). Robert Frost was highly figured as a poet who frequently employed realistic depictions of rural life in New England of the early twentieth century.

To some extent, he was called the spokesman of rural New England. At the age of 86, Robert Frost spoke and performed a reading of his poetry at the inauguration of President John F. Kennedy on January 20, 1961. Two years later, this outstanding poet died in Boston of complications from prostate surgery. He was unique among American poets of the 20th century in simultaneously achieving wide popularity and deep critical admiration. Many of his poems, including "Stopping by Woods on a Snowy Evening", "Birches", "The Death of the Hired Man", "Dust of Snow", "Fire and Ice", and "Home Burial", are widely anthologized. Robert Frost was an intentionally American and traditional poet in an age of internationalized and experimental art. His work led back to aspects of Thomas Hardy, Emily Dickinson, Ralph Waldo Emerson, James Russell Lowell, and to characteristics of William Wordsworth.

Most readers responded readily to Frost's poetry because it was sonorous and presented a sense of despair, of endurance, of failure—of life as many readers had experienced it. It played by poetic rules that rhyme, rhythm, stanza organization reinforced meaning with some key symbols that expressed more than the literal sense of the poem.

Ⅱ. Texts.

Stopping by Woods on a Snowy Evening

Whose woods these are I think I know.
His house is in the village though;
He will not see me stopping here
To watch his woods fill up with snow.

My little horse must think it queer①
To stop without a farmhouse near
Between the woods and frozen lake
The darkest evening of the year.

He gives his harness② bells a shake
To ask if there is some mistake.
The only other sound's the sweep
Of easy wind and downy flake.

The woods are lovely, dark, and deep.
But I have promises to keep,
And miles to go before I sleep,
And miles to go before I sleep.

A Boundless Moment

He halted in the wind, and—what was that
Far in the maples, pale, but not a ghost?
He stood there bringing March against his thought,
And yet too ready to believe the most.

"Oh, that's the Paradise-in-Bloom," I said;
And truly it was fair enough for flowers
Had we but in us to assume in March

---

① queer: 奇怪的,奇异的;古怪的,异常的
② harness: 马具,轭具

Such white luxuriance① of May for ours.
We stood a moment so, in a strange world,
Myself as one his own pretense deceives;
And then I said the truth (and we moved on).
A young beech② clinging to its last year's leaves.

Spring Pools

These pools that, though in forests, still reflect
The total sky almost without defect,
And like the flowers beside them, chill and shiver③,
Will like the flowers beside them soon be gone,
And yet not out by any brook or river,
But up by roots to bring dark foliage④ on.

The trees that have it in their pent-up⑤ buds
To darken nature and be summer woods—
Let them think twice before they use their powers
To blot out⑥ and drink up and sweep away
These flowery waters and these watery flowers
From snow that melted only yesterday.

Ⅲ. **Notes.**

1. "Stopping by Woods on a Snowy Evening", a poem full of imagery and personification, is published in 1923 in Robert Frost's New Hampshire volume. He wrote the new poem "about the snowy evening and the little horse as if I'd had a hallucination" in just "a few minutes without strain." The poem is written in iambic tetrameter in the Rubaiyat stanza created by Edward Fitzgerald. As a whole, the rhyme scheme of the poem is AABA-BBCB-CCDC-DDDD.

2. In the poem "A Boundless Moment", Frost expresses that the present moment is the unbound moment, that is to say, it is a moment of infinite beauty. However, many people often prefer to mix the past experience with the present time, which mostly will result in unforeseen tragedies. The truth is that this year's blossom doesn't need last year's leaves, so people do not

---

① luxuriance: (植物)茂盛的;郁郁葱葱的
② beech:【植】山毛榉
③ shiver: (因寒冷、害怕等)颤抖,哆嗦
④ foliage: 植物的叶子(总称);叶子及梗和枝
⑤ pent-up: 被禁锢的,被压抑的,被抑制的
⑥ blot out: 覆盖,遮住;毁灭

have to cling to the past and should pay more attention to the present.

3. The poem "Spring Pools" is an expression of Robert Frost's feelings towards the quickly passing season of Spring. Meanwhile, life's value doesn't depend on the life-span, but on the contribution to the world. With the poetic devices employed by Frost such as personification, repetition and similes, it is much easier for the readers to understand, appreciate and associate it with other meanings. It seems that this poem reflects life in a profound way.

Ⅳ. Key Words（关键词）.

Iambic: 抑扬格诗体。它是迄今英语诗歌中最常见的音步，从而也被称为最自然的韵律，即一个弱读音节后跟一个重读音节。用这种音步写成的诗行，其节奏鲜明而又持续平缓、畅如流水，更适于表现田园风光恬静素淡的美，这是弗罗斯特在几个诗歌传统音步韵律中最偏爱的一种。

Images of life: 生命意象。在弗罗斯特的诗中，经常会出现大量的关于大自然的意象，这些不起眼的小东西朴实无华而感情含蓄，充满了象征意义，传达了发人深省的人生启示，咏唱出一曲生命的赞歌。弗罗斯特善于运用眼前看似平淡无奇的事物去表达一个深刻的人生哲理，这些看似简单的诗歌往往显现自然与社会、理想与现实的双重关注。

Pastoral: 牧歌。弗罗斯特对古希腊和古拉丁语作家，尤其是忒奥克里托斯和维吉尔的研究，使他打下了写作牧歌的基础，他采用通俗上口的语言、人们熟知的韵律、日常生活中常见的比喻和象征手法，描写新英格兰地区宁静乡村的道德风尚。然而，他对大自然的描写常常蕴涵深刻的、象征性的、甚至是形而上学的意义。

Ⅴ. Questions.

1. In "Stopping by Woods on a Snowy Evening", what tempts the speaker to stay?
2. What does the poet imply to repeat "And miles to go before I sleep"?
3. What is the main theme of the poem "A Boundless Moment"?
4. In the poem "Spring Pools", what is the relationship between the trees and the pools?

Lesson 27　Langston Hughes (1902—1967)

I. A Brief Review.

Born in Joplin, Missouri in 1902, Langston Hughes was an American poet, novelist, playwright, and columnist. His parents separated shortly after his birth, Langston was reared in Lawrence, Kansas, by his grandmother Mary Langston in poverty and loneliness. To battle against a sense of desolation fostered by parental neglect, Hughes sought comfort and company in the wonderful world of books.

图 27　Langston Hughes

While in high school in Cleveland, Ohio, Hughes published his first poem. By the time Hughes enrolled at Columbia University in 1921, he had already started his literary career with his poem "*The Negro Speaks of Rivers*" in the *Crisis*, edited by W. E. B. Du Bois. However, Hughes was unhappy in Columbia. He left after one year and spent the next three years in a succession of menial jobs. He also traveled abroad, working on a freighter down the west coast of Africa and living for several months in Paris before returning to the United States late in 1924. By this time, he was well known in African American literary circles as a gifted young poet, pioneering in the fusion of traditional verse with black artistic forms, especially blues and jazz. He was a leader in the Harlem Renaissance of the twenties and thirties, publishing two verse collections, *The Weary Blues* (1926) and *Fine Clothes to the Jew* (1927), as well as a novel *Not without Laughter* (1930) and an embittered short-story collection *The Ways of White Folks* (1934). With the onset of the depression, Hughes became disillusioned with his wealthy patron, and involved in socialism in the 1930s.

Around 1939, Hughes moved away from the political Left, as the apolitical tone of his autobiography *The Big Sea* (1940) suggested. During the war he supported the Allies with patriotic songs, sketches, and a verse collection, *Shakespeare in Harlem* (1942). However, he continued to vigorously attack racial segregation, especially in his column in the black weekly *Chicago Defender*. In 1947, with Kurt Weill and Elmer Rice on the Broadway opera *Street Scene*, Hughes achieved a major critical success. After that he also continued his work in the theater, pioneering in the gospel musical play.

During his literary career Hughes was widely recognized as the representative of African-American writers and perhaps the most original of black poets, who vividly demonstrated the breadth and depth of his understanding of the American society. What made him outstanding was the deliberate saturation of his work in the primary expressive forms of black mass culture as well as the typical life experiences of African-Americans. In many ways, his art was firmly rooted in race pride and race feeling even though he cherished his freedom as an artist.

Ⅱ. Texts.

The Negro Speaks of Rivers

I've known river:
I've known rivers ancient as the world and older than the
flow of human blood in human veins.

My soul has grown deep like the rivers.

I bathed in the Euphrates① when dawns were young.
I built my hut near the Congo② and it lulled③ me to sleep.
I looked upon the Nile and raised the pyramids above it.
I heard the singing of the Mississippi when Abe Lincoln
went down to New Orleans, and I've seen its muddy
bosom turn all golden in the sunset.

I've known rivers:
Ancient, dusky rivers.

My soul has grown deep like the rivers.

The Weary Blues

Droning④ a drowsy⑤ syncopated⑥ tune,
Rocking back and forth to a mellow⑦ croon⑧,
I heard a Negro play.
Down on Lenox Avenue⑨ the other night

---

① Euphrates: 幼发拉底河
② Congo: 刚果
③ lull: 抚慰，哄
④ drone: （以低沉、单调的声调）谈，说，唱
⑤ drowsy: 欲睡的，半睡的，使人昏昏欲睡的
⑥ syncopate: （音乐的）切分
⑦ mellow: （颜色或声音）柔和的，丰富的
⑧ croon: 低声吟唱
⑨ Lenox Avenue: is a main street in Harlem

By the pale dull pallor① of an old gas light

He did a lazy sway …

He did a lazy sway…

To the tune o' those Weary Blues.

With his ebony② hands on each ivory key

He made that poor piano moan with melody.

O Blues!

Swaying to and fro on his rickety③ stool

He played that sad raggy④ tune like a musical fool.

Sweet Blues!

Coming from a black man's soul.

O Blues!

In a deep song voice with a melancholy tone

I heard that Negro sing, that old piano moan—

"Ain't got nobody in all this world,

Ain't got nobody but ma self.

I's gwine to quit ma frownin'

And put ma troubles on the shelf."

……

I, Too

I, too, sing America.

I am the darker brother.

They send me to eat in the kitchen

When company comes,

But I laugh,

And eat well,

And grow strong.

Tomorrow,

I'll be at the table

When company comes.

---

① pallor: （脸色等的）苍白,灰白
② ebony: 乌木制的,似乌木的
③ rickety: 连接处不牢固的;快要散架的
④ raggy: 粗糙的

Nobody'll dare
Say to me,
"Eat in the kitchen,"
Then.

Besides,
They'll see how beautiful I am
And be ashamed——

I, too, am America.

Ⅲ. Notes.

1. "*The Negro Speaks of Rivers*" celebrates the voice and the soul of the black community in a time of great racial intolerance, injustice, and inequality in America. The poem connects the soul and heritage of the African-American community to four great rivers in the Middle East, Africa, and America. In this way, it charts the journey of African and African-Americans and links this community to the birth of world civilization.

2. In "*The Weary Blues*", the speaker describes an evening of listening to a blues musician in Harlem. With its diction, its repetition of lines and its inclusion of blues lyrics, the poem evokes the mournful tone and tempo of blues music and gives readers an appreciation of the state of mind of the blues musician in the poem.

3. In contrast to the mythical dimension of "*The Negro Speaks of Rivers*", "*I, Too*" is no less powerful in its expression of social injustice.

Ⅳ. Key Words（关键词）.

1. **The Harlem Renaissance:** 哈莱姆文艺复兴。又称"新黑人运动"（The New Negro Movement）。它是指二十世纪二三十年代，以美国纽约黑人的主要居住区哈莱姆为中心，以复兴美国黑人民间文化遗产、获得种族身份、反对种族歧视和振兴美国黑人文化为主要内容。这一时期涌现出了一大批有才华的作家，他们使非裔美国黑人文化得到前所未有的发展。

2. "哈莱姆桂冠诗人"：兰斯顿·休斯是"哈莱姆文艺复兴"的领袖人物，对美国黑人文学和主流文学产生了巨大影响，被誉为"哈莱姆桂冠诗人"。

Ⅴ. Questions.

1. What is the function of the four great rivers in "The Negro Speaks of Rivers"?

2. Can you explain the line "I heard the singing of the Mississippi when Abe Lincoln…. bosom turn all golden in the sunset."

3. Read the lyrics sung by the musician in *The Weary Blues* and explain the deep meaning of them.

Lesson 28　William Carlos Williams (1883—1963)

Ⅰ. A Brief Review.

Born on Sept. 17, 1883, in Rutherford, New Jersey, William Carlos Williams was an American poet closely associated with modernism and imagism. Williams lived in Europe for two years when he was a teenager and received education in Switzerland and France. He returned to the United States and studied in the medical school at University of Pennsylvania, where he met poets Ezra Pound and Hilda Doolittle. Upon graduation in 1906, he interned for two years in New York hospitals and continued to study pediatrics at the University of Leipzig. Since the year of 1910, Williams did his medical career for more than 40 years while he worked as a poet during his spare time, which allowed him to apply the medical experience to his literary works.

图 28　William C. Williams

The poetic life of Williams, at first, was not that successful. His first volume of poetry was defined as derivative and unoriginal by his friend Ezra Pound, who to a great extent, contributed a lot to the starting of Williams' literary career. But Williams didn't give up and continued to dedicate to writing. After a few years, he discovered his original poetic voice and decided to reject the old forms. The poems of his three pivotal volumes—*Al Que Quiere* (1917), *Sour Grapes* (1921), and *Spring and All* (1923)—were marked by a new intensity of vision and a greater subtlety in language and form. He employed images, scenes, and human figures that would generally be considered as ordinary, even antipoetic. However, his unique way of writing poetry made the poems sound more authentic and spontaneous. The later volumes of verse by Williams are *Collected Later Poems* (1950), *Collected Earlier Poems* (1951), and *Desert Music* (1954). His novels include *A Voyage to Pagany* (1928); *White Mule* (1937); *In the Money* (1940); and *The Build-up* (1952). On March 4, 1963, William Carlos Williams died in his birth place, Rutherford. *The William Carlos Williams Reader* (1966) brought together his whole poems and excerpts from his most important prose.

Williams created a body of poetry that celebrated the local American scene while remaining determinedly experimental in its form and language. Perhaps the most immediately striking aspect of Williams' poems was their appeal to the visual imagination. In a 1929 survey, Williams responded that his strongest characteristic was his "sight", and went on to affirm his "ability to be drunk with a sudden realization of things others never notice." One of his most notable contributions to American literature was his willingness to promote the careers of the younger poets who were either tutored or influenced by him.

II. Texts.

Willow Poem

It is a willow when summer is over,
a willow by the river
from which no leaf has fallen nor
bitten by the sun
turned orange or crimson.
The leaves cling and grow paler,
swing and grow paler
over the swirling waters of the river
as if loath① to let go,
they are so cool, so drunk with
the swirl of the wind and of the river—
oblivious② to winter,
the last to let go and fall
into the water and on the ground.

Spring and All

By the road to the contagious hospital③
under the surge of the blue
mottled④ clouds driven from the
northeast——a cold wind. Beyond, the
waste of broad, muddy fields
brown with dried weeds, standing and fallen

patches of standing water
the scattering of tall trees

All along the road the reddish

---

① loath: 不情愿的, 勉强的
② oblivious: 不注意的；未察觉到的, 不知不觉的；不关心的
③ contagious hospital: 传染病医院
④ mottled: 杂色的, 斑驳的

purplish, forked, upstanding, twiggy
stuff of bushes and small trees
with dead, brown leaves under them
leafless vines——

Lifeless in appearance, sluggish①
dazed spring approaches——

They enter the new world naked,
cold, uncertain of all
save that they enter. All about them
the cold, familiar wind——

Now the grass, tomorrow
the stiff② curl of wild carrot leaf
One by one objects are defined—
It quickens: clarity, outline of leaf

But now the stark dignity of
entrance——Still, the profound change
has come upon them: rooted, they
grip down and begin to awaken

Ⅲ. Notes.

1. "Willow Poem" was written in 1921. The main idea of the poem is that although the natural rule forces the willow to give up, it hangs on to life and never gives in to death. It is already the season of autumn when the leaves should have fallen down, but the leaves on the trees show strong will to life. The beauty of perseverance touches a string of the poet, but as he sees it, the willow tree eventually will shed the leaves.

2. "Spring and All" depicts the ordinary scenes on the poet's way to the hospital. The poem is not organized according to any fixed narrative or thematic means and it uses the experimental impulse to create fluid and various relations between objects, ideas, and emotions. The central word of the poem is "imagination", which is a novel way for the poet to take the most ordinary materials and discover the essence of reality.

---

① sluggish: 缺乏活力的,迟钝的
② stiff: 不易弯曲的,硬的

Ⅳ. **Key Words**（关键词）.

Imagism: 意象主义。它是在 20 世纪早期由英美诗人发起的反对维多利亚式伤感主义的一场文学运动，主张使用自由体、普通的语言模式和清晰具体的意象。他们都主张运用朴实精确的视觉意象来清晰地表达诗歌内涵，他们相信自由可以使诗个性得到更佳的表现，诗歌的新韵意味着新思想和艺术创新。意象派诗歌代表人物庞德对威廉斯的诗歌创作有很大的影响。

Free verse: 自由诗。自由诗是诗体的一种，19 世纪末 20 世纪初源于欧洲，其结构自由，段数、行数、字数没有一定规格；语言有自然节奏而不用韵。在美国文学中，惠特曼为自由诗的创始人。它在章节、音步、押韵等方面都比较自由、灵活，没有格律诗那样严格、固定的限制和约束。威廉斯步惠特曼后尘，积极发展了自由诗的形式，所以一些评论家称其为"现代的惠特曼"。

Ⅴ. Questions.

1. What are the symbolic meanings of "willow" and "leaves" in "Willow Poem"?
2. What is the general tone of the poem "Willow Poem"?
3. In "Spring and All", there are no punctuations in the end of each line. Why did Williams use this form?
4. List the images described in "Spring and All" as dead and lifeless.

Lesson 29 Robert Lowell (1917—1977)

Ⅰ. **A Brief Review.**

Born in 1917 in Boston, Massachusetts, Robert Lowell was an American poet and one of the leading figures in American confessional poetry movement. He was descended from a distinguished family with such famous figures as James Russell Lowell, Amy Lowell, another notable New England poet, and A. Lawrence Lowell, a president of Harvard. After graduation from St. Mark's School in Southborough, Robert Lowell studied at Harvard College for two years, where he read many poems by William Carlos Williams. He then transferred to Kenyon College in Gambier, Ohio because of his strong passion for poetry. After that, Lowell made a living by teaching and working in New York City for a short term.

图 29　Robert Lowell

With the publication of *Lord Weary's Castle*, Lowell made his debut and won the Pulitzer Prize in 1947. Lowell's early poems were formal, ornate, and concerned with violence and theology. In 1959, Lowell published his most important single volume, the revolutionary *Life Studies*, in which he perfected what had come to be called "confessional poetry". Expressing the self as the epitome of larger societal dilemmas, his *Life Studies* (1959) was a frank and highly autobiographical volume in the form of both verse and prose. His other poetry collections include *For the Union Dead* (1964), *Near the Ocean* (1967), *The Dolphin* (1973; Pulitzer Prize), *Day by Day* (1977), and *Last Poems* (1977). His dramatic adaptation of Melville's story "Benito Cereno" was part of Lowell's trilogy of plays, *The Old Glory* (1968). Lowell was also an epic poet in the scope and greatness of his poetry. He addressed large questions, and used a multiplicity of forms and styles in his continuing quest. Lowell's literary criticism and autobiographical prose pieces, posthumously collected in *Collected Prose*, received positive reviews for the author's lucid style.

Robert Lowell is always regarded as the representative figure of the Confessional Poets, whose confessional poems are largely based on their family history and personal life. Confessional poetry emphasizes the intimate, and sometimes unflattering, information about details of the poet's personal life. Most confessional poems sound with a tone of suffering and insanity. Lowell's poetry is individualistic and intense, rich in symbolism. His later work indicates a philosophic acceptance of life and the world.

II. Texts.

Skunk Hour①
For Elizabeth Bishop

Nautilus② Island's hermit
heiress still lives through winter in her Spartan cottage;
her sheep still graze above the sea.
Her son's a bishop.   Her farmer
is first selectman in our village,
she's in her dotage③.

Thirsting for
the hierarchic privacy
of Queen Victoria's century,
she buys up all
the eyesores④ facing her shore,
and lets them fall.

The season's ill—
we've lost our summer millionaire,
who seemed to leap from an L. L. Bean
catalogue.   His nine-knot yawl
was auctioned off⑤ to lobstermen.
A red fox stain covers Blue Hill.

And now our fairy
decorator brightens his shop for fall,
his fishnet's filled with orange cork,
orange, his cobbler's bench and awl⑥,
there is no money in his work,
he'd rather marry.

---

① skunk: 臭鼬
② nautilus: 鹦鹉螺
③ dotage: 衰老期,老年糊涂
④ eyesore: 丑陋刺眼之物
⑤ auction off: 把……拍卖掉
⑥ awl: 钻子,尖锥

One dark night,
my Tudor Ford climbed the hill's skull,
I watched for love-cars.　Lights turned down,
they lay together, hull to hull,
where the graveyard shelves on the town. . . .
My mind's not right.

A car radio bleats①,
'Love, O careless Love . . . . ' I hear
my ill-spirit sob in each blood cell,
as if my hand were at its throat . . . .
I myself am hell,
nobody's here—

only skunks, that search
in the moonlight for a bite to eat.
They march on their soles up Main Street:
white stripes, moonstruck② eyes' red fire
under the chalk-dry and spar spire
of the Trinitarian Church.

I stand on top
of our back steps and breathe the rich air—
a mother skunk with her column of kittens swills the garbage pail.
She jabs her wedge-head in a cup
of sour cream, drops her ostrich③ tail,
and will not scare.

Ⅲ. Notes.

1. "Skunk Hour" appears as the last poem in *Life Studies* and is considered by Robert Lowell as the anchor poem of the sequence. This poem, usually cited as the representative of the confessional poems, refers to the social environment in the first four stanzas and expresses the poet's incipient madness in the later four.

2. The poem "Soft Wood" comes from *For the Union Dead*, in which Lowell is defensively suspicious of nostalgia's lyric strategies. In the poem, Lowell seems to present the principle of the

---

① bleat: 咩咩地叫,轻声说
② moonstruck: 神经错乱的,耽于幻想的,多愁善感的
③ ostrich: 鸵鸟

American society that the ideal life just exists in the dream and the real world only permits victor to survive.

Ⅳ. Key Words（关键词）.

The Confessionals: 自白派。它也称为"坦白派",指坦然暴露内心深处隐藏的一切,即使是自私肮脏丑恶卑鄙的东西也暴露无遗,把内心最不可启齿的那一面公开诉说。当时的美国社会处于动荡不安的时期,传统的学院派诗歌对人们的创造力束缚很大,很多诗人处于一种心灵、情绪无处发泄的状态。于是"自白派"等各种诗歌流派如当年的嬉皮士一样,迅速出现并成长。

Pessimism: 悲观主义。在洛威尔的作品中常常充满了怪诞的细节描写和悲凉的情绪色彩。当时的美国社会喧嚣不安,生活环境恶化,传统的清教文化衰退,腐败的社会使得诗人内心十分痛苦,觉得离理想中的生活渐行渐远,对命运抱着悲观态度,但内心的躁动又显示出作者不甘于现状,希望通过诗歌自白内心世界,唤起人们对社会现状的关注。

Image: 意象,洛威尔的诗歌在对自然界、社会生活环境、人物描写的时候,经常会使用恶劣天气、怪异的植物和动物、矿石等意象,还有一些现代人类生活环境恶化所产生的各种意象,如污染、疾病、监狱、墓地等。这些意象体现了现代社会人们追逐利益而忽视精神价值的追求,诗人不苟同于这种精神财富的枯竭,对人们的精神状态感到失望。

Ⅴ. Questions.

1. In the poem "Skunk Hour", what is the symbolic significance of skunk?
2. In the sixth stanza of "Skunk Hour", why does the poet contrast a popular song playing on the car radio with a quote from Milton's *Paradise Lost*: "I myself am Hell."?
3. In "Soft Wood", what is the implied meaning of the last line?

Lesson 30　Allen Ginsberg (1926—1997)

I. A Brief Review.

Born on June 3, 1926 into a Jewish family in Newark, New Jersey, Allen Ginsberg was an important American poet related to the Beat Generation. Ginsberg attended high school in Paterson, New Jersey with the later poet William Carlos Williams (1883—1963) who helped Ginsberg a lot in his poetic creation. When at Columbia University, Ginsberg came across Jack Kerouac, another great writer in the Beat Movement. They were both influenced by William Burroughs (1914—1997) who introduced Ginsberg to get acquainted with some modern writers, such as Kafka (1883—1924), Yeats (1865—1939) and others. Expelled from college due to misbehavior, Ginsberg spent most of his time with William Burroughs and Jack Kerouac and did a variety of odd jobs till he was finally re-admitted to Columbia University. He graduated from the university with high grades in 1948 and furthered his study in literature there. Then he lived in Harlem, where he began to have visions to hear the voice of the English poet William Blake (1757—1827) through reciting his poems. After that, he found the inspiration to wake up the ordinary people.

图 30　Allen Ginsberg

Also, in Harlem, his friend Herbert Huncke stole things to earn the cost of his drug habit and stored them in the apartment of Ginsberg. When the police found these things, Ginsberg unfortunately was sent to jail and almost sentenced. To avoid prosecution, Ginsberg pretended to be insane and was treated in the Columbia Psychiatric Institute where he came across Carl Solomon, to whom Ginsberg's famous poem "Howl" was dedicated. Later, Allen Ginsberg went to San Francisco, where he worked as a successful market researcher. He also made a living by writing book reviews for Newsweek. But he was restless and discontented with the American society. At last, he quitted all his jobs and traveled in Mexico. In 1954 he settled down in San Francisco and joined his old friend Jack Kerouac.

Shortly after *Howl and Other Poems* was published in 1956, it was banned for obscenity. In the 1960s and 70s, Ginsberg went to publish numerous collections of poetry, including *Kaddish and Other Poems* (1961), *Planet News* (1968), and *The Fall of America: Poems of These States* (1973), which won the National Book Award. Ginsberg claimed at one point that all of his work was an extended biography. "Howl" is not only a biography of Ginsberg's experiences before 1955, but also a history of the Beat Generation. "Howl" chronicles the development of many important friendships throughout Ginsberg's life, and sets the stage for Ginsberg to describe his friends Cassidy and Solomon as the typical figures of the era.

Ⅱ. Texts.

Howl

Part I

For Carl Solomon

I saw the best minds of my generation destroyed by madness, starving hysterical naked,
dragging themselves through the negro streets at dawn looking for an angry fix,
angel headed hipsters burning for the ancient heavenly connection to the starry dynamo in the
    machinery of night,
who poverty and tatters and hollow-eyed and high sat up smoking in the supernatural darkness of
    cold-water flats floating across the tops of cities contemplating jazz,
who bared their brains to Heaven under the El and saw Mohammedan angels staggering on
tenement roofs illuminated,
who passed through universities with radiant cool eyes hallucinating① Arkan- sas and Blake-light
    tragedy among the scholars of war,
who were expelled from the academies for crazy & publishing obscene odes on the windows of the
    skull,
who cowered in unshaven rooms in underwear, burning their money in waste baskets and listening
    to the Terror through the wall,
who got busted in their pubic beards returning through Laredo with a belt of marijuana② for New
    York,
who ate fire in paint hotels or drank turpentine in Paradise Alley, death, or purgatoried③ their
    torsos night after night
with dreams, with drugs, with waking nightmares, alcohol and cock and endless balls,
incomparable blind streets of shuddering cloud and lightning in the mind leaping toward poles of
    Canada & Paterson, illuminating all the mo-tionless world of Time between,
Peyote solidities of halls, backyard green tree cemetery dawns, wine drunk-enness over the
    rooftops, storefront boroughs of teahead joyride neon blinking traffic light, sun and moon and
    tree vibrations in the roaring winter dusks of Brooklyn, ashcan rantings and kind king light of

---

①   hallucinate:（尤指由于精神错乱或吸毒而）产生幻觉
②   marijuana: 大麻（尤指与香烟同时吸用）
③   purgatory:（天主教教义）炼狱

mind,

who chained themselves to subways for the endless ride from Battery to holy Bronx on benzedrine①
until the noise of wheels and children brought them down shuddering mouth-wracked and
battered bleak of brain all drained of② brilliance in the drear light of Zoo,

who sank all night in submarine light of Bickford's floated out and sat through the stale beer
afternoon in desolate Fugazzi's, listening to the crack of doom on the hydrogen jukebox,

who talked continuously seventy hours from park to pad to bar to Bellevue to museum to the
Brooklyn Bridge,

a lost battalion of platonic conversationalists jumping down the stoops off fire escapes off
windowsills of Empire State out of the moon,

yacketayakking③ screaming vomiting whispering facts and memories and anecdotes and eyeball
kicks and shocks of hospitals and jails and wars,

whole intellects disgorged in total recall for seven days and nights with brilliant eyes, meat for the
Synagogue④ cast on the pavement,

who vanished into nowhere Zen New Jersey leaving a trail of ambiguous picture postcards of
Atlantic City Hall,

suffering Eastern sweats and Tangerian bone-grindings and migraines of China under junk-
withdrawal in Newark's bleak furnished room,

who wandered around and around at midnight in the railroad yard wonder-ing where to go, and
went, leaving no broken hearts,

who lit cigarettes in boxcars boxcars boxcars racketing through snow toward lonesome farms in
grandfather night,

who studied Plotinus Poe St. John of the Cross telepathy⑤ and bop kabbalah because the cosmos
instinctively vibrated at their feet in Kansas,

who loned it through the streets of Idaho seeking visionary indian angels who were visionary indian
angels,

who thought they were only mad when Baltimore gleamed in supernatural ecstasy,

who jumped in limousines with the Chinaman of Oklahoma on the impulse of winter midnight
streetlight smalltown rain,

who lounged hungry and lonesome through Houston seeking jazz or sex or soup, and followed the
brilliant Spaniard to converse about America and Eternity, a hopeless task, and so took ship

---

① benzedrine: 苯丙胺,一种苏醒剂,〈美〉苯丙胺的商标
② drain of: 把……抽〔带〕走,抽空
③ yackety-yak: 没有意义的谈话,废话
④ Synagogue: 犹太人集会,犹太教会堂,犹太教
⑤ telepathy: 传心术,心灵感应

to Africa,

who disappeared into the volcanoes of Mexico leaving behind nothing but the shadow of dungarees① and the lava and ash of poetry scattered in fireplace Chicago,

who reappeared on the West Coast investigating the FBI in beards and shorts with big pacifist② eyes sexy in their dark skin passing out incompre-hensible leaflets,

who burned cigarette holes in their arms protesting the narcotic tobacco haze of Capitalism,

……

who coughed on the sixth floor of Harlem crowned with flame under the tubercular sky surrounded by orange crates of theology,

who scribbled all night rocking and rolling over lofty incantations③ which in the yellow morning were stanzas of gibberish,

who cooked rotten animals lung heart feet tail borsht & tortillas dreaming of the pure vegetable kingdom,

who plunged themselves under meat trucks looking for an egg,

who threw their watches off the roof to cast their ballot for Eternity outside of Time, & alarm clocks fell on their heads every day for the next decade,

who cut their wrists three times successively unsuccessfully, gave up and were forced to open antique stores where they thought they were growing old and cried,

who were burned alive in their innocent flannel suits on Madison Avenue amid blasts of leaden verse & the tanked-up clatter of the iron regiments of fashion & the nitroglycerine④ shrieks of the fairies of advertising & the mustard gas⑤ of sinister intelligent editors, or were run down by the drunken taxicabs of Absolute Reality,

who jumped off the Brooklyn Bridge this actually happened and walked away unknown and forgotten into the ghostly daze of Chinatown soup alleyways & firetrucks, not even one free beer,

who sang out of their windows in despair, fell out of the subway window, jumped in the filthy Passaic, leaped on negroes, cried all over the street, danced on broken wineglasses barefoot smashed phonograph records of nostalgic European 1930s German jazz finished the whiskey and threw up groaning into the bloody toilet, moans in their ears and the blast of colossal steamwhistles,

……

---

① dungaree: 粗蓝布工装裤,劳动布工装裤
② pacifist: 和平主义者,反战主义者
③ incantation: 咒语,符咒
④ nitroglycerine: 硝化甘油,炸药
⑤ mustard gas: 芥子气(一种糜烂性毒气)

Ⅲ. Notes.

1. The selected text is from the first part of "Howl". This part is the most well-known for the scenes, characters, and situations originating from Ginsberg's personal experiences as well as the group of poets, artists, political radicals, jazz musicians, drug addicts and psychiatric patients, with whom he contacted in the 1950s.

2. "Howl" became one of the most widely read poems of the 20th century, translated into more than twenty-two languages. Allen Ginsberg is always cherished as the pivotal figure among the Beat Generation, who contributed a lot to the counter-cultural movement of the 1960s. His singular use of slang, rhythm, and subject violates the literary rules in the conservative era. Ginsberg became a symbol of rebellion in the 1950s and 1960s. Many critics connect his poetry with his rebellious behaviors in his life and focus on his revolts against the authority.

Ⅳ. Key Words（关键词）.

Beat Generation: 垮掉的一代。它是指第二次世界大战之后出现于美国的一群松散结合在一起的年轻诗人和作家的集合体。该流派的作家都是性格粗犷豪放、落拓不羁的男女青年，他们生活简单、不修边幅，喜穿奇装异服，厌弃工作和学业，拒绝承担任何社会义务，以浪迹天涯为乐，蔑视社会的法纪秩序，反对一切世俗陈规和垄断资本统治，抵制对外侵略和种族隔离，讨厌机器文明，他们永远寻求新的刺激，如纵欲、吸毒、沉沦，以此向传统价值观念进行挑战，因此被称作"垮掉的一代"。

Postwar Period: 战后时期。第二次世界大战后，美国因为在政治、经济和军事上都获得了巨大利益，渐渐称自己为世界第一强国，而且冷战期间更加剧了美国人对于异族的排斥，但是"垮掉派"文人对战后的保守风气感到迷茫，开始质疑和否定传统文化价值观，他们对体验各种极端的生活方式有浓厚的兴趣，许多"垮掉派"文人对东方文明充满兴趣，他们在西方传播了关于禅宗和佛教的种种知识。

Rebellion: 反叛。金斯伯格作为二十世纪五十年代末"垮掉的一代"诗人之一，不论在生活方式或在诗歌风格上，他均与众不同，自成一格，创立了美国新的一代诗风。他是同性恋者，吸过毒，又改信佛教，成了一名"信仰佛教的犹太人"。他在政治、宗教和教育方面挑战主流文化，他向当时盛行的艾略特诗学观及新批评主义提出异议，并开创出一种表达情感的新方式。

Ⅴ. Questions.

1. Why did Ginsberg employ lots of obscene words in the poem?

2. Ginsberg's rebellion, to some extent, made him a controversial figure, so the generation that Ginsberg's poem represented was so different from most Americans. What kind of the spirit does "Howl" capture?

3. What does the last "stanza" mean?

Lesson 31　Elizabeth Bishop (1911—1979)

Ⅰ. A Brief Review.

Born on February 8, 1911 in Worcester, Massachusetts, Elizabeth Bishop was one of the famous female poets in the twentieth century. When she was very young, Bishop suffered from the loss of love of her father and mother. However, her paternal grandparents brought her back to Worcester against her wills. In May 1918, she was taken by her mother's sister and lived with her aunt in South Boston. At that time, her health condition was severely unpleasant, but she attempted to write poetry due to the influence from her aunt's love towards literature.

She traveled to many countries around the world from 1935 to 1937, including France, Spain, North Africa, Ireland, and Italy. The descriptions of her travels and the scenery on route are often seen in her

图 31　Elizabeth Bishop

works. Bishop met Robert Lowell at a dinner party in 1947 and gradually developed a complicated friendship with him. Lowell and Bishop shared several ideas and concepts in common, but they had differences in expressing their feelings. Robert Lowell tended to free his inner thoughts while Bishop always described things objectively to convey her emotion and experience indirectly. Because of the poet Morianne Moore's recommendation to the Houghton Mifflin Prize, Bishop took the chance to publish her manuscript *North and South* in August 1946, introducing the themes of her poetry: geography and landscape, human connection with the natural world, questions of knowledge and perception, and the ability or inability of form to control chaos. Bishop won the Lucy Martin Donnelly Fellowship from Bryn Mawr College in 1950 and an award from the American Academy of Arts and Letters. Elizabeth Bishop's poetry collections include *North & South* (Houghton Mifflin, 1946), *Poems: North &South / A Cold Spring* (1955), *A Cold Spring* (1956), *The Complete Poems:* 1927-1979 (1983), and *Uncollected Poems, Drafts, and Fragments by Elizabeth Bishop* (2006).

In a sense, Bishop's life history would have made her an ideal candidate for the confessional mode. However, Bishop's poetry resists easy classification, and despite her friendship with Lowell and her generational affinities with the confessionals, her work displays a degree of reticence and restraint than that of poets like Lowell, Berryman, Plath, and Sexton. As a woman poet who was a lesbian, virtually all of whose poetic contemporaries were men, she felt marginalized within both literary culture and American culture at large. She is now considered one of the most important American poets of the 20th century.

II. Texts.

The Fish

I caught a tremendous fish
and held him beside the boat
half out of water, with my hook
fast in a corner of his mouth.
He didn't fight.
He hadn't fought at all.
against the cliff behind the house.
The flam① ran down. We saw the pair.

of owls who nest there flying up
and up, their whirling black-and-white
stained bright pink underneath, until
they shrieked up out of sight.

The ancient owls' nest must have burned.
Hastily, all alone.
a glistening armadillo② left the scene,
rose-flecked, head down, tail down,

and then a baby rabbit jumped out,
short-eared, to our surprise.
So soft! —a handful of intangible ash
with fixed, ignited eyes.

Too pretty, dreamlike mimicry!
O falling fire and piercing cry
and panic, and a weak mailed fist
clenched ignorant against the sky!

---

① flam: 谎话,胡扯
② armadillo: 犰狳

Sestina①

September rain falls on the house.
In the failing light, the old grandmother
sits in the kitchen with the child
beside the Little Marvel Stove,
reading the jokes from the almanac②,
laughing and talking to hide her tears.

She thinks that her equinoctial③ tears
and the rain that beats on the roof of the house
were both foretold by the almanac,
but only known to a grandmother.
The iron kettle sings on the stove.
She cuts some bread and says to the child,

It's time for tea now; but the child
is watching the teakettle's small hard tears
dance like mad on the hot black stove,
the way the rain must dance on the house.
Tidying up, the old grandmother
hangs up the clever almanac

on its string. Birdlike, the almanac
hovers half open above the child,
hovers above the old grandmother
and her teacup full of dark brown tears.
She shivers and says she thinks the house
feels chilly, and puts more wood in the stove.

It was to be, says the Marble Stove.
I know what I know, says the almanac.
With crayons the child draws a rigid house
and a winding pathway. Then the child
puts in a man with buttons like tears

---

① Sestina: 六节诗
② almanac: 年鉴,年历,历书
③ equinoctial: 春分或秋分的(暴风雨),赤道的

and shows it proudly to the grandmother.

But secretly, while the grandmother
busies herself about the stove,
the little moons fall down like tears
from between the pages of the almanac
into the flower bed the child
has carefully placed in the front of the house.

Time to plant tears, says the almanac.
The grandmother sings to the marvelous stove
And the child draws another inscrutable① house.

Ⅲ. Notes.

1. The poem "The Unbeliever" is a highly condensed poem of five five-line stanzas. It begins with an enigmatic quotation from *Pilgrim's Progress* (1678, 1684), "He sleeps on the top of a mast." These words are repeated in the first line of the poem. While the top of the mast is a strange place for sleeping in any circumstance, in Elizabeth Bishop's poem it comes to mean that sleeping anywhere is uncanny and strange.

2. The poem "The Fish" is Bishop's most frequently anthologized poem, which justifies the process of a dinghy from plunderer to benefactor by means of the Wordsworthian spiritual practice. In the poem, Bishop deliberately obscures the boundaries between real life and art by the indistinct borders between land and sea, the air and earth of the speaker. For Bishop, nature mastered as static knowledge is a fish out of water. Its beauty and venerability belong to time.

3. "Sestina" is a kind of French form poem, which consists of six six-line stanzas and a three-line envoy. The rule of this form is that the poem has a fixed pattern of end-words which might be arranged in a different sequence. The images in the poem, including the almanac, the old grandmother, the child, the house, and the little moon, all offer the reader a mysterious atmosphere.

Ⅳ. Key Words（关键词）.

Marianne Moore: 玛莉安·莫尔。她出生于密苏里，1905 年进入 Bryn Mawr 学院学习。毕业后，她在卡来尔印第安工业学校执教，直到 1915 年，她开始出版诗歌。莫尔对毕晓普来说，是密友也是精神导师，尤其是莫尔通过描写动植物等普通而具体的生活细节来揭示真理这一手法直接启发了毕晓普后来的诗歌创作。

Sestina: 六节诗。这种诗体结构非常复杂，全诗一共六节，每节共六行，再加三行作结尾，总共三十九行诗。六节中诗行的结尾必须使用相同的六个单词，但这六个单词的排序

---

① inscrutable: 不可理解的，难以解释的

都不相同。美国女诗人毕晓普创作题为《六节诗》的诗歌纪念她的祖母。

Home: 家。伊丽莎白·毕晓普的童年失去了父母,到处漂泊,居无定所,一直处于孤独和被放逐的状态中,所以"家"的概念在其诗歌中时常出现,诗人逐渐认识到童年的家园已经一去不返,失去的天堂不可能被任何东西取代。

Ⅴ. Questions.

1. To most people, it seems very strange to sleep on the top of a mast. What do you think about the action of the man in the poem "The Unbeliever"?

2. What is the symbolic meaning of the fish in the poem "The Fish"?

3. Why did "I" decide to release the fish finally in the poem of "The Fish"?

4. In "Sestina", why does Bishop employ lots of images related to water?

Lesson 32　John Ashbery (1927—)

Ⅰ. **A Brief Review.**

Born in Rochester, New York, on July 28, 1927, John Ashbery has remained a distinguished American poet. As a child, he won an anthology of poetry in a contest, which led him to the discovery that rhyme was not essential to verse. In 1949, Ashbery graduated from Harvard College, where he was a member of the university's literary magazine the *Harvard Advocate*. After that, he received his Master Degree from Columbia University in 1951. From the mid-1950s, he moved to France where he served as the art editor for the European edition of the *New York Herald Tribune*. Ashbery's first collection of poems, *Some Trees* (1956), revealed the influence of W. H. Auden, Wallace Stevens, and many of the French surrealists. In the late 1950s, the critic John Bernard Myers categorized the common traits of Ashbery's avant-garde poetry, as well as that of Kenneth Koch, Frank O'Hara, James Schuyler, Barbara Guest, Kenward Elmslie and others, as constituting a "New York School". Ashbery's subsequent collections include *Houseboat Days* (1977), *As We Know* (1979), *A Wave* (1985), and *And the Stars Were Shining* (1994).

图 32　John Ashbery

In the early 1970s, Ashbery began teaching at Brooklyn College. In the 1980s, he moved to Bard College, where he was the Charles P. Stevenson, Jr., Professor of Languages and Literature, until 2008, when he retired. Since that time, he has continued to win awards, present readings, and work with graduate and undergraduates at many other institutions. He was selected as the poet laureate of New York State from 2001 to 2003, and served for many years as a chancellor of the Academy of American Poets.

Ashbery is a prolific writer who won all three major American poetry prizes (the Pulitzer Prize, the National Book Award, and the National Book Critics Circle Award) for *Self-Portrait in a Convex Mirror* (1975). Ashbery's works are noted for its free-flowing, often disjunctive syntax, extensive linguistic play, and a prosaic, sometimes disarmingly flat or parodic tone. The play of the human mind is the subject of a great many of his poems. In terms of form, the earliest poems show the influence of conventional poetic practice, yet by *The Tennis Court Oath* a much more revolutionary engagement with form appears. In terms of subject matter, his poems are similar to that of his favorite poet, Wallace Stevens. His poems are experimental in style and syntax, strongly visual, and narrative, but typically complex and somewhat obscure.

II. Texts.

Illustration

I

A novice was sitting on a cornice①
High over the city. Angles

Combined their prayers with those
Of the police, begging her to come off it.

One lady promised to be her friend.
"I do not want a friend," she said.

A mother offered her some nylons
Stripped from her very legs. Others brought

Little offerings of fruit and candy,
The blind man all his flowers. If any

Could be called successful, these were,
For that the scene should be a ceremony

Was what she wanted. "I desire
Monuments," she said. "I want to move

Figuratively, as waves caress②
The thoughtless shore. You people I know

Will offer me every good thing
I do not want. But please remember

I died accepting them." With that, the wind
Unpinned her bulky robes, and naked

---

① cornice: (装饰性)飞檐；檐口
② caress: 爱抚，抚摩

As a roc①' s egg, she drifted softly downward
Out of the angels' tenderness and the minds of men.

II
Much that is beautiful must be discarded
So that we may resemble a taller

Impression of ourselves. Moths climb in the flame,
Alas, that wish only to be the flame:

They do not lessen our stature.
We twinkle under the weight

Of indiscretions②. But how could we tell
That of the truth we know, she was

The somber③ vestment? For that night, rockets sighed
Elegantly over the city, and there was feasting:

There is so much in that moment!
So many attitudes toward that flame,

We might have soared from earth, watching her glide
Aloft, in her peplum④ of bright leaves.

But she, of course, was only an effigy⑤
Of indifference, a miracle

Not meant for us, as the leaves are not
Winter' s because it is the end.

III. Notes.
1. Noted for their elegance, originality and obscurity, these lines are characterized by

---

① roc: 大鹏(《一千零一夜》中描绘的传奇巨鸟)
② indiscretion: (言行)不慎重,轻率,草率
③ somber: 阴森的,昏暗的,阴天的,忧郁的
④ peplum: (女式夹克、外衣或上衣腰部以下、作为饰边或荷叶边的)褶襞短裙
⑤ effigy: (人或动物的)雕像,模拟像

arresting images, exquisite rhythms, intricate form, and sudden shifts in tone and subject. His poetry appeals tremendously not because it offers wisdom in a packaged form, but because the elusiveness and mysterious promise of his lines remind us that we always have a future and a condition of meaningfulness to start out toward.

2. The poem "Illustration" is divided into two parts. The first part depicts that a novice is about to commit suicide, and she prefers to pursue the psychological freedom of her own, which means that she is willing to abandon the material enjoyment. The second part implies that unrealistic dream may result in the destruction of everything, and the attractive things often become so dangerous that we may pay more or less for the brilliant scenes, sometimes even our lives.

Ⅳ. Key Words（关键词）.

New York School: 纽约诗派。"纽约诗派"众诗人惟一的共同点是他们喜欢派对,喜欢聚会吃喝,经常在一起神侃。纽约诗派兴起于美国二十世纪六十年代,是美国战后最为重要的诗歌流派之一,它在开拓英语诗歌的疆域的同时,也向世界提供了一位大师级的诗人,即约翰·阿什贝利,其诗歌呈现出了深邃的艺术境界。

Abstract Expressionism: 抽象表现主义。二十世纪四十年代和五十年代起源于纽约的抽象派艺术,旨在表达主观情感,尤其注重即兴创作,如动作绘画,代表人物有杰克逊·波洛克和威廉·德·库宁。阿什贝利的诗歌与抽象表现主义绘画极有渊源,他有时也像波洛克使用颜料那样,把词语当作颜料挥洒,因此词语在他的诗歌中获得了原初的质地和本体论的凸显,而不再仅仅是表意的工具而已。

obscurity: 晦涩。很多读者都会认为阿什贝利的诗歌晦涩难懂,这是因为他把幽默和机智相结合,并时时透露出骨子里的悲凉,有时非常松散随意,有时又极其严格,语言上他糅合了叙述与抒情、经验与玄学等等维度,其复合型写作在拓展意识范围、保持语言活力和对事物的触及能力等方面都给予我们莫大的启示,但是对于读者来说也是一项挑战。

Ⅴ. Questions.

1. What is the implication of the second part of the poem "Illustration"?
2. What is the meaning of the first two lines in the poem "Soonest Mended"?
3. Which aspects of American culture did Ashbery point out in the poem "Soonest Mended"?

Part Five

Fiction and Drama in the 20th Century（2）
第五部　20世纪美国小说与戏剧（Ⅱ）

　　美国在20世纪后半叶经历了许多大的社会变动,从黑人民权运动、反越战运动、女权运动,直到所谓的"文化战争"等等,似乎上演了一出又一出变化莫测的社会悲喜剧。这些变化对于美国文学产生了重要的影响,使之遇到了又一个重要的转折时期。1945年以后,美国社会和经济进入高速发展的轨道,但生活的富庶却掩盖不了各种社会矛盾,冷战的阴影又时时笼罩在人们头上。在这种情况下,美国小说和戏剧出现了一些新的发展态势,例如荒诞派戏剧和黑色幽默小说等等,而一直延续的现实主义潮流仍然影响着不少作家创作出了经典的作品。1951年,塞林格(1919—2010)发表的小说《麦田守望者》迅速引起轰动,小说主人公霍尔顿的反叛举止和放肆言行使他成为当时美国年轻人竞相效仿的偶像。这部小说及时地反映了美国社会风气的逆转,特别是预示了反文化运动在随后年代的高涨。1952年,黑人作家艾里森(1914—1994)出版了小说《隐身人》,深刻批判了少数族裔人群受到的种族歧视,并进一步提出了"寻找自我身份"的时代要求。这两部小说标志了美国文学发展的新趋势,即文学对社会紧迫问题的干预和文学在语言形式上的创新并驾齐驱。在另一方面,美国戏剧的老人新作和新人新作也在不断地突破传统观念的束缚,在关注现实问题的同时也取得了艺术上的开拓创新。

　　美国小说在二战以后出现了蓬勃发展的态势,即作家在整体上达到了思想深刻、艺术精湛的高水平,而他们创作的不少作品确实成为了当代文学的经典,并在国内外文学界获得了广泛的好评和众多的大奖。1948年,诺曼·梅勒(1924—2007)发表了小说《裸者与死者》,对于刚刚过去的第二次世界大战进行了反思,在讲述美军太平洋战争的故事时揭露了权势与人性之间的尖锐矛盾。反思二战的小说还有詹姆斯·琼斯(1921—1977)的《从这里到永恒》(1951)和托马斯·伯格的《柏林疯狂》(1958)等等。约瑟夫·海勒(1923—1999)则在《第22条军规》(1961)中以强烈的黑色幽默叙述揭露了美军内部的贪污腐败和官僚习气,在反讽和粗犷之中显示了思想批判的深度。实际上,美国小说一直具有直面现实和大众化的传统,这一时期的小说还有"垮掉派"作家凯鲁亚克的《在路上》(1957)、卡波特的非虚构小说《冷血》(1966)、女作家卡洛尔·欧茨的《他们》(1969)、欧文·肖的《富人、穷人》(1970)、华莱士·斯太格纳的《旁观鸟》(1976)、约翰·契弗的《短篇故事集》(1978)、约翰·加德纳的《麦克尔森的鬼魂》(1982)、道格拉斯·科普兰的《X一代》(1991)和苏珊·桑塔格的《在美国》(2000)等等。这些作品都从更深的层面揭示了美国社会的种族、性别、时代和阶级的矛盾冲突,塑造了一些生动的现实中人,甚至是"反英雄"的性格,在现代小说技巧的运用中表现了美国作家丰富的艺术想象力和较高的美学品味。与此同时,族裔作家的小说创作也开始涌现,其中以黑人文学首当其冲,率先走向文坛的中心。在艾里森的《隐身人》发表以后,另一位黑人作家詹姆斯·鲍德温(1924—1987)出版了自传体小说《山间倾诉》(1953),对于基督教信仰和种族问题等进行了坦率的阐述,进一步反思了美国社会的基本问题,即种族矛盾和文化冲突等等。这些作品可谓20世纪70年代以后少数族裔作家群体文学繁荣的先声。

在20世纪后半叶的现实主义小说家中,约翰·厄普代克(1932—2009)是一位典型代表。他的"兔子"五部曲集中描写了男主人公安斯特姆在40多年中的悲欢遭遇,是美国当代社会现实和集体心态的真实写照。他从第一部《兔子,跑吧》(1960)再现50年代浮躁心态开始,到第二部《兔子,回家》(1971)和第三部《兔子,富了》(1981)对于越战前后美国社会的剖析,直到在第四部《兔子,休息》(1990)中叙述了主人公的最后死亡,后来又增加了第五部《记忆中的兔子》(2000)来再现历史的记忆等等。这几部系列小说全面展示了美国当代社会变迁的历史长卷,显示了美国文学中现实主义传统和艺术创新的强大生命力。这一时期的小说大家还有获得过诺贝尔文学奖的索尔·贝娄(1915—2005)和艾萨克·辛格(1904—1991)等人。索尔·贝娄在小说《奥吉·玛奇历险记》(1953)中描写了主人公闯荡商界的奇特经历,而在《赫索格》(1964)和《洪堡的礼物》(1975)两部小说中则深入探寻了犹太知识分子的心灵苦旅。艾萨克·辛格以短篇小说见长,他的作品对二次大战再次进行了描述,并反思了当时欧洲屠犹的历史缘由和幸存者的生活。需要指出的是,美国通俗文学的繁荣以及科幻小说的崛起不仅使大众读者获得了更多的阅读选择,而且对于美国文学在艺术技巧上的革新起到了一定的推动作用。例如阿斯莫夫的科幻小说系列《基金会》五部曲(1951—1983)、斯蒂芬·金的惊悚小说《闪灵》(1977)和《黑暗的一半》(1989)等等作品。另外,美国电影电视对于美国当代小说和戏剧的重要作品大多进行了改编并搬上银屏,这使美国文学的经典建构形成了更加广泛的社会基础。

美国戏剧在二战后出现过一段时期的繁荣,一些剧作家大胆地挖掘生活的阴暗面,积极采用了现代戏剧的各种表现手法,产生了不少当代经典戏剧作品。例如,田纳西·威廉斯(1911—1983)的《欲望号街车》(1947)尖锐地揭示了美国社会的阶级矛盾,对南方社会变动中产生的文化冲突给予了深刻的表现。美国剧作家阿瑟·米勒(1915—2005)的《推销员之死》(1949)发表后轰动一时,其中描写了推销员威利老来无着、美国梦碎的悲剧,尖锐地暴露了社会现实中的冷酷一面,其心理描写手法也使该剧赢得了批评家的赞许。另一位戏剧家阿尔比(1928—)在艺术创新中不忘关注现实人生,例如他的荒诞派剧本《动物园的故事》(1959)和《美国梦》(1961)质疑了美国社会的完美,而他的《谁害怕弗吉尼亚·沃尔夫?》(1962)探讨了人生存在的危机,曾在百老汇连续上演达两年之久,使他获得了经典剧作家的声誉。20世纪60年代以来,一些非赢利的小型剧团上演了很多先锋派的戏剧,其中的许多参与者都是年轻的剧作家。例如,芝加哥的大卫·玛米特所写的《美国水牛》(1976)、南方作家贝斯·亨勒的《心中的罪恶》(1979)和山姆·谢泼德的《心灵的谎言》(1985)等等都显示了年轻一代美国剧作家在艺术造诣和思想深度上已经达到了相当高的水准。

Lesson 33　Ralph Ellison (1914—1994)

I. A Brief Review.

Born in Oklahoma in 1914, Ralph Waldo Ellison was a novelist, literary critic, and writer. In 1933, he entered the Tuskegee Institute on a scholarship to study music, majoring in trumpet and embracing both "serious music" and jazz. Later he went to Harlem to study sculpture and photography. His art gifts and composing talents were both outstanding but his literary inclinations finally dominated his artistic ones. When Ellison left Tuskegee for New York City to develop in 1936, he was befriended by Richard Wright, and the latter encouraged him to pursue a career in writing. Beginning with reviews and short stories, Ellison did not begin working on *Invisible Man* until nearly a decade after he began his writing career. Published in 1952, *Invisible Man* explored the theme of man's search for his identity and place in society. By

图 33　Ralph Ellison

tracing the subtle influence of the African-American music, language, folk mythology, clothing styles and sports on the American life, Ellison preferred a linking between the black and the white, or "the unity of American experience beyond all considerations of class, of race, of religion."

Ever since its publication, *Invisible Man* has been highly praised. In 1965, about two hundred literary critics voted it to be the most distinguished novel of the past two decades. Yet despite all the acclaim, *Invisible Man* also incurred much criticism. In the late 1960s, some black activists criticized Ellison's work for being irrelevant to their more activist designs. Irving Howe mildly criticized Ralph Ellison for being "too sanguine about the possibilities of human freedom". However, Ellison answered Howe's charge in the essay "The World and the Jug": "I am a human being not just the black successor to Richard Wright, and there are ways of celebrating my experience more complex than terms like 'protest' can suggest." Therefore, the work is not merely a racial protest novel but goes beyond this. It tends to fall into the theme of the development of youth into maturity, or self-realization.

Ellison began his second novel *Juneteenth* in 1958. It was planned as a trilogy and he toiled over for forty years on it, but it remained unfinished at his death in 1994. Through recording the talk between a white New England senator and a black minister, the author makes an attempt to explore the essence of kinship and race. It seems that the novel intensifies the truth that "African American heritage is an integral part of American culture." In 1964, Ellison published *Shadow and Act*, a collection of essays. He taught literature at several universities including Yale

University, while continuing to work as a novelist. He had been a visiting professor of creative writing, black culture and humanities at different major universities, including Bard College, the University of Chicago and New York University. He died of cancer on April 16, 1994. Today he is still best remembered for his great novel, *Invisible Man*.

II. Texts.

Invisible Man

Prologue

I am an invisible man. No, I am not a spook① like those who haunted Edgar Allan Poe; nor am I one of your Hollywood-movie ectoplasms②. I am a man of substance, of flesh and bone, fiber and liquids—and I might even be said to possess a mind. I am invisible, understand, simply because people refuse to see me. Like the bodiless heads you see sometimes in circus sideshows, it is as though I have been surrounded by mirrors of hard, distorting glass. When they approach me they see only my surroundings, themselves, or figments of their imagination—indeed, everything and anything except me.

Nor is my invisibility exactly a matter of a bio-chemical accident to my epidermis③. That invisibility to which I refer occurs because of a peculiar disposition in the eyes of those with whom I come in contact. A matter of the construction of their *inner* eyes, those eyes with which they look through their physical eyes upon reality. I am not complaining, nor am I protesting either. It is sometimes advantageous to be unseen, although it is most often rather wearing on the nerves. Then too, you're constantly being bumped against by those of poor vision. Or again, you often doubt if you really exist. You wonder whether you aren't simply a phantom in other people's minds. Say, a figure in a nightmare which the sleeper tries with all his strength to destroy. It's when you feel like this that, out of resentment, you begin to bump people back. And, let me confess, you feel that way most of the time. You ache with the need to convince yourself that you do exist in the real world, that you're a part of all the sound and anguish, and you strike out with your fists, you curse and you swear to make them recognize you. And, alas, it's seldom successful.

One night I accidentally bumped into a man, and perhaps because of the near darkness he saw me and called me an insulting name. I sprang at him, seized his coat lapels and demanded that he apologize. He was a tall blond man, and as my face came close to his he looked insolently out of his blue eyes and cursed me, his breath hot in my face as he struggled. I pulled his chin down sharp upon the crown of my head, butting④ him as I had seen the West Indians do, and felt his flesh tear and the blood gush out, and I yelled, "Apologize! Apologize!" But he continued to curse and

---

① spook: 非正式用语,指鬼,幽灵
② ectoplasm: 通灵物
③ epidermis: 表皮
④ butt: 用头猛撞

struggle, and I butted him again and again until he went down heavily, on his knees, profusely bleeding. I kicked him repeatedly, in a frenzy because he still uttered insults though his lips were frothy with blood. Oh yes, I kicked him! And in my outrage I got out my knife and prepared to slit his throat, right there beneath the lamplight in the deserted street, holding him in the collar with one hand, and opening the knife with my teeth—when it occurred to me that the man had not *seen* me, actually; that he, as far as he knew, was in the midst of a walking nightmare! And I stopped the blade, slicing the air as I pushed him away, letting him fall back to the street. I stared at him hard as the lights of a car stabbed through the darkness. He lay there, moaning on the asphalt; a man almost killed by a phantom. It unnerved me. I was both disgusted and ashamed. I was like a drunken man myself, waving about on the weakened legs. Then I was amused: Something in this man's thick head had sprung out and beaten him within an inch of his life①. I began to laugh at this crazy discovery. Would he have awakened at the point of death? Would Death himself have freed him for wakeful living? But I didn't linger. I ran away into the dark, laughing so hard I feared I might rupture myself. The next day I saw his picture in the *Daily News,* beneath a caption stating that he had been "mugged."② Poor fool, poor blind fool, I thought with sincere compassion, mugged by an invisible man!

Most of the time (although I do not choose as I once did to deny the violence of my days by ignoring it) I am not so overtly violent. I remember that I am invisible and walk softly so as not to awaken the sleeping ones. Sometimes it is best not to awaken them; there are few things in the world as dangerous as sleepwalkers. I learned in time though that it is possible to carry on a fight against them without their realizing it. For instance, I have been carrying on a fight with Monopolated Light & Power for some time now. I use their service and pay them nothing at all, and they don't know it. Oh, they suspect that power is being drained off③, but they don't know where. All they know is that according to the master meter back there in their power station a hell of a lot of free current is disappearing somewhere into the jungle of Harlem. The joke, of course, is that I don't live in Harlem but in a border area. Several years ago (before I discovered the advantages of being invisible) I went through the routine process of buying service and paying their outrageous rates. But no more. I gave up all that, along with my apartment, and my old way of life: That way based upon the fallacious assumption that I, like other men, was visible. Now, aware of my invisibility, I live rent-free in a building rented strictly to whites, in a section of the basement that was shut off and forgotten during the nineteenth century, which I discovered when I was trying to escape in the night from Ras the Destroyer. But that's getting too far ahead of the story, almost to the end, although the end is in the beginning and lies far ahead.

The point now is that I found a home—or a hole in the ground, as you will. Now don't jump to the conclusion that because I call my home a "hole" it is damp and cold like a grave; there are

---

① within an inch of his life: 差点要了他的命
② mug: 威胁或殴打某人
③ drain off: 渐渐枯竭

cold holes and warm holes. Mine is a warm hole. And remember, a bear retires to his hole for the winter and lives until spring; then he comes strolling out like the Easter chick breaking from its shell. I say all this to assure you that it is incorrect to assume that, because I'm invisible and live in a hole, I am dead. I am neither dead nor in a state of suspended animation. Call me Jack-the Bear, for I am in a state of hibernation.

My hole is warm and full of light. Yes, *full* of light. I doubt if there is a brighter spot in all New York than this hole of mine, and I do not exclude Broadway, or the Empire State Building on a photographer's dream night. But that is taking advantage of you. Those two spots are among the darkest of our whole civilization—pardon me, our whole *culture* (an important distinction, I've heard) —which might sound like a hoax, or a contradiction, but that (by contradiction, I mean) is how the world moves: Not like an arrow, but a boomerang①. (Beware of those who speak of the *spiral* of history; they are preparing a boomerang. Keep a steel helmet handy.) I know; I have been boomeranged across my head so much that I now can see the darkness of lightness. And I love light. Perhaps you'll think it strange that an invisible man should need light, desire light, love light. But maybe it is exactly because I *am* invisible. Light confirms my reality, gives birth to my form. A beautiful girl once told me of a recurring nightmare in which she lay in the center of a large dark room and felt her face expand until it filled the whole room, becoming a formless mass while her eyes ran in bilious jelly up the chimney. And so it is with me. Without light I am not only invisible, but formless as well; and to be unaware of one's form is to live a death. I myself, after existing some twenty years, did not become alive until I discovered my invisibility.

That is why I fight my battle with Monopolated Light & Power. The deeper reason, I mean: It allows me to feel my vital aliveness. I also fight them for taking so much of my money before I learned to protect myself. In my hole in the basement there are exactly 1,369 lights. I've wired the entire ceiling, every inch of it. And not with fluorescent bulbs, but with the older, more-expensive-to-operate kind, the filament type. An act of sabotage②, you know. I've already begun to wire the wall. A junk man I know, a man of vision, has supplied me with wire and sockets. Nothing, storm or flood, must get in the way of our need for light and ever more and brighter light. The truth is the light and light is the truth. When I finish all four walls, then I'll start on the floor. Just how that will go, I don't know. Yet when you have lived invisible as long as I have you develop a certain ingenuity. I'll solve the problem. And maybe I'll invent a gadget to place my coffeepot on the fire while I lie in bed, and even invent a gadget to warm my bed—like the fellow I saw in one of the picture magazines who made himself a gadget to warm his shoes! Though invisible, I am in the great American tradition of tinkers③. That makes me kin to Ford, Edison and Franklin. Call me, since I have a theory and a concept, a "thinker-tinker." Yes, I'll warm my shoes; they need it, they're usually full of holes. I'll do that and more.

---

① boomerang: 回飞棒
② sabotage: 蓄意破坏
③ tinker: 白铁匠

Now I have one radio-phonograph; I plan to have five. There is a certain acoustical deadness in my hole, and when I have music I want to feel its vibration, not only with my ear but with my whole body. I'd like to hear five recordings of Louis Armstrong① playing and singing "What Did I Do to Be so Black and Blue"—all at the same time. Sometimes now I listen to Louis while I have my favorite dessert of vanilla ice cream and sloe gin. I pour the red liquid over the white mound, watching it glisten and the vapor rising as Louis bends that military instrument into a beam of lyrical sound. Perhaps I like Louis Armstrong because he's made poetry out of being invisible. I think it must be because he's unaware that he is invisible. And my own grasp of invisibility aids me to understand his music. Once when I asked for a cigarette, some jokers gave me a reefer②, which I lighted when I got home and sat listening to my phonograph. It was a strange evening. Invisibility, let me explain, gives one a slightly different sense of time, you're never quite on the beat. Sometimes you're ahead and sometimes behind. Instead of the swift and imperceptible flowing of time, you are aware of its nodes③, those points where time stands still or from which it leaps ahead. And you slip into the breaks and look around. That's what you hear vaguely in Louis' music.

Ⅲ. Notes.

1. *Invisible Man* is an epic-scope novel. With the Prologue, the flashbacks and the Epilogue, the novel presents how a nameless African-American lost his innocence, how he came to gain a mature understanding of the American society and how he planned to act in the future. The black young man tried to find himself an identity in society. The rich symbols in the novel lead to profound understandings of the theme of identity-searching. However, the African-American folktales, songs, the blues, jazz and black traditions permeated in the great work add to its subtlety and complexity.

2. This selection from *Invisible Man* consists of the novel's prologue, revealing two pairs of conflicts, i.e., how the white perceive the black young man and how he perceives himself, the African-American. Ralph Ellison aims to discuss racism and the black struggle for self-dignity and individuality. Ellison created a different type of black people, an educated, articulate, and self-aware young man. The nameless young man, the "hole", the light bulbs and the "Monopolated Light & Power", to name a few in the Prologue, can all be symbolically interpreted.

3. Harlem: is a neighborhood in the New York City borough of Manhattan. It was originally a Dutch village, formally organized in 1658. Since the 1920s, it has been a major African-American residential, cultural, and business center.

---

① Louis Armstrong: (1901—1971) 绰号 Satchmo 或 Pops, 来自美国路易斯安那州新奥尔良地区的爵士乐好手和歌手
② reefer: 大麻烟卷
③ node: 叉点

Ⅳ. Key Words（关键词）.

Racism: 种族主义。种族主义观点认为构成不同种族的遗传因素是决定人类特性和能力的首要因素，并且认为这种种族差异使某一种族具有先天的优越性。种族主义的结果是种族歧视。二战时纳粹杀戮犹太人就是种族主义的一个典型事例。

African-American: 非裔美国人。在美国，有非洲血统的黑人称为非裔美国人，他们是美国最大的少数民族群体。美国在1865年正式废除奴隶制，但种族歧视一直困扰着非裔美国人。二十世纪五六十年代的民权运动大大改善了非裔美国人的社会和经济地位，但非裔美国人仍然在经济、教育、健康等诸多方面仍处于劣势。

Symbol: 象征。通过联想、相似或约定俗成等使某一事物，如一幅画、一个词或一种声音，表现另一种事物。象征是文学创作中常用的手法。例如，鸽子象征和平，狮子象征勇气和力量，玫瑰象征纯洁的爱情等等。艾里森在《隐身人》中大量使用象征手法，这使小说的主题更具深度，但同时这些大量的象征也使小说更为复杂难懂。

Ⅴ. Questions.

1. Explain why the man in this novel is "invisible".
2. Why does Ellison put a prologue before the chapters begin?
3. Does the character in the selected section have name? How do you interpret it?

Lesson 34 Arthur Miller (1915—2005)

Ⅰ. **A Brief Review.**

Born on October 17, 1915 into a German-Jewish family in New York and growing up during the American Depression, Arthur Miller was one of the greatest American playwrights. His father was a manufacturer, whose business collapsed in the crash of 1929 and his mother was a thoughtful reader. After leaving high school, Arthur Miller did a variety of jobs, including working as a farmhand, a truck driver and various jobs in an automobile-parts warehouse for $15 a week and saved up the tuition for the University of Michigan, where he began writing plays and won awards twice. His university years witnessed the Spanish Civil War, the rise of fascism, and the fascination of Marxism as a way to solve the Depression. After graduating in 1938, he returned to New York and for a while wrote radio plays for a living. In 1940 Miller wrote *The Man who Had All the Luck*, which won the Theatre Guild's National Award.

图 34　Arthur Miller

It was in 1947 that Arthur Miller's second Broadway play *All My Sons*, about a manufacturer whose own products caused the death of his son and others during World War II, established him as a playwright. His masterpiece, *Death of a Salesman* was produced two years later. The play was commercially successful and critically acclaimed, bringing Miller a Pulitzer Prize and a Critics' Circle Award. The incarnation of the father-son relationship in the American middle-class family modeled a lot of his later plays. Besides, realism and expressionism, with the vernacular speech of the common characters and the inner psychological analysis are naturally fused in Miller's play. He successfully incorporated the avant-garde into the popular art.

Arthur Miller's play *The Crucible* (1953) is in essence an allegory, in which Miller likened the situation with the House of Un-American Activities Committee to the Salem witch hunt. It discusses the Salem Witch Trials based on the accusation of the twelve-year-old girl Anne Putman and the prosecution by the clergyman Samuel Parris, with nineteen people hanged and one pressed to death. In fact it drew a parallel to the anti-communism "witch-hunts" of McCarthyism of the 1950s, when suspicions were often given credence without evidence, and the level of threat was often greatly exaggerated. Many people suffered unemployment, destruction of the careers, and even imprisonment at that time. The hysteria also touched Miller personally. He was denied a passport and was convicted on contempt charges for refusing to name the so-called Communists.

In 1955, another Pulitzer Prize-winning one-act play, *A View from the Bridge* was produced with *A Memory of Two Mondays*. Meanwhile, Miller's first marriage failed and ended in divorce. He met the glamorous film star Marilyn Monroe and married her. The second marriage lasted three years, ending in another divorce. Miller's *After the Fall* was staged in 1964, which was a semi-autobiography, revealing Miller's views on life, marriage, politics, and some other issues. Arthur Miller was an industrious and prolific playwright. He kept on penning until the new millennium. His later works include: *The Price* (1968), *The American Clock* (1979), *A Life* (1995), *Mr. Peters' Connections* (1999), *The Ride down Mt. Morgan* (1999) and *Echoes Down the Corridor, Collected Essays* 1944-2000 (2000). Miller died of heart failure in 2005, but he has remained very influential as one of the greatest practitioner of the American stage.

II. Texts.

Death of a Salesman

Certain Private Conversations in Two Acts and a Requiem

THE CHARACTERS

WILLY LOMAN
LINDA
BIFF
HAPPY
BERNARD
THE WOMAN
CHARLEY
UNCLE BEN
HOWARD WAGNER
JENNY
STANLEY
MISS FORSYTHE
LETTA

The action takes place in WILLY LOMAN's house and yard and in various places he visits in the New York and Boston of today.

A melody is heard, played upon a flute. It is small and fine, telling of grass and trees and the horizon. The curtain rises.

Before us is the Salesman's house. We are aware of towering, angular shapes behind it, surrounding it on all sides. Only the blue light of the sky falls upon the house and forestage; the surrounding area shows an angry① glow of orange. As more light appears, we see a solid vault of apartment houses around the small, fragile-seeming home. An air of the dream clings to the place, a dream rising out of reality. The kitchen at center seems actual enough, for there is a kitchen table with three chairs, and a refrigerator. But no other fixtures are seen. At the back of the kitchen there is a draped entrance, which leads to the living room. To the right of the kitchen, on a level raised two feet, is a bedroom furnished only with a brass bedstead and a straight chair. On a shelf over the bed a silver athletic trophy stands. A window opens onto the apartment house at the side.

Behind the kitchen, on a level raised six and a half feet, is the boys' bedroom, at present barely visible. Two beds are dimly seen, and at the back of the room a dormer window②. (This bedroom is above the unseen living room.) At the left a stairway curves up to it from the kitchen.

The entire setting is wholly or, in some places, partially transparent. The roof-line of the house is one-dimensional; under and over it we see the apartment buildings. Before the house lies an apron③, curving beyond the forestage into the orchestra④. This forward area serves as the back yard as well as the locale of all WILLY's imaginings and of his city scenes. Whenever the action is in the present the actors observe the imaginary wall-lines, entering the house only through its door at the left. But in the scenes of the past these boundaries are broken, and characters enter or leave a room by stepping "through" a wall onto the forestage.

From the right, WILLY LOMAN, the Salesman, enters, carrying two large sample cases. The flute plays on. He hears but is not aware of it. He is past sixty years of age, dressed quietly⑤. Even as he crosses the stage to the doorway of the house, his exhaustion is apparent. He unlocks the door, comes into the kitchen, and thankfully lets his burden down, feeling the soreness of his palms. A word-sigh escapes his lips —it might be "Oh, boy, oh, boy." He closes the door, then carries his cases out into the living room, through the draped kitchen doorway.

Linda, his wife, has stirred in her bed at the right. She gets out and puts on a robe, listening. Most often jovial, she has developed an iron repression of her exceptions⑥ to WILLY's behavior—she more than loves him, she admires him, as though his mercurial nature, his temper, his massive dreams and little cruelties, served her only as sharp reminders of the turbulent longings within him, longings which she shares but lacks the temperament to utter and follow to their end.

LINDA[hearing Willy outside the bedroom, calls with some trepidation] Willy!
WILLY   It's all right. I came back.
LINDA   Why? What happened?[Slight pause] Did something happen, Willy?

---

① angry: (颜色)刺目的
② a dormer window: 屋顶窗
③ apron: 前舞台口,指戏院中幕前延伸的舞台部分
④ orchestra: 乐池,指剧院里器乐演奏者的位置,紧靠舞台前部并略低于舞台
⑤ dressed quietly: (衣服)朴素的,不张扬的
⑥ exception: 不满,生气

WILLY   No, nothing happened.

LINDA   You didn't smash the car, did you?

WILLY [with casual irritation]   I said nothing happened. Didn't you hear me?

LINDA   Don't you feel well?

WILLY   I'm tired to the death. [The flute has faded away. He sits on the bed beside her, a little numb.] I couldn't make it. I just couldn't make it, Linda.

LINDA [very carefully, delicately]   Where were you all day? You look terrible.

WILLY   I got as far as a little above Yonkers. I stopped for a cup of coffee. Maybe it was the coffee.

LINDA   What?

WILLY [after a pause]   I suddenly couldn't drive any more. The car kept going off onto the shoulder①, y' know?

LINDA [helpfully] Oh. Maybe it was the steering again. I don't think Angelo② knows the Studebaker.③

WILLY   No, it's me, it's me. Suddenly I realize I'm goin' sixty miles an hour and I don't remember the last five minutes. I'm—I can't seem to—keep my mind to it.

LINDA   Maybe it's your glasses. You never went for your new glasses.

WILLY   No, I see everything. I came back ten miles an hour. It took me nearly four hours from Yonkers.

LINDA [resigned]   Well, you'll just have to take a rest, Willy, you can't continue this way.

WILLY   I just got back from Florida.

LINDA   But you didn't rest your mind. Your mind is overactive, and the mind is what counts, dear.

WILLY   I'll start out in the morning. Maybe I'll feel better in the morning. [She is taking off his shoes.] These goddam arch supports are killing me.

LINDA   Take an aspirin. Should I get you an aspirin? It'll soothe you.

WILLY [with wonder]   I was driving along, you understand? And I was fine. I was even observing the scenery. You can imagine, me looking at scenery, on the road every week of my life. But it's so beautiful up there, Linda, the trees are so thick, and the sun is warm. I opened the windshield and just let the warm air bathe over me. And then all of a sudden I'm goin' off the road! I'm tellin' ya, I absolutely forgot I was driving. If I'd've gone the other way over the white line I might've killed somebody. So I went on again — and five minutes later I'm dreamin' again, and I nearly—[He presses two fingers against his eyes.] I have such thoughts, I have such strange thoughts.

LINDA   Willy, dear. Talk to them again. There's no reason why you can't work in New

---

① shoulder: 路肩:沿着路面任意一侧的边界或边缘
② Angelo: 一个机修工
③ Studebaker: 威利·洛曼现在驾驶的汽车品牌

York.

WILLY   They don't need me in New York. I'm the New England man.① I'm vital in New England.

LINDA   But you're sixty years old. They can't expect you to keep travelling every week.

WILLY   I'll have to send a wire to Portland. I'm supposed to see Brown and Morrison tomorrow morning at ten o'clock to show the line②. Goddammit, I could sell them! [He starts putting on his jacket.]

LINDA[taking the jacket from him]   Why don't you go down to the place tomorrow and tell Howard you've simply got to work in New York? You're too accommodating, dear.

WILLY   If old man Wagner③ was alive I'd a been in charge of New York now! That man was a prince, he was a masterful man. But that boy of his, that Howard, he don't appreciate. When I went north the first time, the Wagner Company didn't know where New England was!

LINDA   Why don't you tell those things to Howard, dear?

WILLY[encouraged]   I will, I definitely will. Is there any cheese?

LINDA   I'll make you a sandwich.

WILLY   No, go to sleep. I'll take some milk. I'll be up right away. The boys in?

LINDA   They're sleeping. Happy took Biff on a date tonight.

WILLY[interested]   That so?

LINDA   It was so nice to see them shaving together, one behind the other, in the bathroom. And going out together. You notice? The whole house smells of shaving lotion.

WILLY   Figure it out. Work a lifetime to pay off a house. You finally own it, and there's nobody to live in it.

LINDA   Well, dear, life is a casting off. It's always that way.

WILLY   No, no, some people—some people accomplish something. Did Biff say anything after I went this morning?

LINDA   You shouldn't have criticized him, Willy, especially after he just got off the train. You mustn't lose your temper with him.

WILLY   When the hell did I lose my temper? I simply asked him if he was making any money. Is that a criticism?

LINDA   But, dear, how could he make any money?

WILLY[worried and angered]   There's such an undercurrent in him. He became a moody man. Did he apologize when I left this morning?

LINDA   He was crestfallen④, Willy. You know how he admires you. I think if he finds

---

① I am the New England man: 威利·洛曼负责在新英格兰地区销售货品
② line: 推销的货物的样品
③ old man Wagner: 威利·洛曼现任老板 Howard Wagner 的父亲,也是公司的上任老板
④ crestfallen: 垂头丧气的

himself①, then you'll both be happier and not fight any more.

WILLY   How can he find himself on a farm? Is that a life? A farmhand? In the beginning, when he was young, I thought, well, a young man, it's good for him to tramp around, take a lot of different jobs. But it's more than ten years now and he has yet to make thirty-five dollars a week?

LINDA   He's finding himself, Willy.

WILLY   Not finding yourself at the age of thirty-four is a disgrace!

LINDA   Shh!

WILLY   The trouble is he's lazy, goddammit!

LINDA   Willy, please!

WILLY   Biff is a lazy bum!

LINDA   They're sleeping. Get something to eat. Go on down.

WILLY   Why did he come home? I would like to know what brought him home.

LINDA   I don't know. I think he's still lost, Willy. I think he's very lost.

WILLY   Biff Loman is lost. In the greatest country in the world a young man with such—personal attractiveness, gets lost. And such a hard worker. There's one thing about Biff—he's not lazy.

LINDA   Never.

LINDA[trying to bring him out of it]   Willy, dear, I got a new kind of American-type cheese today. It's whipped.

WILLY   Why do you get American when I like Swiss? WILLY[with pity and resolve]   I'll see him in the morning; I'll have a nice talk with him. I'll get him a job selling. He could be big② in no time. My God! Remember how they used to follow him around in high school? When he smiled at one of them their faces lit up. When he walked down the street … [He loses himself in reminiscences.]

LINDA   I just thought you'd like a change—

WILLY   I don't want a change! I want Swiss cheese. Why am I always being contradicted?

LINDA [with a covering laugh]   I thought it would be a surprise.

WILLY   Why don't you open a window in here, for God's sake?

LINDA[with infinite patience]   They're all open, dear.

WILLY   The way they boxed us in here. Bricks and windows, windows and bricks.

LINDA   We should've bought the land next door.

WILLY   The street is lined with cars. There's not a breath of fresh air in the neighborhood. The grass don't grow any more, you can't raise a carrot in the back yard. They should've had a law against apartment houses. Remember those two beautiful elm trees out there? When I and Biff hung the swing between them?

---

① if he finds himself: 如果他能在生活中找到自己的合适的位置
② big: 显赫的,在地位、财富或重要性方面惹人注目的

LINDA   Yeah, like being a million miles from the city.

WILLY   They should've arrested the builder for cutting those down. They massacred the neighborhood. [lost] More and more I think of those days, Linda. This time of year it was lilac and wisteria. And then the peonies would come out, and the daffodils. What fragrance in this room!

LINDA   Well, after all, people had to move somewhere.

WILLY   No, there's more people now.

LINDA   I don't think there's more people. I think—

WILLY   There's more people! That's what ruining this country! Population is getting out of control. The competition is maddening! Smell the stink from that apartment house! And another one on the other side… How can they whip cheese?

[On Willy's last line, BIFF and HAPPY raise themselves up in their beds, listening.]

LINDA   Go down, try it. And be quiet.

WILLY [turning to Linda, guiltily]   You're not worried about me, are you, sweetheart?

BIFF   What's the matter?

HAPPY   Listen!

LINDA   You've got too much on the ball① to worry about.

WILLY   You're my foundation and my support, Linda.

LINDA   Just try to relax, dear. You make mountains out of molehills.

……

Ⅲ. Notes.

1. *Death of a Salesman* tells the story of how a salesman, who keeps selling goods to distant locations by car for many years, comes to realize that his life has been a failure. He believes in the magic of salesmanship and is obsessed with it, but he seems to have never obtained the respect or the material wealth brought by it as he expects. What is worse, although he places all his hopes on his elder son, Biff, to fulfill his disillusioned dream, both sons prove to be disappointing. He finally commits suicide, in an attempt to bequeath to his family a life insurance.

2. Act One of the play begins with Willy Loman's talk with his wife, Linda, which apparently reflects that Willy keeps falling into a trance while driving as he has formed the habit of contradicting himself. While Biff and Happy's conversation indicates that Biff lives in unsteadiness and is an occasional stealer, whereas Happy is indulged in a dissipated life.

Ⅳ. Key words (关键词).

Disillusionment of "American dream": 美国梦的幻灭。"美国梦"一词首次出现在詹姆斯·特拉斯洛·亚当斯所写的《美国史诗》(1931)一书中。美国梦是一个被众多美国人普遍信仰的信念:在美国只要经过努力和不懈的奋斗,每个人均有机会获得更好的生活。美国梦的宗旨原是指对道德价值和幸福的追求,但这种追求很快就变成了对财富的贪婪追

---

① on the ball: 机灵的,具有成功的潜质的

求。美国的社会现实与梦想常形成强烈的反差,因而生活中也就充满了美国梦破灭的实例,这成为很多美国作家创作的主题。

Realism: 现实主义。文学中的现实主义始于十九世纪法国文学中的一些作品,并一直延续至二十世纪初。现实主义作家力求以"写实"的手法来描写当代社会生活。他们描写日常生活中的琐碎活动和平庸经历,而不愿进行传奇化或程式化的表述。密勒在《推销员之死》中采用现实主义的描写手法,以强化普通人物的日常俗语表达。

Expressionism: 表现主义。二十世纪初,表现主义起源于德国,最初出现在诗歌和绘画领域。表现主义的突出特点是以完全主观的视角来表现世界,极度扭曲现实世界以期得到某种情感效果,并希望清晰地传达出个人的情绪和思想。表现主义者力求表达"活着"的意义和情感体验,而不仅仅是表现客观现实。在《推销员之死》中,密勒很好地把握了时间和空间的流动性,这是表现主义手法的体现。

Ⅴ. Questions.

1. Why do you think Willy came home that day?

2. How does Miller use the skills of Realism and Expressionism in the selected section? Exemplify them.

3. How do you understand the disillusionment of "American dream" represented in this play?

Lesson 35 Edward Albee (1928—)

I. A Brief Review.

Born in Washington D. C. in 1928, Edward Albee was adopted by an affluent couple from New York. He began his writing during his high school days, but was dismissed for playing truant. At the age of twenty, after years of expensive schooling at a number of schools and universities in succession, he went to New York City's Greenwich Village to study avant-garde art. After the troublesome youth, Albee began his career as a playwright in his early thirties. Albee's first major play, *The Zoo Story* (1958) was first staged in Berlin, an experimental play not only bringing him immediate success but also initiating the link between him and the American absurd theatre. The one-act drama presents how a young homosexual tricks a middle-aged, innocent, ordinary man, whom he happens to encounter in a park, into killing him. It reveals the failure of communication between people in the modern world.

图 35 Edward Albee

Another short play, *The Sandbox* (1960), symbolically deals with family relationships between Mommy and Daddy and Grandma. The couple are intriguing to desert the aged Grandma by leaving her on a beach to be picked up by a young man standing for Death. Similar characters appeared later in *The "American Dream"* (1961), which also treats the relationship between a married couple and their mother. As Edward Albee states in the preface to the play, "[It is] an examination of the American Scene, an attack on the substitution of artificial for real values in our society, a condemnation of complacency, cruelty, emasculation, and vacuity; it is a stand against the fiction that everything in this slipping land of ours is peachy-keen." He transcends the "American dream" and goes into the essence of American family. Albee's first full-length play, *Who's Afraid of Virginia Woolf?*, produced in 1962, is generally considered his greatest dramatic achievement. Albee's plays also include: *Tiny Alice* (1964), *A Delicate Balance* (1966), *Box and Quotations from Chairman Mao Tse-tung* (1968), *All Over* (1971), *Seascape* (1975) and others.

In general, his works are considered well-crafted, often unsympathetic examinations of the modern condition. His early plays focus on the discussion of modern man's predicament, such as human loneliness, the unwillingness or inability to communicate, and the spiritual waste land. He is always labeled as an American absurdist playwright. Although he denies this identity, his worldview is existential; he makes good use of repetitions, clichés and other inventive handling of dialogue; moreover, his plays are usually progressive in plot and the endings always bring the stories to unexpectedness. In the new century, he continues the American experimentation with basically realistic theatre in his new works, such as *The Goat: Or, Who is Sylvia?* (2002). Albee has won three Pulitzer Prizes so far, a Special Tony Award for Life-time Achievement and many other awards.

Ⅱ. Texts.

Who's Afraid of Virginia Woolf?

GEORGE: ... Now, take our son①...

HONEY: Who?

GEORGE: Our son ... Martha's and my little joy!

NICK (*Moving toward the bar*): Do you mind if I ...?

GEORGE: No, no; you go right ahead.

MARTHA: George ...

GEORGE (*Too kindly*): Yes, Martha?

MARTHA: Just what are you doing?

GEORGE: Why, Love, I was talking about our son.

MARTHA: Don't.

GEORGE: Isn't Martha something? Here we are, on the eve of our boy's homecoming, the eve of his twenty-first birthday, the eve of his majority ... and Martha says don't talk about him.

MARTHA: Just ... don't.

GEORGE: But I want to, Martha! It's very important we talk about him. Now bunny② and the ... houseboy or stud③ here, whichever he is ... don't know much about junior, and I think they should.

MARTHA: Just ... don't.

GEORGE (*Snapping his fingers at* NICK): You. Hey, you! You want to play bringing up baby, don't you!

NICK (*Hardly civil*): Were you snapping at me?

GEORGE: That's right. (*Instructing him*) You want to hear about our bouncy boy.

NICK (Pause; then, shortly): Yeah; sure.

---

① take our son: 就拿我们的儿子来说吧

② bunny: bunny 是儿童对小兔子的昵称,在美国俚语中也指可爱的女郎。本剧中指 Honey,她个性温和,长相平平。Nick 因为她怀孕而和她结婚

③ houseboy or stud: houseboy 指"男仆",而 stud"种马",在美国俚语中指性欲旺盛的男子。乔治一直怀疑妻子与迪克有染却有没有证据,因此经常试探

GEORGE (*To* HONEY): And you, my dear? You want to hear about him, too, don't you.

HONEY: Whom?

GEORGE: Martha's and my son.

HONEY: Oh, you have a child? (MARTHA *and* NICK *laugh uncomfortably*)

GEORGE: Oh, indeed; do we ever! Do you want to talk about him, Martha, or shall I? Hunh?

MARTHA (*A smile that is a sneer*): Don't, George.

GEORGE: All rightie. Well, now; let's see. He's a nice kid, really, in spite of his home life; I mean, most kids'd grow up neurotic, what with① Martha here carrying on the way she does: sleeping 'til four in the P. M., climbing all over the poor bastard, trying to break the bathroom door down to wash him in the tub when he's sixteen, dragging strangers into the house at all hours …

MARTHA (*Rising*): O. K. YOU!

GEORGE (*Mock concern*): Martha!

MARTHA: That's enough!

GEORGE: Well, do you want to take over?

HONEY (*To* NICK): Why would anybody want to wash somebody who's sixteen years old?

NICK (*Slamming his drink down*): Oh, for Christ's sake, Honey!

HONEY (*Stage whisper*): Well, why?!

GEORGE: Because it's her baby-poo②.

MARTHA: ALL RIGHT!! (*By rote; a kind of almost-tearful recitation*) Our son. You want our son? You'll have it.

GEORGE: You want a drink, Martha?

MARTHA (*Pathetically*): Yes.

NICK (*To* MARTHA *kindly*): We don't have to hear about it … if you don't want to.

GEORGE: Who says so? You in a position to set the rules around here?

NICK (*Pause; tight-lipped*): No.

GEORGE: Good boy; you'll go far. All right, Martha; your recitation, please.

MARTHA (*From far away*③): What, George?

GEORGE (*Prompting*): "Our son …"

MARTHA: All right. Our son. Our son was born in a September night, a night not unlike tonight, though tomorrow, and twenty … one … years ago.

GEORGE (*Beginning of quiet asides*): You see? I told you.

MARTHA: That was an easy birth …

GEORGE: Oh, Martha; no. You labored…how you labored.

---

① what with: 考虑到
② -poo: 该后缀此处表示乔治的轻蔑与不屑
③ from far away: 神情恍惚,心不在焉

MARTHA: That was an easy birth, once it had been ... accepted, relaxed into.

GEORGE: Ah ... yes. Better.

MARTHA: That was an easy birth, once it had been accepted, and I was young.

GEORGE: And I was younger ... (*Laughs quietly to himself*)

MARTHA: And I was young, and he was a healthy child, a red, bawling child, with slippery firm limbs ...

GEORGE: Martha thinks she saw him at delivery ...

MARTHA: With slippery, firm limbs, and a full head of black, fine, fine hair which, oh, later, later, became blond as the sun, our son①.

GEORGE: He was a healthy child.

MARTHA: And I had wanted a child ... oh, I had wanted a child.

GEORGE (*Prodding her*): A son? A daughter?

MARTHA: A child! (*Quieter*) A child. And I had my child.

GEORGE: Our child.

MARTHA (*With great sadness*): Our child. And we raised him ... (*Laughs, briefly, bitterly*) yes, we did; we raised him...

GEORGE: With teddy bears and an antique bassinet from Austria ... and no nurse.

MARTHA: With teddy bears and transparent floating goldfish, and a pale blue bed with cane at the headboard when he was older, cane which he wore through ... finally ... with his little hands ... in his ... sleep ...

GEORGE: ... nightmares ...

MARTHA: ... sleep ... He was a restless child...

GEORGE (*Soft chuckle, head-shaking of disbelief*): ... Oh Lord...

MARTHA: ... sleep... and a croup tent... a pale green croup tent, and the shining kettle hissing in the one light of the room that time he was sick ... those four days ... and animal crackers, and the bow and arrow he kept under his bed ...

GEORGE: ... the arrows with rubber cups at their trip ...

MARTHA: ... at their trip, which he kept beneath his bed ...

GEORGE: Why? Why, Martha?

MARTHA: ... for fear ... for fear of ...

GEORGE: For fear. Just that: for fear.

MARTHA: (*Vaguely waving him off; going on*) ... and ... and sandwiches on Sunday night, and Saturdays ... (*Pleased recollection*) ... and Saturdays the banana boat, the whole peeled banana, scooped out on top, with green grapes for the crew, a double line of green grapes, and along the sides, stuck to the boat with toothpicks, orange slices ... SHIELDS.

GEORGE: And for the oar?

MARTHA (*Uncertainly*): A ... carrot?

---

① as the sun, our son: sun 和 son 同音,构成双关语

GEORGE: Or a swizzle stick, whatever was easier.

MARTHA: No. A carrot. And his eyes were green … green with … if you peered so deep into them … so deep … bronze … bronze parentheses around the irises… such green eyes!

GEORGE: … blue, green, brown …

MARTHA: … and he loves the sun! … He was tan before and after everyone … and in the sun his hair … became … fleece.

GEORGE (*Echoing her*): … fleece …

MARTHA: … beautiful, beautiful boy.

GEORGE: Absolve, Domine, animas omnium fidelium defunctorum ab omni vinculo delictorum. ①

MARTHA: … and school … and summer camp … and sledding … and swimming …

GEORGE: Et gratia tua illis succurrente, mereantur evadere judicium ultionis. ②

MARTHA (*Laughing, to herself*): … and how he broke his arm … how funny it was… oh, no, it hurt him! …but, oh, it was funny … in a field, his very first cow, the first he'd ever seen … and he went into the field, to the cow, where the cow was grazing, head down, busy … and he moo'd at it! (*Laughs ibid*) He moo'd at him, all three years of him, and he ran, startled, and he stumbled … Fell … and broke his poor arm. (*Laughs, ibid*) Poor lamb.

GEORGE: Et lucis aeternae beautitudine perfrui. ③

MARTHA: George cried! Helpless… George… cried. I carried the poor lamb. George snuffling beside me, I carried the child, having fashioned a sling … and across the great fields.

GEORGE: In Paradisum deducant te Angeli. ④

MARTHA: And as he grew … and as he grew… oh! So wise! … he walked evenly between us… (*She spreads her hands*) … a hand out to each of us for what we could offer by way of support, affection, teaching, even love … and these hands, still, to hold us off a bit, for mutual protection, to protect us all from George's … weakness … and my necessary greater strength… to protect himself … and *us*.

GEORGE: In memoria aeterna erit Justus: ab auditione mala non timebit. ⑤

MARTHA: So wise; so wise.

NICK (*To GEORGE*): What is this? What are you doing?

GEORGE: Shhhhh.

HONEY: Shhhhh.

---

① Absolve, Domine, animas omnium fidelium defunctorum ab omni vinculo delictorum:（拉）天主,求你赦免所有虔诚者的一切罪行(杨敦惠译)。本句出自《安魂曲》中的《联想曲》

② Et gratia tua illis succurrente, mereantur evadere judicium ultionis:（拉）借着你的慈悲之助,希望他们能够逃脱惩罚式的判决。出处同上

③ Et lucis aeternae beautitudine perfrui:（拉）并享有永生的快乐

④ In Paradisum deducant te Angeli:（拉）愿天使引导你进入天堂。出自《安魂曲》中的《在天堂》

⑤ In memoria aeterna erit Justus: ab auditione mala non timebit:（拉）正直的人将留存于不朽的回忆中；他将不畏邪恶的审听(杨敦惠译)。本句出自《安魂曲》中的《阶台经》

NICK (*Shrugging*): O. K.

MARTHA: So beautiful; so wise.

GEORGE (*Laughs quietly*): All truth being relative.

MARTHA: It was true! Beautiful; wise; perfect.

GEORGE: There's a real mother talking.

HONEY: (*Suddenly; almost tearfully*) I want a child.

NICK: Honey…

HONEY (More forcefully): I want a child!

GEORGE: On principle?

HONEY (in tears): I want a child. I want a baby.

MARTHA: (Waiting out the interruption, not really paying it any mind) Of course, this state, this perfection … couldn't last. Not with George … not with George around.

GEORGE (Mock awe): Sorry … mother.

NICK: Can't you be still?

GEORGE (Making a sign at NICK): Dominus vobiscum.①

MARTHA: Not with George around. A drowning man takes down those nearest. George tried, but, oh, God, how I fought him. God, how I fought him.

GEORGE (A satisfied laughs): Ahhhhhhh.

MARTHA: Lesser states can't stand those above them. Weakness, imperfection cries out against strength, goodness and innocence. And George tried.

GEORGE: How did I try, Martha? How did I try?

MARTHA: How did you … what? … No! No … he grew … our son grew … up; he is grown up; he is away at school, college. He is fine, everything is fine.

GEORGE (Mocking): Oh, come on, Martha!

MARTHA: No. That's all.

GEORGE: Just a minute! You can't cut a story off like that, sweetheart. You started to say something … now you say it!

MARTHA: No!

GEORGE: Well, I will.

MARTHA: No!

GEORGE: You see, Martha, here, stops just when the going gets good … just when things start getting a little girl; she really is. Not only does she have a husband who is a bog … a younger-than-she-is bog albeit … not only does she have a husband who is a bog, she has as well a tiny problem with spirituous liquors—like she can't get enough …

MARTHA (Without energy): No more, George.

GEORGE: … and on top of all that, poor weighed-down girl, PLUS a father who really doesn't give a damn whether she lives or dies, who couldn't care less *what* happens to his only

---

① Dominus vobiscum: (拉)愿主与你们同在

daughter ... on the top of all that she has a *son*. She has a son who fought her every inch of the way, who didn't want to be turned into a weapon against his father, who didn't want to be used as a goddamn club whenever Martha didn't get things like she wanted them!

MARTHA (Rising to it): Lies! Lies!!

GEORGE: Lies? All right. A son who would *not* disown his father, who came to him for advice, for information, for love that wasn't mixed with sickness—and you know what I mean, Martha!—who could not tolerate the slashing, braying① residue that called itself his MOTHER. MOTHER? HAH!!

MARTHA (*Cold*): All right, you. A son who was so ashamed of his father he asked me once if it—possibly—wasn't true, as he had heard, from some cruel boys, maybe, that he was not our child; who could not tolerate the shabby failure his father had become ...

GEORGE: Lies!

MARTHA: Lies? Who would not bring his girl friends to the house ...

GEORGE: ... in shame of his mother ...

MARTHA: ... of his father! Who writes letters only to me!

GEORGE: Oh, so you think! To me! At my office!

MARTHA: Liar!

GEORGE: I have a stack of them!

MARTHA: YOU HAVE NO LETTERS!

GEORGE: And you have?

MARTHA: He has no letters. A son ... a son who spends his summers away... away from his family... ON ANY PRETEXT... because he can't stand the shadow of a man flickering around the edges of a house...

GEORGE: ... who spends his summers away... and he does! Who spends his summers away because there isn't room for him in a house full of empty bottles, lies, strange men, and a harridan② who...

MARTHA: Liar!!

GEORGE: Liar?

MARTHA: ... A son who I have raised as best I can against ... vicious odds, against the corruption of weakness and petty revenges ...

GEORGE: ... A son who is, deep in his gut, sorry, to have been born...

...

GEORGE: All fight. (Pause) Time for bed.

MARTHA: Yes.

GEORGE: Are you tired?

MARTHA: Yes.

---

① bray: 大声而刺耳地发出声响
② harridan: 形容枯槁(或脾气暴躁)的老妇人,名声不好的老泼妇

GEORGE: I am.

MARTHA: Yes.

GEORGE: Sunday tomorrow; all day.

MARTHA: Yes. (A long silence between them) Did you … did you … have to?

GEORGE (Pause): Yes.

MARTHA: I don't know.

GEORGE: It was … time.

MARTHA: Was it?

GEORGE: Yes.

MARTHA (Pause): I'm cold.

GEORGE: It's late.

MARTHA: Yes.

GEORGE (Long silence): It will be better.

MARTHA (Long silence): I don't … know.

GEORGE: It will be … maybe.

MARTHA: I'm … not … sure.

GEORGE: No.

MARTHA: Just … us?

GEORGE: Yes.

MARTHA: I don't suppose, maybe, we could…

GEORGE: No, Martha.

MARTHA: Yes. No.

GEORGE: Are you all right?

MARTHA: Yes. No.

GEORGE (Puts his hand gently on her shoulder; she puts her head back, and sings to her, very softly): Who's afraid of Virginia Woolf

     Virginia Woolf

     Virginia Woolf,

MARTHA: I … am … George …

GEORGE: Who's afraid of Virginia Woolf…

MARTHA: I … am … George … I … am …

(GEORE nods, slowly)

(Silence; tableau①)

CURTAIN

---

① tableau: 场景,一幕场景中的一个插曲,此时舞台上所有演员都在他们各自的位置上静止下来,片刻后再次恢复先前的动作

Ⅲ. Notes.

1. *Who's Afraid of Virginia Woolf?* is Edward Albee's first three-act play. It was awarded the New York Drama Critics Circle Award for best new play in 1963. It was also nominated for six Tony Awards and won five. No Pulitzer Prize for drama was awarded this year after one judge rejected the nominated play, labeling it "a filthy play", and Committee members resigned in protest. *Who's Afraid of Virginia Woolf?* is set on the campus of a small, New England university. It presents one night drinking of a middle-aged professor and his wife, joined by a new math professor and his silly wife. Through verbal torturing against one another, they eventually achieve catharsis.

2. In the first act, "Fun and Games", the couple fight and humiliate each other, transforming their guests into at once their audience, their pawns, as well as the means to complete their story. In the second act, "Walpurgisnacht", the couple even seduce their guests to tell their secrets and reveal their true selves. In the last act, "The Exorcism", all four characters' secrets have been revealed and purged. The guests go home and the couple try to rebuild their relationship.

Ⅳ. Key Words (关键词).

Marriage: 婚姻。婚姻是美国人珍视的价值观之一。婚姻是作家探讨两性关系和社会现实的绝佳领域。阿尔比在《谁害怕弗吉尼亚·沃尔夫?》中批判性地分析了婚姻,揭示出婚姻可能是为逃避现实而制造出的产物。乔治和玛莎本是相互关爱的一对夫妻,但他们的婚姻却渐渐演变成一场恶战。

Sexuality: 性。性是女性主义研究、性别研究等多个研究领域关注的主题,也是文学创作中经常涉及的内容。从古至今,关于两性之间先天形成的或后天追加的异同,人们一直在不断地研究和探讨。但关于性的描写多为隐晦的;直白的性描写则被视为淫秽。《谁害怕弗吉尼亚·沃尔夫?》中对性不加任何掩饰的描述使该剧引起了巨大争议,也使阿尔比错失了当年的普利策奖。

Religion: 宗教。它是最古老的文学创作母题之一,无论是颂扬还是贬抑,对宗教的描写可以说贯穿整个文学发展史。宗教是探讨人性的理想场域,因而一直以来它都是作家乐于在作品中表现的内容。阿尔比的《谁害怕弗吉尼亚·沃尔夫?》中折射出浓郁的宗教色彩。

Ⅴ. Questions.

1. How do you understand marriage after reading the selected section?
2. What do you think of Albee's attitude toward religion in this play?
3. How do you interpret the title of this play?

Lesson 36 Joseph Heller (1923—1999)

I. A Brief Review.

图 36 Joseph Heller

Born in New York's Coney Island in 1923, Joseph Heller was an American satirical novelist, short story writer, and playwright. Fatherless, he grew up with his Russian-immigrant mother and two older half-siblings. Though he had witnessed the aftermath of the Depression, he himself was well protected by a close-knit Jewish-Italian neighborhood. He enlisted in the United States Air Force in the Second World War and served as a bombardier. Later he received an A. B. from New York University and M. A. from Columbia University. He enjoyed a long career as a writer and a teacher. His best-selling books include *Something Happened* (1974), *Good as Gold* (1979), *Picture This* (1988), *God Knows* (1984), and *Closing Time* (1994). His first novel, *Catch-22* (1961), remains his most influential masterpiece, the title of which has entered the English lexicon to stand for a dilemma with no way out. His other works center on the lives of various members of the middle class and remain exemplars of modern satire.

Catch-22 is a grotesquely comic novel of Captain Yossarian, an American bombardier stationed in Italy at the end of World War II. Obsessed with the fear that everyone around him is trying to kill him, he is eager to complete the missions and then go home. Moreover, the colonel on the base of the US Air Force keeps raising the number of the missions, so that he has no choice but to stay. When he discovers that insane pilots will be discharged from military service, he pleads Doctor Daneeka to ground him on the basis of insanity but is told that according to army regulation Catch-22, anyone who claims that he is insane actually has proved that he is obviously sane, for only sane person could claim that he is insane for dodging flying missions. Therefore, although the symbolic novel allows for different understandings of its themes, one of them must be the absurdity of bureaucracy. The United States Air Force Academy even uses the novel to "help prospective officers recognize the dehumanizing aspects of bureaucracy."

The alternating play of humor and terror in the novel to depict the paradox in modern society marks Joseph Heller's contribution as the representative of black humor. Interestingly, his work does predict the Vietnam War and part of its aftermath, that is, the disillusionment about the military that many Americans experienced. Heller is generally regarded as one of the best post-World War II satirists.

Ⅱ. Texts.

Snowden

……

They gave Yossarian total anesthesia and knocked him out. He woke up thirsty in a private room, drowning in ether fumes. Colonel Korn was there at his bedside, waiting calmly in a chair in his baggy, wool, olive-drab① shirt and trousers. A bland, phlegmatic② smile hung on his brown face with its heavy-bearded cheeks, and he was buffing the facets of his bald head gently with the palms of both hands. He bent forward chuckling when Yossarian awoke, and assured him in the friendliest tones that the deal they had made was still on if Yossarian didn't die. Yossarian vomited, and Colonel Korn shot to his feet at the first cough and fled in disgust, so it seemed indeed that there was a silver lining to every cloud, Yossarian reflected, as he drifted back into a suffocating daze. A hand with sharp fingers shook him awake roughly. He turned and opened his eyes and saw a strange man with a mean face who curled his lip at him in a spiteful scowl and bragged, "We've got your pal, buddy. We've got your pal."

Yossarian turned cold and faint and broke into a sweat.

"Who's my pal?" he asked when he saw the chaplain sitting where Colonel Korn had been sitting.

"Maybe I'm your pal," the chaplain answered.

But Yossarian couldn't hear him and closed his eyes. Someone gave him water to sip and tiptoed away. He slept and woke up feeling great until he turned his head to smile at the chaplain and saw Aarfy there instead. Yossarian moaned instinctively and screwed his face up③ with excruciating④ irritability when Aarfy chortled and asked how he was feeling. Aarfy looked puzzled when Yossarian inquired why he was not in jail. Yossarian shut his eyes to make him go away. When he opened them, Aarfy was gone and the chaplain was there. Yossarian broke into laughter when he spied the chaplain's cheerful grin and asked him what in the hell he was so happy about.

"I'm happy about you," the chaplain replied with excited candor and joy. "I heard at Group that you were very seriously injured and that you would have to be sent home if you lived. Colonel Korn said your condition was critical. But I've just learned from one of the doctors that your wound is really a very slight one and that you'll probably be able to leave in a day or two. You're in no danger. It isn't bad at all."

Yossarian listened to the chaplain's news with enormous relief. "That's good."

"Yes," said the chaplain, a pink flush of impish⑤ pleasure creeping into his cheeks. "Yes,

---

① olive-drab: 深绿褐色的
② phlegmatic: 冷静的、冷淡的
③ screw up: 振作
④ excruciating: 极度痛苦的
⑤ impish: 顽皮的

that is good."

Yossarian laughed, recalling his first conversation with the chaplain. "You know, the first time I met you was in the hospital. And now I'm in the hospital again. Just about the only time I see you lately is in the hospital. Where've you been keeping yourself?"

The chaplain shrugged. "I've been praying a lot," he confessed. "I try to stay in my tent as much as I can, and I pray every time Sergeant Whitcomb leaves the area, so that he won't catch me."

"Does it do any good?"

"It takes my mind off my troubles," the chaplain answered with another shrug. "And it gives me something to do."

"Well that's good, then, isn't it?"

"Yes," agreed the chaplain enthusiastically, as though the idea had not occurred to him before. "Yes, I guess that is good." He bent forward impulsively with awkward solicitude. "Yossarian, is there anything I can do for you while you're here, anything I can get you?"

Yossarian teased him jovially. "Like toys, or candy, or chewing gum?"

The chaplain blushed again, grinning self-consciously, and then turned very respectful. "Like books, perhaps, or anything at all. I wish there was something I could do to make you happy. You know, Yossarian, we're all very proud of you."

"Proud?"

"Yes, of course. For risking your life to stop that Nazi assassin. It was a very noble thing to do."

"What Nazi assassin?"

"The one that came here to murder Colonel Cathcart and Colonel Korn. And you saved them. He might have stabbed you to death as you grappled with him on the balcony. It's a lucky thing you're alive!"

Yossarian snickered sardonically when he understood. "That was no Nazi assassin."

"Certainly it was. Colonel Korn said it was."

"That was Nately's girl friend. And she was after me, not Colonel Cathcart and Colonel Korn. She's been trying to kill me ever since I broke the news to her that Nately was dead."

"But how could that be?" the chaplain protested in livid and resentful confusion. "Colonel Cathcart and Colonel Korn both saw him as he ran away. The official report says you stopped a Nazi assassin from killing them."

"Don't believe the official report," Yossarian advised dryly. "It's part of the deal."

"What deal?"

"The deal I made with Colonel Cathcart and Colonel Korn. They'll let me go home a big hero if I say nice things about them to everybody and never criticize them to anyone for making the rest of the men fly more missions."

The chaplain was appalled and rose halfway out of his chair. He bristled① with bellicose② dismay. "But that's terrible! That's a shameful, scandalous deal, isn't it?"

"Odious③," Yossarian answered, staring up woodenly at the ceiling with just the back of his head resting on the pillow. "I think 'odious' is the word we decided on."

"Then how could you agree to it?"

"It's that or a court-martial, Chaplain."

"Oh," the chaplain exclaimed with a look of stark④ remorse, the back of his hand covering his mouth. He lowered himself into his chair uneasily. "I shouldn't have said anything."

"They'd lock me in prison with a bunch of criminals."

"Of course. You must do whatever you think is right, then." The chaplain nodded to himself as though deciding the argument and lapsed into embarrassed silence.

"Don't worry," Yossarian said with a sorrowful laugh after several moments had passed. "I'm not going to do it."

"But you must do it," the chaplain insisted, bending forward with concern. "Really, you must. I had no right to influence you. I really had no right to say anything."

"You didn't influence me." Yossarian hauled himself over onto his side and shook his head in solemn mockery. "Christ, Chaplain! Can you imagine that for a sin? Saving Colonel Cathcart's life! That's one crime I don't want on my record."

The chaplain returned to the subject with caution. "What will you do instead? You can't let them put you in prison."

"I'll fly more missions. Or maybe I really will desert and let them catch me. They probably would."

"And they'd put you in prison. You don't want to go to prison."

"Then I'll just keep flying missions until the war ends, I guess. Some of us have to survive."

"But you might get killed."

"Then I guess I won't fly any more missions."

"What will you do?"

"I don't know."

"Will you let them send you home?"

"I don't know. Is it hot out? It's very warm in here."

"It's very cold out," the chaplain said.

"You know," Yossarian remembered, "a very funny thing happened—maybe I dreamed it. I think a strange man came in here before and told me he's got my pal. I wonder if I imagined it."

"I don't think you did," the chaplain informed him. "You started to tell me about him when I

---

① bristle: 发怒
② bellicose: 好战的
③ odious: 可憎的、令人作呕的
④ stark: 完全的、十足的

dropped in earlier."

"Then he really did say it. 'We've got your pal, buddy,' he said. 'We've got your pal.' He had the most malignant manner I ever saw. I wonder who my pal is."

"I like to think that I'm your pal, Yossarian," the chaplain said with humble sincerity. "And they certainly have got me. They've got my number and they've got me under surveillance, and they've got me right where they want me. That's what they told me at my interrogation."

"No, I don't think it's you he meant," Yossarian decided. "I think it must be someone like Nately or Dunbar. You know, someone who was killed in the war, like Clevinger, Orr, Dobbs, Kid Sampson or McWatt." Yossarian emitted a startled gasp and shook his head. "I just realized it," he exclaimed. "They've got all my pals, haven't they? The only ones left are me and Hungry Joe." He tingled with dread as he saw the chaplain's face go pale. "Chaplain, what is it?"

"Hungry Joe was killed."

"God, no! On a mission?"

"He died in his sleep while having a dream. They found a cat on his face."

"Poor bastard," Yossarian said, and began to cry, hiding his tears in the crook of his shoulder. The chaplain left without saying goodbye. Yossarian ate something and went to sleep. A hand shook him awake in the middle of the night. He opened his eyes and saw a thin, mean man in a patient's bathrobe and pajamas who looked at him with a nasty smirk① and jeered.

"We've got your pal, buddy. We've got your pal."

Yossarian was unnerved. "What the hell are you talking about?" he pleaded in incipient② panic.

"You'll find out, buddy. You'll find out."

Yossarian lunged③ for his tormentor's throat with one hand, but the man glided out of reach effortlessly and vanished into the corridor with a malicious laugh. Yossarian lay there trembling with pounding pulse. He was bathed in icy sweat. He wondered who his pal was. It was dark in the hospital and perfectly quiet. He had no watch to tell him the time. He was wide-awake, and he knew he was a prisoner in one of those sleepless, bedridden nights that would take an eternity to dissolve into dawn. ……

Ⅲ. Notes.

1. *Catch*-22 is noted for its strong atmosphere of black humor, which is exemplified in misplace events, incongruous details, extravagant puns, and lexical distortions. It breaks away from the traditional war fiction and the concept of patriotism or heroism. It mixes horror with comic absurdities to assail authority and bureaucracy.

2. This excerpt is taken from Chapter 41. Yossarian awakens in the hospital where several

---

① smirk: 假笑
② incipient: 初期的, 开始的
③ lung: 突击

unqualified doctors are preparing to perform unnecessary surgery on him. The chaplain visits Yossarian and praises him for protecting the colonel from a Nazi assassin. Yet Yossarian recognizes the lie and refuses to corporate with him. Later, a mysterious man in a bathrobe seizes him and keeps on tormenting him.

Ⅳ. Key Words（关键词）.

Black humor novel: 黑色幽默小说。在美国,黑色幽默小说于二十世纪五六十年代异军突起,它是喜剧或讽刺类型的一个分支。这种戏剧类型以幽默或讽刺的方法描写通常被认为是禁忌的主题,并保持这些主题的严肃性。黑色幽默小说希望引读者发笑,同时希望读者感受到某种不安。1964 年由斯坦利·库布里克导演的电影《奇爱博士》就是典型的黑色幽默故事。海勒在《第二十二条军规》中将黑色幽默艺术特征发挥到极致。

Paradox: 悖论。似是而非、自相矛盾的观点。将相互矛盾的陈述组合起来,以凸显由这种不合理、不协调所造成的讽刺效果。《第二十二条军规》就是以悖论为基础进行叙述的。悖论加强了《第二十二条军规》的黑色幽默效果,也使小说对体制的控诉更加透彻深入。

Ⅴ. Questions.

1. Describe the term "Catch-22" in your own words.
2. Is there any version of Catch-22 in our daily life?
3. Can you obtain a sense of Black Humor through reading the text?

Lesson 37 John Updike (1932—2009)

I. A Brief Review:

Born in Reading, Pennsylvania in 1932, John Hoyer Updike was an American novelist, poet, short story writer, art critic, and literary critic. Updike was also gifted at drawing and caricature. After graduating laude from Harvard and studying art for one year at Oxford, he began to work for *The New Yorker* in 1955 and since then his affinity with the magazine remained intermittently the whole of his life. As one of the most prolific American writers, he is noted for his works' "patience, leisure and craft". His most famous work is his Rabbit series. The heroes of the stories are adolescents facing and adjusting to the fast changing, environments and

图 37 John Updike

social realities. In total, he has produced over 60 books, including many novels, short story collections, children books, 6 books of poetry, a play, a vast store of book reviews and other prose writings. *The Centaur* (1963) was Updike's most ambitious novel which won the National Book Award in 1964.

The Rabbit series include: *Rabbit, Run* (1960), *Rabbit Redux* (1971), *Rabbit Is Rich* (1981), *Rabbit at Rest* (1990), and the novella *Rabbit Remembered* (2001). The series chronicle the life of Harry "Rabbit" Angstrom over the course of several decades, from young adulthood to his death. Each book in the sequence covers one decade: the 1950s, the 1960s, the late 1970s, and the 1980s. In the first book readers find a fading basketball star who is unsatisfied with his career and family life, attempting to get rid of the constraints but actually leads to a series of sentimental and irresponsible results. In the second book, the chaotic state of the United States is exemplified in Harry's home. Besides the recurring themes of guilt, sex, and death, the second novel touches on issues of the Vietnam War and the black rebellions. The third book examines Harry's persistent problems and complicated life as he is getting into his old age. The fourth book turns to the present society and deals with social issues such as AIDs, drug abuse and diet. Throughout the series, Angstrom becomes a reflection of social transformations during each of the four decades. Both *Rabbit Is Rich* and *Rabbit at Rest* received the Pulitzer Prize. He died of cancer on January 27, 2009.

Also worth mentioning is *Couples* (1964) which created a national sensation with its portrayal of the complicated sex-lives of a set of young married couples in the suburbs. The interwoven themes of sex and religion make the novel remain on the best-seller lists for over a year. Other recurrent themes in John Updike's writing include clash of generations and death. He often combines them in the American Protestant small-town middle class family life. Updike won an array of awards. As the third American to win a second Pulitzer Prize in fiction writing, Updike is considered one of the greatest American fiction writers of his generation.

Ⅱ. Texts.

Separating

……

Now it was here. A Friday. Judith was reacclimated; all four children were assembled, before jobs and camps and visits again scattered them. Joan thought they should be told one by one. Richard was for making an announcement at the table. She said, "I think just making an announcement is a cop-out. They'll start quarrelling and playing to each other instead of focussing. They're each individuals, you know, not just some corporate obstacle to your freedom."

"O. K. , O. K. I agree." Joan's plan was exact. That evening, they were giving Judith a belated welcome-home dinner, of lobster and champagne. Then, the party over, they, the two of them, who nineteen years before would push her in a baby carriage along Tenth Street to Washington Square①, were to walk her out of the house, to the bridge across the salt creek, and tell her, swearing her to secrecy. Then Richard Jr. , who was going directly from work to a rock concert in Boston, would be told, either late when he returned on the train or early Saturday morning before he went off to his jobs; he was seventeen and employed as one of golf-course maintenance crew. Then the two younger children, John and Margaret, could, as the morning wore on, be informed.

"Mopped up②, as it were," Richard said.

"Do you have any better plan? That leaves you the rest of Saturday to answer any questions, pack, and make your wonderful departure."

"No," he said, meaning he had no better plan, and agreed to hers, though it had an edge of false order, a plea for control in the semblance of its achievement, like Joan's long chore lists and financial accountings and, in the days when he first knew her, her too copious lecture notes. Her plan turned one hurdle for him into four—four knife-sharp walls, each with a sheer blind drop on the other side.

All spring he had been morbidly conscious of insides and outsides, of barriers and partitions. He and Joan stood as a thin barrier between the children and the truth. Each moment was a partition, with the past on one side and the future on the other, a future containing this unthinkable *now*. Beyond four knifelike walls a new life for him waited vaguely. His skull cupped a secret, a white face, a face both frightened and soothing, both strange and known, that he wanted to shield

---

① Washington Square: 位于纽约市曼哈顿地区格林威治村
② mop up: 俚语,指收尾工作

from tears, which he felt all about him, solid as the sunlight. So haunted, he had become obsessed with battening down the house against his absence, replacing screens and sash cords, hinges and latches—a Houdini① making things snug before his escape.

The lock. He had still to replace a lock on one of the doors of the screened porch. The task, like most such, proved more difficult than he had imagined. The old lock, aluminum frozen by corrosion, had been deliberately rendered obsolete by manufacturers. Three hardware stores had nothing that even approximately matched the mortised hole its removal (surprisingly easy) left. Another hole had to be gouged, with bits too small and saws too big, and the old hole fitted with a block of wood—the chisels dull, the saw rusty, his fingers thick with lack of sleep. The sun poured down, beyond the porch, on a world of neglect. The bushes already needed pruning, the windward side of the house was shedding flakes of paint, rain would get in when he was gone, insects, rot, death. His family, all those he would lose, filtered through the edges of his awareness as he struggled with screw holes, splinters, opaque instructions, minutiae② of metal.

Judith sat on the porch, a princess returned from exile. She regaled them with stories of fuel shortages, of bomb scares in the Underground, of Pakistani workmen loudly lusting after her as she walked past on her way to dance school. Joan came and went, in and out of the house, calmer than she should have been, praising his struggles with the lock as if this were one more and not the last of their chain of shared chores. The younger of his sons, John, now at fifteen suddenly, unwittingly handsome, for a few minutes held the rickety screen door while his father clumsily hammered and chiselled, each blow a kind of sob in Richard's ears. His younger daughter, having been at a slumber party, slept on the porch hammock through all the noise—heavy and pink, trusting and forsaken. Time, like the sunlight, continued relentlessly; the sunlight slowly slanted. Today was one of the longest days. The lock clicked, worked. He was through. He had a drink; he drank it on the porch, listening to his daughter. "It was so sweet," she was saying, "during the worst of it, how all the butcher's and bakery shops kept open by candlelight. They're all so plucky and cute. From the papers, things sounded so much worse here—people shooting people in gas lines, and everybody freezing."

Richard asked her, "Do you still want to live in England forever?" Forever: the concept, now a reality upon him, pressed and scratched at the back of his throat.

"No," Judith confessed, turning her oval face to him, its eyes still childishly far apart, but the lips set as over something succulent and satisfactory. "I was anxious to come home. I'm an American." She was a woman. They had raised her; he and Joan had endured together to raise her, alone of the four. The others had still some raising left in them. Yet it was the thought of telling Judith—the image of her, their first baby, walking between them arm in arm, to the bridge—that broke him. The partition between himself and the tears broke. Richard sat down to the celebratory meal with the back of his throat aching; the champagne, the lobster seemed phases

---

① Harry Houdini (1874—1926), 匈牙利裔美国魔术师,擅长脱身术表演
② minutia(e): 细枝末节

of sunshine; he saw them and tasted them through tears. He blinked, swallowed, croakily joked about hay fever①. The tears would not stop leaking through; they came not through a hole that could be plugged but through a permeable spot in a membrane, steadily, purely, endlessly, fruitfully. They became, his tears, a shield for himself against these others—their faces, the fact of their assembly, a last time as innocents, at a table where he sat the last time as head. Tears dropped from his nose as he broke the lobster's back; salt flavored his champagne as he sipped it; the raw clench at the back of his throat was delicious. He could not help himself.

His children tried to ignore his tears. Judith on his right, lit a cigarette, gazed upward in the direction of her too energetic, too sophisticated exhalation; on her other side, John earnestly bent his face to the extraction of the last morsels—legs, tail segments—from the scarlet corpse. Joan, at the opposite end of the table, glanced at him surprised, her reproach displaced by a quick grimace②, of forgiveness, or of salute to his superior girl of strategy. Between them, Margaret, no longer called Bean, thirteen and large for her age, gazed from the other side of his pane of tears as if into a shop-window at something she coveted—at her father, a crystalline heap of splinters and memories. It was not she, however, but John who, in the kitchen, as they cleared the plates and carapaces away, asked Joan the question: *"Why is Daddy crying?"*

Richard heard the question but not the murmured answer. Then he heard Bean cry, "Oh, no-oh!" —the faintly dramatized exclamation of one who had long expected it.

John returned to the table carrying a bowl of salad. He nodded tersely at his father and his lips shaped the conspiratorial words "She told."

"Told what?" Richard asked aloud, insanely.

The boy sat down as if to rebuke his father's distraction with the example of his own good manners and said quietly, "The separation."

Joan and Margaret returned; the child, in Richard's twisted vision, seemed diminished in size, and relieved, relieved to have had the boogeyman③ at last proved real. He called out to her—the distances at the table had grown immense—"You knew, you always knew," but the clenching at the back of his throat prevented him from making sense of it. From afar he heard Joan talking, levelly, sensibly, reciting what they had prepared: it was a separation for the summer, and experiment. She and Daddy both agreed it would be good for them; they needed space and time to think; they liked each other but did not make each other happy enough, somehow.

Judith, imitating her mother's factual tone, but in her youth off-key④, too cool, said, "I think it's silly. You should either live together or get divorced."

Richard's crying, like a wave that has crested and crashed, had become tumultuous, but it was overtopped by another tumult, for John, who had been so reserved, now grew larger and

---

① hay fever: 花粉病
② grimace: 鬼脸
③ boogeyman: 具有超人力量的恶巫。很多父母告诉孩子,如果他们表现不好这个恶巫就会抓他们
④ off-key: 不相符的

larger at the table. Perhaps his younger sister's being credited with knowing set him off. "Why didn't you *tell* us?" he asked, in a large round voice quite unlike his own. "You should have told us you weren't getting along."

Richard was startled into attempting to force words through his tears. "We do get along, that's the trouble, so it doesn't show even to us—" "That we do not love each other" was the rest of the sentence; he couldn't finish it.

Joan finished for him, in her style. "And we've always, *especially*, loved our children."

John was not mollified①. "What do you care about us?" he boomed. "We're just little things you had." His sister's laughing forced a laugh from him, which he turned hard and parodistic②: "Ha ha ha." Richard and Joan realized simultaneously that the child was drunk, on Judith's homecoming champagne. Feeling bound to keep the center of the stage, John took a cigarette from Judith's pack, poked it into his mouth, let it hang from his lower lip, and squinted like a gangster.

"You're not little things we had," Richard called to him. "You're the whole point. But you're grown. Or almost."

The boy was lighting matches. Instead of holding them to his cigarette (for they had never seen him smoke; being "good" had been his way of setting himself apart), he held them to his mother's face, closer and closer, for her to blow out. Then he lit the whole folder—a hiss and then a torch, held against his mother's face. Prismed by tears, the flame filled Richard's vision; he didn't know how it was extinguished. He heard Margaret say, "Oh stop showing off," and saw John, in response, break the cigarette in two and put the halves entirely into his mouth and chew, sticking out his tongue to display the shreds to his sister.

Joan talked to him, reasoning—a fountain of reason, unintelligible. "Talked about it for years… our children must help us… Daddy and I both want…" As the boy listened, he carefully wadded a paper napkin into the leaves of his salad, fashioned a ball of paper and lettuce, and popped it into his mouth, looking around the table for the expected laughter. None came. Judith said, "Be mature," and dismissed a plume of smoke.

Richard got up from this stifling③ table and led the boy outside. Though the house was in twilight, the outdoors still brimmed with light, the long waste light of high summer. Both laughing, he supervised John's spitting out the lettuce and paper and tobacco into the pachysandra④. He took him by the hand—a square gritty hand, but for its softness a man's. Yet, it held on. They ran together up into the field, past the tennis court. The raw banking left by the bulldozers was dotted with daisies. Past the court and a flat stretch where they used to play family baseball stood a soft green rise glorious in the sun, each weed and species of grass distinct as illumination on parchment. "I'm sorry, so sorry," Richard cried. "You were the only one who

---

① mollified: 平静的
② parodistic: 讽刺性模仿的
③ stifling: 非常炎热或气闷的,几乎令人窒息的
④ pachysandra: 富贵草

ever tried to help me with all the goddam jobs around this place."

Sobbing, safe within his tears and the champagne, John explained, "It's not just the separation, it's the whole crummy year, I *hate* that school, you can't make any friends, the history teacher's a scud①."

They sat on the crest of the rise, shaking and warm from their tears but easier in their voices, and Richard tried to focus on the child's sad year—the weekdays long with homework, the weekends spent in his room with model airplanes, while his parents murmured down below, nursing their separation. How selfish, how blind, Richard thought; his eyes felt scoured. He told his son, "We'll think about getting you transferred. Life's too short to be miserable."

They had said what they could, but did not want the moment to heal, and talked on, about the school, about the tennis court, whether it would ever again be as good as it had been that first summer. They walked to inspect it and pressed a few more tapes more firmly down. A little stiltedly, perhaps trying to make too much of the moment, to prolong it, Richard led the boy to the spot in the field where the view was best, of the metallic blue river, the emerald marsh, the scattered islands velvet with shadow in the low light, the white bits of beach far away. "See," he said. "It goes on being beautiful. It'll be here tomorrow."

"I know," John answered, impatiently. The moment had closed.

Back in the house, the others had opened some white wine, the champagne being drank, and still sat at the table, the three females, gossiping. Where Joan sat had become the head. She turned, showing him a tearless face, and asked, "All right?"

"We're fine," he said, resenting it, though relieved, that the party went on without him.

……

III. Notes.

1. "Separating" is one of John Updike's best short stories, illustrating the emotional impact that the dissolution of a marriage has on a family. The story focuses on Richard and Joan's separation, which has long been discussed and decided without mentioning the exact reason except that Richard might have been having an affair. The story is about how to inform the separation to their four teenage children. Through the three pairs of conflicts between Richard and his wife, between Richard and the children, and between Richard and himself respectively, Updike depicts an incompatible family: Joan, the wife, is endowed with male idiosyncrasy as cool and calm, whereas Richard appears sensitive and fragile. It is all the same for the four children: both girls take the news calmly while the two boys are relatively more impulsive.

2. "Separating" is a perfect example to indict that John Updike is excellent in portraying the "middleness" in America. The domestic life of a typical American family, the recreation, the public space, the economy, and religion together with the character development of the protagonist, and the reversal of the male and female characters in emotions and actions are just

---

① scud: 学生俚语,飞毛腿

episodes of American middle class life. Besides, the ample use of symbols and euphemisms add to the exquisiteness and complexity of the story.

Ⅳ. Key Words（关键词）.

American middle class: 美国中产阶级。在美国,中产阶级指那些介于极度富有的阶级和无技能的劳工阶级以及失业人群之间的人,包括商人、专业人士、办公室文员以及众多的技术型工人。除了职业和经济地位外,"中产阶级"一词还用于描述某种特定的价值观和态度。由于通常受过良好的教育,有固定的职业和不错的经济收入,社会地位也相对较高,因而美国中产阶级的生活比较稳定。但他们也面对着来自社会、家庭及内心的各种各样的压力和问题。厄普代克对美国中产阶级生活的刻画细致深入,他的作品从不同侧面反映美国中产阶级所面临的问题。

Family conflict: 家庭冲突。作为社会体制中可能是最小单位的冲突类型,家庭冲突一直的文学作品反映和探讨的对象。家庭冲突中表现出的矛盾和问题可能是社会生活中矛盾和问题的集中体现。它或者以细小的冲突展现社会体制中大的矛盾的某些方面,或者以升华的冲突形式浓缩表现社会体制中矛盾和问题。无论如何,家庭冲突绝不单纯是一个家庭的问题。

Ⅴ. Questions.

1. Why does Updike use the present continuous tense in the title?
2. How do the children react to the news of their parents' separation?
3. Can you find any traits that are specific to the American middle class family?

Lesson 38 Saul Bellow (1915—2005)

Ⅰ. A Brief Review.

Born into a Russian-Jewish family in Lachine, Quebec in 1915, Saul Bellow was one of the famous American authors. He was educated at the University of Chicago and Northwestern University, majoring in anthropology and sociology. Later, he taught related courses at Minnesota, Princeton, New York University and elsewhere.

Saul Bellow's first novel, *Dangling Man*, was published when he was twenty-nine. It was written in the form of a journal about a young man waiting to be inducted to the army with his reflections on the relationship between civilian and military life. *The Adventures of Augie March* and *Henderson the Rain King* appeared in the 1950s. The first is a picaresque novel as well as a "novel of development", while

图 38 Saul Bellow

the second is a philosophical quest. His two important novels include *Herzog* (1964) and *Mr. Sammler's Planet* (1970). The former discusses how a Jewish intellectual deals with his relationship between himself and his wife, his children, his friend as well as his career, whereas the latter is a grim novel of social turmoil. *Humboldt's Gift* (1975) depicts how the narrator is helped out of difficulty by his friend and deals with the relationship between art and power in contemporary America. He also published three novellas, *The Bellarosa Connection* (1989), *A Theft* (1989), and *The Actual* (1997). Although much of Saul Bellow's writing focuses on the theme of Jewish life and identity, many of his heroes are characters struggling to pursue their individualism with persistence and resistance, which in a sense transcends the American experience.

Saul Bellow is the only writer to have been nominated for the National Book Award six times and won three times. He was awarded the Pulitzer Prize and the Nobel Prize for Literature "for the human understanding and subtle analysis of contemporary culture that are combined in his work." According to the Swedish Nobel Committee, his writing was characterized by "exuberant ideas, flashing irony, hilarious comedy and burning compassion… the mixture of rich picaresque novel and subtle analysis of our culture, of entertaining adventure, drastic and tragic episodes in quick succession interspersed with philosophic conversation, all developed by a commentator with a witty tongue and penetrating insight into the outer and inner complications that drive us to act, or prevent us from acting, and that can be called the dilemma of our age."

Ⅱ. Texts.

Looking for Mr. Green

Whatsoever thy hand findeth to do, do it with thy might...①

Hard work? No, it wasn't really so hard. He wasn't used to walking and stair-climbing, but the physical difficulty of his new job was not what George Grebe felt most. He was delivering relief checks② in the Negro district③, and although he was a native Chicagoan this was not a part of the city he knew much about—it needed a depression to introduce him to it. No, it wasn't literally hard work, not as reckoned in foot-pounds④, but yet he was beginning to feel the strain of it, to grow aware of its peculiar difficulty. He could find the streets and numbers, but the clients were not where they were supposed to be, and he felt like a hunter inexperienced in the camouflage of his game. It was an unfavorable day, too—fall, and cold, dark weather, windy. But, anyway, instead of shells in his deep trenchcoat pocket he had the cardboard of checks, punctured for the spindles of the file, the holes reminding him of the holes in player-piano paper. And he didn't look much like a hunter, either; his was a city figure entirely, belted up in this Irish conspirator's coat. He was slender without being tall, stiff in the back, his legs looking shabby in a pair of old tweed pants gone through and fringy at the cuffs⑤. With this stiffness, he kept his head forward, so that his face was red from the sharpness of the weather; and it was an indoors sort of face with gray eyes that persisted in some kind of thought and yet seemed to avoid definiteness of conclusion. He wore sideburns that surprised you somewhat by the tough curl of the blond hair and the effect of assertion in their length. He was not so mild as he looked, nor so youthful; and nevertheless there was no effort on his part to seem what he was not. He was an educated man; he was a bachelor; he was in some ways simple; without lushing, he liked a drink; his luck had not been good. Nothing was deliberately hidden.

He felt that his luck was better than usual today. When he had reported for work that morning he had expected to be shut up in the relief office at a clerk's job, for he had been hired downtown as a clerk, and he was glad to have, instead, the freedom of the streets and welcomed, at least at first, the vigor of the cold and even the blowing of the hard wind. But on the other hand he was not getting on with the distribution of the checks. It was true that it was a city job; nobody expected you to push too hard at a city job. His supervisor, that young Mr. Raynor, had practically told him that. Still, he wanted to do well at it. For one thing, when he knew how quickly he could deliver a batch of checks, he would know also how much time he could expect to clip for himself. And

---

① 本句出自《圣经》中的《传道书》，原句为"Whatsoever thy hand findeth to do, do it with thy might; for there is no work, nor device, nor knowledge, nor wisdom, in the grave whither thou goest".
② relief checks: 福利支票
③ the Negro district: 这里指 Cottage Grove 和 Ashland 之间的区域。
④ foot-pound: 尺磅，功的单位
⑤ cuff: 裤脚底部向上折叠的翻边

then, too, the clients would be waiting for their money. That was not the most important consideration, though it certainly mattered to him. No, but he wanted to do well, simply for doing-well's sake, to acquit himself decently of a job because he so rarely had a job to do that required just this sort of energy. Of this peculiar energy he now had a superabundance; once it had started to flow, it flowed all too heavily. And, for the time being anyway, he was balked. He could not find Mr. Green.

So he stood in his big-skirted trenchcoat with a large envelope in his hand and papers showing from his pocket, wondering why people should be so hard to locate who were too feeble or sick to come to the station to collect their own checks. But Raynor had told him that tracking them down was not easy at first and had offered him some advice on how to proceed. "If you can see the postman, he's your first man to ask, and your best bet①. If you can't connect with him, try the stores and tradespeople around. Then the janitor and the neighbors. But you'll find the closer you come to your man the less people will tell you. They don't want to tell you anything."

"Because I'm a stranger."

"Because you're white. We ought to have a Negro doing this, but we don't at the moment, and of course you've got to eat, too, and this is public employment. Jobs have to be made. Oh, that holds for me too. Mind you, I'm not letting myself out. I've got three years of seniority on you, that's all. And a law degree. Otherwise, you might be back of the desk and I might be going out into the field this cold day. The same dough② pays us both and for the same, exact, identical reason. What's my law degree got to do with it? But you have to pass out these checks, Mr. Grebe, and it'll help if you're stubborn, so I hope you are."

"Yes, I'm fairly stubborn."

Raynor sketched hard with an eraser in the old dirt of his desk, left-handed, and said, "Sure, what else can you answer to such a question. Anyhow, the trouble you're going to have is that they don't like to give information about anybody. They think you're a plain-clothes dick③ or an installment collector, or summons-server or something like that. Till you've been seen around the neighborhood for a few months and people know you're only from the relief."

It was dark, ground-freezing, pre-Thanksgiving weather; the wind played hob with the smoke, rushing it down, and Grebe missed his gloves, which he had left in Raynor's office. And no one would admit knowing Green. It was past three o'clock and the postman had made his last delivery. The nearest grocer, himself a Negro, had never heard the name Tulliver Green, or said he hadn't. Grebe was inclined to think that it was true, that he had in the end convinced the man that he wanted only to deliver a check. But he wasn't true. He needed experience in interpreting looks and signs and, even more, the will not to be put off or denied and even the force to bully if need be. If the grocer did know, he had got rid of him easily. But since most of his trade was with

---

① best bet: 最好的办法
② dough: 在美国俚语中指钱
③ dick: 在美国俚语中指侦探

reliefers, why should he prevent the delivery of a check? Maybe Green, or Mrs. Green, if there was a Mrs. Green, patronized another grocer. And was there a Mrs. Green? It was one of Grebe's great handicaps that he hadn't looked at any of the case records. Raynor should have let him read files for a few hours. But he apparently saw no need for that, probably considering the job unimportant. Why prepare systematically to deliver a few checks?

But now it was time to look for the janitor. Grebe took in the building in the wind and gloom of the late November day—trampled, frost-hardened lots on one side; on the other, an automobile junk yard and then the infinite work of Elevated frames, weak-looking, gaping with rubbish fires; two sets of leaning brick porches three stories high and a flight of cement stairs to the cellar. Descending, he entered the underground passage, where he tried the doors until one opened and he found himself in the furnace room. There someone rose toward him and approached, scraping on the coal grit and bending under the canvas-jacketed pipes.

"Are you the janitor?"

"What do you want?"

"I'm looking for a man who's supposed to be living here. Green."

"What Green?"

"Oh, you maybe have more than one Green?" said Grebe with new, pleasant hope. "This is Tulliver Green."

"A crippled man."

The janitor stood bent before him. Could it be that he was crippled? Oh, God! what if he was. Grebe's gray eyes sought with excited difficulty to see. But no, he was only very short and stooped. A head awakened from meditation, a strong-haired beard, low, wide shoulders. A staleness of sweat and coal rose from his black shirt and the burlap sack he wore as an apron.

"Crippled how?"

Grebe thought and then answered with the light voice of unmixed candor, "I don't know. I've never seen him." This was damaging, but his only other choice was to make a lying guess, and he was not up to it. "I'm delivering checks for the relief to shut-in① cases. If he weren't crippled he'd come to collect himself. That's why I said crippled. Bedridden, chair-redden—is there anybody like that?"

This sort of frankness was one of Grebe's oldest talents, going back to childhood. But it gained him nothing here.

"No suh②. I've got four buildin's same as this that I take care of. I don't know all the tenants, leave alone the tentants' tenants. The rooms turn over so fast, people movin' in and out every day. I can't tell you."

The janitor opened his grimy lips but Grebe did not hear him in the piping of the valves and the consuming pull of air to flame in the body of the furnace. He knew, however, what he had said.

---

① shut-in: 因病弱而被关在屋内的人
② suh: 即 sir

"Well, all the same, thanks. Sorry I bothered you. I'll prowl around upstairs again and see if I can turn up someone who knows him."

Once more in the cold air and early darkness he made the short circle from the cellarway to the entrance crowded between the brickwork pillars and began to climb to the third floor. Pieces of plaster ground under his feet; strips of brass tape from which the carpeting had been torn away marked old boundaries at the sides. In the passage, the cold reached him worse than in the street; it touched him to the bone. The hall toilets ran like springs. He thought grimly as he heard the wind burning around the building with a sound like that of the furnace, that this was a great piece of constructed shelter. Then he struck a match in the gloom and searched for names and numbers among the writings and scribbles on the walls. He saw WHOODY-DOODY GO TO JESUS, and zigzags, caricatures, sexual scrawls, and curses. So the sealed rooms of pyramids were also decorated, and the caves of human dawn.

The information on his card was, TULLIVER GREEN—APT 3D. There were no names, however, and no numbers. His shoulders drawn up, tears of cold in his eyes, breathing vapor, he went the length of the corridor and told himself that if he had been lucky enough to have the temperament for it he would bang on one of the doors and bawl out "Tulliver Green!" until he got results. But it wasn't in him to make an uproar and he continued to burn matches, passing the light over the walls. At the rear, in a corner off the hall, he discovered a door he had not seen before and he thought it best to investigate. It sounded empty when he knocked, but a young Negress answered, hardly more than a girl. She opened only a bit, to guard the warmth of the room.

"Yes suh?"

"I'm from the district relief station on Prairie Avenue. I'm looking for a man named Tulliver Green to give him his check. Do you know him?"

No, she didn't; but he thought she had not understood anything of what he had said. She had a dream-bound, dream-blind face, very soft and black, shut off. She wore a man's jacket and pulled the ends together at her throat. Her hair was parted in three directions, at the sides and transversely①, standing up at the front in a dull puff.

"Is there somebody around here who might know?"

"I jus' taken this room las' week."

He observed that she shivered, but even her shiver was somnambulistic② and there was no sharp consciousness of cold in the big smooth eyes of her handsome face.

"All right, miss, thank you. Thanks," he said, and went to try another place.

Here he was admitted. He was grateful, for the room was warm. It was full of people, and they were silent as he entered—ten people, or a dozen, perhaps more, sitting on benches like a parliament. There was no light, properly speaking, but a tempered darkness that the window gave, and everyone seemed to him enormous, the men padded out in heavy work clothes and

---

① transversely: 横切地
② somnambulistic: 梦游般地

winter coats, and the women huge, too, in thick sweaters, hats, and old furs. And, besides, bed and bedding, a black cooking range, a piano piled towering to the ceiling with papers, a dining-room table of the old style of prosperous Chicago. Among these people Grebe, with his cold-heightened fresh color and his smaller stature, entered like a schoolboy. Even though he was met with smiles and good will, he knew, before a single word was spoken, that all the currents ran against him and that he would make no headway①. Nevertheless he began. "Does anybody here know how I can deliver a check to Mr. Tulliver Green?"

"Green?" It was the man that had let him in who answered. He was in short sleeves, in a checkered shirt, and had a queer, high head, profusely overgrown and long as a shako②; the veins entered it strongly from his forehead. "I never heard mention of him. Is this where he live?"

"This is the address they gave me at the station. He's a sick man, and he'll need his check. Can't anybody tell me where to find him?"

He stood his ground and waited for a reply, his crimson wool scarf wound about his neck and drooping outside his trenchcoat, pockets weighted with the block of checks and official forms. They must have realized that he was not a college boy employed afternoons by a bill collector, trying foxily to pass for a relief clerk, recognized that he was an older man who knew himself what need was, who had had more than an average seasoning in hardship. It was evident enough if you looked at the marks under his eyes and at the sides of his mouth.

"Anybody know this sick man?"

"No suh." On all sides he saw heads shaken and smiles of denial. No one knew. And maybe it was true, he considered, standing silent in the earthen, musky human gloom of the place as the rumble continued. But he could never really be sure. ……

Ⅲ. Notes.

"Looking for Mr. Green" is taken from *Mosby's Memoirs and Other Stories* (1968). It gives an account of George Grebe's effort in delivering relief checks to shut-in cases in South Chicago. Aged thirty-five, a former classical language instructor and reduced to be a relief check deliverer due to the Great Depression, George Grebe meant to do the job well but was hampered on his first day. Superficially, it is a realistic description of the hardship a relief worker has undergone. While in essence, it is a modern man's search of his own identity in relationship between reality and appearance. The short story explores the interwoven issues of race, class and gender. It is a good introduction to Saul Bellow's fiction. Grebe himself is idealistic, educated, slightly ambiguous, and therefore a typical Bellow hero.

Ⅳ. Key Words（关键词）.

Jewish literature: 犹太文学。犹太作家不仅创作出独特的犹太文学,并且为他们所居

---

① headway: 进展
② shako: 筒状军帽

住国家的民族文学做出了极大的贡献。犹太作家或用意第绪语(Yiddish,犹太人使用的国际语言)创作,或用英语或其他某种语言创作。犹太文学已经形成了自己的经典,并在世界文学中占有重要的一席之地。美国犹太文学是美国文学不可缺少的重要部分,包括菲利普·罗思、索尔·贝娄等犹太作家已经成为公认的美国经典作家。

Depression: 大萧条,是指始于 1929 年、延续至 30 年代末或 40 年代初的美国经济大萧条。这是一次世界范围的经济低迷,也是二十世纪持续时间最长、波及范围最广、影响程度最深的萧条。它起源于美国;美国股票价格下跌并最终造成 1929 年 10 月 29 日股票崩盘(著名的"黑色星期二")。这一情况迅速席卷世界各国,社会失业率剧增,人民生活受到巨大影响。大萧条不仅对美国人民的生活造成影响,并且对人们的内心形成巨大的冲击。

Ⅴ. Questions.

1. What is the plight of an idealistic contemporary man in face of the harsh reality? Is he a victim or a master?

2. In what sense does Saul Bellow identify with his characters?

3. Does Saul Bellow suggest any solution to the problems of his characters?

Part Six

Postmodernism and Ethnic Literature
第六部 后现代主义和族裔文学

20世纪70年代以后,西方社会进入了后工业化时代,计算机信息技术改变了千家万户的生活方式,也使文学艺术受到了极大的挑战。在这样的背景下,欧洲和美国都出现了后现代主义的文学思潮,许多文学理论家如约翰·巴思(1930—)等主张开辟新的创作道路,运用新的表现手法来挽救文学的衰落。更多的作家写出了一批有代表性的后现代主义作品,这些作品已经或正在进入当代经典的行列,例如美国作家纳博科夫(1889—1997)的《微暗的火》(1962)和托马斯·品钦(1937—)的《万有引力之虹》(1973)等小说创作。另一方面,美国社会在越战结束以后进入了一个更加多元开放的时代,族群矛盾在多元化社会里出现一定程度的缓解,而众多少数族裔作家的涌现也为美国文学的多元创作奠定了基础。事实上,一些族裔作家如黑人女作家托尼·莫里森(1931—)和犹太裔作家索尔·贝娄等都是诺贝尔文学奖获得者,而亚裔、拉美裔和印第安裔的新人新作更是令人刮目相看。可以说,从20世纪70年代一直到21世纪初,美国文学一方面延续了传统的现实主义和大众化的创作倾向,另一方面就是后现代主义文学创作和族裔文学的崛起,这两种倾向预示了美国文学在新世纪的发展趋势。

1967年,约翰·巴思在论文《枯竭的文学》中指出,面对新媒体艺术的挑战,美国文学必须另辟蹊径,摆脱文学创作的枯竭状态。他自己也身体力行,在小说《烟草商人》(1960)、《迷失在开心馆中》(1968)和《喀迈拉》(1972)等作品中大量运用了实验性的写作技巧,例如反身评论、戏仿、拼贴以及碎片化等等后现代艺术手法,在美国文学界引起了很大的反响。20世纪80年代初,詹明信全面阐述了后现代主义文化理论,伊哈布·哈桑在《走向后现代的观念》一文中也具体论述了后现代文学的历史沿革和创作特征。这些理论话语对于美国后现代文学的发展起了重要的推动作用,很多年轻作家积极运用后现代主义的创作技巧,取得了令人瞩目的成就。在美国后现代作家中,冯尼古特(1922—2007)是一位独出心裁的作家,他在《五号屠场》(1968)和《冠军的早餐》(1973)等作品中充分发挥了后现代艺术的表现力,在嬉笑怒骂的叙述中让人感受到战争的冷酷和现实的荒谬。除了上面提到的一些作家以外,巴塞尔姆的碎片化长篇叙事《白雪公主》(1967)和威廉·加斯运用戏仿和元小说技巧的《隧道》(1995)等等是当代美国后现代文学的重要成果。另外,近年来E. L. 多克托罗(1931—)的《上帝之城》(2000)和《进军》(2005)等小说在后现代艺术语境中深入批判了人类本性中的贪婪和虚伪,而唐·德里罗则在看似无深度的琐碎叙事《白色噪音》(1984)里讽刺了唯利是图的社会风气和颓废堕落的人生焦虑。时至今日,后现代主义作为一种文学思潮已经过了高峰期,但是后现代文学的许多艺术技巧和文体构思却在新一代作家的写作中变得日益纯熟,与现代主义和其他流派的艺术技巧一样都已成为当代作家创作的必备参照系。

　　在后现代主义文学经历了数十年的发展之时,美国少数族裔文学也蓬勃兴旺,佳作连连。族裔文学繁荣的一个基本原因在于当代美国多元化社会的形成,这使众多的少数族裔作家有机会在文学领域里展露自己的艺术创造才华。族裔文学的两个基本主题就是"族群寻根"和"美国梦寻",而不同民族和族群的文化历史轨迹则决定了族裔文学作品的丰富多彩。从种族分布、文化渊源和艺术成就上看,美国族裔文学可以分为五大类型,即欧裔白人作家群、非裔黑人作家群、犹太裔作家群、亚裔作家群和拉丁—印第安裔作家群等等。在这些族群作家中,近年来出现了不少艺术创作的佼佼者,其中一些作家更是取得了世界性的声誉。在欧裔作家群中,除了前面提到的现实主义和后现代主义重要作家和诗人之外,科马克·麦卡锡(1933—)的西部小说《骏马》(1992)等组成的"边境三部曲"重振了西部文学,显示了美国文学特有的边疆雄浑之风;弗雷泽的小说《冷山》(1997)再次对美国内战的历史进行了反思,提出了人道主义的理想主题。在非裔作家群中,除了托尼·莫里森的小说《最蓝的眼睛》(1970)、《宠儿》(1987)和《爱》(2003)以外,还有艾丽丝·沃克的书信体小说《紫色》(1982)、伊斯梅尔·里德的《春季日语班》(1992)和葆拉·马歇尔的《女儿们》(1991)等小说。犹太裔作家群历来名家辈出,除了索尔·贝娄和其他已经提到的作家以外,菲利浦·罗思的《人性的污点》(2000)和马拉默德的《修配工》(1966)等等也是犹太裔作家的重要作品。在亚裔作家群中,华裔作家汤亭亭(1940—)是一位开创性的族裔女作家,她的传记体小说《女勇士》(1976)重新塑造了中华民族的文化和历史,而印度裔作家幕克吉的小说《茉莉花》(1989)更为亚裔文学增添了光彩。在拉丁—印第安裔作家群中,印第安部落文化养育的女作家西尔克(1948—)的小说《死者年鉴》(1991)预言了欧洲人全部离开美洲的前景,使之成为一部政治寓言小说;而墨西哥裔的作家希斯内罗丝(1954—)的中篇叙事《芒果街的小屋》(1994)则赢得了读者和评论家的广泛赞誉。总之,美国族裔文学正在成为新世纪美国文学创作队伍的中坚,特别是在全球化时代的文学想象中,族裔文学已经成为美国文学的重要组成。事实上,美国建国伊始就是一个多种族和多族裔的多元化社会,美国文学也在日益变得多元化:它既有艺术创作技巧的多姿多彩,也有主题思想的多重思考,还有文化语境的多元共存。这些创作特征的形成表明了美国文学经典建构的新动向,也对我们全面认识美国文学的历史发展轨迹具有十分重要的标识意义。

Lesson 39 John Barth (1930—)

I. A Brief Review.

Barth was born in Maryland in 1930. His family was deeply rooted in a rural community, and his father was the proprietor of a combination candy store/restaurant. In his youth, Barth attended Cambridge High School, where he played the drums in the band and wrote a column for the school paper. Barth transferred to Johns Hopkins University in the fall of 1947, and changed his major to writing and journalism. He graduated with a major in creative writing in 1951 and earned his M. A. at the same university one year later.

图 39 John Barth

Barth began his writing career with *The Floating Opera* and *The End of the Road*, two straightforward tales that dealt wittily with controversial topics, suicide and abortion respectively. While at Penn State University, Barth wrote four novels. *The Floating Opera* was the first written in 1955. In 1966, Barth completed his fourth novel, *Giles Goat-Boy*, a book of 800 pages. The novel soon became a *New York Times* Best-Seller. A year before that, Barth left Penn State University for a position of a professor of English at the State University of New York at Buffalo. *Giles Goat Boy* was Barth's satirical allegory, presenting the modern world as an academic campus on which the progress of the first programmed man takes place. The novel, parodying mythic archetypes, enhanced Barth's reputation as a postmodern exponent of self-reflective "metafiction."

Barth's next book, *Chimera*, won the National Book Award after his two previous nominations for *The Floating Opera* and *Lost in the Funhouse*. *Lost in the Funhouse* (1968) was a collection of experimental short fiction, which sold twenty thousand copies in hardcover and was nominated for a National Book Award. Barth became one of the most well-known post-Vietnam-war writers. *Chimera* (1972) came out as Barth's short fiction collection, including well-known tales with reflexive discussion of the composition difficulties of the author—Barth himself—thus making the act of writing a part of the volume's theme. While writing these books, Barth was also discussing the theoretical problems of fiction writing.

Barth is now recognized as a pioneer of American postmodern literature. "The Literature of Exhaustion" (1967) is Barth's influential essay, in which Barth defines the postmodernist writer as one who "confronts an intellectual dead end and employs it against itself to accomplish new human work." Barth's books often examine the relationship between language and reality, and he is one of the most important figures in twentieth-century American literature. Barth now resides in Baltimore with his wife Shelly, and teaches at the Johns Hopkins University.

Ⅱ. Texts.

Chimera①

Dunyazadiad

1

"At this point I interrupted my sister as usual to say, 'You have a way with words, Scheherazade②. This is the thousandth night I've sat at the foot of your bed while you and the King made love and you told him stories, and the one in progress holds me like a genie's gaze. I wouldn't dream of breaking in like this, just before the end, except that I hear the first rooster crowing in the east, et cetera, and the King really ought to sleep a bit before daybreak. I wish I had your talent.'

"And as usual Sherry replied, 'You're the ideal audience, Dunyazade③. But this is nothing; wait till you hear the ending, tomorrow night! Always assuming this auspicious King doesn't kill me before breakfast, as he's been going to do these thirty-three and a third months.'

"'Hmp,' said Shahryar④. "Don't take your critics for granted; I may get around to it yet. But I agree with your little sister that this is a good one you've got going, with its impostures that become authentic, its ups and downs and flights to other worlds. I don't know how in the world you dream them up.'

"Artists have their tricks,' Sherry replied. We three said good night then, six goodnights in all. In the morning your brother went off to court, enchanted by Sherry's story. Daddy came to the palace for the thousandth time with a shroud under his arm, expecting to be told to cut his daughter's head off; in most other respects he's as good a vizier as he ever was, but three years of suspense have driven him crackers in this one particular—and turned his hair white, I might add, and made him a widower. Sherry and I, after the first fifty nights or so, were simply relieved when Shahryar would hmp and say, 'By Allah, I won't kill her till I've heard the end of her story'; but it still took Daddy by surprise every morning. He groveled gratitude per usual; the King per usual spent the day in his durbar, bidding and forbidding between man and man, as the saying goes; I climbed in with Sherry as soon as he was gone, and per usual we spent our day sleeping in and making love. When we'd had enough of each other's tongues and fingers, we called in the

---

① Chimera: 喀迈拉,希腊神话中的狮头、羊身、蛇尾的吐火女妖
② Scheherazade: 山鲁佐德,《一千零一夜》中自愿向国王献身的宰相的女儿
③ Dunyazade: 敦亚佐德,山鲁佐德的妹妹
④ Shahryar: 山鲁亚尔,《一千零一夜》中的暴君,为报复而每晚强暴一个妙龄少女,次日清晨便将其处死。后被山鲁佐德的故事所征服而停止杀戮

eunuchs, maidservants, mamelukes, pet dogs and monkeys; then we finished off with Sherry's Bag of Tricks: little weighted balls from Baghdad, dildoes from the Ebony Isles and the City of Brass, et cetera. Not to break a certain vow of mine, I made do with a roc-down tickler from Bassorah, but Sherry touched all the bases. Her favorite story is about some pig of an ifrit who steals a girl away on her wedding night, puts her in a treasure-casket locked with seven steel padlocks, puts the casket in a crystal coffer, and puts the coffer on the bottom of the ocean, so that nobody except himself can have her. But whenever he brings the whole rig ashore, unlocks the locks with seven keys, and takes her out and rapes her, he falls asleep afterward on her lap; she slips out from under and cuckolds him with every man who passes by, taking their seal rings as proof; at the end of the story she has five hundred seventy-two seal rings, and the stupid ifrit still thinks he possesses her! In the same way, Sherry put a hundred horns a day on your brother's head: that's about a hundred thousand horns by now. And every day she saved till last the Treasure Key, which is what her story starts and ends with.

"Three and a third years ago, when King Shahryar was raping a virgin every night and killing her in the morning, and the people were praying that Allah would dump the whole dynasty, and so many parents had fled the country with their daughters that in all the Islands of India and China there was hardly a young girl fit to fuck, my sister was an undergraduate arts-and-sciences major at Banu Sasan University. Besides being Homecoming Queen, valedictorian-elect, and a four-letter varsity athlete, she had a private library of a thousand volumes and the highest average in the history of the campus. Every graduate department in the East was after her with fellowships—but she was so appalled① at the state of the nation that she dropped out of school in her last semester to do full-time research on a way to stop Shahryar from killing all our sisters and wrecking the country.

"Political science, which she looked at first, got her nowhere. Shahryar's power was absolute, and by sparing the daughters of his army officers and chief ministers (like our own father) and picking his victims mainly from the families of liberal intellectuals and other minorities, he kept the military and the cabinet loyal enough to rule out a coup d'état. Revolution seemed out of the question, because his woman-hating, spectacular as it was, was reinforced more or less by all our traditions and institutions, and as long as the girls he was murdering were generally upper-caste②, there was no popular base for guerrilla war. Finally, since he could count on your help from Samarkand, invasion from outside or plain assassination were bad bets too: Sherry figured your retaliation would be worse than Shahryar's virgin-a-night policy.

"So we gave up poly sci (I fetched her books and sharpened her quills and made tea and alphabetized her index cards) and tried psychology—another blind alley. Once she'd noted that your reaction to being cuckolded by your wife was homicidal rage followed by despair and abandonment of your kingdom, and that Shahryar's was the reverse; and established that that was

---

① appalled: 感到惊骇的,表示憎恶的
② upper-caste: 指上层社会;统治阶层

owing to the difference in your ages and the order of revelations; and decided that whatever pathology was involved was a function of the culture and your position as absolute monarchs rather than particular hang-ups in your psyches, et cetera—what was there to say?

"She grew daily more desperate; the body-count of deflowered and decapitated Moslem girls was past nine hundred, and Daddy was just about out of candidates. Sherry didn't especially care about herself, you understand—wouldn't have even if she hadn't guessed that the King was sparing her out of respect for his vizier① and her own accomplishments. But beyond the general awfulness of the situation, she was particularly concerned for my sake. From the day I was born, when Sherry was about nine, she treasured me as if I were hers; 1 might as well not have had parents; she and I ate from the same plate, slept in the same bed; no one could separate us; I'll bet we weren't apart for an hour in the first dozen years of my life. But I never had her good looks or her way with the world—and I was the youngest in the family besides. My breasts were growing; already I'd begun to menstruate: any day Daddy might have to sacrifice me to save Sherry.

"So when nothing else worked, as a last resort she turned to her first love, unlikely as it seemed, mythology and folklore, and studied all the riddle/puzzle/secret motifs she could dig up. 'We need a miracle, Doony,' she said (I was braiding her hair and massaging her neck as she went through her notes for the thousandth time), 'and the only genies I've ever met were in stories, not in Moormans'-rings and Jews'-lamps. It's in words that the magic is—Abracadabra②, Open Sesame, and the rest—but the magic words in one story aren't magical in the next. The real magic is to understand which words work, and when, and for what; the trick is to learn the trick.'

"This last, as our frantic research went on, became her motto, even her obsession. As she neared the end of her supply of lore, and Shahryar his supply of virgins, she became more and more certain that her principle was correct, and desperate that in the whole world's stock of stories there was none that confirmed it, or showed us how to use it to solve the problem. 'I've read a thousand tales about treasures that nobody can find the key to,' she told me; 'we have the key and can't find the treasure.' I asked her to explain. 'It's all in here,' she declared—I couldn't tell whether she meant her inkstand or the quill she pointed toward it. I seldom understood her any more; as the crisis grew, she gave up reading for daydreaming, and used her pen less for noting instances of the Magic Key motif in world literature than for doodling the letters of our alphabet at random and idly tickling herself.

"'Little Doony,' she said dreamily, and kissed me: 'pretend this whole situation is the plot of a story we're reading, and you and I and Daddy and the King are all fictional characters. In this story, Scheherazade finds a way to change the King's mind about women and turn him into a gentle, loving husband. It's not hard to imagine such a story, is it? Now, no matter what way she finds—whether it's a magic spell or a magic story with the answer in it or a magic anything—it

---

① vizier: 维齐(旧时一些穆斯林国家的高官)
② Abracadabra:（表演魔术、施魔法时所念的咒语）阿布拉卡达布拉

comes down to particular words in the story we're reading, right? And those words are made from the letters of our alphabet: a couple-dozen squiggles① we can draw with this pen. This is the key, Doony! And the treasure, too, if we can only get our hands on it! It's as if—as if the key to the treasure is the treasure!"

"As soon as she spoke these last words a genie appeared from nowhere right there in our library-stacks. He didn't resemble anything in Sherry's bedtime stories: for one thing, he wasn't frightening, though he was strange-looking enough: a light-skinned fellow of forty or so, smooth-shaven and bald as a roc's egg. His clothes were simple but outlandish; he was tall and healthy and pleasant enough in appearance, except for queer lenses that he wore in a frame over his eyes. He seemed as startled as we were—you should've seen Sherry drop that pen and pull her skirts together!—but he got over his alarm a lot sooner, and looked from one to the other of us and at a stubby little magic wand he held in his fingers, and smiled a friendly smile.

"'Are you really Scheherazade?' he asked. 'I've never had a dream so clear and lifelike! And you're little Dunyazade—just as I'd imagined both of you! Don't be frightened: I can't tell you what it means to me to see and talk to you like this; even in a dream, it's a dream come true. Can you understand English? I don't have a word of Arabic. O my, I can't believe this is really happening!'

III. Notes.

1. *Chimera* is one of Barth's best novels. It consists of three interconnected novellas — one about Scheherazade from *A Thousand and One Nights*, one about the Greek hero Perseus, and one about the lesser-known Greek hero Bellerophon. The Dunyazadiad is a retelling of the framing story of Scheherazade. The story is told from the point-of-view of Scheherazade's younger sister Dunyazad. Its characterization as metafiction can be understood as a result of the use of several literary devices, most notably the introduction of the author as a character and his interaction with Scheherazade and Dunyazade.

2. The author appears from the future and expresses his admiration for Scheherazade and the 1001 Nights as a work of fiction. Barth retells this tale from varying perspectives, examining the myths' relationship to reality and their resonance with the contemporary world.

IV. Key Words(关键词).

Metafiction: 元小说。这是后现代文学中"关于小说的小说"。元小说的基本特征是把叙事建立在作者与文本的对话之中：在构筑小说幻象的同时又公开评论自身的虚构特性，从而使读者意识到小说并非现实生活的摹本，而只是作家编撰的故事。后现代主义元小说对小说这一文学形式和叙述本身进行反思、解构和颠覆，在叙事和语言上导致了传统小说及其叙述方式的解体，并确定了自己的合法化方式。《喀迈拉》由《敦亚佐德》、《英仙座流星》和《勃勒罗丰》三个中篇故事组成，是一部典型的元小说，是关于自身创作的小说，三个

---

① squiggles: 弯弯曲曲的线条；潦草的笔迹

中篇故事自我指涉和相互指涉,作者巴思也隐身其中。

Parody: 戏仿。它源自后现代主义流派中的叙事技巧,是仿造、仿拟的意思,从修辞意义上说,戏仿就是戏谑的仿造,罗兰·巴尔特将其解释为"引用和参考"。戏仿也常被称为反讽引用,被认为是后现代主义至关重要的文学创作手法。后现代主义作家运用戏仿的写作手法不但使所戏仿的内容合法化,而且颠覆了所戏仿的内容。神话和传奇是巴思重要戏仿的对象,在模仿的过程中加进自己的创意,创造出一个充满了滑稽、嬉戏和讽刺意味的艺术世界。小说《喀迈拉》中对古代神话名著的题材、人物、内容进行了一系列滑稽、嘲讽乃至荒诞的模仿。

Ⅴ. **Questions.**

1. In *Chimera*, how does John Barth create the story of postmodernism?
2. Can you find evidence on the method of parody in the text we choose from *Chimera*?
3. How do you interpret the role the author himself plays in the story?

Lesson 40   Kurt Vonnegut (1922—2007)

Ⅰ. A Brief Review.

Vonnegut was born in Indianapolis, Indiana, to the second-generation of German-American parents. He graduated from Shortridge High School in Indianapolis in May 1940, and was accepted to attend Cornell University beginning that fall. At Cornell, he served as an assistant managing editor and associate editor for the student newspaper, the *Cornell Daily Sun*, and majored in chemistry. While at Cornell, Vonnegut enlisted in the U. S. Army, which transferred him to the Carnegie Institute of Technology and the University of Tennessee to study mechanical engineering.

图 40　Kurt Vonnegut

Kurt Vonnegut's experience as a soldier and prisoner of war had a profound influence on his later work. When he served with the 106th Infantry Division, Vonnegut was captured during the Battle of the Bulge on December 19, 1944. Imprisoned in Dresden, Vonnegut was chosen as a leader of the POWs because he spoke some German. As a prisoner, he witnessed the fire bombing of Dresden in February 1945, an air strike that destroyed most of the city. This experience was the inspiration for his famous novel, *Slaughterhouse-Five*, and became a central theme in at least six of his other books. After the war, Vonnegut studied anthropology at Chicago University from 1944 to 1947, but his M. A. thesis was rejected. However, in 1971 the anthropological department accepted his novel *Cat's Cradle* (1963) in lieu of a thesis and awarded him the degree of M. A. On April 11, 2007, Vonnegut died in Manhattan, following a fall and brain injuries at his Manhattan home several weeks earlier.

Vonnegut's frequent use of elements of fantasy made him classified by some critics as a writer of science fiction. His work did not attract significant critical interest until the mid-1960s, when increasing disillusionment with American society led to widespread admiration for his penetrating satires. His reputation was greatly enhanced in 1969 with the publication of *Slaughterhouse-Five*, a vehemently antiwar novel that appeared during the peak of protest against American involvement in Vietnam. In his works, the fantastic settings serve primarily as a metaphor for modern society, which Vonnegut views as absurd to the point of being surreal, and as a backdrop for Vonnegut's central focus: the hapless human beings who are struggling with both their environments and themselves.

In the works written after *Slaughterhouse-Five*, Vonnegut shifted his thematic concerns to the problems of contemporary society as exemplified in *Breakfast of Champions* (1973) and *Lonesome*

No More (1976). The two novels examine the widespread feelings of despair and loneliness that result from the loss of traditional values in the United States. Although many of these works are highly regarded, many critics suggest that Vonnegut's narrative style, which includes the frequent repetition of distinctive phrases, the use of colloquial words, and a digressive manner, becomes formulaic in some of his later works. Nevertheless, Vonnegut remains one of the most esteemed American satirists——a modern-day Mark Twain. Noted for their frank and insightful social criticism as well as their innovative style, his works present an idiosyncratic yet compelling vision of modern life in the US.

II. Texts.

Breakfast of Champions

Preface

The expression "Breakfast of Champions" is a registered trademark of General Mills, Inc., for use on a breakfast cereal product. The use of the identical expression as the title for this book is not intended to indicate an association with or sponsorship by General Mills, nor is it intended to disparage their fine products.

The person to whom this book is dedicated, Phoebe Hurty, is no longer among the living, as they say. She was an Indianapolis widow when I met her late in the Great Depression. I was sixteen or so. She was about forty.

She was rich, but she had gone to work every weekday of her adult life, so she went on doing that. She wrote a sane and funny advice-to-the lovelorn column for the Indianapolis *Times*, a good paper which is now defunct①.

Defunct.

She wrote ads for the William H. Block Company, a department store which still flourishes in a building my father designed. She wrote this ad for an end-of-the-summer sale on straw hats: "For prices like this, you can run them through your horse and put them on your roses".

Phoebe Hurty hired me to write copy for ads about teen-age clothes. I had to wear the clothes I praised. That was part of the job. And I became friends with her two sons, who were my age. I was over at their house all the time.

She would talk bawdily② to me and her sons, and to our girlfriends when we brought them around. She was funny. She was liberating. She taught us to be impolite in conversation not only about sexual matters, but about American history and famous heroes, about the distribution of wealth, about school, about everything.

I now make my living by being impolite. I am clumsy at it. I keep trying to imitate the impoliteness which was so graceful in Phoebe Hurty. I think now that grace was easier for her than

---

① defunct: 已灭绝的,不再起作用的
② bawdily: 喧嚣地,猥琐地

it is for me because of the mood of the Great Depression. She believed what so many Americans believed then: that the nation would be happy and just and rational when prosperity came.

I never hear that word anymore: *Prosperity*. It used to be a synonym for *Paradise*. And Phoebe Hurty was able to believe that the impoliteness she recommended would give shape to an American paradise.

Now her sort of impoliteness is fashionable. But nobody believes anymore in a new American Paradise. I sure miss Phoebe Hurty.

As for the suspicion I express in this book, that human beings are robots, are machines: It should be noted that people, mostly men, suffering from the last stages of syphilis①, from *locomotor ataxia*, were common spectacles in downtown Indianapolis and in circus crowds when I was a boy.

Those people were infested with carnivorous little corkscrews which could be seen only with a microscope. The victim's vertebrae② were welded together after the corkscrews got through with the meat between. The syphilitics seemed tremendously dignified—erect, eyes straight ahead.

I saw one stand on a curb at the corner of Meridian and Washington Streets one time, underneath an overhanging clock which my father designed. The intersection was known locally as "The Crossroads of America."

This syphilitic man was thinking hard there, at the crossroads of America, about how to get his legs to step off the curb and carry him across Washington Street. He shuddered gently, as though he had a small motor which was idling inside. Here was his problem: his brains, where the instructions to his legs originated, were being eaten alive by corkscrews. The wires which had to carry the instructions weren't insulated anymore, or were eaten clear through. Switches along the way were welded open or shut.

This man looked like an old, old man, although he might have been only thirty years old. He thought and thought. And then he kicked two times like a chorus girl.

He certainly looked like a machine to me when I was a boy.

I tend to think of human beings as huge, rubbery test tubes, too, with chemical reactions seething inside. When I was a boy, I saw a lot of people with goiters③. So did Dwayne Hoover, the Pontiac dealer who is the hero of this book. Those unhappy Earthlings had such swollen thyroid glands that they seemed to have zucchini squash growing from their throats.

All they had to do in order to have ordinary lives, it turned out, was to consume less than one-millionth of an ounce of iodine every day.

My own mother wrecked her brains with chemicals, which were supposed to make her sleep. When I get depressed, I take a little pill, and I cheer up again.

And so on.

---

① syphilis: 梅毒(一种性传播疾病)
② vertebrae: 动物的椎骨
③ goiters: 甲状腺肿

So it is a big temptation to me, when I create a character for a novel, to say that he is what he is because of faulty wiring, or because of microscopic amounts of chemicals which he ate or failed to eat on that particular day.

What do I myself think of this particular book? I feel lousy about it, but I always feel lousy about my books. My friend Knox Burger said one time that a certain cumbersome novel "… read as though it had been written by Philboyd Studge." That's who I think I am when I write what I am seemingly programmed to write.

Ⅲ. Notes.

1. *Breakfast of Champions* or *Goodbye Blue Monday* is a 1973 novel by Kurt Vonnegut. Set in the fictional town of Midland City, it is the story of "two lonesome, skinny, fairly old white men on a planet which was dying fast." One of these men, Dwayne Hoover, is a normal-looking but deeply deranged Pontiac dealer and Burger Chef franchise owner who becomes obsessed with the writings of the other man, Kilgore Trout, taking them for literal truth. Trout, a largely unknown pulp science fiction writer who has appeared in several other Vonnegut novels, looks like a crazy old man but is in fact relatively sane.

2. As the novel opens, Trout journeys toward Midland City to appear at a convention where he is destined to meet Dwayne Hoover and unwittingly becomes crazy. *Breakfast of Champions* trips through American mindset of the early 1970s. Its deadpan irony satirizes the party line on just about everything, from sex and racism to the Vietnam War and the meaning of the "American dream".

Ⅳ. Key Words(关键词).

Black humour: 黑色幽默。是西方后现代派文学中的一个十分重要的流派,对西方文学有着广泛而深刻的影响。冯尼古特是这一流派的代表性作家之一。"黑色幽默"小说突出描写人物周围世界的荒谬和社会对个人的压迫,以一种无可奈何的嘲讽态度表现环境和个人(即"自我")之间的矛盾,并把这种矛盾加以放大、扭曲,变形,使它们显得更加荒诞不经、滑稽可笑,同时又令人感到沉重和苦闷。"黑色幽默"作家往往塑造一些乖僻的"反英雄"人物,借他们的可笑言行影射社会现实,表达作家对社会问题的观点。"黑色幽默"作家也常常打破传统叙述模式,把严肃的哲理和插科打诨混成一团,但小说的情节之间往往缺乏逻辑联系。

collage: 拼贴。这是后现代文学创作的主要手法之一。"拼贴"一词源自绘画,后被作家所借用,指将各种典故、引文、描述等混合使用,将不同作家作品中的词语、句子、段落掺杂在一起。这种将毫不相干的碎片构成一个文本的叙事方法打破了传统小说的理性叙述方式,让读者感到强烈的震撼。在后现代作家看来,整个世界是由片断构成的,片断之和构成不了一个整体,代表了破碎的现实。因此,后现代主义小说不去追踪人类整体性的历史叙述,也不去探求永恒而内在的存在真谛,而是倾向于追求话语的解构和重构。《冠军的早餐》对这一创作手法的运用极具代表性。

Ⅴ. **Questions.**

1. Do you think that Phoebe Hurty would believe that the impoliteness she recommended would give shape to an American paradise?

2. Why does Vonnegut claim that all human beings are robots?

3. After reading the novel, can you figure out the meaning of the title *Breakfast of Champions*?

Lesson 41　Toni Morrison (1931—)

Ⅰ. A Brief Review.

Born in 1931, Toni Morrison was one of the four children of George Wofford, who led the whole family from the south to evade racism. Since her childhood, she was exposed to the influence of the black folklores her father told her and was always so fascinated by the stories in the black community that she later explored further in her works such as *Beloved* (1987). Morrison was received as an undergraduate in Howard University in Washington D. C. as soon as she finished high school. It was then that she changed her name to Toni. After graduating from Howard, she continued her

图 41　Toni Morrison

master degree at Cornell University and earned a Master of Fine Art degree. Not long after her graduation, she began her teaching and editing career for Random House. Among her numerous awards, this member of the American Academy of Arts and Letters was mostly remembered by Pulitzer Prize in 1987 and Nobel Prize in 1993.

In 1975 her novel *Sula* (1973) was nominated for the National Book Award, and her third novel, *Song of Solomon* (1977), won the National Book Critics Circle Award. In 1987 Morrison's novel, *Beloved*, won the Pulitzer Prize for fiction and the American Book Award, and was adapted into film of the same name in 1998. The Nobel Prize for Literature statement reads: Toni Morrison, "who in novels characterized by visionary force and poetic import, gives life to an essential aspect of American reality." Toni Morrison was the first black woman to receive Nobel Prize for Literature. Her novels, such as *The Bluest Eye*, *Song of Solomon*, and *Beloved*, were well known for their epic themes, vivid dialogue, and richly detailed black characters. Although her novels typically concentrated on black women, Morrison did not identify her works as feminist as she stated: "I don't think it should be substituted with matriarchy."

Morrison's works are famous for rich images, poetic narration, and impressive depiction of characters and settings of Black American communities. Though most of her works are written from a female point of view about African American stories with various inspirations from folklores or news that she learned, she did write once from a male perspective in *Song of Solomon*, a novel compared with *Roots* by Alex Haley. Her recent novel is *Love* published in 2003, a novel that has aroused the public attention toward Morrison's critical stance against any type of oppression and exploitation regardless of people's race and gender.

Ⅱ. Texts.

Beloved

Not quite in a hurry, but losing no time, Sethe and Paul D climbed the white stairs. Overwhelmed as much by the downright luck of finding her house and her in it as by the certainty of giving her his sex, Paul D dropped twenty-five years from his recent memory. A stair step before him was Baby Suggs' replacement, the new girl they dreamed of at night and fucked cows for at dawn while waiting for her to choose. Merely kissing the wrought iron① on her back had shook the house, had made it necessary for him to beat it to pieces. Now he would do more.

She led him to the top of the stairs, where light came straight from the sky because the second-story windows of that house had been placed in the pitched ceiling② and not the walls. There were two rooms and she took him into one of them, hoping he wouldn't mind the fact that she was not prepared; that though she could remember desire, she had forgotten how it worked; the clutch and helplessness that resided in the hands; how blindness was altered so that what leapt to the eye were places to lie down, and all else—door knobs, straps, hooks, the sadness that crouched in corners, and the passing of time—was interference.

It was over before they could get their clothes off. Half-dressed and short of breath, they lay side by side resentful of one another and the skylight above them. His dreaming of her had been too long and too long ago. Her deprivation had been not having any dreams of her own at all. Now they were sorry and too shy to make talk.

Sethe lay on her back, her head turned from him. Out of the corner of his eye, Paul D saw the float of her breasts and disliked it, the spread-away, flat roundness of them that he could definitely live without, never mind that downstairs he had held them as though they were the most expensive part of himself. And the wrought-iron maze③ he had explored in the kitchen like a gold miner pawing through pay dirt was in fact a revolting clump of scars. Not a tree, as she said. Maybe shaped like one, but nothing like any tree he knew because trees were inviting; things you could trust and be near; talk to if you wanted to as he frequently did since way back when he took the midday meal in the fields of Sweet Home. Always in the same place if he could, and choosing the place had been hard because Sweet Home had more pretty trees than any farm around. His choice he called Brother, and sat under it, alone sometimes, sometimes with Halle or the other Pauls, but more often with Sixo, who was gentle then and still speaking English. Indigo with a flame-red tongue, Sixo experimented with night-cooked potatoes, trying to pin down exactly when to put smoking-hot rocks in a hole, potatoes on top, and cover the whole thing with twigs so that by the time they broke for the meal, hitched the animals, left the field and got to Brother, the potatoes would be at the peak of perfection. He might get up in the middle of the night, go all the way out

---

① wrought iron: 锻铁,熟铁
② pitched ceiling: 尤指房屋阁楼上倾斜的屋顶
③ maze: 指迷宫

there, start the earth-over by starlight; or he would make the stones less hot and put the next day's potatoes on them right after the meal. He never got it right, but they ate those undercooked, overcooked, dried-out or raw potatoes anyway, laughing, spitting and giving him advice.

Time never worked the way Sixo thought, so of course he never got it right. Once he plotted down to the minute a thirty-mile trip to see a woman. He left on a Saturday when the moon was in the place he wanted it to be, arrived at her cabin before church on Sunday and had just enough time to say good morning before he had to start back again so he'd make the field call on time Monday morning. He had walked for seventeen hours, sat down for one, turned around and walked seventeen more. Halle and the Pauls spent the whole day covering Sixo's fatigue from Mr. Garner. They ate no potatoes that day, sweet or white. Sprawled near Brother, his flame-red tongue hidden from them, his indigo face closed, Sixo slept through dinner like a corpse. Now there was a man, and that was a tree. Himself lying in the bed and the "tree" lying next to him didn't compare.

Paul D looked through the window above his feet and folded his hands behind his head. An elbow grazed Sethe's shoulder. The touch of cloth on her skin startled her. She had forgotten he had not taken off his shirt. Dog, she thought, and then remembered that she had not allowed him the time for taking it off. Nor herself time to take off her petticoat, and considering she had begun undressing before she saw him on the porch, that her shoes and stockings were already in her hand and she had never put them back on; that he had looked at her wet bare feet and asked to join her; that when she rose to cook he had undressed her further; considering how quickly they had started getting naked, you'd think by now they would be. But maybe a man was nothing but a man, which is what Baby Suggs always said. They encouraged you to put some of your weight in their hands and soon as you felt how light and lovely that was, they studied your scars and tribulations①, after which they did what he had done: ran her children out and tore up the house.

She needed to get up from there, go downstairs and piece it all back together. This house he told her to leave as though a house was a little thing—a shirtwaist or a sewing basket you could walk off from or give away any old time. She who had never had one but this one; she who left a dirt floor to come to this one; she who had to bring a fistful of salsify② into Mrs. Garner's kitchen every day just to be able to work in it, feel like some part of it was hers, because she wanted to love the work she did, to take the ugly out of it, and the only way she could feel at home on Sweet Home was if she picked some pretty growing thing and took it with her. The day she forgot was the day butter wouldn't come or the brine in the barrel blistered her arms.

At least it seemed so. A few yellow flowers on the table, some myrtle③ tied around the handle of the flatiron holding the door open for a breeze calmed her, and when Mrs. Garner and she sat down to sort bristle, or make ink, she felt fine. Fine. Not scared of the men beyond. The

---

① tribulations: 忧患，苦难，磨难
② salsify: 蒜叶婆罗门参(可作蔬菜食用)
③ myrtle: 爱神木，香桃木(一种灌木)

five who slept in quarters near her, but never came in the night. Just touched their raggedy hats when they saw her and stared. And if she brought food to them in the fields, bacon and bread wrapped in a piece of clean sheeting, they never took it from her hands. They stood back and waited for her to put it on the ground (at the foot of a tree) and leave. Either they did not want to take anything from her, or did not want her to see them eat. Twice or three times she lingered. Hidden behind honeysuckle she watched them. How different they were without her, how they laughed and played and urinated and sang. All but Sixo, who laughed once—at the very end. Halle, of course, was the nicest. Baby Suggs' eighth and last child, who rented himself out all over the county to buy her away from there. But he too, as it turned out, was nothing but a man.

"A man ain't nothing but a man," said Baby Suggs. "But a son? Well now, that's somebody."

It made sense for a lot of reasons because in all of Baby's life, as well as Sethe's own, men and women were moved around like checkers. Anybody Baby Suggs knew, let alone loved, who hadn't run off or been hanged, got rented out, loaned out, bought up, brought back, stored up, mortgaged, won, stolen or seized. So Baby's eight children had six fathers. What she called the nastiness of life was the shock she received upon learning that nobody stopped playing checkers just because the pieces included her children. Halle she was able to keep the longest. Twenty years. A lifetime. Given to her, no doubt, to make up for hearing that her two girls, neither of whom had their adult teeth, were sold and gone and she had not been able to wave goodbye. To make up for coupling with a straw boss for four months in exchange for keeping her third child, a boy, with her—only to have him traded for lumber in the spring of the next year and to find herself pregnant by the man who promised not to and did. That child she could not love and the rest she would not. "God take what He would," she said. And He did, and He did, and He did and then gave her Halle who gave her freedom when it didn't mean a thing.

Ⅲ. Notes.

The text is selected from chapter 2 of *Beloved*. Toni Morrison focuses her accusation of whites' cruelty to blacks rather on the blacks' internal experiences than on the facts. Chapter 2 begins with Paul D and Sethe rushing upstairs to have meeting, but the past rushes over them and both are caught in flashbacks of Sweet Home. Sethe recalls how Baby Suggs lost all her children to slavery and how Halle sold himself for her freedom "when it didn't mean a thing."

Ⅳ. Key Words(关键词).

Collective memory: 集体记忆。小说《宠儿》的叙事结构以女黑奴塞丝的回忆为主线。塞丝为什么要杀死自己的女儿;包括塞斯在内的黑奴在"甜蜜之家"都经历了些什么;为什么塞丝杀女的理由全然是爱。当塞丝心头的隐秘和疼痛随着小说的情节慢慢展开的时候,一个灾难性的种族集体记忆就呈现在了人们的眼前。小说由此为饱受奴隶制精神残害的黑奴们写就了一部血淋淋的心灵史。

deprivation:《宠儿》中黑人面对的是被追杀、贩卖、蹂躏、玷污的命运。在白人的世界里，黑人奴隶是被剥夺的对象。被剥夺是塞丝及其他黑奴自始至终无法摆脱的梦魇。从身体到灵魂，从欲望到情爱，塞丝无时无刻不生活在被剥夺的心灵体验中。通过昭示这种被剥夺的痛苦体验，莫里森从一个崭新的视域控诉了万恶的奴隶制对黑人，尤其是对黑人女性的惨无人道地摧残，以及这种摧残对黑人族群身心所造成的旷日持久的影响。

Ⅴ. **Questions.**

1. In the text, what does the wrought-iron maze refer to?
2. How did Baby Suggs lose all her children?
3. From Sethe's memories, can you briefly figure out her experience in the past?

Lesson 42　　Maxine Hong Kingston (1940—)

Ⅰ. **A Brief Review.**

Maxine Hong Kingston is a Chinese American author and Professor Emeritus at the University of California, Berkeley, where she graduated with a BA in English in 1962. Kingston has contributed to the feminist movement with her memoir *The Woman Warrior*, which discusses gender and ethnicity and how these concepts affect the lives of women. Kingston received the National Book Award in 1981 for her novel *China Men*.

图 42　Maxine Hong Kingston

Published in 1989, *Tripmaster Monkey* was the first novel written by Maxine Hong Kingston. The story follows Wittman Ah Sing, an American graduate of University of California, Berkeley of Chinese ancestry in his adventures around San Francisco during the 1960s. Heavily influenced by the Beat Movement, and exhibiting many prototypical symptoms of postmodernism, the book retains numerous themes, such as ethnicity and prejudice, addressed in Kingston's other works. The novel is rampant with allusions to pop-culture and literature, especially the Chinese novel, *Journey to the West*.

Wittman Ah Sing is the protagonist of the novel, with his name being a reference to Walt Whitman. The novel mainly follows his actions and changing attitudes towards his ancestry and life in general. Taña De Weese is a woman who meets Wittman at a wild party, eventually marrying him in order that Wittman can avoid being drafted to fight in the Vietnam War. She is a white American and introduces Wittman to her parents, which signifies Wittman's increasing comfort with white American culture. Nanci Lee attended the University of California, Berkeley and dates Whittam at the beginning of the novel. However, their shared culture does not promote their relationship into marriage.

Her writing style mainly consists of elements typical of postmodernism, especially a disjointed story line. The book is written entirely in stream of consciousness form and it is difficult to tell what is happening in reality versus only in Wittman's mind. There are constant references to the Chinese language, American literature, and English literature. Some of the stylistic elements are similar to those in *The Woman Warrior*.

In an interview published in *American Literary History*, Kingston disclosed her admiration for Walt Whitman, Virginia Woolf, and William Carlos Williams, who were inspirational influences for her work, shaping her analysis of gender studies. Kingston said of Walt Whitman's work, "I like the rhythm of his language and the freedom and the wildness of it. It's so American. … And also I love that throughout *Leaves of Grass* he always says 'men and women,' 'male and female.' He's so different from other writers of his time, and even of this time."

Ⅱ. Texts.

Tripmaster Monkey

Trippers and Askers

Maybe it comes from living in San Francisco, city of clammy humors and foghorn that warn and warn. —omen, o-o-men. O dolorous omen, o dolorous omens—and not enough sun, but Whitman Ah Sing considered suicide every day. Entertained it. There slid beside his right eye a black gun. He looked side-eyed for it. Here it comes. He actually crooked his trigger finger and—bang! —his head breaks into pieces that fly far apart in the scattered universe. Then blood, meat, disgusting brains, mind guts, but he would be dead already and not see the garbage.

The mouth part of his head would remain attached. He groaned. Hemingway had done it in the mouth. Wittman was not el pachuco loco①. Proof: he could tell a figment from a table. Or a tree. Being outdoors, in Golden gate park, he stepped over to a tree and knock-knocked on it. Lit a cigarette. Whose mind is it that doesn't suffer a loud takeover once in a while? He was aware of the run of his mind, that's all. He was not making plans to do himself in, and no more willed these seppuku② movies—no more conjured up that gun—than built this city. His cowboy boots, old brown Wellingtons, hit its pavements hard. Anybody serious about killing himself does the big leap off the Golden Gate. The wind or shock knocks you out before impact. Oh, long before impact. So far, two hundred and thirty-five people, while taking a walk along on the bridge—a mere net between you and the grabby ocean—had heard a voice out of the windy sky—Laurence Olivier③ asking them something: "To be or not to be?" And they'd answered, "Not to be," and climbed on top of the railing, fingers and toes roosting on the cinnabarine steel. They take the side of the bridge that faces land. And the City. The last city. Feet first. Coit Tower giving you the finger all the way down. Wittman would face the sea. And the setting sun. Dive. But he was not going to do that. Strange. These gun pictures were what was left of his childhood ability to see galaxies. Glass cosmospheres there had once been, and planets with creatures, such doings, such colors. None abiding. In the chronicle, a husband and wife, past eighty, too old to live, had shot each other with a weak gun, and had had to go to a doctor to have the bullets prized out of their ears. And a Buddhist had set fire to himself and burned to death on purpose④; his name was Quang Duc. Quang Duc. Remember. In the cremations along the Ganges, the mourners stay with the

---

① el pachuco loco: (西裔墨西哥人俚语)指穿着俗艳的疯子
② seppuku: 日本人的剖腹自杀
③ Laurence Olivier: 英国演员(1907—1989),莎士比亚名剧《哈姆雷特》中饰演王子
④ a Buddhist had set fire to himself and burned to death on purpose: 越战期间越南僧人为抗议政府而进行的自焚事件

burning body until its head pops. Pop.

Today Wittman was taking a walk on a path that will lead into the under path beneath the gnarly tree. In fact, the park didn't look half bad in the fog beginning to fall, dimming the hillocks that domed like green-grey moons rising or setting. He pulled the collar of his pea coat higher and dragged on his cigarette. He had walked this far into the park hardly seeing it. He ought to let it come in, he decided. He would let it all come in. An old white woman was sitting on a bench selling trivets "@ – dollar ea. ," which a ducky and a bunny pointed out with gloved fingers. She lifted her head and turned her face toward Wittman's; her hands were working one more trivet out of yarn and bottle caps. Not eyelids exactly but like skin flaps or membranes covered her eye sockets and quivered from the empty air in the holes or with efforts to see. Sockets wide open. He looked at her thick feet chapped and dirty in zoris①. Their sorry feet is how you can tell crazy people who have no place to go and walk everywhere.

Wittman turned his head, and there on the ground were a pigeon and a squatting man, both puking. He looked away so that he would not himself get nauseated. Pigeons have milk sacs in their throats. Maybe this one was disgorging milk because last night a wind had blown in from the ocean and blown its squabs out of their nest, and it was milking itself. Or does that happen in the spring? But in California in the fall as well? The man was only a vomiting drunk. This walk was turning out to be a Malte Laurids Brigge② walk. There was no helping that. There is no helping what you see when you let it all come in; he hadn't been in on building any city. It was already cold, soon the downside of the year. He walked into the tunnel.

Heading toward him from the other end came a Chinese dude from China, hands clasped behind, bow-legged, loose-seated, out on a stroll——that walk they do in kung fu movies when they are full of contentment on a sunny day, As luck would have it, although there was plenty of room, this dude and Wittman tried to pass each other both on the same side, then both on the other, sidestepping like a couple of basketball stars. Wittman stopped dead in his tracks, and shot the dude a direct stink-eye. The F. O. B.③ stepped aside. Following, straggling, came the poor guy's wife. She was coaxing their kid with sunflower seeds, which she cracked with her gold tooth and held out to him. 'Ho sick, la. Ho sick,,, she said. "Good eating. Good eats." Her voice sang, rang, banged in the echo-chamber tunnel. Mom and shamble-legged kid were each stuffed inside of about ten homemade sweaters. Their arms stuck out fatly. The mom had on a nylon or rayon pantsuit. ("Ny-longe. Mm lon doc." "Nylon-made. Lasts forever." "No!" said the kid. Echoes of "No!" Next there came scrabbling an old lady with a cane. She also wore one of those do-it-yourself pantsuit outfits. On Granny's head was a cap with a pompon that matched everybody's sweaters. The whole family taking cheap outing on their day off. Immigrants. Fresh Off the Boats out in public. Didn't know how to walk together. Spitting seeds. So uncool. You

---

① Zoris: 指露趾的凉鞋
② Malte Laurids Brigge: 奥地利诗人瑞纳·玛利亚诗作中从悲惨走向极乐的主角
③ F. O. B: Fresh off the boat. 指新近的移民者

wouldn't mislike them on sight if their pants weren't so highwater, gym socks white and noticeable. F. O. B. fashions—highwaters or puddlecuffs. Can't get it right. Uncool. Uncool. The tunnel smelled of mothballs—F. O. B. perfume.

On the tunnel ceiling, some tall paint-head had sprayed, "I love my skull." And somebody else had answered, "But oh you kidney!" This straighter person had prime-coated in bone-white a precise oval on the slope of the wall, and lettered in neat black, "But oh you kidney!"

He would avoid the Academy of Sciences, especially the North American Hall. Coyotes and bobcats dead behind glass forever. Stuffed birds stuffed inside their pried-open mouths. He was never going to go in there again. Claustro. Dark except for the glow of fake suns on the "scenes." Funeral-parlor smell seeping through the sealant.

Don't go into the Steinhart Aquarium either. Remember The Lady from Shanghai①? The seasick cameras shoot through and around the fishtanks at Orson Welles and Rita Hayworth saying goodbye. The fish are moving, unctuously moving.

No Oriental Tea Garden either. "Oriental." Shit.

Ⅲ. Notes.

1. Wittman Ah Sing, the protagonist of the novel, with his name being a reference to Walt Whitman. Set in the San Francisco Bay Area during the 1960's, Wittman Ah Sing is conflicted over his Chinese ancestry. He looks down upon the immigrants from China, refers to them as fobs, and believes that Asian-Americans know little about the culture of the countries their ancestors came from.

2. As time goes on, Wittman become more and more upset at the racism towards Asian people. His thoughts become more fixated on the similarities between himself and the character of a monkey king, Sun Wukong. Wittman is bothered by the perception that his culture is considered Asian, instead of Western. He can not shake off thinking about the racism and prejudice in American society. He is angry at the discrimination faced by non-white Americans, yet he is also embarrassed by the behavior of recent Chinese immigrants.

Ⅳ. Key Words(关键词).

spiritual suffering: 精神折磨。小说主人公惠特曼·阿新受过正规高等教育,是在美国文化中长大的华裔第五代。他一直强调自己是有中国血统的美国人,既鄙视他的华裔同族身上种种的"陋习",又痛斥那些把华裔美国人当作"他者"的白人。正是从自身的经历、生存环境中,阿新渐渐体会到自己的"中国人"、"美国人"与"华裔美国人"的多重身份。也正是这种多重身份让阿新困窘无比,备受精神折磨。

Lost in identity: 身份迷失。小说中阿新处处感受到现实生活中少数民族被排斥于美国白人主流社会之外的"他者"地位。处于东西两种文化的浸染中,阿新无以回避地迷失于

---

① Shanghai: 指1948年由奥尔森·威勒斯执导并主演的影片。该片主要角色并非亚洲人而是俄罗斯人

"我是谁?"这一少数族裔集体意识中至关重要的命题。而以当代社会中自我身份的迷失为起点,美国少数族裔开始了寻找自我家园,重构民族身份的种种艺术创作。

V. Questions.

1. What motivates Wittman Ah Sing to think about so much about death?
2. What kind of impression does the F. O. B leave to Wittman Ah Sing?
3. Can you give a brief description to the writing style of Maxine Hong Kingston?

Lesson 43　Leslie Marmon Silko (1948—)

Ⅰ. A Brief Review.

Leslie Marmon Silko is a Native American writer of the Laguna Pueblo tribe, and one of the key figures in the second wave of the Native American Renaissance. She received the MacArthur Foundation "Genius" Grant in 1981, and won prizes, fellowships, and grants from such sources as the National Endowment for the Arts and The Boston Globe. She was the youngest writer to be included in *The Norton Anthology of Women's Literature* for her story "Lullaby."

Born on March 5, 1948 in Albuquerque, New Mexico, Silko is 1/4 Laguna Pueblo Native American, and the rest of her ancestry being European American and Mexican American. Her father used to be a noted photographer but her family's house was at the edge of the reservation——and figuratively, therefore her family was not allowed to participate in various rituals of the pueblo societies. However, she was educated by her grandmother and aunts, who told her the traditional stories of the Laguna people, and as a result she was always identified with the native part of her ancestry. She attended a Catholic school in Albuquerque, and went on to receive a BA from the University of New Mexico in 1969. She briefly attended law school before leaving to pursue her literary career.

图 43　Leslie Marmon Silko

Silko's first novel *Ceremony* (1977) describes a dispossessed mixed-blood veteran of World War II, who restores his own psychological balance and returns to the Indian community through the use of Native American myths and rituals. *Ceremony* narrates nonchronologically the protagonist's experiences of the war with interweaving free verse poetry and narrative prose. The story is set primarily in the years following World War II and revolves around Tayo, a veteran of mixed white and Laguna heritage who returns to the reservation. Silko incorporates Laguna myths and historical incidents, reflecting the Pueblo's abiding connection to the natural world. Critics applaud *Ceremony* as "one of the most realized works of fiction devoted to Indian life that has been written in this country."

Published in 1981, *Storyteller* is a hybrid collection of poetry, short stories and family photographs compiled by Silko. The collection contains fictional stories about her family and tribal traditions. *Storyteller* contains three of Silko's most commonly-anthologized stories, "Yellow Woman," "Lullaby" and "Tony's Story." One such story, "Yellow Woman," is based on traditional abduction tales. Similarly, *Lullaby* tells an interesting story with a strong sense of Pueblo legends.

In 1991, *Almanac of the Dead* was published and attracted many critics and scholars immediately. The almanac of the title is an ancient Mayan book of prophecy, which describes the invasion of white Europeans and the decline of Mayan culture. The novel, set in the near future, is about twins, Lecha and Zeta, mixed-blood Yaquis who piece together the story from the book and converge on Tucson to await apparently apocalyptic changes that are believed to occur in future. Critics praise both the main theme of Silko's narration and her experimentation with artistic innovations. Many critics admire Silko's ability to integrate a powerful nostalgia for the Native American past with a recognition that Native Americans must adapt themselves to the changing society while never forsaking their bond with the land and their heritage.

II. Texts.

Lullaby

The sun had gone down but the snow in the wind gave off its own light. fit; came in thick tufts like new wool-washed before the weaver spins it. Ayah reached out for it like her own babies had, and she smiled when she remembered how she had laughed at them. She was an old woman now, and her life had become memories. She sat down with her back against the wide cottonwood tree, feeling the rough bark on her back bones; she faced east and listened to the wind and snow sing a high-pitched Yeibechei song. Out of the wind she felt warmer, and she could watch the wide fluffy snow fill in her tracks, steadily, until the direction she had come from was gone. By the light of the snow she could see the dark outline of the big arroyo① a few feet away. She was sitting on the edge of Cebolleta Creek, where in the springtime the thin cows would graze on grass already chewed flat to the ground, in the wide deep creek bed where only a trickle of water flowed in the summer, the skinny cows would wander, looking for new grass along winding paths splashed with manure.

Ayah pulled the old Army blanket over her head like a shawl. Jimmie's blanket—the one he had sent to her. That was a long time ago and the green wool was faded, and it was unraveling on the edges. She did not want to think about Jimmie. So she thought about the weaving and the way her mother had done it. On the wall wooden loom set into the sand under a tamarack tree for shade. She could see it clearly. She had been only a little girl when her grandma gave her the wooden combs to pull the twigs and burrs from the raw, freshly washed wool. And while she combed the wool, her grandma sat beside her, spinning a silvery strand of yarn around the smooth cedar spindle, Her mother worked at the loom with yarns dyed bright yellow and red and gold. She watched them dye the yarn in boiling black pots full of beeweed petals, juniper berries, and sage. The blankets her mother made were soft and woven so tight that rain rolled off them like birds' feathers. Ayah remembered sleeping warm on cold windy nights, wrapped in her mother's blankets on the Hogan's sandy floor.

---

① arroyo: 被水冲出的沟壑

The snow drifted now, with the northwest wind hurling it in gusts. It drifted up around her black overshoes—old ones with little metal buckles. She smiled at the snow which was trying to cover her little by little. She could remember when they had no black rubber overshoes, only the high buckskin leggings that they wrapped over their elk hide moccasins. If the snow was dry or frozen, a person could walk all day and not get wet; and in the evenings the beams of the ceiling would hang with lengths of pale buckskin leggings, drying out slowly.

She felt peaceful remembering. She didn't feel cold any more. Jimmie's blanket seemed warmer than it had ever been. And she could remember the morning he was born. She could remember whispering to her mother, Who was sleeping on the other side of the hogan①, to tell her it was time now. She did not want to wake the others. The second time she called to her, her mother stood up and pulled on her shoes; she knew. They walked to the old stone hogan together, Ayah walking a step behind her mother. She waited alone, learning the rhythms of the pains while her mother went to call the old woman to help them. The morning was already warm even before dawn and Ayah smelled the bee flowers blooming and the young willow growing at the springs. She could remember that so clearly, but his birth merged into the births of the other children and to her it became all the same birth. They named him for the summer morning and in English they called him Jimmie.

It wasn't like Jimmie died. He just never came back, and one day a dark blue sedan with white writing on its doors pulled up in front of the boxcar shack where the rancher let the Indians live. A man in a khaki uniform trimmed in gold gave them a yellow piece of paper and told them that Jimmie was dead. He said the Army would try to get the body back and then it would be shipped to them; but it wasn't likely because the helicopter had burned after it crashed. All of this was told to Chato because he could understand English. She stood inside the doorway holding the baby while Chato listened. Chato spoke English like a white man and he spoke Spanish too. He was taller than the white man and he stood straighter too. Chato didn't explain why; he just told the military man they could keep the body if they found it. The white man looked bewildered; he nodded his head and he left. Then Chato looked at her and shook his head, and then he told her, "Jimmie isn't coming home anymore," and when he spoke, he used the words to speak of the dead. She didn't cry then, but she hurt inside with anger. And she mourned him as the years passed, when a horse fell with Chato and broke his leg, and the white rancher told them he wouldn't pay Chato until he could work again. She mourned Jimmie because he would have worked for his father then; he would have saddled the big bay horse and ridden the fence lines each day, with wire cutters and heavy gloves, fixing the breaks in the barbed wire and putting the stray cattle back inside again.

She mourned him after the white doctors came to take Danny and Ella away. She was at the shack alone that day they came. It was back in the days before they hired Navajo women to go with them as interpreters. She recognized one of the doctors. She had seen him at the children's clinic

---

① Hogan: 纳瓦霍人用原木和泥筑成的居所

at Canoncito about a month ago. They were wearing khaki uniforms and they waved papers at her and a black ball-point pen, trying to make her understand their English word. She was frightened by the way they looked at the children, like the lizard watches the fly. Danny was swinging on the tire swing on the elm tree behind the rancher's house, and Ella was toddling around the front door, dragging the broomstick horse Chato made for her. Ayah could see they wanted her to sign the papers. And Chato had taught her to sign her name. It was something she was proud of. She only wanted them to go, and to take their eyes away from her children.

She took the pen from the man without looking at his face and she signed the papers in three different places he pointed to. She stared at the ground by their feet and waited for them to leave. But they stood there and began to point and gesture at the children. Danny stopped swinging Ayah could see his fear. She moved suddenly and grabbed Ella into her arms; the child squirmed, trying to get back to her toys. Ayah ran with the baby toward Danny; she screamed for him to run and then she grabbed him around his chest and carried him too. She ran south into the foothills of juniper trees and black lava rock. Behind her she heard the doctors running, but they had been taken by surprise, and as the hills became steeper and the cholla cactus were thicker, they stopped. When she reached the top of the hill, she stopped to listen in case they were circling around her. But in a few minutes she heard a car engine start and they drove away. The children had been too surprised to cry while she ran with them. Danny was shaking and Ella's little fingers were gripping Ayah's blouse.

She stayed up in the hills for the rest of the day, sitting on a black lava boulder in the sunshine where she could see for miles all around her. The sky was light blue and cloudless, and it was warm for late April, The sun warmth relaxed her and took the fear and anger away. She lay back on the rock and watched the sky. It seemed to her that she could walk into the sky, stepping through clouds endlessly. Danny played with little pebbles and stones, pretending they were birds eggs and then little rabbits. Ella sat at her feet and dropped fistfuls of dirt into the breeze, watching the dust and particles of sand intently. Ayah watched a hawk soar high above them, dark wings gliding; hunting or only watching, she said not know. The hawk was patient and he circled all afternoon before he disappeared around the high volcanic peak the Mexicans called Guadalupe.

Late in the afternoon, Ayah looked down at the gray boxcar shack with the paint all peeled from the wood; the stove pipe on the roof was rusted and crooked. The fire she had built that morning in the oil drum stove had burned out. Ella was asleep in her lap now and Danny sat close to her, complaining that he was hungry; he asked when they would go to the house. "We will stay up here until your father comes," she told him, "because those white men were chasing us." The boy remembered then and he nodded at her silently.

If Jimmie had been there he could have read those papers and explained to her what they said. Ayah would have known then, never to sign them. The doctors came back the next day and they brought a BLA① policeman with them. They told Chato they had her signature and that was ail

---

① BIA: Bureau of Indian Affairs 美国印第安事务管理局

they needed. Except for the kids. She listened to Chato sullenly; she hated him when he told her it was the old woman who died in the winter, spitting blood; it was her old grandma who had given the children this disease. "They don't spit blood," she said coldly. "The whites lie." She held Ella and Danny close to her, ready to run to the hills again. "I want a medicine man first," she said to Chato, not looking at him. He shook his head, "It's too late now. The policeman is with them. You signed the paper." His voice was gentle.

It was worse than if they had died: to lose the children and to know that somewhere, in a place called Colorado, in a place full of sick and dying strangers, her children were without her. There had been babies that died soon after they were born, and one that died before he could walk. She had carried them herself, up to the boulders and great pieces of the cliff that long ago crashed down from Long Mesa; she laid there in the crevices of sandstone and buried them in fine brown sand with round quartz pebbles that washed down the hills in the rain. She had endured it because they had been with her. But she could not bear this pain. She did not sleep for a long time after they took her children. She stayed on the hill where they had fled the first time, and she slept rolled up in the blanket Jimmie had sent her. She carried the pain in her belly and it was fed by everything she saw: the blue sky of their last day together and the dust and pebbles they played with, the swing in the elm tree and broomstick horse choked life from her. The pain filled her stomach and there was no room for food or for her lungs to fill with air. The air and the food would have been theirs.

She hated Chato, not because he let the policeman and doctors put the screaming children in the government car, but because he had taught her to sign her name. Because it was like the old ones always told her about learning their language or any of their ways: it endangered you. She slept alone on the hill until the middle of November when the first snows came. Then she made a bed for herself where the children had slept. She did not lie down beside Chato again until many years later, when he was sick and shivering and only her body could keep him warm. The illness came after the white rancher told Chato he was too old to work for him anymore, and Chato and his old woman should be out of the shack by the next afternoon because the rancher had hired new people to work there. That had satisfied her. To see how the white man repaid Chato's years of loyalty and work. All of Chato's fine-sounding English talk didn't change things.

……

The storm passed swiftly. The clouds moved east. They were massive and full, crowding together across the sky. She watched them with the feeling of horses—steely blue-gray horses startled across the sky. The powerful haunches pushed into the distances and the tail hairs streamed white mist behind them. The sky cleared. Ayah saw that there was nothing between her and the stars. The light was crystalline. There was no shimmer. No distortion through earth haze. She breathed the clarity of the night sky; she smelled the purity of the half moon and the stars. He was lying on his side with his knees pulled up near his belly for warmth. His eyes were close now, and in the light from the stars and the moon, he looked young again.

She could see it descend out of the night sky: an icy stillness from the edge of the thin moon.

She recognized the freezing. It came gradually, sinking snowflake by snowflake until the crust was heavy and deep. It had the strength of the stars in Orion, and its journey was endless. Ayah knew that with the wine he would sleep. He would not feel it. She tucked the blanket around him, remembering how it was when Ella had been with her; and she felt the rush so big inside her heart for the babies. And she sang the only song she knew to sing for babies. She could not remember if she had ever sung it to her children, but she knew that her grandmother had sung it and her mother had sung it:

> The earth is your mother,
> she holds you.
> The sky is your father,
> he protects you.
> Sleep,
> sleep.
> Rainbow is your sister,
> she loves you.
> The winds are your brothers,
> they sing to you.
> Sleep,
> sleep.
> We are together always
> We are together always
> There never was a time
> when this
> was not so.

III. Notes.

The text is from *Storyteller*. *Lullaby* depicts Native American culture in collision with a white culture that has dominated and oppressed the native people. Silko's story illustrates the sense of loss experienced by one Native American woman at the hands of white authority figures. As the main character, Ayah looks back on the most devastating events of her life. The death of Jimmie, and the removal of Ella and Danny from her home are her most painful sufferings because they represent not just the loss of loved ones but the loss of an entire culture to the hands of white culture. She mourns the loss of tradition, language, and family experienced by many Native Americans in the twentieth century. At the same time, Ayah, as many of Silko's characters, is able to combine traditional culture with modern elements in order to make meaning in her life.

IV. Key Words(关键词).

Lullaby: 摇篮曲。在这部小说中,摇篮曲代表着印第安文化的血脉与传承,在白人文化一点点蚕食印第安人精神领地的时候,获知与巩固本民族文化身份的最主要手段之一就是固守本民族的文化遗产。而作为一代代印第安人口头传承的摇篮曲则完美地体现着印第安人的文化财富。它也是印第安人的精神堡垒和反抗白人文化殖民的最有力的武器。

A sense of pain: 痛楚感。小说女主人公阿娅在其生命历程中对痛苦的感悟构成了小说的情感基调。印第安女性的痛苦源自于她生命中的挚爱被一次次的夺走而她对此却无能为力。她的亲人,她赖以存在的文化乃至环境都因白人的入侵而被剥夺殆尽。阿娅每一次的痛苦经历都是对白人野蛮侵略的控诉。

Language dominance: 语言强势。小说中阿娅的恐惧和无助从一个方面体现了白人语言对印第安人生活的强势介入和破坏。主导印第安人生活的本族语言被边缘化象征着印第安民族被边缘化。陌生的强势语言蛮横地摆弄着印第安人尤其是女性的命运,同时将印第安人的一切摆在了"他者"的地位。阿娅的屈辱感很重要的一方面来自于她认识到自己对白人语言的畏惧和屈从。

Ⅴ. Questions.

1. Who is Jimmie and how did he die?

2. In this story, Chato is an important character. Would you give an analysis of his personality?

3. How do you interpret the significance of the lullaby at the end of the story?

Lesson 44　E. L. Doctorow (1931—)

I. A Brief Review.

Born in the Bronx, New York, Doctorow was named after the great poet and short story writer Edgar Allen Poe, who had also lived in the Bronx. His parents were fond of music and came from second-generation of immigrants who descended from Russian Jews. Doctorow attended public grade schools and the Bronx High School of Science. He then enrolled at Kenyon College in Gambier, Ohio, a liberal arts school known to be a hub of literary studies. After earning his undergraduate degree with honors in 1952, Doctorow moved to graduate program in English drama at New York's Columbia University in the autumn of 1952. There he was introduced to the work of the German Romantic playwright Heinrich Von Kleist, whose writing had a profound effect on young Doctorow.

图 44　E. L. Doctorow

After serving in the army, Doctorow returned to New York, where he got a job as an "expert reader" for Columbia Pictures. His responsibilities included reading a novel each day and writing a 1200-word critique evaluating its cinematic potential. Doctorow acknowledged that the job gave him insights into the structure and pacing of novels that he would later use in his own writing. Since 1969, Doctorow has devoted his time to writing and teaching at several colleges and universities, including the University of California, Irvine; Yale University Drama School; and Princeton University. He has made his permanent home at New York University where he holds the Glucksman Chair in American Letters.

In 1960, Doctorow published his first novel, *Welcome to Hard Times*. A Western genre story, the novel was narrated from the point of view of the mayor of a frontier town of Hard Times, in the form of a series of journal entries. *Ragtime* (1975), was one of the most highly anticipated and critically acclaimed novels of 1976, as well as one of the fastest selling and most popular American books of all time. *Ragtime* uses historical figures as characters (J. P. Morgan, Emma Goldman, and many others), but it interweaves these personalities with a fictional narrative in order to expose a more ominous political and cultural threat that is always central to Doctorow's general critique of American life. *Ragtime* received the first National Book Critics Circle Award for fiction in 1976 and the Arts and Letters Award given by the American Academy and National Institute of Arts and Letters.

Although his fiction reflected mainly on historical facts, Doctorow stated his preference to "mingle the Marvelous" with the real. Doctorow explored several genres of fiction: western, science-fiction, historical, and science-detection mystery, which not only provoked critical thought but also achieved commercial success. A post-modern novelist, Doctorow has been portrayed as a literary descendant of Nathaniel Hawthorne and Edgar Allan Poe: a teller of tales that both reflect the writer's time and heritage. His recent books include *City of God* (2000) and *The March* (2005), the former is highly appreciated as a profound reflection on human beings' destiny and the latter won the National Book Critics Circle Award in 2005.

Ⅱ. Texts.

The Leather Man

They're nothing new, you can read about the Leather Man, for instance, a hundred years ago making his circuit through Westchester, Connecticut, into the Berkshires in the summer, seen sitting on the roadside, glimpsed in the woods, he had these regular stops, caves, abandoned barns, riverbanks under the iron bridges in mill towns, the Leather Man, a hulk①, colossally dressed, in layers of coats and shawls and pants, all topped with a stiff hand-fashioned leather outer armor, like a knight's, and a homemade pointed hat of leather, he was ten feet tall, an apparition. Of course it's the essence of these people that they're shy, they scurry at the sign of confrontation, never hurt a soul. But it was said of this fellow that when cornered he would engage in quite rational conversation, unlearned of course, with no reference to current events, and perhaps with a singular line of association that might strike one at times as not sequential, not really reasonably sequential on first audit②, but genial nonetheless, with transitions made by smile or the sincere struggle for words; even the act of talking, one assures, is something you can lose the knack of. So there is a history. And though the country of western New England or the farmlands in the north Midwest will still find one asleep in the plains, a patch of wheat flattened in his contours, say, and although they're common enough in the big cities, living in doorways, wiping your windshields with a dirty rag for a quarter, men, or carrying their bags, smoking butts from the gutters, women, or the communities of them, living each in a private alcove underground between subway stations, in the nests of the walls alongside tracks, or down under the tracks in the hollows and nooks of the electric cable conduits, what is new is the connection they're making with each other, some kind of spontaneous communication has flashed them into awareness of each other, and hell, they may as well have applied to the national endowment as a living art form, there is someone running them but I don't know who.

I don't know who and I don't know why. Conceivably it's a harmless social phenomenon, like all the other forms of suffering, that is to say not planned for a purpose but merely a natural function of everything else going, and maybe it is heartless to look askance at suffering, to be

---

① hulk: 指高大粗笨的人
② audit: 指旁听

suspicious of it, Southern church blacks, welfare recipients, jobless kids around the pool halls and so on, but that's the job, that's our role, I don't think I have to justify it. We know how danger grows, or for that matter large intangible events, spiritual events, there were five six hundred thousand, yes? at that farmer's field twenty years ago, and fifty of them were us, you remember, one part per ten thousand, like the legal chemistry for a preservative, one part per ten thousand to keep the thing from turning bad. I was there myself and enjoyed the music. My favorite was Joan C. Baez①, the most conservative of musicians, ultraliberal pacifist peacenik②, remember peaceniks? That was a coining we did ourselves and gave it to some columnist, in Denver I think it was, spread like wildfire. But she sang nice, early in the game, everyone stoned on sun, chemical toilets still operative…

We found a girl there, incidentally, who was doing these strange spastic pantomimes that drew a real crowd. Beginning with her arms over her head. Brought her elbows down over the boobs, seemed to push the elbows out, pushing at something, and then one arm went around the back of the neck, and then all these gyrations of the head, it was the weirdest thing, as if she was caught in something, a web, a net, so intense, so concentrated, the crowd, the music disappeared, and then she went down on her knees and knelt through her arms like they were some kind of jump rope, and then when her arms were behind her, that was not right, she tried to get out that way, get out, she was getting out of something, enacting the attempt, face all twisted and red to get out, you see. So we took some pictures, and then we diagrammed the action and what we came up with was very interesting, it was someone in a straitjacket③, it was the classic terror enacted of someone straitjacketed and trying to break free. Now, who can you think of, the person who in fact could do that, the person who could get out of straitjackets, who was that? he said.

Houdini④.

That's right. Houdini, it was one of his routines, getting out of the kind of straitjacket to break the heart.

……

To do hermitage, the preference for one's own company. Picture yourself in such solitude, in natural surroundings, say, the classical version. Build a hut in the woods, split your own logs, grow things, ritualize daily subsistence, listen to the wind sing, watch the treetops dance, feel the weather, feel yourself in touch with the way things are. You remember your Thoreau. There's a definite political component to avoiding all other human beings and talking on the coloration of your surroundings, invisible as the toad on the log. Whatever the spiritual content, it is the action hiding out, you see these guys hide out. So the question is, why? It may be a normal life directed

---

① Joan C. Baez: 拜耶兹(Joan Baez,1941—),美国民歌歌唱家,曾积极参加反对越战活动
② Peacenik: 这里指反战运动分子
③ straitjacket: 指束身衣,紧身衣
④ Houdini: 胡迪尼(Harry Houdini,其名叫 Ehrich Weiss,1874—1926),美国魔术家。犹太血统

by powerful paranoidal impulses, or it may be a paranoid① life that makes sense given the particular individual's background. But something has happened. If he is hiding, I want to know why.

But supposing on the other hand we all seek to impose the order we can manage, the more public the order the better we are known. Politicians are known. Artists are known. They impose public order. But say you are some hapless fellow, you can't keep a job, the wife nags, the children are vicious, the neighbors snigger. Down in your basement, though, you make nice things of wood. You make a bookshelf, you make a cabinet, sawing and planning, sanding, fitting, gluing, and you construct very fine, you impose that order, that is the realm of your control. You make a bigger cabinet. You make a cabinet you can walk into. You build it where nobody will watch you. When it is done, you walk inside and lock the door.

Before we break for lunch, let me propose this idea. You have them walking into their boxes and locking the door the door behind them. Fine. But two people do that and you have a community. You see what I'm saying? You can make a revolution with people who have nothing to do with each other at the same time. There is a theory, for instance, that the universe oscillates②. It is not a steady beaming thing, nor did it start with a bang. It expands and contracts, inhales and exhales, it is either growing larger than you can imagine or imploding toward a point. The crucial thing is its direction. If things come apart enough, they will have started to come together.

Members of the class: feral children, hermits, street people, gamblers, prisoners, missing persons, forest-fire wardens, freaks, permanent invalids, recluses, autistics, road tramps, the sensory deprived. (See also astronauts.)

We borrowed an ordinary precinct car and went looking for one. Contact on Fourteenth Street and Avenue A, time of contact ten-thirteen P. M. Subject going east on southside Fourteen Street. White, female, indeterminate age. Wearing WWII-issue khaki greatcoat③ over several dresses, gray fedora over blue watch cap, several shawls, some kind of furred shoes overlaid with galoshes. Stockings rolled to ankles over stockings. Pushing two-wheeled grocery cart stuffed with bags, sacks, rags, soft goods, broken umbrellas. Purposeful movements. Subject went directly from public trash receptacles to private trash deposits in doorways, seemed interested in anything made of cloth. Subject sat down to rest, back to fence, East Fifteenth Street. This is the site of Consolidated Edison generating plant. Subject slept several hours on sidewalk in twenty-degree weather. At four A. M. awakened by white male derelict urinating on her.

Ⅲ. Notes.

"The Leather Man" is selected from Doctorow's *Lives of the Poets: Six Stories and a*

---

① paranoid: 患偏执症的
② oscillates: 振动,摆动
③ WWII-issue khaki greatcoat: 二战时配发的咔叽布大衣

Novella. The subject of "The Leather Man" is isolation. In this story, Doctorow creates the guys who deliberately hide out from the normal world. The narrator tells us that there is a history about all these leather men. Doctorow pursues the answer to the question of peoples' isolation from one another. By creating the image of these outcasts even without certain names, Doctorow intends to distance the seemingly familiar American life because all characters involved in the story are estranged from their originally accepted stands.

Ⅳ. Key Words(关键词).

Anti-hero: 反英雄。它指现代小说或戏剧中其品行与读者心目中严肃文学作品里传统的主角或英雄形象相去甚远的主要角色。与伟大、高尚、威严或英勇的英雄形象相反,反英雄体现的是卑鄙、下流、消沉、无能或奸诈的人物品行。这一形象大量出现在二战后反映梦幻破灭的荒诞派或黑色幽默等文学作品中。在多克托罗的《皮男人》里,主人公皮男人像是百年前神话中的人物,衣着像个骑士,来去匆匆如幽灵,是一些流浪汉、厌世者和无家可归者,是非常典型的反英雄形象。

Theme of alienation: 异化专题。它指人同自己的本质、劳动产品或社会现实极度疏离的状态。欧美文学中对这一主题的关注由来已久。进入二十世纪后半叶,随着资本主义的发展与二战对人类社会的空前破坏,这一主题受到文学创作的极大关注。在《皮男人》里,多克托罗通过塑造"皮男人"这一群体形象,表达了对异化主题的深度关切。

Ⅴ. Questions.

1. Who is the narrator, or who are the narrators, of the story? How would you describe the narrative voice?
2. In what way does the Leather Man matter to the author and all of us readers?
3. What is the essential significance of the Leather Man?

Lesson 45 Cormac McCarthy (1933—)

Ⅰ. A Brief Review.

Born in Rhode Island, 1933, McCarthy was the third of six children (the eldest son) in the family. In 1937, the family moved to Knoxville, where his father became a lawyer for the Tennessee Valley Authority. McCarthy was raised a Roman Catholic and attended Catholic High School in Knoxville. He went to the University of Tennessee in 1951—52, majoring in liberal arts. McCarthy joined the U. S. Air Force in 1953, and returned to the University of Tennessee four years later. He left school without earning a degree and moved with his family to Chicago where he wrote his first novel, *The Orchard Keeper*, which was published in 1965.

McCarthy's novels include *The Orchard Keeper* (1965), *Child of God* (1974), *Blood Meridian* (1985), and *All the Pretty Horses* (1992; National Book Award), which

图 45 Cormac McCarthy

is his best-known work and the first book in his "Border Trilogy". His next two books in the triad are *The Crossing* (1994) and *Cities of the Plain* (1998). Recently he published two important novels: *No Country for Old Men* (2005); and *The Road* (2006; Pulitzer Prize).

Like its predecessors, McCarthy's third novel *Child of God* (1974) is set in eastern Tennessee and centers on a demented backwoodsman who is, among others things, a murderer and a necrophilia. McCarthy's artistic treatment prompts comparison with the work of the ancient Greek playwrights for its deep religious feeling and stubborn insistence on the mystery of existence. In 1985, *Blood Meridian* was published. This story is about a Tennessee boy traveling in Texas in the 1840s and the main character joins a band of irregulars to fight in Mexico and then falls in with a band of outlaws. Critics compare the book with American classics such as *Moby-Dick* in its unremitting look at the shady side of the American character. *Blood Meridian* was among *Time* Magazine's poll of 100 best English-language books published between 1923 and 2005.

McCarthy finally received widespread recognition in 1992 with the publication of *All the Pretty Horses*, which won the National Book Award and the National Book Critics Circle Award. *All the Pretty Horses* focuses on Cole and Rawlins who set off into pastoral Mexico in this novel, which vividly re-creates the world of Mexican bandits and Texas ranchers. As the first part of McCarthy's Border trilogy, it is praised by critics for endowing the genre of the western with literary grandeur while maintaining lucid and accessible prose.

McCarthy's next book, *No Country for Old Men*, was published in 2005. The novel stayed with the western setting and themes, yet moved to a more contemporary period. It was adapted into a film of the same name by the Coen Brothers, winning four Academy Awards and more than 75 film awards globally. *The Road* was published in 2006 and won international acclaim and the Pulitzer Prize for literature. Literary critic Harold Bloom named him as one of the four major American novelists of his time, along with Don DeLillo, Thomas Pynchon and Philip Roth. He is frequently compared by modern reviewers to William Faulkner in terms of their sophisticated observation and nostalgic representation of the rural life in the South.

II. Texts.

All the Pretty Horses

……

In the evening he saddled his horse and rode out west from the house. The wind was much abated① and it was very cold and the sun sat blood red and elliptic under the reefs of bloodred cloud before him. He rode where he would always choose to ride, out where the western fork of the old Comanche road coming down out of the Kiowa country to the north passed through the westernmost section of the ranch and you could see the faint trace of it bearing south over the low prairie② that lay between the north and middle forks of the Concho River. At the hour he'd always choose when the shadows were long and the ancient road was shaped before him in the rose and canted light like a dream of the past where the painted ponies and the riders of that lost nation came down out of the north with their faces chalked and their long hair plaited and each armed for war which was their life and the women and children and women with children at their breasts all of them pledged in blood and redeemable in blood only. When the wind was in the north you could hear them, the horses and the breath of the horses and the horses' hooves③ that were shod in rawhide and the rattle of lances and the constant drag of the travois④ poles in the sand like the passing of some enormous serpent and the young boys naked on wild horses jaunty as circus riders and hazing wild horses before them and the dogs trotting with their tongues aloll and foot-slaves following half naked and sorely burdened and above all the low chant of their traveling song which the riders sang as they rode, nation and ghost of nation passing in a soft chorale across that mineral waste to darkness bearing lost to all history and all remembrance like a grail the sum of their secular and transitory and violent lives.

He rode with the sun coppering his face and the red wind blowing out of the west. He turned south along the old war trail and he rode out to the crest of a low rise and dismounted and dropped the reins and walked out and stood like a man come to the end of something.

---

① abate: 指风势的减弱
② prairie: 指北美地区的大草原
③ hooves: hoof 的复数形式,指马,牛等的蹄
④ travois: 在这里指小路

There was an old horse skull in the brush and he squatted and picked it up and turned it in his hands. Frail and brittle. Bleached paper white. He squatted in the long light holding it, the comic book teeth loose in their sockets. The joints in the cranium like a ragged welding of the bone plates. The muted ran of sand in the brain box when he turned it. What he loved in horses was what he loved in men, the blood and the heat of the blood that ran them. All his reverence and all his fondness and all the leanings of his life were for the ardent hearted and they would always be so and never be otherwise.

He rode back in the dark. The horse quickened its step. The last of the day's light fanned slowly upon the plain behind him and withdrew again down the edges of the world in a cooling blue of shadow and dusk and chill and a few last chitterings of birds sequestered in the dark and wiry brush. He crossed the old trace again and he must turn the pony up onto the plain and homeward but the warriors would ride on in that darkness they'd become, rattling past with their stone-age tools of war in default of all substance and singing softly in blood and longing south across the plains to Mexico. THE HOUSE was built in eighteen seventy-two. Seventy-seven years later his grandfather was still the first man to die in it. What others had lain in state in that hallway had been carried there on a gate or wrapped in a wagon sheet or delivered crated up in a raw pine board box with a teamster standing at the door with a bill of lading. The ones that came at all. For the most part they were dead by rumor. A yellowed scrap of newsprint. A letter. A telegram. The original ranch was twenty-three hundred acres out of the old Meusebach stravoisurvey of the Fisher-Miller grant, the original house a one room hovel① of sticks and wattle. That was in eighteen sixty-six. In that same year the first cattle were driven through what was still Bexar County and across the north end of the ranch and on to Fort Sumner and Denver. Five years later his great-grandfather sent six hundred steers over that same trail and with the money he built the house and by then the ranch was already eighteen thousand acres. In eighteen eighty-three they ran the first barbed wire. By eighty-six the buffalo were gone. That same winter a bad die-up. In eighty-nine Fort Concho was disbanded.

His grandfather was the oldest of eight boys and the only one to live past the age of twenty-five. They were drowned, shot, kicked by horses. They perished in fires. They seemed to fear only dying in bed. The last two were killed in Puerto Rico in eighteen ninety-eight and in that year he married and brought his bride home to the ranch and he must have walked out and stood looking at his holdings and reflected long upon the ways of God and the laws of primogeniture. Twelve years later when his wife was carried off in the influenza epidemic they still had no children. A year later he married his dead wife's older sister and a year after this the boy's mother was born and that was all the horning that there was. The Grady name was buried with that old man the day the northern blew the lawn chairs over the dead cemetery grass. The boy's name was Cole. John Grady Cole.

---

① hovel: 指异常简陋的小屋

Ⅲ. Notes.

In *All the Pretty Horses*, Cormac McCarthy begins his Border Trilogy with a coming of age tale that is a departure from the bizarre richness and mysterious violence of his early novels, yet in many ways preserves the mystery and the richness in a more understated form. This novel follows a young man's journey to the regions of the unknown. John Grady Cole, more heroic than the protagonists of McCarthy's earlier novels, confronts the evil that is an inescapable part of the universe as well as the evil that grows out of his own ignorance and pride. His story is told in a style often restrained and simple, embedded with lyrical passages that echo his dreams and memory.

Ⅳ. Key Words(关键词).

Border Trilogy: 边境三部曲。麦卡锡以其边境三部曲《骏马》(1992),《穿越》(1994)和《平原上的城市》(1998)等奠定了他在当代美国文坛上的大师地位。这些发生在美墨边境地区的动人叙事描写了梦魇般的历史、令人颤栗的暴力,还有壮阔雄浑的西部风光,被评论家称为"地狱与天堂的交响曲",是可与福克纳、斯坦贝克等小说家的杰作相比肩的当代美国文学经典。

pastoral scenes: 田园风光。麦卡锡钟情于田园荒野生活,曾经游居得克萨斯、新墨西哥、亚利桑那、田纳西及墨西哥等地。这些地方的生活经历成了其小说故事的主要素材:美丽如画的田园,人烟稀少的沙漠,残酷激烈的冒险,以及简洁有力的语言。麦卡锡的作品具有一种感觉和想象的力量。这种力量出于他对自然和人生的感受和探求,对于年轻生命中甘苦喜乐的真实细致的体验,对于未来的期待和向往。

Ⅴ. Questions.

1. Discuss briefly McCarthy's language style in the novel.

2. Why does McCarthy set his story at the border? Do you think that border means something special to the writer?

3. After you read the selected section of the novel, can you tell the history of Cole family's ranch?

参 考 文 献

陈安著:《新英汉美国小百科》,上海:上海译文出版社,2000 年。
董衡巽主编:《美国文学简史》(修订本),北京:人民文学出版社,2003 年。
江宁康:《美国当代文学与美利坚民族认同》,南京:南京大学出版社,2008 年。
刘海平、王守仁主编,张冲、朱刚、杨金才、王守仁等主撰:《新编美国文学史》,上海:上海外语教育出版社,1999—2002 年。
萨克文·伯科维奇主编,孙宏等译:《剑桥美国文学史》,北京:中央编译出版社,2005 年。
陶洁主编:《美国文学选读》(第二版),北京:高等教育出版社,2005 年。
童明著:《美国文学史》,北京:外语教学与研究出版社,2008 年。
杨仁敬等著:《美国文学简史》,上海:上海外语教育出版社,2008 年。
张冲主编:《美国文学选读》,上海:复旦大学出版社,2008 年。

Baym, Nina. et al ed. *The Norton Anthology of American Literature*, Vol. 1 and Vol. 2, Sixth Edition. New York: W. W. Norton, 2003.

Beach, Christopher. *Introduction to Twentieth-Century American Poetry*. Cambridge: Cambridge UP, 2003.

Borland, Bruce. ed. *America Through the Eyes of Its People*, 2nd edition. New York: Longman, 1997.

Doren, Charles Van, ed. *Webster's American Biographies*. Springfield, Mass.: Merriam-Webster Inc., 1984.

Hart, James D. ed. *The Oxford Companion to American Literature*, Fifth Edition. Oxford University Press & Beijing: Foreign Language Teaching and Research Press, 1993.

Lauter, Paul et al ed. *The Heath Anthology of American Literature*, Vol. 1 and Vol. 2, 3rd Edition. Boston: Houghton Mifflin Company, 1998.

Patton, Venetria. *Background Readings for Teachers of American Literature*. Boston: Bedford/St. Martin's, 2006.

VanSpanckeren, Kathryn. *Outline of American Literature*. US Information Agency, 2000.

Spark Notes: http://www.sparknotes.com
The Free Library: http://www.thefreelibrary.com
The Literature Network: http://www.online-literature.com
Wikipedia: http://en.wikipedia.org/wiki

后　记

　　本教材《美国文学经典教程》借鉴了当代两本重要的美国文学选集:《诺顿美国文学选集》和《西斯美国文学选集》的编写体例,把选文的范围上溯到早期印第安人的民间口头文学,下延至近年来的美国当代文学名著。教材共选编了45位作家的文学作品,按年代把这些作家及选文分为六个部分共45课加以组合。每个部分前面有简明扼要的中文概述,每课再分为短评、选文、题解、关键词和思考题五项内容,并加上了一些必要的生词注释。本教材主要供大学本科生和研究生使用,教学时间大约需要一学期或延至一学年,也可以从各部分中选读若干作家作品进行专题学习。

　　本教程由南京大学英语系江宁康主编,其他高校的几位老师参加了编写工作。具体分工如下:江宁康(南京大学)负责全书策划、统稿、校改和中文概述撰写,并编写了第1—5、11—12、19—20、25、27、39—45课。程爽(哈尔滨师范大学)编写第33—38课。丁建宁(南京师范大学)编写第16—18课。郝桂莲(云南师范大学)编写第6—7、21—24课。叶英(四川大学)编写第8—10、14—15课。朱丽田(东南大学)编写第13、26、28—32课。另外,高巍、项歆妮、孔小纲和王华等也参加了后期的统稿和校改工作。马涛和王晶协助我做了核对校样的工作。本教程编写者参考了有关的美国文学选集和重要论著,并参考了一些相关的公共网站文献进行改写编撰。

江宁康
2010.11